HE'S OUT THERE (EXPANDED EDITION)

J.L. Taylor

Monkey Tales Publishing

ISBN: 979-8-9942274-8-0

Cover design by: Art Painter
Library of Congress Control Number: 2018675309
Printed in the United States of America

This book is dedicated to my wife, Michelle Bigos-Taylor, and my three daughters, Maddy, Jossy, and Katelyn. Thank you all for being part of my life, I love you all so much!

Each year 1,100 people, on average, get lost in the wilderness of the Pacific Northwest of the United States. 90% of those that become lost are found alive, 8% are located deceased, and the other 2% simply vanish without a trace.

CONTENTS

PREFACE

This expanded edition includes new chapters bridging the events of Book One and Book Two, additional character development, and newly revealed lore not present in the original release.

PROLOGUE

He enters quietly.

Not like the others. No shouting. No smoke. No shiny tools. He walks with care, low, deliberate. He smells of sap, salt, leather. Not fear. Not yet.

But it doesn't matter.

He crossed the boundary.

The wind brought word before his foot touched soil. The birds warned. The roots stirred. The lake went still.

This place is not for him.

I rise from the dark, from the branches twisted into a labyrinth where light does not reach. Bones line the floor, hang from limbs, scraped and gnawed clean. The earth is tight with old silence.

The water speaks. Ripples that do not belong. I feel it against my skin, movement where there should be none.

He is near.

There is no hate in me. Only memory. The bloodline I was

shaped to protect. The line they drew in ash and bone, in fire long forgotten by their kind.

He does not know this place was once sacred.
He does not know what still lives in its shadow.

But I know.
And I remember.
And I will keep it.

Even from him.

HE'S OUT THERE (EXPANDED EDITION)

CHAPTER 1: IT BEGINS

Venu Vanakar stepped out of the luxury SUV and into the cold, pine-scented air. He stretched his arms high overhead, spine arching until he felt the satisfying pop between his shoulders. A long breath slipped from his lungs as he shook out the stiffness of the drive.

Tall and broad-shouldered, with a few days' worth of stubble that carved shadows into his high cheekbones, Venu looked every bit the seasoned adventurer. His olive-green tactical pants and scuffed boots bore the wear of countless trails. A tan knit sweater peeked from beneath a bright green North Face jacket, the fabric flecked with bits of dried grass and pine needles.

After a moment of stillness, he turned back to the SUV and opened the rear door. From the backseat, he pulled a bright red knit cap and tugged it down over his thick black hair, smoothing it with both hands. He scratched at his beard absently, then reached for his pack.
The backpack came out in a single practiced motion. He slung it over his shoulders, adjusted the straps, and with one final glance at the vehicle, pressed the lock button on the key fob. The SUV gave a muted chirp as the doors clicked shut behind him.

Venu reached into the front pocket of his jacket and pulled out a napkin. He unfolded it carefully, smoothing it against his palm.

A crude map stared back at him. Just a few shaky lines and a scribbled instruction: *"walk 50m to R/of gate."* He looked toward the secured gate up ahead, then took two deliberate steps in its direction before veering right. The napkin was folded again with the same care he'd used to open it, then tucked back into his jacket.

Leaving the gravel road behind, he stepped into the thick brush that had overtaken the fence line. Scotch broom clawed at his pants. Dogwoods crowded in close. The tall grass clung to his leg around his legs, wild and damp.

Venu stayed tight to the fence. In places, the growth pressed so close he had to shoulder his way through it. The mesh of the chain-link felt cold against his arm through the sleeve of his jacket. Every step forward felt like a minor negotiation with the land.

Finally, he found it.

The opening in the fence was barely a few feet wide, just enough chain-link cut and peeled back to allow someone through. The jagged edges curled like broken teeth.

He frowned.

The backpack came off first, passed through the opening with a grunt of effort. Then he turned sideways, braced a hand on the cold metal, and began to squeeze himself into the gap.

Halfway through, the tug came with a sudden catch at his back. Venu stopped. His jacket had snagged.

He reached behind with his hand, fingers searching for the stubborn patch of fabric. He tried coaxing it loose gently.

Then not so gently.

A rip tore through the silence.

“Shit,” he muttered, twisting to inspect the torn seam along his jacket.

He slung his pack over one shoulder and faced the woods beyond the fence.

With a breath drawn deep into his chest, Venu moved forward toward the abandoned logging camp.

CHAPTER 2: HIDDEN LAKE

Venu walked through the camp, stepping carefully around the rusting equipment scattered across the clearing—old generators, fuel drums, a toppled scaffold. The machines were covered in moss and half-swallowed by the earth, the forest slowly reclaiming them.

He stopped near the center of camp.

Around him there was nothing but silence.

The skeletal remains of old structures loomed, empty and sagging. Fog crept along the treetops, settling low around the perimeter. Venu turned in a slow circle, eyes scanning the woods. Every path in seemed swallowed by gray mist. Then he saw it. A break in the trees revealed an old access road, barely visible, leading up into the foothills, vanishing into fog.

He reached into his pocket and pulled out the napkin again, unfolding it with fingers slightly damp from the cool mist. The ink had begun to smudge at the edges. Venu traced the faint line with his index finger, following it from a crude box labeled *MAIN* , curving up and to the left.

His finger stopped.

He looked up, comparing map to landscape. Something didn't quite line up, but it was close. He frowned, folded the napkin, and returned it to his pocket.

He turned toward the main building.

It loomed larger than the rest, but it too was dead, windows boarded up from the outside, the front doors chained shut. Something about it felt...fortified. It wasn't just abandoned, it had been *sealed.*

Venu moved briskly around the left side of the building. Tools lay haphazardly scattered in the grass...flashlights, a dented lunchbox, even a jacket stiff with mildew. It was as if whoever left hadn't expected to leave for good.

He paused at the edge of the tree line.

A breeze stirred the leaves. Something creaked above him, but it was only a branch swaying under its own weight. To the left, he spotted it: a faded yellow swing gate, its arm lowered across the narrow access road leading deeper into the forest.
Venu approached the gate, cautiously. He looked out at the access road before him, then back towards the logging camp. Doubt flickered in his eyes.

Then, without a word, he stepped past the gate and began his hike up the road.

The fog thickened as he went.

Each step crunched softly beneath Venu's boots, the gravel muffled by damp earth and fallen pine needles. The forest around him was alive with the chittering of birds and the occasional rustle of squirrels darting through the underbrush, but none of them sounded close. It was as if they watched from a distance, unwilling to come near the road.

Venu moved briskly, glancing down at his smartwatch now and then, checking time. Each step peeled away another layer of work week stress. Out here, the deadlines couldn't touch him. No cell service meant no Slack pings, no "quick" phone calls that lasted hours. Here, outdoors, he found the peace and solitude that eluded him during the week.

He welcomed it. Needed it.

The constant grind culture at his job had become a constant. Ten to twelve hour days stacked against each other in the frenzied weeks leading up to each new feature release. Most launches were disasters anyway, bug-filled and held together with the digital equivalent of duct tape and baling wire. He was coding over the rotted out foundation of a legacy system that was beyond repair.

Still, the money was good. More than good.

At thirty, Venu's net worth had already crossed into low seven figures. He was liquid, too, as multiple accounts bumped up against FDIC insurance caps. His financial advisor called him "strategically independent". His parents said it was a good start. But Venu knew better.

What he really was...was exhausted.

Working for a Chinese e-commerce giant came with its own price. On paper, he was part of the global team. In practice, he was a brown Indian man in a Mandarin speaking club. The racism was rarely overt, but it was constant, woven into slights, smirks, and the exclusion from any conversations that actually mattered.

Aside from these hikes, he had no work-life balance. He was always on. Always reachable. Calls came in at midnight. Texts pinged 24/7. Sleep was shallow, when he had time to sleep at all.

He paused at a bend in the trail to catch his breath. A soft breeze pushed through the branches.

Venu reached into his jacket pocket and pulled out the napkin. The creases had deepened and the ink was now slightly smudged. He smoothed it flat against his thigh and then smiled.

He thought of the man who gave the map to him.

Venu certainly hadn't expected to talk to anyone last night, let alone someone like him. He looked like the kind of guy who fixed things with his hands and drank cheap beer out of cans.

Venu had been sitting alone at the bar, nursing a Jack & Coke while thumbing through photos on his camera when he approached, nodded, and asked, "Is that a Sony or a Canon?"

That was it.

Next thing he knew, they'd been talking for hours about wildlife, the deep woods, and long stretches of silence and what it did for the mind. Venu had been cautious at first, uncertain if he was humoring him or genuinely interested. But there was something in his voice that was direct, weathered, and unsentimental, that drew him in.

They had next to nothing in common. Mike had grown up nearby and stayed. Venu had spent the better part of his adult life in high-rise apartments and code sprints.

They didn't align religiously, politically, or socially. But none of that mattered. What they did share was an appreciation for natural beauty and the outdoors.
Near the end of the conversation, he drew Venu the napkin map. He told him about an old trail leading to a glacial lake up in the foothills. He said it was the quietest and most beautiful place he'd ever known.

Venu looked back down at the napkin and began to walk. He kept one eye on the crude map, the other scanning the forest to his left. Step after step, his breath visible in the cool air, he searched.

Then he saw it.

A weathered green steel post, barely rising above the ferns. Near its top, three yellow plastic ribbons fluttered faintly in the breeze—tattered, frayed, almost swallowed by the surrounding growth.

Venu stopped. A faint smile touched his lips. On my way, buddy, he thought to himself.

He stepped off the access road and into the underbrush. The transition was immediate as gravel gave way to the sponge-soft floor of the forest, thick with sword ferns, Oregon grape, vanilla leaf, and clusters of stinging nettles.

The air felt heavier as he neared the trees. Quieter.

He moved cautiously, testing each step. Rocks and hidden ruts threatened to roll an ankle, and the forest felt like it had no intention of helping him.
Past the post now, Venu paused and stared into the woods ahead.

The trees stood close together, tall, unmoving, and ancient. Light filtered through the canopy in fractured shafts. The silence pressed in, deeper here, as though even the birds didn't follow him past the ribbons.

He swallowed. Took a breath. And stepped deeper into the trees.

Venu refolded the napkin map, pressing the creases flat with his thumb before sliding it back into his jacket pocket. He took one last glance behind him—at the road, the post, the known world—and then stepped into the woods. There was no path. Just uneven ground swallowed by ferns and fallen limbs, and trees that stood like sentinels, their trunks slick with moss, their branches knitting a ceiling far above. The light dimmed almost instantly.

Venu moved carefully, each step deliberate. The forest gave him nothing, not even so much as hint of direction. He scanned the trees ahead, eyes narrowing as he searched for something, anything, that matched what he'd been told to look for. Twigs snapped beneath his boots. A branch brushed against his arm like a skeletal hand. He kept moving. Then ahead, a splash of color.

A single tree stood out from the rest. Several strands of yellow ribbon clung to its trunk, tied haphazardly but still visible. The plastic had faded under weather and time, but it held. It was real. It was something.

Venu exhaled, not realizing he'd been holding his breath. Relief flickered across his face. He adjusted his pack on his shoulders and pressed forward, deeper into the trees.

Another ribbon. Venu spotted it several meters ahead, faded

yellow plastic ribbon wrapped around the trunk of a narrow pine. He made his way toward it, careful not to slip on the moss-covered roots that snaked through the forest floor.

When he reached the tree, he shrugged off his backpack and unzipped the main compartment. From inside, he pulled out an empty sandwich bag. He then slid the carefully folded map into the plastic bag before tucking it into an interior pocket for safekeeping. He stood for a moment, letting his eyes wander across the forest. It was quiet here. Not silent, but hushed, as if the trees themselves were leaning in to try and listen to his thoughts.

Leaves rustled overhead in the light wind. A bird chirped once, then fell quiet. In the filtered sunlight, the forest glowed—the canopy above broke just enough to cast long, shimmering beams of silver light through the branches. The moss growing on the trunks of smaller hardwoods and pines glowed emerald green in the sunlight.

Sweat dampened the collar of Venu's sweater. He took a short break, dropping his pack at his feet and pulling out a water bottle. He drank, wiped his mouth, then took another long swallow, eyes still scanning the woods as he did. He slipped off his coat and tied it through the straps of his pack. Digging through one of the outer pouches, he pulled out a small packet of Kirkland trail mix. He leaned against a low boulder, chewing slowly, listening.

When he finished, he carefully folded the empty wrapper and slid it into the front pocket of his pants. Leave no trace.

The forest around him remained still.

He slung the pack over his shoulders, tightened the straps, and checked his watch. A bit behind schedule. Time to move.

Venu picked up his pace, boots pattering softly over loam and fallen pine needles. Every few dozen steps he paused, scanning ahead for the telltale flash of yellow. Occasionally, he checked the compass on his watch, correcting his bearing before continuing deeper.

The terrain began to shift—less undergrowth, more old-growth trees. The light grew brighter ahead. He pushed forward with a renewed sense of urgency and excitement.

Suddenly, he stepped through the tree line and froze.
Venu stood at the edge of a clearing, eyes wide, breath caught in his throat. The awe on his face said everything: he'd found it.

The lake appeared all at once, as if the trees had parted just for him.

Its water was a cloudy ice blue and dense with glacial silt, untouched and perfectly still. Not even a breeze disturbed the surface. The only movement came in the form of tiny ripples near the center, where a lone trout occasionally broke the water, snapping at the insects that skimmed just above it. To the northeast, snowcapped ridges rose like ancient stone guardians, their white peaks framed against a pale blue sky.

The scene was unbothered by time.

Venu set down his backpack beside a fallen log and lowered himself onto the weathered wood. After a moment, he reached down, hefted the pack into his lap, unzipped the top carefully as if he were performing a quiet ritual. From within, he pulled a padded black camera case and unlatched it with a soft click.

The digital camera nestled inside gleamed in the daylight. He removed it with practiced hands, adjusting dials and settings almost instinctively. After a moment, he selected a lens from the case, attached it with a satisfying twist, and raised the camera to his eye.

Click. Click.
The shutter sounded soft and deliberate, like the moment demanded reverence.

After capturing several frames, Venu stood and followed the curve of the shoreline toward a small meadow on the western edge of the lake. Wild grasses swayed in the breeze, golden against the soft green moss and algae that lined the water's edge.

He stepped carefully onto a partially submerged log that extended into the lake, balancing himself before lifting the camera again. From here, the mountains and sky framed the water perfectly. He snapped a few more photos, each one a quiet meditation.

Then he paused. Lowered the camera.

A slow smile crossed his face. He turned in a slow circle, letting the moment imprint itself on him as much as he tried to capture it with the lens.

For now, it was his alone.

Venu returned to his backpack and crouched beside it, lifting the camera case to begin packing it away. His fingers moved methodically—lens detached, body wrapped, zippers sealed. Then he stopped.

He glanced over his shoulder, eyes narrowing. The wind had

shifted. Or maybe it had simply stopped.

A hush had fallen over the lake, like someone had dropped a blanket over the sound. No birds. No distant chittering of squirrels in the trees or rustling of leaves. Just the faint, constant hum of insects.

He stood slowly and scanned the tree line.
Nothing moved. But something felt… off.

From the side pocket of his pack, he pulled out a peanut butter sandwich wrapped in wax paper. He stared at it for a moment —then, without taking a bite, returned it to the pack.

His gaze drifted back to the lake, still placid and beautiful.

A sharp crack echoed behind him.

Venu spun around, his heart punching against his ribs.
Nothing. Only trees. Stillness.

But the air had changed. It felt thicker now, humid and close, charged like the moment before a thunderstorm. The incessant buzzing of insects was louder than before, no longer background noise, but suffocating, static, and dense.

He slung the backpack over one shoulder, then the other, hands fumbling with the straps. His eyes never stopped moving—scanning the woods, the shadows, the places between the trees.
Something was wrong. He didn't know what. But his body did.

Venu turned and stepped back into the forest, his pace quickening as he tightened the pack against his shoulders. The shadows seemed darker now. The path back felt less certain.

He didn't look back.

CHAPTER 3: THE WOODS

Back in the woods, Venu moved quickly. He weaved from one yellow-ribboned tree to the next, trying to retrace the steps he'd taken earlier that day. The markers, once comforting, now felt sparse. Too far apart. Too easy to miss.

His boots struck the forest floor with heavy, uncertain steps. Twigs snapped beneath his soles, and low branches clawed at his arms and chest. Every few seconds, he glanced behind him—nothing. But his breath came fast, shallow, and sweat clung to his face like glue.

Crack!

A thick branch snapped off to his right, the sound sharp and sudden.

Venu's head whipped in the direction of the noise. He froze.

The woods were utterly still.

His chest rose and fell rapidly. He wrinkled his nose—there was something in the air now, sour and pungent, like rotting meat and wet fur. He held his breath, listening.

Nothing.

No wind. No birds. No insects. The forest had gone mute. He took a hesitant step forward toward the next ribboned tree. His eyes darted through the trees, scanning every shadow. He *felt* eyes on him—felt the weight of a gaze too massive, too intent.

Another branch snapped behind him, but closer this time. He stopped. Every muscle in his body tensed. A wave of cold dread surged through him, and he reached out with one trembling hand to brace himself against the nearest tree. The bark was rough and wet beneath his palm.

Something was moving through the woods. And it was huge. Without warning, a rock that was roughly the size of a volleyball, whistled through the air and missed his head by inches. It slammed into a tree behind him with a *thud* so deep it echoed.

Venu ran.

Branches whipped his face, snagged his clothing, tore at his skin. He broke through brambles and low limbs, eyes wild, searching frantically for the next yellow ribbon.

He tripped and hit the ground hard, thorns and branches slicing across his face and hands. He scrambled up instantly, bleeding, gasping, driven by pure terror. Behind him, the forest *moved* with a heavy, deliberate, and unrelenting malice.

It was following him, crashing through the trees with methodical violence, it stalked, not sprinted. It didn't need to run.

Venu pushed harder, lungs burning, legs screaming. He heard it shift left, then right—keeping pace. *Playing with him.*

A second rock tore through the air, slamming into a tree less than a foot away. Bark exploded in a burst of splinters. The indent it left was deep, malicious and inhuman.

Venu didn't stop.

He couldn't.

Venu could see the access road through the trees—a narrow ribbon of pale gravel in the distance, lit like salvation. His breath came in ragged bursts, each one scraping at his throat. His legs churned, fueled by panic more than strength, his lungs screamed for air.
He burst from the tree line and stumbled onto the gravel with all the grace of a collapsing scarecrow. His boots skidded, stones crunching beneath his weight. He staggered a few more steps, bent at the waist, hands braced on his knees as he gasped for air.

Then he turned, slowly, to look back into the forest.

The trees stood silent.

But he knew it was still there.

Venu straightened, swaying on legs that barely obeyed him. He began to limp-run down the access road toward the logging camp—arms pumping, feet dragging, body threatening to buckle with every step.

Behind him, something massive exploded from the trees.

The forest itself seemed to exhale.

Venu didn't look back.

He ran harder.

A *sharp whistle* in the air.

Impact.
A heavy blow struck him squarely between the shoulder blades with brutal precision. It felt like a sledgehammer slammed into his spine.

Venu was airborne for half a second before the ground stole him back.

He hit hard, face-first in the gravel, the wind knocked entirely from his lungs. He gasped, but nothing came. His limbs twitched uselessly, flailing as he struggled to flip over. Dirt filled his mouth. Blood dripped from his nose. His chest heaved in silence, his lungs refusing to work. Tears welled in his eyes. He tried to scream, but only a ragged gasp came out.

Footsteps, heavy and measured, smashed into the gravel behind him.

Venu rolled onto his back, wheezing, vision swimming. The blue sky spun above him, indifferent. His arms scrambled for purchase, trying to drag himself away, his boots scuffing against the road as panic fully set in.

Behind him, the footsteps grew louder.

It was close.

The footsteps closed in, slow, crushing, and final. A sound, deep and primal, hung in the air. Not just a grunt, but something that wasn't meant to be heard by human ears.
Venu barely had time to flinch before he was lifted off the

ground with violent ease. His backpack tore free from his shoulders, straps snapping with a loud *pop* . He dropped back to the gravel in a heap, gasping as his ribs slammed into the earth.

He blinked through sweat and blood, just in time to see his backpack hurled down the road. It spun through the air before crashing to the ground several meters in front of him.

He was yanked violently upward again.

His feet left the ground. The sky opened above him, tall trees framing a blur of blue. For a split second, he was weightless, suspended in the still air, his body limp in something else's grasp.

Time seemed to freeze.

He was whipped downward with brutally crude force. The last thing Venu saw was the gravel rushing up toward his face.

And then nothing.

CHAPTER 4: HIGH RISE

A slight Indian man sat alone on a leather sofa, eyes locked on the massive flatscreen mounted above the fireplace. His posture was rigid, but his face told another story. Grief and exhaustion pulled at his features, dark circles bloomed under his eyes.

Vikram Vanakar.

He wore a maroon cashmere V-neck sweater, tailored black slacks, and bright red socks. No shoes. His beard was deliberate and neatly unshaven in a way that suggested style once mattered, though today it looked more like neglect and mourning.

On the screen, a local newscaster recited the facts in a flat tone:

"The search for a missing Bellevue man was called off today. Venu Vanakar left his home over three weeks ago for what was supposed to be a routine day hike but never returned. His vehicle was found parked near a trailhead on
the outskirts of Glacier, Washington, but there were no signs of Venu anywhe—"

The screen blinked off with a sharp *click*.

“Bullshit,” Vikram muttered, voice thick with anger.

He tossed the remote onto the sofa and crossed to the fireplace. A row of photographs lined the mantle. All of them were of Venu, sunlit and smiling, frozen in time atop distant peaks and misty ridgelines. His brother had hiked across three continents, but it was Washington’s wilderness he had loved most.

Vikram picked up one of the frames.

Venu stood near a snow-fed lake, arms outstretched, the jagged spires of the Enchantments rising behind him.

He looked tired but happy, the way only hikers looked after earning a summit.

Vikram’s eye twitched. He walked to the center of his brother's condo, still holding the picture. Floor-to-ceiling windows framed a view of the city skyline, the Space Needle off in the distance, just off center, like it had been staged. The air smelled of cedar and espresso. Every surface gleamed - sleek, modern, and expensive.

Of course it did.

Venu had always been better at everything. A better student. A better developer. He understood code like other people understood music or language. Vikram had tried to keep up, taking the same classes as Venu, but he struggled. Venu made it look effortless.

And it wasn't just code and academics.

Venu was better looking. More poised. Self-assured and better with people. He made their parents beam in a way Vikram never could. Not that they said it outright, but Venu was their favorite. They bragged about him at parties and family gatherings. His photos sat framed in every room back home. Venu was the one with the right grades, the right job, the right condo. He was the golden child.

Vikram had spent years being measured against him.

Teachers, aunties, neighbors all used Venu as the benchmark. Hell, even he had done it, compared himself to his brother and he always fell short.

He turned towards the mantle, his eyes landing back on the series of framed photos. Vikram stared at the faces, the backdrops, the quiet peace that radiated from them.
How the hell could Venu walk away from all this? The condo, the job, the goddamn imported soap in the bathroom. How did someone with all of this walk away and then vanish in the woods? How?

He realized he was clutching the frame in his hand so tightly his knuckles had gone white.

He set the photo back in its place and exhaled long and low. Without a word, he turned and walked into the kitchen. The stainless steel of the Sub-Zero refrigerator reflected him faintly as he opened the door, the chill escaping in a quiet rush.

"You always had great taste, Venu..." Vikram murmured to the open fridge. He reached inside and pulled out a lone bottle of Michelob Ultra. A tired smirk tugged at the corner of his mouth. He popped the cap and took a long drink. His face wrinkled into a grimace.
"...but not when it comes to beer," he added, lowering the

bottle.

He dumped the rest down the sink, the fizzing sound briefly filling the silence. The bottle landed in the recycling bin with a hollow clink.

Vikram picked up his phone from the counter and tapped to replay the message he'd received the day before. The voice was calm, polite, almost painfully gentle.

“Hello, Vikram. This is sheriff E.J. Baker with the Whatcom County Sheriff's Office. I was just calling to let you know how sorry I am that we weren't able to locate your brother. We were able to recover your brother's backpack. Please come by my office at any time to pick it up or give me a call and we can arrange to have it sent to you. Again, I'm terribly sorry.”

The message ended.

Vikram stared at the screen for a long beat. The silence that followed was heavier than the message itself.

He set the phone down, grabbed the black Burberry jacket draped over the back of a leather bar stool, and headed toward the front door. Before reaching it, he paused, turning to take in the apartment one last time.

It was unmistakably Venu's. Every detail was carefully curated, clean, modern, touched with comfort and intention. A space lived in and earned.

"You worked hard for all of this, bro," Vikram said softly. His voice was steadier now. “I'm gonna find you...and bring you home.”

He slipped his feet into a pair of brown leather loafers and

opened the door. The hallway outside was quiet and brightly lit, washed in the low hum of recessed lighting.
As he pulled the door shut behind him and turned the key in the lock, his shoulders slumped slightly. His head dipped forward as if the weight of his brother's disappearance had settled into his bones.

He hadn't taken more than a few steps down the hall when a door creaked open behind him. "Venu! Venu, you're..." Vikram turned.
A woman stood just outside the apartment across the hall. Fit, early thirties, dressed head-to-toe in sleek, expensive athleisure. Her blonde hair was pulled into a loose ponytail.

She froze when she saw him.

"Oh. I'm so sorry," she said, her voice faltering. "I thought for a second you were Venu. I was really hoping you were Venu... I heard the door to his apartment close and I just—"

"Yeah," Vikram said, offering a tired smile. "I used to get that a lot growing up. 'Why aren't you Venu?'"

"No, no... not like that." She stepped a little closer, arms folded across her chest. "I heard the search was called off and thought maybe...seeing you in the hallway just... I don't know. I was hoping he was okay."

Vikram nodded, softening. "I get it. I'm Vikram—Venu's younger and less adventurous brother."

He extended a hand. She reached out, hesitated just for a second, then took it.

"I'm Becca. I live across the hall. Venu and I used to go on little hikes together. He was... is... very sweet."

Her eyes glassed over, and she quickly brushed at them with the sleeve of her hoodie. She looked up at him, her voice suddenly more fragile.
"I'm sorry. I am. Venu was just...a really great person."

"Yeah," Vikram said, his voice quieter now. "He is. Thank you."

He stepped back, glanced toward the elevators. "I should get going. Driving up to Whatcom County—sheriff's office. They found his backpack."

Becca nodded, arms still crossed tightly. "Drive safe. And... if you need anything. Seriously. Let me know."

"I will. Thanks." He gave her a small smile. "Take care." He turned and walked to the elevators. Pressed the down button.

Behind him, he could feel Becca still standing there. When he turned to look, she was watching him, her expression unreadable.

He offered a half smile and a nod.

The elevator chimed twice.

Vikram stepped inside and hit the button marked for the parking garage. The doors slid closed, the hallway slipping away behind him.

Inside the elevator, Vikram stood alone.

He leaned his back against the mirrored wall, buried his face in the crook of his right arm. The fabric of his jacket muffled the soft, uneven sound of his breathing.

He was crying.

Not loudly. Not dramatically. Just the kind of quiet, exhausted weeping that escaped when no one else was watching.

The elevator descended.

CHAPTER 5: DETLEF SCHREMPF

The driver's side door of the Audi S5 opened, Vikram stepped out. He wore the same clothes from earlier that day — the maroon cashmere sweater, black slacks, bright red socks tucked into brown leather loafers. The Burberry jacket was now buttoned all the way to the top, the collar turned slightly against the cool wind. He cut a slender but striking figure as he closed the door behind him and surveyed the building ahead.

The entrance to the sheriff's office was unassuming, the kind you could walk past without noticing. The lettering across the door, once bold in gold and blue paint, now looked chipped and sun-faded: *Whatcom County Sheriff's Office*.

Vikram paused at the threshold, hand hovering near the door handle.

A breath in. A breath out.

Then he pulled the door open and stepped inside.

The sheriff's office was nondescript and practical in the way rural buildings often were, with no effort made to impress. Just inside the entrance, the air smelled faintly of dust, stale coffee, and old paper.

Two dented filing cabinets stood against the back wall, the beige paint chipped at the corners. In the center of the room sat a squat reception desk, an institutional relic that looked like it had been salvaged from a government auction in the early 2000s, maybe earlier. Its laminate surface was dull with age and wear.

Behind the desk sat a young deputy. Very young. He didn't look older than twenty-one. His uniform hung awkwardly off his shoulders, a size too big, as though he'd borrowed it from an older sibling. His cheeks were flushed pink, and a faint band of peach fuzz lined his upper lip, valiantly attempting to become a mustache.

He stared intently at a computer monitor, brow furrowed with the kind of concentration usually reserved for gaming or an intense game of solitaire.

To the right of the desk, a small office sat tucked behind a closed door. A water cooler stood guard beside it, flanked by a low bookcase that held a Keurig coffee machine, a stack of Styrofoam cups, a disorganized pile of coffee pods, and a scattering of sugar packets and sweeteners.
Above the bookcase, a mounted deer head looked down at the room with glassy indifference, its antlers wide and imposing. Below it hung a wooden sign, clearly handmade. Burned into the wood in uneven block letters were the words: *The buck stops here.*

Vikram stepped through the threshold, the door clicking softly shut behind him.

The young deputy looked up, blinking once, startled from

whatever screen had held his focus.

"Hey there," he said with a friendly nod. "How can I help you?"

"Oh, yeah... I'm here to see Sheriff Baker," Vikram said. "I'm Venu's brother. The sheriff said I could come down to pick up Venu's backpack."

The deputy stood, and Vikram blinked in surprise. The kid was *tall*—not just tall but looming. Standing up, he was a full head above most people Vikram had met.

"Wow," Vikram said, catching himself. "You are tall. Sorry. You probably hear that a lot. It's just... sitting down, you don't look as tall. Probably because you're sitting."

The deputy chuckled. "No worries. Yeah, I heard that a lot growing up. I hit six-two in eighth grade. Ended up at six-seven by senior year."

"Did you play basketball at all? I mean..."

"I did," the deputy said, nodding. "Stopped after high school, though. Tweaked my knee a few times senior year. That didn't stop me from playing at the next level though."

Vikram raised an eyebrow. "No? Where'd you play?"

The deputy grinned. "Well, what stopped me from playing at the next level was an epic lack of talent. It was easy dominating around here against stocky lumberjack kids."

Vikram laughed. "I bet! You kinda look like a young Detlef Schrempf. Minus the flattop, the German accent, and the tragic off-court wardrobe choices."

The deputy's face twisted in thought. "I don't think I know who that is."

"Detlef Schrempf. Sixth-man phenom, small forward out of Germany. Played in Seattle in the mid-90s with those amazing Sonics teams that *never* won a championship." Vikram's voice grew animated—genuine affection in every word. "I'm a huge basketball junkie. Got obsessed with the '90s Sonics."

"I'll look him up," the deputy said, smiling. "YouTube probably has a bunch of clips."
"Do it. You won't be disappointed. Who knows, it might inspire you to get back in the game. There's gotta be a school around here that needs a six-seven forward."

"Yeah, maybe the middle school out in Monroe," the deputy said. "Forgot to mention: the only skill I have is being tall. Can't shoot, dribble, or pass."

"Rebound?" Vikram offered.

"Only if it falls right into my hands, guy. I can't jump either."

"Well hey, at least you've got hands, right?"

The deputy held up his hands. "Nimble as bricks."

They both laughed.

Just then, the office door to the right creaked open. A man stepped out, his uniform pressed, sharp creases, silver badge. He was older, mid-fifties at least, but his hair was immaculately styled, and his bright blue eyes gave him a youthful spark beneath the weight of authority and calculation. The sheriff.

Deputy Grimes straightened, clearing his throat. “Sheriff, this is... I’m sorry, I don’t think I ever caught your name.”

“I don’t think I ever introduced myself,” Vikram said.
The sheriff raised an amused brow. “The way you two were carrying on, I figured you’d be on a first-name basis by now.”

Vikram smiled, offering his hand. “Vikram. Venu’s brother. You left me a message yesterday.”

“Right. Of course. I’m sorry about your brother,” the sheriff said, his tone softening. “Come on into my office. I’ve got a couple forms you’ll need to sign.”

He paused, gesturing toward the coffee setup.

“Water? Coffee? That’s about all we’ve got.”

“I’m good, thank you,” Vikram replied. “But I do have some questions...”

“I bet you do. Let’s talk in the office.” He turned toward the door. “Deputy, hold any calls that come in.”

“You got it, Sheriff,” Grimes replied. "Name's Grimes, by the way."

Vikram nodded, then followed Baker through the door, the warmth of the earlier banter giving way to the quiet, leaden weight of unfinished business.

CHAPTER 6: PUSH PINS

The sheriff's office was small and utilitarian, more function than comfort. A family photo sat on the desk, Sheriff Baker with his wife and two teenage daughters, all smiling in a sunlit backyard.

Each wall was pinned with large aerial maps of the surrounding region, some curling at the edges. One map, directly behind the desk, was studded with colored pushpins, the red and blue dots scattered like a strange constellation.

In the far corner of the room, on a low table, sat Venu's backpack.

It looked strangely intact. Zipped. Upright. As if it had just been set down by its owner moments ago. Only the torn straps betrayed the violence it was witness to.

"Please," Sheriff Baker said, gesturing to the chair in front of the desk.

Vikram pulled the chair out, its metal legs scraping softly against the tile floor. The burnt-orange vinyl seat was cracked in places. He sat down, but his eyes kept drifting back to the backpack.

Baker rounded his desk, picked the backpack up carefully, then moved to the map with the pins.

"We found this on an access road in a remote area outside of town," he said, pointing to a blue pin on the northern edge of the map.

Vikram leaned forward slightly.

The sheriff traced his finger several inches to the left and down. "And this is where your brother's car was spotted a few days ago."

He turned back toward Vikram, brow furrowed. "We have no idea what he was doing out there. That area's private property. The road leading in is unmaintained, overgrown, and about as far from anything useful as you can get. Do you know why he would've gone out there?"

Vikram shook his head. "No. I was hoping *you* could tell me. The news said his car was found near a trailhead."

Baker gave a dry laugh. "The news condensed it into a thirty-second soundbite. The unabridged version is: we found your brother's backpack in a restricted section of the Snoqualmie National Forest. Privately owned, no public trails. Did he mention anything to you about going out there?"

"No. Just said he couldn't hang out that weekend, said he was heading out for a day hike near Glacier. Said he needed to 'do his thing.'"

"Do his thing?"

"Yeah...take pictures. Post them to his socials. He's got a solid following," Vikram explained. "He'd post these mystery photos and ask people to guess where they were taken. He didn't like the obvious spots. He was always chasing something new, some place no one had seen before."

The sheriff raised a skeptical eyebrow. "Well... you lost me at social media. My daughters like that Chinese TicTac stuff. Makes no sense to me."

"TikTok," Vikram corrected with a faint smile. "Chinese TikTok."

Baker smirked, shook his head, placed the tattered backpack on the small table, and returned to his desk. The leather chair let out a soft creak as he sat and leaned back, sizing Vikram up like he was solving a puzzle he didn't quite have the box for. Then he leaned forward again, hands flat on the desk.

"Okay then," he said. "Your brother picked one hell of a remote wilderness area for a day hike. How he even found that spot's a mystery."

He drew a long breath through his nose, exhaled hard through his mouth, and gave a slow shake of his head.

"His phone pinged a cell tower a few miles from where we found the car. Grimes spotted the vehicle, just off the side of the road. From there, we tried to determine if he'd entered the logging camp nearby. Got lucky again and found tracks and broken scotch broom near the fence line."

Vikram's hands clenched subtly in his lap. The backpack still sat on the table between them. Quiet. Waiting.

Sheriff Baker leaned back in his chair, hands folded loosely in front of him. His eyes drifted toward the backpack on the table, then back to Vikram.

“We found his SUV on a logging road that hasn’t seen regular use in years," Baker said. "It was just sitting there, locked up tight. No other tire tracks leading in, no signs of a struggle. Looked like it had been there a while.”

As the sheriff spoke, his mind pulled back to the memory of that day.

***

The cold drizzle, the droplets streaking down the dark metallic paint of the SUV. The ground beneath the vehicle was damp, but hardpacked. Moss had begun to curl at the edges of the tires. Dirt traced slow rivers across the quarter panels and rear window. He had walked a slow circle around the vehicle, checking each door handle. Locked. Undisturbed.

Deputy Grimes had been standing a few yards away, near the gate to the logging camp, squinting through the mist. “You think he climbed the fence and went in there?” Grimes had asked.

Baker had stepped away from the car, rubbing the back of his neck.

“Well, let’s see,” he said, voice low and measured. “His car is here. Been here a while, by the looks of it. Last I checked, this ain't a park-and-ride. No other vehicles. No other tracks. And if foul play was involved... I doubt the bad guys would leave a hundred-thousand-dollar SUV untouched.”

He glanced toward the camp’s perimeter. Razor wire lined the entire top of the fence. Chains wrapped the gate, sealing it off from the outside and inside.

“I’d say he went in,” he added. “Just gotta figure out how. Check the perimeter. I’ll update SAR.”

Grimes moved toward the gate, testing the heavy locks. “If he climbed this, he’d have to be Spider-Man to clear that wire,” he muttered.

Baker returned to the patrol vehicle and lifted the radio receiver. “We found the missing hiker’s vehicle,” he said, flatly. “Yeah. No, I doubt it’s another case. How many folks out here drive a fancy SUV like this? Sending coordinates now. Bring the dogs. I’ve got a bad feeling.”

He hung up, slammed the door shut, and walked back toward the fence. The mist hadn’t let up. Dew clung to the fence like sweat, heavy on the air.

Tracking would be hard.

He joined the deputy in walking the perimeter. It didn’t take long. A patch of scotch broom had been crushed near the base of the fence. Another few steps and there were more bent stems, flattened plants. A faint trail. Subtle, but real.

“Hey,” he called over his shoulder. “I think I’ve watched enough episodes of *Alone* to spot a path through the brush when I see one. Our guy went this way.”

Grimes joined him, and together they followed the faint trail until they reached the breach in the chain-link fence.

Both men stood still for a moment.

Then Baker noticed something—a scrap of fabric, caught on the metal. He pulled it free and turned it over in his hand. He looked to the side. No tracks past the cut. Just brush, undisturbed.

"Guess this is where he went through," Baker said, holding up the fabric. "Probably caught his jacket here."

Grimes shifted beside him, eyes on the camp beyond. "We going in?"

***

The memory slipped away, leaving only the quiet of the sheriff's office. Baker exhaled and leaned back in his chair. "Once we spotted the breach in the fence, we figured it was worth checking the buildings. Maybe your brother found shelter, got turned around...maybe he was holed up inside."

He didn't elaborate. Silence stretched between him and Vikram. Baker traced the faux woodgrain of his desk as the images of that day returned.

***

Grimes and Baker walked in silence back to the sheriff's vehicle, the mist curling low over the access road. Baker popped the rear hatch of his Explorer, the metallic clank of tools rising into the stillness as he rummaged through a mess of gear.

Behind him, Deputy Grimes stood at the gate, staring into the camp beyond. His gaze drifted upward, past the rusted equipment and sagging roofs, up toward the treeline and the thick mist beyond it.

He shifted his weight, scuffed the gravel with the toe of his boot, hands resting on his hips.

"What do you think brought him out here?" he asked softly.

The question hung in the air like breath in the cold.
"Your guess is as good as mine," Baker thought.

He slammed the hatch shut and stepped around the vehicle, bolt cutters in hand."Let's get those chains off and take a look around."

Grimes nodded, and they approached the fence together.

Baker leaned into the first lock, angling the cutters, and with a heavy *clunk*, the chain dropped to the ground.

He repeated the process with the second lock, then dragged the tangled chain free from the gates.

The air beyond the fence felt different, quieter somehow.
Not the silence of a still morning, but something heavier and expectant.

The sheriff pushed one side of the gate open, the metal creaking in protest. Grimes did the same with the opposite side.

They stepped through.

Inside, the logging camp was nothing but a ghost of abandoned equipment slouched in rust, buildings were half-swallowed by moss and brush. The fog seemed thicker now, muting color and sound.

Neither man spoke.

They moved deeper into the logging camp, boots moving steadily across the damp gravel and broken pinecones. The place felt long abandoned, though nothing had collapsed, just suspended in time.

"The timber company bailed out in a hurry," Grimes said, glancing around at the half-forgotten machinery. "Why'd they cut outta here so fast?"

Baker walked slow, hands in his jacket pockets, eyes sweeping the haphazard sprawl of generators, fuel drums, and a loader with its claw still raised like it was frozen mid-motion.

"Probably trying to stay three steps ahead of lawsuits," he said.

Grimes frowned. "Environmentalists?"

"That," Baker replied, "and... there were a lot of worker injuries. In a short amount of time."

Grimes gave him a look but didn't push. They continued toward the cluster of administrative buildings near the center of the camp.

"What's with all the security, though?" Grimes asked. "Gates, concrete barriers, cameras. That's a lot for a place that was shut down due to worker's comp claims."

Baker stopped and took in the camp with a slow, sweeping look. The place was unnaturally silent. Even the birds seemed to avoid it.

"I think they planned to reopen once the legal stuff cooled off," he said. "That's why the gear's still here. Just waiting."

They approached the first of the buildings. The exterior was intact, if weathered. A heavy chain was looped through the door handles and secured with a rusting padlock. Grimes gave it a tug. Nothing moved.

"If they're all sealed like this," Grimes said, "we can probably rule out our hiker camping out inside."

Baker grunted, then stepped over to one of the boarded-up windows. He worked at a corner with his fingers, trying to peel it back. No luck. He stepped back and inspected the frame.

"These boards are screwed in. Not nailed," he muttered.

"Bit of overkill," Grimes said.

"Yeah," Baker murmured. "Maybe..."

His voice drifted off as he turned away from the building. A subtle shift in the air had caught his attention. He waved to get Grimes' attention. "Let's split up. Check the rest of the doors. Then we'll head back to the vehicles. SAR should be here soon."

Grimes nodded and peeled off toward the west side of the camp.

Baker moved between the buildings, following a gravel path that led past the largest structure. It was the same one Venu had approached. As he stepped around the corner, the fog shifted, clearing just enough to expose the swing gate that blocked the access road beyond the camp.

He stopped.

Something was there.

Just past the gate.

A flicker, maybe just a shape. But *something large* moving through the trees. It didn't make a sound, but it moved with purpose, not drifting like fog, not the sway of trees in wind. Baker flinched. His head jerked back instinctively.

Grimes looked up from across the camp, his eyes locking on the sheriff.

“You good?” he called.

Baker didn’t answer immediately. The shape had vanished. He stared at the space beyond the gate. The forest beyond was still again, wrapped in its blanket of mist.

No noise.
Just silence.

Too much of it.

Grimes’s voice cut through the stillness. “Hey… you see something out there?”

Baker stood silent. His eyes lingered on the space just beyond the gate, where the mist had closed back in.

“No,” he said finally. “I don’t think so. Just the fog playing tricks.”

He turned, his voice low and tight. “Let’s wrap this up and get back to the truck.”

They started walking, the gravel shifting underfoot in steady rhythm. Grimes glanced sideways at the sheriff, noting the tight line of his jaw and the way his eyes kept scanning the trees.

“You sure you didn’t see something?”

Baker didn't look at him. "Yep. I'm sure. Don't ask me again."

The two men walked in silence for a few paces. The forest pressed close, thick with fog. The logging camp behind them was already fading into gray.

Grimes frowned. "When we were checking those buildings earlier...I don't know. A couple times it felt like something was watching us from out in the trees."

Baker grunted, noncommittal.

"All this mist and fog dampens sound," he said. "Plays tricks. Makes everything feel closer than it is. Once it burns off, that feeling will go away."

"Yeah," Grimes said slowly. "I guess so."

He looked down at the trail, then back up at the woods flanking the road.

"But you know the feeling I mean, right?" he continued. 'That weird buzz, like the hair on your neck's about to stand up? Did you feel that?"

"Nope," said Baker.

"I did," replied Grimes, a bit more emphatically than intended.

They reached the main gate. The chains lay limp where they'd fallen earlier, curled like discarded snakes on the gravel.

Baker walked through first, his boots hitting the road with a heavy finality. He paused, tilted his head back, and looked up at the sky. The fog still hung thick, but there were hints of light filtering through the gray.

He shook his head.

"This fog'll burn off soon," he muttered. "Search and Rescue should be here any minute. Let's look alive."

Grimes said nothing. Just followed, eyes drifting back toward the woods.

Two orange-and-white crew cab trucks rolled in to the access road behind the sheriff's Explorer, the tires sliding across the gravel as they came to a halt.

Sheriff Baker stepped back from the gate and gave a wave.

The trucks hissed and settled. Doors opened. Slammed shut. A team of six Search and Rescue personnel climbed out, men and women in matching khaki pants, long-sleeve work shirts, and orange safety vests. They moved with purpose, immediately heading to the truck beds to pull gear from locked compartments. A stocky man with sun-creased skin and salt-and-pepper hair approached.

"Wade," Sheriff Baker called out. "How are ya?"

"Doin' well, Sheriff," Wade Coombs replied. The two men shook hands. Deputy Grimes stepped in and offered his own.

"Deputy Grimes solvin' crimes!" Wade said with a grin.

Grimes grinned back. "I do my best, Wade."

Wade turned his gaze toward the thick forest beyond the fence. "Our missing hiker out there somewhere?"

"That's how it's looking," Baker said.

“Well, we’ve got the dogs. We’re ready." Wade nodded towards the SUV. "I take it that’s the hiker’s vehicle?”

“Yep,” Baker said. “Let the dogs get a nose full before heading in. We think we’ve got his entry point over by the east fence line."

The dog handler approached with two Labrador retrievers in bright yellow harnesses marked WORKING DOG. The dogs were alert, tails wagging furiously, eager to move.

The handler, a woman in her late twenties with bright blue eyes and shoulder-length strawberry blonde hair tied into a low ponytail, walked them over with practiced ease. Sheriff Baker recognized her from the SAR roster—Deanna Moore, one of the more experienced handlers in the county.

She offered a polite nod. Baker bent down instinctively, hand outstretched to scratch behind one of the dog’s ears—then stopped himself midmotion. “Hard not to pet these pups, Deanna” he said with a sheepish grin. “But I know they’re on the clock.”

Deanna smiled. “They look playful, sure, but trust me, they’re just ready to work.” She looked down at the dogs proudly.

Baker could still see the glint of pride in her eyes as he blinked back to the present. Across from him, Vikram sat silently in the vinyl chair, his fingers worrying a loose thread in his jacket cuff.

He didn’t interrupt, but the look on his face had shifted.

Less grief. More focus.

***

Vikram's voice pulled him back to present.

"You said the dogs got Venu's scent from the SUV?" Vikram asked. "How?"

The sheriff didn't miss the edge in his voice—quiet, but sharpening.

"That's right," he said carefully. "Some liberties were taken with your brother's rig."

Vikram lifted an eyebrow.

The sheriff sucked on his teeth, then continued. "Grimes popped the driver's side lock with a slim jim. That was the only way we could guarantee the dogs would get what they needed to track your brother's movements. We can talk about what they found... or didn't... in a minute. Just wanted you to have the whole picture."

Vikram nodded as Sheriff Baker continued.

The memory unfolded as he spoke:

***

Deanna straightened, giving the dogs a quick scan. "They caught a good scent off the SUV," she said. "Point us in the right direction, and I'll let them get after it."

Baker gave a nod and motioned for her to follow. Wade Coombs let out a sharp whistle.

"All right, folks, let's move! Let's keep it tight behind the dogs," he called out.

The SAR crew fell in behind them, stepping through the open gates and into the fog-drenched camp.

"Hey, Deanna," Grimes said, falling into step beside her.

She glanced over. "Hey, Grimes."

Grimes gave a shy smile, then looked down at his boots.

Deanna didn't say anything, but her mouth twitched at the corners.

Grimes cleared his throat and gestured ahead. "He came in over here through a cut section of fence. I'll show you."

From behind, Baker muttered, "I bet you will…"
Grimes shot the sheriff an embarrassed look, but Deanna was smiling now, clearly amused. He relaxed a little and led her to the spot where the fence had been breached.

"There you go," he said. "You can see where he, uh...where me and the sheriff trampled through the foliage. It's a safe bet that's where he ent..."

"We got it from here, Grimey," Deanna said, cutting him off gently.

She knelt beside the dogs, unhooking their leashes from the harnesses. The two Labradors stood poised, muscles coiled, eyes focused.

"Find!" she commanded.

They shot off like arrows, noses low, weaving a purposeful path from the fence line toward the buildings. The rest of the team filtered through the camp's open gate while Baker, Grimes, and Deanna followed through the cut section in the fence.

The dogs led them on a winding path through the camp until they arrived at the rear of the largest building. There, the overgrown access road stretched out into the mist.

"Stay," Deanna called. The dogs halted immediately, heads up and alert, tails rigid.

Baker caught up, eyeing them with quiet curiosity.

"They didn't go near any of the buildings," he said. "Except that one."

Deanna gave a half-nod, her eyes on the tree line. "Our guy's not here. He went up this road."

She turned to Baker, smiling playfully. "But hey, if you want to search the buildings, knock yourself out."

"I'll trust the dogs," Baker said. "Deputy and I already checked the doors and windows. All sealed up tight."

Deanna gave the dogs a firm nod. "Find."

They launched forward again, up the narrow road and into the woods, with the rest of the team in pursuit.

CHAPTER 7: BEAR WITH ME

Baker took a deep breath and continued, his voice measured and steady.

***

They'd been on the access road for a while now, hiking steadily into thicker, wilder country. Fog still clung to the treetops, but the sun had begun to break through in places.

"Where was this guy going?" Wade Coombs asked, adjusting his pack and wiping sweat from his brow. "We've been on this road at least two miles."

Grimes nodded. "Sheriff and I were wondering the same thing."

Deanna walked a few steps ahead, the two Labradors weaving along the road's shoulder, sniffing and focused.

"They aren't thinking this is just a long-ass walk, are they?" Wade asked, smirking.

"My dogs are working," Deanna said. "They'll let me know if they lose the scent. Or find something."
Wade let out a low whistle. "All right. Just feels like a long haul

for a day hike. He didn't bring camping gear, right?"

"Nope," Grimes said. "Not that we know of."

Suddenly, the dogs broke into a sprint, tearing up the road ahead, barking low and anxious.

"They found something!" Deanna called out, breaking into a run. "Let's go!"

The team scrambled to follow, boots pounding as they chased the dogs up the incline. One hundred meters ahead, the two Labradors had stopped and were hovering just a half meter from a backpack lying squarely in the middle of the access road.

Venu's backpack.

The dogs whined, tails lowered, their posture shifting from excitement to unease. Deanna reached them seconds later and gave the "finish" command. The dogs immediately returned to her side, heads down, ears twitching.

Baker arrived next, crouching over the pack. He inspected the torn straps, the punctures along one side, the way it had landed—askew, but not dropped.

Grimes slipped on a pair of latex gloves and joined him, kneeling beside the sheriff. "We got a crime scene here?"

Baker shook his head. "I don't think so."

He turned the backpack over slowly, examining the frayed fabric. "Something tore this off him."

Around them, the SAR team began to fan out, instinctively

scanning for signs, trails, or anything that might lead them further.

“Hey, over here!” one of the crew shouted, waving them over.

The team jogged to the spot, about twenty feet off the road, where the ferns had been trampled and grass bent sharply toward the trees.

“Someone definitely came through here recently,” the team member said. “Look at this trail...blades broken, underbrush smashed. I bet he wandered off here.”

Grimes frowned. “Then why’s his backpack out in the middle of the road?”

Another team member, closer to the trees, turned back to the group.

“Not to be a downer,” he said, “but maybe something dragged him off.”

“Yeah,” the first added. “There’s cougars and shit out here.”

Wade looked to Baker. “Sheriff?”

“It’s possible,” Baker said, his voice even. “And over here...looks like signs of a struggle.”

He was staring down at the dirt near the road. One rock stood out among the small gravel, darker and stained with something that didn’t match the rain-slicked surface. It was larger than thc others and heavy enough to do damage.

Baker furrowed his brow and squatted beside it.

"This job would be a hell of a lot easier if it didn't rain so much out here," he muttered. "Deanna, see if your dogs can check the area where your folks are clustered."

"Got it," she said, and moved to lead the dogs forward. But as they approached the area, the dogs resisted. Their tails dropped further. Their bodies tensed. They dug their paws into the gravel and refused to move.

"What's up with the dogs?" Wade asked.
Deanna crouched beside them, speaking gently. "I don't know. Something's got them spooked. It's okay," she whispered, stroking one of their necks. "Easy, easy…"

"Look, we can head in without the dogs if..." The team member stopped mid-sentence.

Snap.
A sharp crack of breaking branches echoed from the woods.

Snap. Snap.

It was getting closer fast.

The team froze. The dogs began barking wildly, tails low, backing away from the trees. Deanna's grip tightened on their leashes.

Grimes and Baker were already stepping forward, hands on their sidearms.

A blur of movement exploded from the tree line. A massive black bear burst into the clearing, barreling into the nearest team member and knocking him flat on his back. The man screamed as the bear clamped its jaws down into his left shoulder.

Five gunshots rang out, sharp and close.

Then silence.

Baker and Grimes stood with their weapons drawn, eyes locked on the fallen bear. It didn't move.

The injured team member writhed on the ground, moaning in pain, blood blooming across his shirt.

"We need to get him to a hospital," Wade said quickly. "I've got enough in the kit to slow down the bleeding, but we gotta get him to the trucks fast."

"Okay," Baker said, already holstering his weapon. "Get to work."

"Roger that."

Wade dropped to his knees and opened the first aid kit strapped to his pack, working with practiced calm.

Deanna was there a second later. "Hey, buddy," Deanna said gently. She knelt beside the injured man, her voice calm, but her eyes sharp and focused. "I need you to try and relax, okay? We're gonna get you out of here."

"Argh..." The team member groaned, his face twisted in pain. "This friggin' hurts. You think that bear had rabies?"

Deanna looked up, caught Grimes's eye.

Grimes gave a small shrug, his expression unreadable.

"Let's not worry about that right now," Deanna said.

“Yeah,” Grimes added, stepping closer. “We’re getting you out of here. The doctors will take care of the rest.”

“How’s it going, Wade?” Deanna asked, shifting slightly to give him more room to work.

“Good,” Wade said, tightening a final bandage. “Just about done here.”
He pressed a hand to the man’s arm. “You’re gonna have to stand for me, buddy.”

The injured man groaned, but with help, he got to his feet. He swayed, knees buckling for a moment before finding his balance.

“You’ve lost some blood,” Deanna said. “You’re a little shook up.”

“That’ll happen,” the man muttered through clenched teeth, “when a fucking *rabid bear* attacks you.”

“We don’t know if it had rabies,” she said, steady but kind. “Wade and I are going to start walking you back to the trucks. We’ll get you to the hospital and get that bite looked at properly.”

She gave him a nod and motioned for Wade. The two began guiding the injured man back down the road, the rest of the team falling into quiet formation behind them. Deanna's dogs trotted loyally by her side.

Grimes lingered behind, stepping over to where Baker still stood, unmoving, his eyes fixed on the bear’s corpse. The animal lay splayed in the gravel, its thick fur matted and patchy, ribs faintly visible beneath its hide. Its lips were curled back from broken yellow teeth, gums blackened in places, eyes cloudy.

Baker didn't say anything at first. He just stared.

"Black bears don't normally act like that," Grimes said finally. "But this one came right at us. No bluff. Just straight in." Grimes studied the carcass. "It's late in the season," he said slowly. "And this one looks… off. Sick, maybe. Could be rabies. He's still a big fella though."

"Yeah." Baker nodded, then sighed through his nose. "Let's get Fish and Wildlife up here. They'll need to haul this thing out, run some tests."

He looked down the road, toward the fading shapes of the others.

"They'll probably need four-wheelers to get it out." Baker turned to Grimes, his tone shifting back into official cadence. "Make a call to the logging company's corporate office. Tell them we found our missing hiker on their property. They'll need to come secure the fence."

Grimes turned toward him, confused. "Wait, we found our missing hiker?"

Baker met his eyes. "Dollars to donuts," he said, "that bear got to him. He ran, it caught the backpack, tore it off… then dragged him back into the woods."

He said it plainly. With authority.

But his eyes drifted toward the trees again.

And he didn't look convinced.

Grimes didn't move. "Shouldn't we confirm that's what happened?" he asked. "Find the body?"

Baker rounded on him. "Christ, Grimey! You saw what that bear did to that guy, didn't you? Damn near tore his arm off before we even knew what the hell was happening."

He gestured back toward the logging road, voice rising. "You think we're going to find a body? No. We're not finding a *fucking* body. That's the reality."

He paused, chest heaving slightly.

"Collect the backpack, notify next of kin, and call off the search. It's over."

Grimes held his ground. "That just seems a bit presumptuous, don't you think?"

Baker's face reddened. His voice dropped, low and sharp. "If you want to go out into those woods on a goddamn body recovery mission, be my guest. But I'm telling you, whatever's left of that hiker is either in that bear's belly or being picked clean by every other critter in the forest."

He turned away, muttering something under his breath as he started walking back toward the rest of the team.

Grimes stood in silence, eyes still scanning the forest. Something about it didn't feel right.

It hadn't all day.

***

The thought lingered as Baker leaned forward in the present, folding his hands across the desk. “Some might call this speculation,” he began carefully, “but all evidence points to your brother crossing paths with that bear.”

He paused.

“That bear wasn’t right. Too aggressive. Not afraid of people. We took it down right near where we found Venu’s backpack...it was probably guarding it.”

He glanced at Vikram, reading his face. “It severely injured a Search and Rescue worker.”

Vikram’s brow furrowed. “But there was no sign of Venu. Just… his backpack?”

Baker’s eyes flicked to the side. “Look, son… I don’t know how to say this without sounding insensitive.”

“Just say it,” Vikram said. “Please.”

Baker exhaled, more through his nose than his mouth. “After a couple of days... there really isn’t much left after an animal attack out in these woods. Bears, mountain lions, coyotes. Scavengers. Nature doesn’t leave things behind.”

Vikram shifted in his seat, eyes glossing as the sheriff’s words began to settle in. Too many details. Too much certainty.

Baker caught himself, straightened, softened his language. “We believe the encounter happened on the access road. There were signs of a struggle, even after the rain. The bear was undernourished. Old. Probably couldn’t fight off other predators once it brought the body into the woods.”

He studied Vikram for a moment. "You sure you want to hear this?"

Vikram's voice was barely above a whisper. "So the bear killed my brother, dragged his body off into the woods, and ate him? That's what you're saying?"

"Yes," Baker said.

Vikram stared down at his hands, then turned to the wall map. He let out a long, unsteady sigh.

"A friggin' bear ate my brother." He looked back at Baker. "Did anyone cut the bear open? Like… in *Jaws* ?"

Baker nodded. "We did. Nothing out of the ordinary in the digestive tract. But that doesn't mean much. Black bears process fast."

He sighed and spoke softly. "This can't be easy for you." Vikram swallowed. "Are you sure he's dead? You said you didn't find anything conclusive in the bear. He could still be out there. Hurt. Alive."

The sheriff's expression was firm. "It's been over four weeks. The weather's dropping below freezing at night. If there was any chance Venu was still out there, I'd be in those woods right now."

The two men sat in silence for several beats, the weight of it all hanging in the room like fog.

Finally, Baker shifted in his seat and gestured toward the pack resting on the table.

"Your brother's backpack is yours to take. His camera's intact. There's a few other personal effects inside."

"Thanks," Vikram said, voice brittle. He wiped his eyes quickly and stood. "Is there a motel nearby? Not a bed and breakfast or anything with... morning scones. Just... quiet. I don't feel like driving home tonight."

Baker gave a faint smile. "Twenty minutes out. No breakfast. No Wi-Fi. It's about as basic as they come."

"Perfect," Vikram muttered. "Guess I'll grab the backpack and get out of your way."

"Anytime," Baker said. "Give me a call if you think of anything else to ask. But I think we've covered it all."

Vikram slung the backpack over his shoulder. As he reached the office door, he paused. His eyes drifted to the map on the wall. Then back to Baker.

"What was he doing out there, Sheriff?"

Baker's face didn't change. "I have no idea. Like I said, I was hoping you could tell me."

Vikram pursed his lips, gave a faint nod, and walked out. On his way through the lobby, he passed Deputy Grimes at the front desk.

"Hit me up if you're ever in Seattle," Vikram said, managing half a smile. "We'll shoot around."

Grimes perked up. "Sounds good. Take care." Vikram stepped out into the fading light.

In the quiet that followed, Sheriff Baker emerged from his

office and stood beside the front desk. He stared at the door for a long moment.

Grimes slowly turned in his chair, hands folded.

The sheriff shook his head. “Well,” he muttered. “That was that.”

Grimes leaned back in his chair, watching the door settle shut behind Vikram.

“Yeah,” he said, after a moment. “You think he bought it?”

The sheriff didn’t answer right away. He stood there, still staring at the door, lips pressed into a thin line.

“Even if he didn’t,” Baker said finally, voice quiet but firm, “I don’t think he’s the type to do anything about it.”

Grimes nodded slowly, but something in his eyes suggested he wasn’t so sure.

Neither of them spoke for a long while.

CHAPTER 8: 80S NIGHT

Vikram sat on the edge of the motel bed, staring down at the contents of his brother's backpack.

The room was bright, but not cheerful. Everything inside looked like it hadn't been updated since the early days of the George H.W. Bush administration. The comforter was a faded swirl of pink and aqua, the fixtures dull gold, worn down to the base metal in places. The table and chairs were the kind of oak veneer that tried too hard to look expensive. Only the television—a 43" flatscreen mounted above a chipped dresser —betrayed any sense of modernity.

On the bed in front of him, the backpack's contents were spread out like puzzle pieces. Vikram methodically sorted through them, placing uneaten granola bars and foil-wrapped energy gels in a pile off to the side.

He picked up a pair of Venu's gloves and slipped one on, flexing his fingers. Too tight. He smirked.
"Still had those freaky little hands, huh?" he murmured, chuckling to himself. An old inside joke. One of a hundred. He tossed the gloves aside and unzipped the camera case. Inside was Venu's DSLR, worn but well cared for. Vikram held it for a moment, heavy in his hands, then pressed the power button.

Nothing.

He dug around in the case and found the charger, then fumbled with the battery for longer than he cared to admit before finally removing it and sliding it into the dock. He plugged it into the wall beside the nightstand and set the camera back in its case with a sigh.

The analog alarm clock read 8:36 PM. The slow blink of its red digits felt louder than it should have.

Vikram pulled the backpack closer and began checking the smaller pockets. Lip balm. Travel sunscreen. More energy gels.

He held one up and squinted.

"Did you ever eat actual food, bro?" he muttered.

Then, in one of the interior compartments, his hand brushed plastic.

He pulled out a sandwich bag.

Inside was a crumpled bar napkin. The ink was slightly smeared, but still legible. A crude map had been drawn in blue ballpoint pen, along with a short set of instructions:

Pull off at mile marker... front gate... hole in fence... fence post... yellow ribbon.

Vikram turned the napkin over.

The bar's name was stamped in faded black ink across the back. *The Thirsty Badger.*

His breath caught for half a second. He fumbled for his phone, thumb swiping quickly to Instagram. Venu's profile was still up.

Scrolling. Scrolling. There it was.

A photo of a low-slung building with a gravel lot. The caption: *Badger Time!*

Then he shot up from the bed.

He moved quickly—shoes, jacket, keys—all muscle memory. He dropped into a dingy upholstered chair, yanked his shoes on, and was out the door a heartbeat later.

The name of the bar was still bouncing around in Vikram's head by the time he hit the highway.
It was one of those places Venu talked about after weekend road trips, the kind of bar that probably hadn't changed much over the last two decades. Maybe longer.

GPS led him there.

Fifteen minutes and three right turns later, Vikram pulled into a gravel lot with two trucks, a Subaru Outback, and what he was pretty sure was a hearse that had been converted into someone's daily driver.

The bar sat low and wide at the edge of a strip of thinning trees, the neon beer signs in the window humming faintly against the night.

Vikram sighed, turned off the engine, and checked his reflection in the rearview mirror.

The Burberry jacket wasn't doing him any favors.

He exited the car and walked toward the front door, then hesitated. "Do I really want to go in here?" he quietly asked himself. Muted classic rock spilled out from the bar. Vikram took a deep breath and then stepped inside.

The wall to the right of the entrance was covered in flyers for local events, lost dogs, used kayaks for sale, acoustic shows promising $3 cover and “vibes.” In the upper corner, above a bulletin for a stolen pressure washer, were several Missing Person notices.
Vikram stopped. Each flyer had a photo of smiling hikers, dates, trail names. "Last seen..." printed in bold type beneath them.

He didn’t linger long.

The interior was dim but warm, lit by low amber bulbs and the flicker of a muted flat-screen playing a regional college basketball game. The place wasn’t full, but it was *occupied* by a handful of regulars planted in time-worn booths or leaning on the bar, each nursing drinks with the comfort of habit.

Vikram knew immediately he stood out.

The Burberry jacket. The city energy. The quiet unease that followed him in like static. A dozen eyes flicked toward him and then looked away.

Nobody seemed to care.

Still, he felt like he had wandered into someone else’s story. He moved toward the bar, willing himself to stay cool, confident.
It helped when he noticed the bartender.
She wasn’t what he expected.

Slender, brunette, probably mid-thirties. She wore glasses, her hair tied back, a towel slung over one shoulder as she dried pint glasses with steady, practiced hands. She looked more like a grad student than a small-town bartender, more NPR than NRA.

Beth.

Vikram felt himself relax, just slightly.

He picked a spot a few seats down from her and slid into place. As he reached for the menu tent, his fingers misjudged the distance and his left hand knocked it off the bar and onto the floor with a soft *thwap*.

The bartender raised an eyebrow without looking away from the billiards area.

"There's better ways to get my attention if you want something," she said.

Vikram's face flushed. "Oh no—I'm sorry. I wasn't trying to get your attention. I mean, I *was* ... 'cause I want to order something. But I wasn't throwing that around or anything, I just have this weird monovision contact lens prescription and sometimes my depth perception is off and I knock stuff over when I reach for..."

She cut him off.

"Jesus, dude," she said. "I was just messing with you."

She gave him a smirk, tossing the towel on the bar. "What'll you have, monovision?"

CHAPTER 9: THE BAR

Vikram scanned the tap handles with mild dread. "Do you have anything that isn't an IPA?" he asked. "IPAs give me heartburn. And they taste like rusty pipe water."

Beth didn't miss a beat. "You know what rusty pipe water tastes like?"

"Yeah," Vikram said. "It tastes like terrible IPAs. And I'm from India, so I've tasted lots of terrible water."

She laughed. It was an easy, unfiltered kind of laugh. "Think you can handle a Blue Moon?"

"Sure," he said. "But save the orange slice for after soccer practice."

"Beth," she said, still smirking as she reached for a glass under the bar.

"Vikram," he replied.

Beth poured the beer like she'd done it ten thousand times. She slid it across the bar without spilling a drop.

"Kitchen's about to close," she said. "If you want food, now's the time."

Vikram opened the menu and gave it the kind of panicked

glance reserved for final exams and fast food drive-thrus. "Uh… turkey club?"

Beth tilted her head. "Are you asking or ordering?"

"Both? I mean, may I have a turkey club?"

She smirked. "Of course," she said. "Fries?"

"Chips?"

Beth raised an eyebrow. "Are you using the British colloquialism for fries because you're making some half-assed commentary on colonialism…or do you actually want chips?"

Vikram grinned. "Chips, please. Or 'crisps' as they say in England."

"Sure thing, smart ass."

Beth disappeared through the swinging door to the kitchen. Vikram turned in his seat, slowly taking in the bar's interior as Tom Petty's "*The Waiting*" rolled out of the jukebox. Most of the regulars kept to themselves, faces lit in amber glow. In the back corner, a man sat alone in a booth, silent amid the low din.

He looked to be in his mid-50s, with a thick, solid frame that filled out his well worn flannel jacket. His beard, streaked with gray, matched the close shave of his scalp. Quiet strength hung on him, and he appeared to be the kind of man that could snap a wrench, or a neck, without much effort. But it was his eyes that held Vikram. They carried no sadness, only the heaviness of years unsaid, regret that had taken root and made itself at home.

He caught Vikram staring.

The look he sent back could've been menace or curiosity. Vikram decided not to find out. He turned back to the bar.

Beth reappeared with his order. "Here you go. Turkey club with chips. Anything else?"

"No, thank you. I'm good."

He picked at a few chips, then carefully deconstructed the sandwich like it was an engineering problem.

"You know," he said between bites, "I love club sandwiches, but there's no way to eat one without unhinging your jaw. Very unbecoming of a gentleman like me."

Beth gave him a sideways look. "You're right. But also? No one gives a shit how you eat that sandwich...unless you ask me for a knife and fork. Then we'll have problems."

He raised his hands in mock surrender. "Ha, ha. No fork required."

Beth drifted down the bar to break up some light drama at the pool table, then crossed to the booth where the solitary man sat. She leaned in, exchanged a few quiet words, then returned to the bar.

She paused behind the counter, studying Vikram. "Hey, question for you."

He looked up. "Shoot."

"Are you at all related to that hiker who went missing a few weeks back?"

Vikram pushed his plate aside. Beth picked it up and slid it into the bus bin, but her eyes stayed on him.

"Yeah," he said quietly. "He's my brother. Why?"

Beth shrugged. "Just wondering."

"Did he come in here?" Vikram pressed. "Did you meet him? Maybe you can help me with this?"

He stood, reaching into his jacket pocket. From a plastic sandwich bag, he pulled out the bar napkin. He unfolded it and laid it flat, bar logo facing her first. Then he flipped it, revealing the crude hand-drawn map sketched on the back. She picked the napkin up from the bar, scanning the logo first, her brows drawing together in confusion as she examined the map on the opposite side.

"I didn't draw this," she said, shaking her head slowly. "And I've never seen it before." Her eyes lifted to meet his. "Where'd you get this?"

Vikram's voice softened. "My brother's backpack. It was in a plastic bag, tucked away in an inside pocket."

Beth let out a long breath and tapped her fingers along the bar's edge, her mind working.

"Yeah," she said. "He's been here a few times. Kinda looks like you..."

"...but taller and better looking?" Vikram offered, smiling.

"I didn't say that," Beth said, her voice soft. "I said he *looked* like you. Yeah, he's come in here a few times, actually. Always after hiking. Had a way of looking like he belonged here and didn't, all at once."

She paused, her eyes flicking toward the far booth. "Last time was maybe a day or two before he disappeared. He had dinner, sat at the bar for a while. Then—somehow— got *Mike* back there to talk to him." She nodded subtly in that direction. "They talked for a while. Then your brother left. Quiet, like always."

She picked up a towel and began drying a pint glass with slow, thoughtful movements. "He was kind. Thoughtful. The kind of guy you remember."

She looked up. "I'm sorry about what happened."

Vikram nodded once, silently. A moment passed. "Mike's his name?"

"Yep," Beth said. "He comes in here a lot. Doesn't say much. But like I said, he really hit it off with your brother. Think I even saw him smile a couple of times while they talked."

Vikram turned, slow and casual, trying not to be obvious. Mike's eyes were already on him. Vikram quickly looked back to Beth. "He looks terrifying."

Beth grinned. "Yeah, he looks mean. But he's a good guy. Just been through a lot, and it all shows on that face of his."

Vikram stood from the barstool. "Do you think he's the one who drew this map?"

"That'd be my guess," Beth said. "They were tucked in that booth a long time. Don't remember anyone else joining them."

Vikram picked the napkin off the bar. "Wish me luck."

He walked toward the booth where Mike sat, drink untouched, fingers steepled beneath his chin like he'd been waiting. He looked up as Vikram approached, his face equal parts caution and calculation.

Vikram hesitated at the edge of the booth, unsure. The napkin felt heavier now in his hand. He cleared his throat. "I...uh...I think you talked to my brother Venu a few weeks ago. He had this."

He placed the napkin gently on the table, unfolding it so the map and logo were clearly visible. He didn't slide it, didn't push it, he set it down like it might shatter.

Mike studied the napkin. Then he looked up at Vikram.

"Hey," he said, voice flat but not hostile. "I'm Mike. Good to meet you."

He unfolded his hands and placed them on the table. "You wanna take a breath and maybe not hover?"

Vikram blinked, flustered. He hadn't realized how tense his posture had become. Around them, conversation had quieted just enough to notice.

He glanced back toward Beth. She gave a small nod, a mix of *you're fine* and *keep going.*

Vikram slid into the booth across from Mike, trying to appear less rattled than he felt.

Mike's eyes lingered on the napkin, the familiar creases, the blue ballpoint scrawl, the faded bar logo. The map was the kind of thing, Vikram realized, you only make for someone you trust.

Mike looked back up at Vikram, his expression carefully neutral. “Right,” he said, voice low. “I remember him. Quiet guy. Had questions about local hiking spots.”

He tapped the napkin once, casual, though it felt like anything but. “So,” Mike said, meeting Vikram's gaze. “What exactly is it you're hoping to find out?”

CHAPTER 10: BUILDING A MYSTERY

Vikram shifted in the booth, his hands resting lightly on the edge of the table. His voice came out low, uncertain. "I, um...I just want to understand how my brother ended up with this map."

Mike studied him for a moment. His brow lifted slightly in calculation. "I drew it," he said simply. "For Venu."

Vikram blinked. "You...you drew this?"

"Yeah."

There was a pause, and then Vikram gave a small, almost embarrassed huff of a laugh. "It's...not great. You'd make a terrible cartographer, Mike."

Mike didn't smile. He didn't respond at all.
He just leaned back in the booth and let the silence settle. "Your brother came in here a few weeks back," he said eventually. "Sat right where you did at the bar. Was flipping through that nice camera of his. I came over to order a drink and caught a glimpse of one of the photos on the display. I said something. Complimented it. We got to talking."

Vikram nodded, following along.

Mike continued, "He said he was tired of taking the same pictures everyone else was taking. You know...Mount Rainier, the Cascades, the usual Instacart fodder. Wanted something different. Remote."

"It's called Instagram," Vikram said, softly correcting. "Instacart's for groceries."

Mike's lips twitched, maybe the ghost of a smirk. "Right. Instagram."

He looked down at the napkin again.

"I told him about this lake up in the foothills, more of a big pond, actually," Mike said. "Real secluded. Unreal. Water clear as glass. On a good day, you get the mountain rising up right behind it like something out of a painting."

He picked the napkin up from the table, angling it toward the overhead light as if trying to retrace the moment he had drawn it.
"Not many people know about it. It's on private company land. Hard to get to. I used to work up that way, so…I knew a route. Drew him the map. Gave him the directions. He said he'd come back after his hike and show me what he got."

Mike's voice grew quieter. "He never came back."

Vikram swallowed hard. "No. He didn't."

"I'm sorry, kid."

Vikram looked down at his hands. "I've been hearing that a lot lately." He took a slow breath, let it out unevenly. "What's so special about that lake?"

Mike shrugged. "The color, mostly. Clear blue water like you've never seen. Whole area's kind of surreal. Like someone forgot to tell it the world changed."

Vikram nodded, unsure what to say. His voice was almost a whisper. "And you told Venu about it?"

"I'm no photographer, but he showed me some of his stuff on that Insta thing, and I was impressed," Mike said. "He seemed like the kind of guy who'd get it. Who'd appreciate the remoteness." He hesitated. "Figured he'd keep quiet about it's location."

Vikram's eyes flicked down at the napkin, at the scrawled notes he already knew by heart — front gate... hole in fence... yellow ribbon. He looked back up. "How'd you know about the hole in the fence?"

Mike stilled for just a second.

"I cut it," he said finally. "Went in a few years back after the logging company shut everything down and left their equipment behind. I figured no one would miss a few pieces of scrap. I went in, salvaged what I could, sold it off. Let's just leave it at that."

Vikram blinked. "So...outdoor B&E. Got it."

His tone wasn't mocking, it was tired. Defeated. Like the shape of his brother's final days had been drawn in by strangers, piece by piece, and all Vikram could do now was trace the lines.

Mike picked up his glass, swirled the ice and took a drink. He then set it down again and slid it toward the edge of the table. He gave Beth a subtle nod for a refill.

The moment lingered.

And there was more, Vikram could feel it. But Mike wasn't offering it freely.

Not yet.

Mike placed the napkin on the table and leaned back in the booth, eyes on his glass. "The company used to pay for regular patrols of that area," he said. "Stopped maybe five or six years ago."

Vikram furrowed his brow. "Regular patrols, like rent-a-cops? That's expensive. If they cared that much about the equipment, why not just move it?"

Mike shrugged. "I have no idea, kid. It's private land. I think they were more worried that people would hole up in the buildings...squatters, junkies, whatever. But nobody noticed when someone slipped in and made off with a couple chainsaws from a storage shed in the back. Cameras haven't worked in a long time. Rumor was the camp would re-open sooner than later, but that day never came."

Vikram nodded absently. He reached for the napkin map and began folding it back into its plastic bag. Beth returned with another drink for Mike, setting it down carefully on a coaster.

"You good?" she asked, glancing at Vikram.

He smiled weakly. "Yeah. I should probably get going. I'm staying at that motel the 80s never forgot out on the edge of town."

Beth chuckled, then drifted away.

Mike raised his glass in a small, parting gesture. “Good meeting you. And…I’m sorry about your brother.”

Vikram hesitated, the plastic bag still in his hand.

He looked up. His voice was quiet, but steady. "Mike… I’m going up there tomorrow. To the lake.”

Mike didn’t react.

“I need to see it,” Vikram continued. “The last place Venu was. I just...” he swallowed, “I just want to understand. Seems pretty remote, kinda nervous about going up, but I'm going to do it. Bravery is moving forward even when you're scared...so...yeah.”

Mike’s gaze stayed fixed on the glass in his hand. “I’m not going up there, if that's what you're tiptoeing around.”

“You sent him there,” Vikram said, not accusing, just matter of fact. “You thought it was worth seeing. You told him it was special.”

“I’ve already seen it,” Mike said flatly. “Don’t need to go back.”

Vikram looked down at the table, not noticing he had clenched the plastic bag with the map in his hand. “I don’t know the terrain. Or what to expect. I didn't even bring hiking gear, so I have to pick some up in the morning.” He looked at Mike, his voice wavering. “Please. Just…help me get up there. I’m not asking for a full guided tour.”

Mike exhaled through his nose. “Not happening.”

Vikram took a step back from the table, exasperated. "Dude! You went back there to steal stuff, but you won't take me to see the last place my brother was alive? The place you sent him to? That's horseshit. This is an opportunity for you to do the right thing!"

Mike didn't respond, he sat stoically, unmoved.

Vikram gathered up his jacket. “Okay,” he said, voice small, but tense. “I’ll be at the front gate tomorrow. Eleven. If you change your mind.”

Vikram moved toward the front door, hesitated, and glanced back once. “For what it’s worth… you kinda scare me. A little. But that shouldn't stop you from taking me up there.”

He gave a half-hearted smile and walked out of the bar.

Mike sat in silence.

Beth came over and slid into the seat Vikram had just left.

She watched the door for a moment before looking at Mike. Mike leaned back in the booth, sighed. "He wanted me to take him up to Hidden Lake. Wanted closure, whatever that means. Told him no."

“You can’t let him go up there alone,” she said. “He doesn’t know what he’s doing.”

“He’s not my problem,” Mike muttered.

Beth leaned forward. “He kinda is. You sent Venu up there. The least you can do is help his brother get some closure.”

Mike didn't answer. He picked up his glass, drained it, and set it down harder than necessary.

Beth didn't back off. "Did you see his hands? His nails were manicured."

Mike stood abruptly, pulling out his wallet. He tossed a pair of twenties on the table and turned toward the door. "He should stay the hell out of there then," he said. "They got the bear that killed his brother, end of story. He should let it go."

Beth's voice followed him. "You know damn well it wasn't..."

Mike spun back, slamming a hand down on the table. The impact rattled the glassware, and one fell, shattering on the floor.

The bar fell quiet. Only the jukebox kept going—Tom Petty singing about an American girl.

Mike leaned across the table, jaw clenched.
"*Don't.*"

A burly man near the pool table stepped forward, cue stick in hand.

"You alright, Beth?" he said. "How about giving her some room there, Mike?"

The pool cue wavered in the bar patron's hand, part bravado, part hesitation.

Mike turned slowly, squaring his broad frame toward the man.

“How ’bout you stay the fuck outta this,” he said coldly. “Unless you’re real curious what it feels like to have that stick shoved up your ass.” His voice wasn’t raised. He didn’t need to raise it. “Go back to your game,” he added. “Mind your own goddamn business.”

Beth stood, hand raised just enough to signal calm.

“It’s good,” she said lightly. “We’re just having a friendly little conversation about right and wrong and accountability. Nothing to see here, right Mike?”

The pool player looked between them, weighing his odds. A beat passed. Then he stepped back, slowly, lowering the cue.

Beth gave him a nod. “Appreciate it.”
Mike glanced down at the table, then back toward the door. “If the kid goes up there,” he muttered, “he goes up there. I doubt the sheriff left the gate wide open. Kid will see the locks, that the fence was repaired, and turn around. No harm done.”

Beth raised an eyebrow. “You’re making a lot of assumptions, Mike. If he goes up there alone, and something happens. That'll be two on you. Brothers.”

Mike didn’t answer.

He started toward the door, steps thudding heavily across the bar's old hardwood floor.

“Either way,” he said without turning, “not my problem.” He reached the door, paused, then turned just enough to raise his voice. “And hey—”

The pool player looked up.

"Next time one of you comes at me with a stick," Mike said, tone flat and deadly, "make sure you're ready to leave here with half of it jammed in your skull." The door swung open.

"Fuuuuuuck you, Mike!" someone shouted after him.
He didn't respond.

He was already gone.

CHAPTER 11: RATTATOUIE

Mike entered the kitchen through the garage like he'd done a thousand times before. He flipped on the light switch and set his keys on the counter. The kitchen was
spotless, almost astringently neat. There was no clutter, everything was in its place. He paused, letting the silence settle around him. Aside from the steady hum of the refrigerator, the house was completely still.

It hadn't always been this way.

He thought back to when his daughter was younger, his "little chef," always at his side in the kitchen, helping him cook by tossing in chopped tomatoes or onions as he sautéed. They were inseparable, always off on one adventure or another. Even through her teenage years, they remained a team.

The divorce changed that.

She was devastated, and threw herself into school as a coping mechanism. She took college-level courses as a high school junior, and graduated at seventeen with both her diploma and an associate's degree. A far cry from his own academic path—he'd barely scraped through high school with a 2.0 GPA, passing a required math class on the literal last day of his senior year. Without that, he would've spent the summer in remedial classes just to graduate.

Even after the dust from the divorce settled, they stayed close. Road trips to visit his parents outside Salt Lake City. Just the two of them, nothing but the open road. They hiked through Arches, Zion, and Bryce Canyon.

Those were good memories—cherished ones.

Then came the falling out.

It seemed so small now, so trivial. But sharp, painful words had been exchanged, words they could never take back. The damage was done. The things they said were etched into each other like scars on stone. Time might dull the edges, but the marks would always remain.

She left for college two years ago.

Since then, they'd spoken maybe three times—quick, obligatory calls on birthdays and holidays. Texts were rare, and when they did come, they were brief and impersonal.

He missed her.

His life now, if it could be called that, was more solitary than lonely. He had his books and his weights. Occasionally, he'd join a few of his National Park coworkers on hikes, though most of them were half his age. Still, they respected his ability to tackle steep terrain and even set the pace.

The closest thing he'd had to a new friend was the night he met Venu. And look how that turned out. The kid was dead. Now his brother was sniffing around, and from what Mike could tell, he was nothing like Venu.

He made his way to the bathroom off his bedroom—also spotless—and washed his face, brushed his teeth. He stared at himself in the mirror. His face looked like it had
aged five years in the past few days. He looked old. Tired. Maybe even defeated.

Everything he touched seemed to fall apart.

He undressed, climbed into bed, and stared up into the darkness.

His thoughts drifted back to Venu—and the decision to give him that map.

Why did you do that, he asked himself. He had no answer.

He closed his eyes and waited for sleep to take him.

CHAPTER 12: HAND CANNON

The road narrowed as Vikram veered off the highway, tires sliding over mud and gravel between two massive concrete blocks. Fog hugged the treetops, clinging low like it hadn't moved since the day Venu disappeared.

It was early, the sun struggling to break through the clouds, and the world felt muffled and gray.

The stereo hummed the last lines of *"The Outdoor Type"* by The Lemonheads, a little too on-the-nose.

Vikram smiled anyway.

He was dressed like a catalog ad—yellow and black North Face jacket zipped to the chin, matching beanie, new black tactical pants, brand-new hiking boots, and a yellow mock turtleneck under a black tech shirt.

He slowed the vehicle as he navigated around the makeshift barriers. He turned slowly around a bend. Waiting for him there was a mid-2010s maroon Ford F-150 pickup.

Mike stepped out from behind the truck, arms crossed.

Vikram braked, parked, and all but bounced out of his Audi.

"I *knew* you'd show," he said, grinning. "Good to see you doing the right thing, guy!"

Mike gave him a long once-over, then shook his head. "You look like a bumblebee." He sighed. "Jesus, kid… what else did you buy?"

Vikram popped the trunk like it was a grand reveal.

"Check it out," he said, waving him over.

Mike followed, muttering, "You know these German cars are a real pain in the ass to service..." He stopped short.
His eyes dropped into the trunk, scanning the mountain of gear crammed inside. His shoulders sagged a little. "Well," he muttered, "the fellas at Cascade Supply had themselves a helluva day, huh?"

"I got a camping stove," Vikram said, already digging through his haul, "a tent, sleeping bag, sleeping pad, these heat-and-eat meal packs—someone swore the turkey à la king was legit—extra clothes, a couple lanterns, waterproof matches, a ferro rod, and..."

He pulled it out with both hands, proud.
"...this big-ass knife. It's a replica of Rambo's in *First Blood*."

Mike looked at the knife. Blinked. Didn't say a word about it. Instead: "Did you get a backpack?"

Vikram's expression changed instantly.

His shoulders dropped. "Shit. I knew I forgot something. We gotta go back to town."

Mike turned, already walking toward his truck. “We’re not going back to town, you idiot. I brought a spare. Kinda figured you’d forget something fundamental.”

He popped open the backseat and pulled out a small, light blue backpack. One of the outer pockets was adorned with a slightly faded Elsa from *Frozen* patch. He handed it to Vikram. “Here. Load the first aid kit, ferro rod, some food, water, and that big ass knife. Maybe extra socks.”

Vikram looked at it like it was radioactive. “Are you serious right now? I'm not using that 'Frozen' backpack!”

Mike held the backpack out toward Vikram, “You don’t really have a choice. Who the hell’s gonna see it out here besides me? It's a sturdy backpack, used to be my daughter's.”

Vikram hesitated. “Used to be your daughter's? Is she...dead?"
Mike rolled his eyes. “No, dumbass. She’s away at school with a fake ID and a Fireball Whisky habit. Get your gear squared away. We’re burning daylight.”

Vikram grumbled but started stuffing gear into the Elsa backpack.

Mike returned to his truck, grabbing a larger, worn-in pack from the front seat. When Vikram walked over, pack on his shoulders, still muttering about how ridiculous he looked, he caught sight of what Mike was doing.
The older man stood at the tailgate, calmly loading rounds into a large-caliber revolver. Smith & Wesson. Heavy. Practical. Brutal.

Vikram stopped cold. “Whoa. What’s with the friggin’ hand cannon, Mike?”

Mike snapped the cylinder shut with a clean *click*, then holstered it on his right hip.

He turned to face Vikram, dead calm. "You said you wanted to be prepared. I'm not taking any chances," Mike said, tapping the revolver holstered on his hip. "There's mountain lions and bears out here."

Vikram raised an eyebrow. "Do I get a gun?"
Mike didn't answer.

"Wait, don't tell me," Vikram added. "You brought the one your daughter used. The grip's covered in *My Little Pony* stickers and shoots glitter rounds. That's the one I get, right?"

Mike chuckled. "Nope. You don't get a gun. You've never fired a gun outside of a video game." He patted the weapon again. "This thing would tear your arm clean off."

"The video game part's accurate," Vikram muttered. "But still hurtful."

"You ready?"

Vikram nodded. "As I'll ever be."

They walked toward the main gate. New heavy duty chains and padlocks secured the entrance. Vikram looked up at the rusted security cameras posted above. Their lenses were dusty, unmoving dead eyes on steel poles. He reached out, cautiously touching the fence with his fingertips, half-expecting a jolt. Nothing. He leaned in, pressing his face close to the links, trying to see what lay beyond.

Through the gaps, the old logging camp spread out like a forgotten military installation—quiet, still, half-swallowed by fog and time.

"Not gonna lie," Vikram said quietly. "I'm glad you're here with that mini howitzer."

He shook the fence a little, testing it.
"So... how exactly are we getting in here? Where's your chainsaw stealing hole in the fence?"

Mike had already turned. "Follow me."

They started along the fence line, pushing through damp overgrowth—scotch broom, ferns, and tangled dogwood. The trees thickened just slightly here, obscuring the perimeter. After a few minutes, they reached the spot where the chain link had been peeled back.

Mike shook his head, chuckling under his breath.

"Lazy sons of bitches," he said. "Didn't even bother patching it."

He pushed through the gap, ducking slightly. Vikram followed, careful not to snag the straps of his Elsa backpack. On the other side, the logging camp opened before them— rows of low-slung boarded up buildings, weathered metal siding dull under the gray sky. The mist moved between them like it had a mind of its own.

Vikram looked around uneasily.

"You sent my brother to *this* place?" he said. "It's like walking into a *Silent Hill* cut scene."

Mike said nothing. Just kept walking.

CHAPTER 13: THE ROAD

“It’ll burn off soon,” Mike said, glancing up at the lowhanging mist. “Let’s get going. We’ve got a couple miles of access road ahead of us.”

They started walking through the remains of the logging camp. Vikram’s eyes darted from one abandoned building to the next, taking in the boarded-up windows and metal siding streaked with rust. He wondered if Venu had stopped here, if he’d felt the same tension Vikram did now, something electric in the air, buzzing beneath the quiet.

Vikram slowed, falling a few meters behind as he turned to look at a toppled portable generator.

“Pick up the pace, kid,” Mike called over his shoulder. “I’d like to start back before sundown.”

"Aye aye, captain,” Vikram said, mock saluting.

Mike didn’t break stride. “We’re on dry land, dipshit. And I was never in the Navy.”

Vikram jogged a few steps to catch up. “Sorry, my dude. Just trying to keep it light.”

“And don't call me dude.”

"Then stop calling me kid. My name's Vikram. You can call me Vik."

Mike let out a low breath through his nose. "How 'bout we try keeping it quiet for a while?" he said. "Listen to nature while we hike, Vik."

Vikram nodded. "I can do that."

They reached the swing gate and hopped over it one after the other. The gravel road beyond curved gently into the trees, disappearing into fog and pine.

They walked on, the only sounds their footsteps and the soft murmur of the forest around them.

A camera would've caught them from the front—two silhouettes pushing steadily up the gravel road, one tall and quiet, the other layered in high-end outdoor gear and already starting to sweat.

Birds chirped overhead in the canopy, their song drifting through the mist. The steady crunch of boots on gravel filled the silence between them.
"So," Vikram finally said, breath just a little uneven,
"where did your daughter go to school?"

Mike glanced at his watch.

"Six minutes."

Vikram blinked. "Six minutes?"

"That's how long you went without talking," Mike said.
"Didn't think you'd make it past five."

Vikram grinned, undeterred. “So? Where?”

“WSU." Mike was quiet for a moment. "She wants to be a vet," he said like he was trying to make something come true.

“That’s cool. Fixing up poodles and Komodo dragons and stuff.”

Mike allowed himself a small smile. “She’s always loved animals.”

Vikram looked over at him. “You see her much?”

“Nope,” Mike said flatly. “We had a falling out a couple years back, right before she left. Don’t talk much. Maybe a birthday or Christmas text. That’s about it.”

“A falling out?” Vik asked.

Mike nodded. “You’ll find this hard to believe, but I can be difficult. Stubborn. She made some choices I didn’t agree with and I told her so. She’s stubborn too. We dug in. Neither of us has budged.”

Vikram was quiet for a few steps, then said, “You should call her.”

Mike gave him a look.

“I’m serious,” Vikram continued. “You’re like the old guy in *Home Alone*, you know, the guy with the shovel? Kevin was scared of him at first, but it turns out he was just sad because he hadn’t talked to his son in years. Had some fight. Kevin tells him to call his son and at the end of the movie, he does, then boom! His kid’s at the house for Christmas with his whole family. I'm tearing up just talking about it."

Mike raised an eyebrow.

"Point is," Vikram said, undeterred, "you've gotta be the bigger person. Call her."

"Wow, you really turned me around with that Home Alone story," Mike replied, sarcasm dripping off every word.

"C'mon, Mike!" Vikram exclaimed. "You can't go the rest of your life not talking to your daughter, that's crazy! Whatever choice she made that got you all fired up can't be that big of a deal. Give her a call when we get back."
They walked in silence a few steps, then, "I'll think about it," Mike muttered.

The incline steepened as they continued up the road, and Vikram's steps began to drag. He looked up the long stretch ahead and groaned. "This uphill walking sucks. How much farther?"

Mike pressed on, not slowing his pace. "Little over a mile, mile and a half."

Vikram's mouth dropped open. "That's on top of what we've already hiked. Damn, Mike."

"You'll live," Mike said. "Just keep walking."

They trudged onward. Vikram's legs ached with every step, but Mike moved like the climb had barely registered. Until he stopped abruptly, turning in a small circle as his gaze swept the trees. He tapped the face of his smart watch, swiping through the screens until the distance traveled appeared on the display.

“We should be close,” he said. “There’s a fence post with yellow ribbons out here somewhere, left side of the road.
Keep your eyes peeled.”

Vikram moved to the edge of the road, hands resting on top of his head, breathing slightly heavier now. His expression twisted with mild annoyance. “What color is this magical fence post again?”

“Green,” Mike said. “Maybe some white paint near the top. There’ll be a couple yellow ribbons tied to it. You’ll know it when you see it.”

Vikram raised an eyebrow. “So I’m looking for a green post with a splash of white and yellow ribbons. Among the millions of green and yellow things growing beside this road. Great.”

Mike shot him a look but said nothing. He checked his watch again, then sighed. “It’ll be close to the road. Just past the drainage ditch.”

They moved carefully, scanning the brush. Every few steps, they’d stop to peer into the undergrowth, eyes adjusting to the dim light under the canopy. After a few minutes, Mike pointed. “There it is. Just like I said.”

The post was leaning at an awkward angle, barely visible through the tangle of brush. The ribbons were frayed and sun-bleached, more gray than yellow, but still recognizable.

“Yeah,” Vikram muttered, “it jumps right out at you.”

Mike dropped his pack onto a patch of gravel and rolled his

shoulders.

“Let’s take a minute. Eat something, drink some water. It’s easier to grab a bite out here than in there.”

Vikram stopped beside him, eyes scanning the wall of forest. “So this is where Venu followed the ribbons?”

Mike nodded. “This is it. Those woods are dense...dark, uneven, easy to lose your footing or your direction. There's lots of roots, low limbs, thick undergrowth. Watch your step. You don’t look like you weigh much, but I’m not hauling you out of there if you snap an ankle.”

As if summoned by the warning, a sharp crack echoed through the trees on the opposite side of the road—branches snapping, twigs breaking, something large was moving fast. And it was coming right at them.

Mike’s arm shot out, palm open. *Be still.*
Vikram froze.

The sound got louder, closer. Whatever it was, it was crashing through the woods at full speed. Mike stepped in front of Vikram, his body tense, drawing the revolver from his hip in one smooth motion. He cocked the hammer, eyes locked on the tree line.

A second later, a massive bull elk burst from the underbrush, hooves hammering the ground. It paused briefly in the road about ten meters away, steam rising from its nostrils. It gave them a brief, uninterested glance, then galloped up the road. Mike lowered his arm, uncocked the revolver, and returned it to the holster in a slow, controlled motion. He let out a long breath.
Vikram exhaled too, sharper and more audible. He shook his

head and let out a quick, incredulous laugh. "Jesus, you were really going to shoot that deer." He glanced at Mike, then up the access road where the elk had disappeared. "That deer was huge, though. Didn't think they were that big."

“It was an elk, not a deer.” Mike replied.

“Eh, elk, deer—same difference, no?” Vikram asked.

“Not really.”

They stood in silence for a moment. Then Mike nodded toward the gravel. “Grab something to eat. Get some water. We’ve still got a ways to go.”

Vikram unshouldered his backpack and knelt, unzipping the top. He pulled out a small bag of trail mix and a neon green pouch of Sour Skittles. Tearing it open, he poured a handful into his palm and tossed them into his mouth.

His face instantly puckered.

Mike glanced over. “What the hell are you eating?”

“Sour Skittles,” Vikram said, grinning as he shook the pouch. “They’re amazing. Want to try some?”

Mike gave him a dubious look, but extended his palm anyway. Vikram poured a small handful into it. Mike studied the brightly colored candy with visible skepticism, then popped them into his mouth.

His face twisted almost immediately—eyes squinting, lips pursed as the sourness hit.

“These are awful,” he muttered. “They’re making my teeth

hurt."

He unscrewed the lid of his Hydroflask, took a swig, swished the water in his mouth, and spat it onto the grass growing beside the road.

"How the hell do you eat those?"

"You have to toughen up," Vikram said, laughing. "They're instant energy. I could run a marathon on these alone."

Mike didn't look convinced.

"Come on," Vikram added, slinging on his backpack. "Get that pack back on, big fella. Let's get to that lake."

Mike's humor faded as he turned to face the woods. He adjusted the straps on his pack, cinched it tight. "Let's do this."

They stepped off the road and into the trees.

CHAPTER 14: THE TREES

Within a few meters, the canopy swallowed the sunlight. Then the first yellow ribbon appeared on the trunk of a scraggly pine, faded but visible.

"There," Mike said. "Should be easy to spot the rest."

They moved deeper into the woods, the air growing thick and humid. Vikram followed closely, carefully stepping over downed limbs and weaving through undergrowth. For several minutes, neither of them spoke, the only noise their footsteps and the subtle breath of the forest surrounding them.

Eventually, Vikram broke the silence.

"So... what happened with your daughter? If you don't mind me asking."

Mike didn't answer. Just kept walking.
"You don't have to tell me," Vikram said. "I just thought maybe I could offer some thoughtful insight or advice. I don't have kids, but I'm not exactly new to pissing people off."

He sighed.

"Venu and I didn't talk for weeks before he went missing. We had a huge fight. He was going to leave his engineering job to work retail at REI or something like that. Or maybe go off and be a forest ranger. I couldn't believe it. Our parents sacrificed so much so we could go to good schools, get real careers. That's not something you just walk away from. I asked if he wanted to talk about it more, but he had made plans for a day hike. He said we could talk more about it when he got back."

A heavy silence hung between Vikram and Mike.

"Maybe being happy doing something he loved mattered more to him than making money," Mike said.

"That's bullshit," Vikram shot back. "Money gave him the freedom to do all this hiking and adventuring in the first place. He was making high six figures. That's why he could buy the gear, take the trips. You know how much I spent yesterday? Over three grand, and I'm not even *good* at this stuff."

Mike gave a quiet shrug. "I don't know, Vik. Sometimes money's more of a boat anchor than you think, especially if you need it to maintain a life you don't even like." He paused, then added, "Ever hear the saying, 'Having nothing is almost like having it all'?"

Vikram snorted. "No. Because it's stupid. What's that even supposed to mean?"

Mike smiled faintly. "Not sure. It's from a Todd Snider song. I think it just means if you're not tied down by a job, a house, or a lifestyle then you're free in ways other people aren't."

"That's boomer nonsense," Vikram muttered.

"Maybe," Mike said. "Maybe not."

A sharp, resonant *crack* echoed through the trees. It was the unmistakable sound of wood striking wood—once, clean and loud.

They both stopped.
The forest fell eerily silent. No birds, no squirrels. Just the faint drip of water from the trees and the breath in their chests.

"What was that?" Vikram whispered. "Someone else out here?"
"I doubt it," Mike replied. "Probably just a dead limb falling."

Neither of them moved. They scanned the trees, waiting. After a long, breathless beat, sound returned to the forest. A bird called in the distance. Then another. The normal soundtrack of the woods returned, cautiously.

Mike adjusted his pack. "Come on. We've got another mile or so."

They continued deeper into the woods, each step accompanied by the soft crackle of twigs and leaves underfoot. The air grew cooler, the light dimmer. Thick moss clung to the tree trunks and limbs.

"So," Vikram said, quieter now, "you and your daughter… you said it was a disagreement?"

"You're just not going to let this go, are you?" Mike's voice was low. "Yeah, she made some choices I didn't agree with, and I let her know I didn't agree with them."

"With all the subtlety of a chainsaw?" Vikram asked.

Mike shook his head, a faint smile crossing his mouth. “That sounds about right. Let's leave it at that for now.”

They continued moving through the forest. Branches clawed at their sleeves as they ducked and weaved, the sharp snap of twigs and the dry crunch of old leaves and pine needles the only soundtrack to their steps.

Vikram glanced sideways at Mike, the quiet gnawing at him. “So...” he said casually, brushing a fern aside. “You got a girlfriend, Mike?”

Mike snorted. “Hell no.”

Vikram raised an eyebrow. “Why not?”

Mike shrugged without breaking stride. “No interest. Got burned bad in my divorce. Once was enough.”

“Ah,” Vikram said, grinning. “That explains the permascowl.” He waited a beat. “What about Beth?”

Mike stopped mid-step, turning to face him with narrowed eyes. “What about her?”

Vikram kept his tone light, teasing. “She seems cool. Sharp. Clearly puts up with your charming personality.”

Mike shook his head and pushed forward again, eyes on the path. “That’s not happening.”

“Why not?”

“Because I’m not interested in dating!" Mike snapped.

Vikram laughed, hands raised. “Alright, alright! Just saying...

Beth seems like someone who could actually handle you."

Mike shook his head, "Dating takes work that I'm not up for. I'm set in my ways. She's probably set in hers. We'd wind up annoying each other."
Vikram rolled his eyes. "Isn't being annoyed with your partner a main feature of relationships? And no offense, Mike...but from what I can tell, your life seems kind of lonely."

A small laugh from Mike. He stopped to look at Vikram. "Yeah? Maybe I'd rather be lonely than annoyed. Did you consider that?"

Vikram furrowed his brow, shook his head in disgust. "No, Mike, I didn't consider that because it's a garbage take."

"Maybe it is, maybe it isn't," said Mike, "but it's my choice.
Let's keep moving, we're wasting daylight."

They hiked on, the conversation fading into the rhythm of boots on soil and the distant rustle of the forest.

"You know," Vik muttered, "old, LONELY, people sure love saying stuff like, 'We're wasting daylight.'"

Mike didn't even turn around. "Enough."

CHAPTER 15: THE LAKE

They stepped out of the trees and into the clearing, the lake appeared before them just as Mike described—still, serene, impossibly blue. The surface was glass, reflecting the snow-dusted ridges of the Cascades like a portal to another world. A few scattered sunbeams cut through the thinning mist, touching the lake with gentle light.

Vikram stopped in his tracks. His eyes widened. He opened his mouth to speak, but nothing came out. His chest rose and fell with emotion, and his lips pressed into a tight line as his eyes filled with tears.

He took a few slow steps forward, boots squishing into the damp earth. Then he turned back toward Mike. "This is beautiful," he said, voice soft and cracking. "No wonder you sent Venu up here. His pictures don't do it justice. And Venu could *take* pictures."

Mike gave a small nod, looking out over the lake with his arms crossed.
"Yeah," he said. "It's special. Not many people know about it. We used to come up here and fish. Before the camp shut down, anyway. After that… well. That was that."

Vikram glanced at the water, then the trees, then up at the

mountain again. "I want to walk where Venu walked," he said quietly. "Or where I think he walked. Based on his pictures. I think it might help me find some kind of closure."

Mike looked hesitant. He checked the time on his watch, then up at the sky, gauging the angle of the sun. Eventually, he gave a reluctant nod.

"Go ahead," he said. "Just don't take too long. I don't want to be walking back through the woods after dark."

Vikram smirked. "Why? Are there monsters out here?"

At the word *monsters*, Mike's eye flicked away, just for a moment. He didn't answer right away.

"No monsters," he said at last. "I just don't like the woods at night. Hard enough getting around in daylight."

With a small smile, Vikram turned and began walking the lake's perimeter. He stopped a few times to stare out at the view, taking it all in. Once, he tilted his head back and simply breathed. Another time, he lowered his head and clasped his hands together—whether in prayer or reflection, it was hard to tell.

Mike stayed back near the trailhead, sitting on a fallen log. He kept one eye on Vikram and the other on the forest. His hands tapped nervously against his thighs. After a moment, he pulled off his backpack and dug around for something to eat.

He tore open a pack of peanut butter crackers and ate quickly, washing it down with gulps from his battered Hydroflask. He had just finished when he heard it.

"Mike!"

Vikram's voice, distant but clear.

"Mike! Come here! Hurry!"

Mike shot to his feet, cursing under his breath. "Shut up, kid," he muttered. "Shut the hell up."

Vikram's voice called again, louder.
"Mike! Mike!"

"Fuck," Mike hissed, slinging his pack over his shoulder and jogging around the lake's edge. He found Vikram near the far tree line, pacing, eyes wide with urgency.

"What?" Mike said, slightly winded. "What is it?"
"Do you see it?" Vikram said, pointing into the woods. "Do you?"

"See *what* ?" Mike followed his line of sight, hand already hovering near the revolver at his hip.

"Right there," Vikram said, voice insistent. "Beside that big tree. In the shrubs. You can't miss it."

Mike squinted his eyes. The forest ahead was dense, saturated in greens and browns.

But then—he saw it.

A flash of *red* in the brush. Small, half-concealed, but unmistakably out of place. It was a sharp contrast against the sea of moss, bark, and shadow.

Mike's hand tightened around the revolver grip. "I see it."

“That’s Venu’s beanie,” Vikram said, eyes fixed on the flash of red nestled in the shrubs. “I *know* it. He wore that thing everywhere. You could spot him like Waldo in any outdoor picture —always that bright red hat.”

He started forward, instinctively, feet pressing into the damp moss covered earth.

Mike reached out and grabbed his arm, firm and urgent.
“Let’s get out of here, Vik,” he said. “It’s getting late.”

“Not until I grab that beanie,” Vikram replied, voice sharp. “I *have* to get it.”

“I don’t think so,” said Mike, gripping Vikram's arm harder.

“Let go, Mike. I’m getting it, then we can go.”

Mike tightened his grip even more. “You don’t know what else you might find over there, okay? It might be something you *don’t want to see.*”

Vikram paused. The tension in his shoulders loosened for just a moment, but his eyes never left the beanie. Then he yanked free.

“Dammit,” Mike muttered.

Vikram was already moving—pushing through ferns, ducking under a low limb. Mike chased after him, boots snapping on fallen twigs and pine needles. They reached the sapling at nearly the same time.

The beanie hung like an ornament, snagged perfectly on a thin, wiry branch. It looked intentional. As if someone had placed it there.

Vikram hesitated, hand inches away. Then he gently pinched the edge and pulled it free.

At first, it seemed fine. Weathered, a little damp, but familiar. His breath hitched in his throat as he turned it over in his hands.

Then his fingers stiffened.

The knit fabric had hardened in places. A texture that didn't belong.

He rotated it slowly and stopped when he saw the dark, jagged stain across the back of the beanie—dried, rust-colored, unmistakable.

Blood.

Vikram's hands trembled. The beanie slipped from his grasp and fell silently to the forest floor.

He stood there, unmoving, as the truth washed over him like ice water.

"He's really dead," he said softly.

Mike's voice came from behind him low and steady.
"He is, Vik."

The forest went still. No wind, no birds, just the quiet truth hanging between them.

"We should head out," Mike added gently.
Vikram didn't respond. He just stared down at the beanie, as

if some part of him was still hoping it would mean something else.

But it didn't. Not anymore.

CHAPTER 16: THE LAIR

"Stupid fucking bear," Vikram muttered, swiping tears from his cheeks with the sleeve of his jacket. "Venu..." He looked up again, his eyes scanning the shadows. They froze. There, several meters ahead, something bright and out of place peeked through the brush.
His heart leapt.

"There's his coat!" Vikram shouted, already moving toward it.

Mike caught up quickly, his voice tight. "Vik—wait."

But Vikram was already at the tattered remains of the bright green North Face jacket. It hung limply from a low branch, shredded in several places. Stiff patches of dried blood marred the synthetic fabric.

"What's his stuff doing all the way up here, Mike?" Vikram demanded, voice rising.

Mike stood beside him, eyes low. "The bear probably dragged him back here."

Vikram shook his head. "That doesn't make sense. His backpack was on the road. You're saying a bear dragged him ...what, all the way *back* up here? Through *that* ?" He gestured toward the dense forest behind them. "He was over two hundred pounds, Mike. Solid muscle. You saw him. A bear wouldn't haul him uphill through the woods like this."

"Bears will protect a kill," Mike said quietly. "Especially if there's competition around."

"It just seems like a lot of effort," Vikram murmured, eyes sweeping the forest floor. "And if Venu was dragged, his beanie would've come off *way* earlier. We've been getting snagged on branches left and right."

He took another step forward and spotted more.

Another strip of jacket, caught on a bramble ahead. "There's more of his jacket..."

Mike's tone sharpened. "We don't have time for this, Vik. We need to go."

But Vikram was already moving again, his eyes wide, jaw clenched.

"Vik," Mike hissed, his voice low and harsh. "C'*mon*! We'll come back with the sheriff."
Vikram turned, a desperate fire in his eyes. "He's out there, Mike. Part of him is still out there."

Mike's shoulders tensed. "I know you want closure, but there's a chance you'll see something you don't want to see. We have to get out of here."

Vikram pressed deeper into the woods, following the silent trail of torn fabric like breadcrumbs through a tunnel of moss and shadows. Mike cursed under his breath and followed, glancing up at the twisted canopy above them. The branches seemed to bend in unnatural ways, forming a woven ceiling that filtered the light into pale green gloom. The trees grew tighter, their trunks leaning in towards them as if threatening to close them off from the world behind them.

Vikram moved with purpose now, head down, boots careful on the narrow game trail. And then...

“There.”

He stopped and pointed.

Ahead, in a clearing no bigger than a small bedroom, lay a pile of clothing. Tattered, stained, and still. The buzzing of flies rose in the silence like a siren.

Mike caught up and grabbed Vikram’s arm. He shook his head, eyes steady, voice no louder than a whisper. “You *don’t* want to go over there,” he said. “Your brother is gone. We need to head back.”
Vikram looked at him, eyes blazing, possessed, and brimming with tears.

“You don’t understand,” he said softly. “I *have to*.”

Mike let out a breath and released his grip. His gaze fell to the ground.

Vikram approached the pile slowly, picking up a long stick from the forest floor. With trembling hands, he extended it outward and nudged at the remains of the jacket.

The buzzing grew louder.

He looked up and everything inside him froze. His breath caught in his throat. Time stood still, vision tunneled. His body went rigid as the reality before him took shape in fragmented horror.

There, propped on a jagged tree stump, was a *head* , his brother's head. Decomposed, sunken, almost unrecognizable, but unmistakably Venu. His features contorted in death, lips pulled back slightly, teeth exposed in a grotesque half-snarl.

Surrounding the stump were piles of bones, antlers, skulls, rib cages. Some were clearly from deer and elk.
Some were not.

Human ribs. Shattered femurs. A partially intact spinal column curled beside the stump like a fossilized serpent. It wasn't just a resting place. It was a shrine. A nest. A *lair* .
Vikram screamed.

Mike surged forward and clamped a hand over his mouth, dragging him backward as birds exploded from the canopy above.

" *Shhh!* " Mike hissed, eyes wide and scanning the trees.
"Don't make a sound!"

Vikram thrashed briefly in his grip, then fell limp, tears streaming down his face as he stared at the clearing. Mike tightened his grip around Vikram's shoulders, holding him fast, voice low and trembling now.

"Shut up," Mike hissed, voice low but urgent, inches from Vikram's ear. "Do you understand me? *Shut up.* We have to start moving. The whole fucking mountain knows we're here now. *Move it!* "

Vikram's voice was breaking apart. "Mike, bears don't... they don't *do that.* They just eat, right? They're *bears.* Why would a bear—why would it *decorate* —why would it take *trophies? Bears don't do that, Mike!* "

"I know," Mike snapped. "Move. We gotta move. *Go.* " His hand hovered near the revolver. And for the first time since Vikram met him, Mike looked afraid.

Not startled. Not cautious. Afraid.

He shoved Vikram ahead of him, nearly carrying him through the dense underbrush, pushing him away from the clearing, away from the stump, the bones, the head. Branches clawed at their arms like crooked, skeletal fingers, as if the forest itself was trying to hold them back. Thorns bit at them like sharp, unrelenting teeth, drawing blood with each step. The air was thick and fetid, choked with decay and something older, heavier.

Vikram stumbled, collapsing onto the forest floor with a choked sob.

Mike didn't hesitate. He dropped to one knee and slid his arms under Vikram's armpits, hauling him upright. The two of them half-ran, half-fell out of the tree line and onto the shoreline of the lake. The sudden openness felt jarring.

They were exposed.

Mike looked across the lake, eyes scanning the tree line where they had entered less than an hour ago. The sunlight was already thinning, retreating behind the mountaintops like it, too, wanted no part of this place.

"Mike..." Vikram's voice was shaking. "What *was* that? You said you knew it wasn't a bear. So, what did that?"

"I don't know," Mike said. "And I'm not sticking around to find out. We have to get out of here, now . Do you have bear spray in that pack?"

Vikram shook his head. "No. And even if I did you just said it wasn't a bear."

He was spinning, scanning the trees. The shoreline. The rocks. His hands clenched and unclenched. Something was wrong, worse than before.

"Something's watching us," Vikram whispered. "I can feel it. Jesus, what is that smell?"

"Just your imagination," Mike muttered, but his voice was tight, strained. He didn't believe it either.

The woods went dead quiet. No birds. No wind. Just the buzzing of insects and their own ragged breathing.

Crack.
A branch broke somewhere behind them.

Mike's head snapped toward the sound, one hand hovering over the grip of the revolver at his hip. He scanned the trees, trying to triangulate the noise.

Then another snap, this time from the *opposite* direction.

It was closer.

"Mike..." Vikram's voice was barely audible. They both froze. Ahead of them, deep in the tree line, something moved . A shift of shadow. A silhouette too massive, too wrong to be human. It stepped— no , glided — between the trees, just beyond the reach of sunlight.

Mike's hand gripped the revolver.
His face had gone pale.

"It's not going to let us out that way," he said, almost to himself.

"What?" Vikram's voice was climbing into panic. "What's not letting us out? What are you saying?"

"We have to run," Mike whispered, his voice a thread of urgency. "Back toward the den. Swing around. Try to get back to the lake from the other side—*go!*
"

A sudden *whistle* sliced through the silence. A rock the size of a grapefruit screamed past them and slammed into the ground with a wet *thud,* spraying mud and water into the air.

"*RUN!!!*" Mike roared. "*MOVE!*"

They ran.

CHAPTER 17: THE CLIMB

They crashed back into the deep woods, branches whipping against their faces, underbrush pulling at their legs. Mike led the charge, plowing ahead with desperate purpose. Vikram was only a few steps behind, lungs burning, heart hammering in his chest.

As they approached the grotesque clearing where Venu's remains had been left, Vikram skidded to a stop.

"Mike! I'm not going back in there," he panted, voice raw with panic.

Mike turned, chest heaving, face pale with fear.

"We have to , Vik," he said. "We need to find high ground so we don't..."

WHIZZ–THUD!

Another rock tore through the trees and smashed into the foliage beside them, kicking up dirt and leaves.
"...so we don't get *hit by a rock! Move it!* "

Vikram screamed as they bolted through the lair again, his eyes catching the gory stump, the impossibly still face of his brother one final time. He clenched his eyes shut and ran harder.

Mike shouted ahead. "This way...we'll cut across, scramble up that hill and try to circle back to the lake."

They veered left, the forest darkening as they entered a patch of heavy firs. The ground began to slope upward sharply. Both men dropped low and used their hands to pull themselves up, grabbing exposed roots and slick branches.

Dirt crumbled underfoot, but they climbed.

Minutes passed. Minutes that felt like hours.

They reached the top of the ridge, their chests heaving, legs shaking, and collapsed to their knees. Below them, the forest was still.

Mike was the first to speak.

"Catch your breath," he said, his voice low and grave. "Then we keep moving."

Vikram turned to him, eyes wide, his face pale with sweat and disbelief. "What *was* that, Mike? That wasn't a bear. Bears don't throw rocks. They don't make nests out of bones. They don't..." His voice cracked. "They don't hunt people. That wasn't a bear. Was it a person? What the hell was it?"

Mike scanned the tree line around them, every muscle tense. Then he looked at Vikram.

"You won't believe me if I tell you," he said. "We need to move. Stay on the ridge...we're a harder target up here. We'll work our way around, try to drop back down closer to the lake." He gestured down the hill behind them. "There's ravines on both sides. One of them's that den we climbed out of. Watch your footing. The brush hides drop-offs."

Vikram stared at him. "What made that den, Mike?" His voice was high, trembling. "Fucking *Bigfoot* ?"

Mike gave him a sharp look—about to say something—but the words died in his throat.

Something moved in the forest below, heavy and deliberate.

Mike turned, eyes scanning the slope. " Move," he said. "Stay close to me."

They kept to the ridge, weaving around trees, ducking under limbs. The ground was uneven, broken by roots and sudden dips. At times, they nearly lost the path, but Mike kept them moving, eyes darting between the terrain and the forest below.

For several minutes, there was nothing but their footsteps. No birds. No wind. Just the dry rasp of their breathing and the steady thud of their boots.

There was another crack of movement from the trees below.

Louder this time.

Vikram didn't speak. Mike looked back once, eyes full of something Vikram hadn't seen in the man before - fear and recognition.

CHAPTER 18: FACE TO FACE

After nearly thirty minutes of scrambling on the ridge, Vikram faltered. He staggered sideways, caught himself, and hunched over, gasping. "Mike...I gotta stop. Just for a second..."

Mike stopped and wheeled around. His voice was low but urgent. "Grab a quick drink. *Quick.* We need to get out of this clearing. He'll pick us off with rocks out here."

Vikram, still bent over, wiped sweat from his brow. "You keep saying *he.* Do you *know* this thing? I feel like you're not telling me everything..."

Before Mike could answer, a sharp *snap* echoed through the forest—clean and close. Both men froze. Mike's revolver was in his hand in a flash, hammer cocked, his stance solid and practiced.

Another noise burst from behind them. Closer this time. Tree limbs *cracking,* trunks shaking as something *charged* toward them through the underbrush.

Mike instinctively stepped in front of Vikram, his left arm braced like a shield.

THWACK.

A rock the size of a softball came screaming from the woods and smashed into Vikram's back. He cried out and dropped to his knees, his breath ripped from his lungs. Mike stood over him, gun raised, scanning the trees. His jaw was tight, his finger just off the trigger, steady and calm.

The forest went silent.

Vikram gasped. "Mike... did I die? It feels like I died. I couldn't... breathe..."

"Stay quiet," Mike said sharply. "He's still out there."

"There it is again, *he.* Why do you keep saying that? Why not *it?* " Vikram looked up, his eyes wide with realization. "It's a Bigfoot, right?"

"Just shut up, Vik. Please. Shut up."

Mike's revolver tracked the forest as his nose twitched.

"God, that smell," Vikram said, gagging.

"He's upwind," Mike muttered. Then he turned his head slightly, eyes narrowing. "Get ready to ru—"

A shape exploded from the trees ahead—tall, broad, and *moving fast.* Trees bent and swayed in its wake. The thing charged with terrifying speed, an inhuman mass of muscle and rage.

Mike barely had time to react.
BOOM.

The first shot hit its right shoulder—it jerked, but didn't slow.

BOOM.

The second slug caught it in the ribs. It let out a thunderous, wet *snarl* that sounded less like pain and more like rage.

BOOM.
The third shot missed entirely, echoing off the trees like a firecracker. Time froze.

The air felt charged, heavy and brittle. Mike and Vikram stood rooted to the ground, unable to move or speak, locked in a moment of suspended reality.

Twenty meters ahead, the creature was in full view for the first time.

It was enormous, easily seven and a half feet tall. Its frame was a grotesque monument to muscle and brutality, covered in thick, matted fur that clung to its skin in oily clumps. Elongated limbs flexed with sinew and primal strength, its massive hands were capped with sharp, jagged claws.

But it was the eyes that terrified. Forward-facing. Intelligent. Burning with a primitive malice.

The creature scanned them, its heavy brow furrowed in suspicion and rage. Then, its expression shifted. It blinked and tilted its massive head downward, registering something for the first time.

Blood and pain.

A dark bloom stained the fur just beneath its right shoulder, where Mike's first shot had struck. The creature stared at the wound as if not quite understanding how it had come to be.

Its enormous hand rose and gently touched the ragged flesh.

The fury returned.

The eyes narrowed. A deep, guttural snarl rolled from its chest and then erupted into a howl—pure rage, raw and unholy. The sound tore through the trees like a shockwave. It bared its teeth, all of them, lips curled high to expose massive upper and lower canines like a gorilla in full display. Whatever human glint that had lingered in its features vanished, replaced by something purely animal, primal, and furious.

And then—it was gone. It bounded off into the trees in a blur of movement that defied its size. Mike fired again, and again, emptying the revolver into the forest.

Silence.

Leaves floated gently to the ground where the creature had vanished. The smell of gunpowder and something darker, fouler, clung to the air.

Vikram exhaled hard, wide-eyed and trembling. “You shot it!”

Mike didn’t look away from the tree line as he spoke. “I don’t think any of those shots were fatal.”

He popped open the cylinder of his revolver and one by one, dropped the spent casings into the front pocket of his pants with methodical care.

“But...” he added, “he’s hurt. And I don’t think he’s ever been hurt before. Not like that." Mike paused for a moment, then, "And I don't think he liked it."

Vikram let out a shaky laugh. “Is there anything that likes getting shot? I got hit by a rock, Mike, and I *hated* it.”

Mike didn’t smile. He focused on reloading. “We gotta move. He’ll be back. He's hurt, but still fast..and pissed off. We’ll cut over the ridge and head down. We're about three or four miles from the camp.”

Vikram stepped closer, frustration rising through his fear. “No. No, screw that. I’m not taking another step until you tell me what you know. You’ve been using *he* this entire time. That thing wasn’t a bear. That was Bigfoot. And you *knew it.* You knew it wasn’t some animal that killed my brother.”

Mike holstered the revolver, his jaw flexing.

“I’ll tell you everything I know,” he said finally. “but not here. Not now. This clearing is death. We have to get out.” He tilted his head, eyes locked on Vikram.

Vikram stared for a long beat. Then he nodded. Together, they turned and moved, slipping into the shadows beneath the trees. The forest thickened around them again, darker now.

And somewhere out there, the thing that killed Venu was bleeding.

And watching.

“Stick close to me,” Mike said, voice low but firm. “Don’t go wandering off. This is true old growth. Get turned around in here, and you’re not getting unturned.”

Vikram glanced around nervously. The trees were ancient

towering giants cloaked in moss and shadow. The trail, if there was one, was more suggestion than path.

“If we get separated,” Mike continued, “don’t call out. Don’t yell for me. Just find the sun and head west. You’ll hit the camp or the fire service road eventually.”

Vikram froze. "Wait, what? Mike, I won't last half an hour out here on my own." His voice was anxious and tight. "Why can't I call out?"

Mike turned to face him, eyes steady. "Because if you call out, it'll know we're split up. It'll come for the one making noise...it's not just big, it's friggin' smart too."

“Great,” Vikram muttered. “So head west and hope for the best. Or follow the sun.”

Vikram pointed to a tree with moss growing nearly from root to canopy. “Wait, can’t I just follow the moss? Doesn’t that grow on the north side or something? I can use that to navigate too, right?”

Mike shook his head. “Maybe where you’re from. Out here moss grows on whatever it damn well pleases. North, south, upside down. All these trees are blanketed in the stuff.”

Vikram stared at the trees, his voice a notch more bitter. “Everything I learned about the woods in grade school is bullshit.”

Then he cut to the real question.

“Speaking of bullshit,” he said, “start talking. Why did you send my brother to the lake when you knew something was out here. You said *he* . You knew.”

Mike kept walking. His boots crunched softly over a patch of fallen needles. He didn't answer.

"Well?" Vikram prompted, close on his heels. "You going to say something, or do I have to start throwing rocks, too?"

"I didn't think it was still alive," Mike said finally, stopping mid-step. "Last I heard, it was over. When the logging camp shut down, the stories just... stopped. Nothing. Not even from the security contractors when they'd come into town."

He paused, looking into the trees as if the past was written there.

Vikram stepped up beside him, quieter now. "What are you talking about?"
Mike turned, motioned for him to follow, and started walking again.

"I'll explain," he said. "But not while we're standing still. Let's move."

The two men descended deeper into the woods, shadows tightening around them, the silence pressing in like a heavy fog. Whatever secrets Mike carried, they were leading Vikram further away from the world he knew—and closer to something primal, hidden, and waiting.

CHAPTER 19: BACK STORY

Mike didn't speak for several paces. The only sounds were their footsteps stepping through the old growth forest and the distant trill of a bird calling out in the high canopy. Finally, he let out a long breath.

"We started experiencing weird vandalism about a year before the camp shut down," he said. "Nothing big at first. Just tools getting tossed down the hillside. Windows cracked on the Caterpillars, seat cushions ripped. Real random stuff. It was small, but deliberate."

Vikram glanced over. "So not stuff animals would do?"

Mike shook his head. "Not unless the bears up here learned how to throw axes and toss toolboxes."

He continued walking, his voice steady but distant. "Management figured it was environmentalists. Some of them had already made noise about our operation. They started offering overtime to guys willing to stay overnight, guard the site and act as loss prevention. Replacing broken equipment starts to add up after a while. I signed up. Figured I'd get paid extra to drink a few beers, shine a flashlight around, and if any tree-huggers showed up, maybe teach one a lesson."

Vikram raised an eyebrow. "You were gonna rough up some hippies?"

Mike gave a faint, humorless smile. ""I wasn't looking for a fight. Just wanted to scare off whoever it was that was messing with productivity and my wallet. I had a shotgun loaded up with rock salt. Learned that trick from a groundskeeper I worked for in high school. Hurts like hell but doesn't kill you. Thought I was being clever." They walked on. Mike came to an abrupt halt.

Vikram tensed. "What? Did you hear something?"

Mike shook his head, but his eyes were far away. "No. Just...remembering."

They resumed walking, slower now.

"Third night out there, I smelled it before I saw anything. And yeah, it was *that* smell. Same one we caught a whiff of earlier. Like a skunk took a bath in hot garbage. I was sitting on the front end of a parked Cat. Had a beer cracked open. Felt something. A presence. That instinctual thing...like the air around you folds in." He paused again.
"I spun around with my mag light, thinking I'd catch someone sneaking up behind me. Nothing. Just empty trees and that stench. But I knew I wasn't alone. I heard a grunt. Deep. Heavy. Thought, *hell, it's a bear. A big one.*" He adjusted the strap on his pack and kept moving.

"I started backing up toward the cab, trying to keep calm. I could hear it circling. Limbs snapping under its weight. Slow steps, deliberate. It wasn't moving like a bear, but it wasn't moving like a person either. It was something in between."

Vikram looked over, studying the lines of tension in Mike's face. He wasn't just recounting. He was reliving.

Mike continued. "I climbed into the cab and racked the shotgun. Loud, on purpose. Figured the sound alone would scare whatever it was. I sat there in the dark, listening. Then..." He snapped his fingers. The sound echoed.

"...the first rock shattered the windshield. Big as a cantaloupe. Glass went everywhere. I panicked and fired straight through the hole. Didn't hit anything. Another rock hit the side panel a second later. I turned, fired again...damn near blinded myself with salt fragments ricocheting off the metal. It just kept coming...branches and rocks just pounding on the cab. I slid down onto the floor and didn't move."

Vikram's voice was hushed. "How'd you get out?"

Mike looked at him, the memory of that night still haunting the corners of his expression. He slowed, eyes distant.

A long pause.

Mike's voice grew quieter, but the tension in his jaw tightened as the words began to pour out like steam from a long-sealed valve.

"I could hear it walking toward the Caterpillar," he said. "Whatever it was, it wasn't trying to sneak up on me anymore. The smell got worse too, rotting meat and wet fur. It was... thick...got into your mouth when you breathed."

Vikram listened, wide-eyed, trying to keep pace both with Mike's story and their careful descent through the trees.

"Then it started screaming and rocking the Cat from side to

side like it weighed nothing. The whole thing was shaking...s-teel and hydraulics moaning under the pressure. I just laid there on the damn floorboard, trying not to piss myself, when the door ripped open."

Mike stopped, swallowed hard.

"It had hands," he said, quieter now. "Big hands. I could see them in the dark, reaching in. I fired everything I had, rock salt or not. It was just reflex. I know I hit its arm, maybe even clipped its face. Because it screamed. Not like anything I've ever heard. Not human. Not animal. Something else. Same sound we heard today." He looked at Vikram.

"Then it ran. And so did I."

They kept walking. Vikram's voice was almost reverent.
"Did you report all of this?"

Mike nodded slowly. "Reported everything...well, almost everything. Left out the part about me curled up in a ball on the floor. Told the rest straight. They said it was probably a bear."

"A bear," Vikram repeated flatly.

"Yeah," Mike said, voice dry. "And I believed it. Or I wanted to. Because anything else seemed... impossible."
He sighed, adjusted the straps on his pack again.

"But things didn't stop. Not long after that, one of the re-planting crews - the guys who went in after the clear-cut to plant new saplings - they started talking about feeling watched. Not once or twice, but every day. One guy said he caught sight of something watching from the trees, just the shape of it, the outline, and refused to go back up."

Vikram didn't interrupt, just let Mike keep going.

"Then a few weeks later, two guys disappeared. Surveyors. Their job was to hike a thousand meters up past where your brother would've turned off for the lake, take some measurements to maybe build out a second camp. They never came back. SAR went up. Only found their helmets and equipment. Said it was a mountain lion that got 'em." Mike snorted softly.

Vikram's voice was tight. "Do you think the logging company knew what was really happening?"

Mike paused. Thought about it.

"Hard to say. Maybe. But after that, things got worse. There was a mountain biker from town that used to ride up the access road for training. Good kid. Tough. Never came back from one of his rides. We went out looking, found what was left of his bike a few miles up the road. Frame twisted. Tires shredded like something gnawed through them." He took a deep breath.

"Didn't find him either. Not then. Search and Rescue called it after three days. Said it was too dangerous. But the team that went out, they came back spooked. Said they felt watched, eyes on them the whole time."

Vikram stopped walking. "What happened to the biker?"

Mike looked at him, eyes dark.

"Day four, someone found what was left of him hanging on the swing gate behind the camp."

Vikram blinked. "The gate we passed?"

Mike nodded. "His head. His insides. Draped over the gate like someone—or *something*—was sending a message."

Vikram's voice cracked. "What did they tell the family?"

Mike shrugged. "Same thing they told everyone. That he was attacked by a wild animal. That it was tragic. That they were sorry."

He shook his head.

"No one mentioned the part about the... display. Or the fact his injuries didn't line up with any bear mauling anyone had ever seen. No claw marks. He was torn apart."

Silence lingered between them. The wind shifted, bringing with it that same sour, earthy smell from earlier. Both men picked up their pace without needing to say anything.

Mike exhaled hard through his nose, like the wind had been knocked out of him just from remembering.

"All I know," he said slowly, "is that after they found what was left of that biker, everything changed. The very next morning, a crew showed up—people none of us had ever seen before. They didn't speak to anyone, didn't ask questions. Just came in and started taking over everything."

He paused. Vikram could feel a shift in Mike's tone, more cautious now, like he was threading carefully through memory and consequence.

"The rest of us were told to stay put. They gave us a list of chores of menial crap, all of it. Clean this, inventory that. Nobody left the perimeter."

He turned to look at Vikram, face dark in the growing shadows of the trees.

"Then came the fencing. Razor wire. Cameras. Orders to move all personal vehicles to town. They said the road would be closed soon. A bus would bring us to work from that point forward. Weird as hell. Everyone was on edge."

Vikram didn't say anything. He didn't need to.

"There was a meeting," Mike continued. "Upper management flew in. Said the camp was closing due to ongoing threats from environmental extremists, pending lawsuits, and... for good measure, they threw in some story about the spotted owl. Said they didn't want to risk further disruption to the habitat. PR-friendly reason, right? Makes 'em look noble."

He scoffed and rubbed his eyes, as if the memory still itched at the back of his skull.

"They kept a skeleton security crew behind for a while, said contractors would install the cameras and other surveillance. Promised the camp would be monitored twenty-four-seven. Then they handed us our final paychecks... and a thick-ass NDA."

Vikram frowned. "An NDA?"

"Yeah," Mike said. "Multi-page document that basically said if you so much as whispered a word about anything you'd seen or even thought you'd seen, you'd lose every cent of your severance. Worse, they'd come after *everything* . Not just the payout, but lawsuits, legal fees...they made sure we knew they had the muscle to ruin us." He gave a bitter laugh.

"Worked too. The money was good. Real good. Enough that a few of the older guys just retired. The younger ones blew it on trucks, motorcycles, dumb shit. A couple of them moved away. One of 'em became an engineer. None of them ever said a damn word."

Mike shifted the pack on his back and looked away. "I put some of it aside for my daughter. Bought a small house just outside of town. Lost the rest in the divorce. I took odd jobs for a few years, then landed that glorified park ranger gig."

He fell quiet for a long moment before adding, "It's been mostly quiet since. People still go missing around here, but that happens anywhere hikers go too far off trail. Nothing like what we saw before."

Vikram stared hard at Mike. The air between them felt taut, like a wire ready to snap.

"Until you decided to send my brother up here," he said, his voice low and bitter. "Then it got loud again."

Mike didn't flinch. He met Vikram's glare and nodded once, solemnly.

"Yeah," he said. "Quiet... until Venu."

Vikram shook his head. "After all that—everything you just told me—I still don't understand *why*, Mike. Why would you send him up here?"

Mike opened his mouth, then closed it again. He clicked his tongue and looked ahead into the thick forest. His voice, when it finally returned, was barely above a whisper.

"I honestly thought the creature was dead," he said, voice

rough. “Or gone. Maybe both. That lake wasn’t unknown, Vik. Guys from camp used to hike there to fish or cool off when they didn’t want to go into town. How do you think all those yellow ribbons got there? And yeah… when your brother was at the bar, the way he talked about nature, the wilderness—man, I knew he’d love it up here. That lake is special. You saw it. I figured a day hike would be harmless. That’s it. No more.”

Mike paused, looked up into the trees. "Old timers in town, when they heard the camp was shutting down, started whispering again about the creature. But always past tense. Like it came through once every few years. Caused hell, then disappeared. Like it belonged to the land, but didn’t live here. Transitory, I guess. The camp operated for over a decade without any incidents."

Vikram stared at him, silent. His eyes searched Mike’s face for even a flicker of sincerity.

“Look,” Mike went on, his tone edging defensive, “remember when I told you I came back here years ago to salvage equipment? That was only half true. I wasn’t just after old gear. I wanted to see if that feeling was still there, of being watched...to make sure the nightmare was gone.”

He kept walking. “I hiked the same access road you and I came up today. Even made it up to where the surveyors were attacked. And it was quiet. Dead quiet. Just deer and birds. No weird feelings. Nothing off. The camp was intact, everything like we had left it. None of the boards on the window were torn off, no windshields busted out on the vehicles. It was like the whole damn spell that thing cast over this place had...evaporated...and the creature had moved on.”

Vikram took a step closer, his voice low, barely contained. “That still doesn’t explain why you sent Venu up here. There's something you're not telling me."

Mike's mouth opened, closed. Then he snapped, not out of anger, but exasperation.

"I don't know what the hell you want me to say, Vik! I just laid it all out for you!" His voice bounced off the trees, startling a bird from the canopy above.

Vikram stepped in front of Mike, "You gave me the back story of this place, that's it. Why did you send Venu up here alone knowing all of that?"

Mike pushed past Vikram, then spun around to face him again. "You want me to say I used your brother as bait? Fine. I'll say it. Is that what you want to hear? That I sent him up here hoping maybe he'd feel something—sense something — that'd prove I wasn't crazy after all? That some part of me needed to know whether the monster was still out here? There. You got it. You happy now?"

"No," Vikram said. His voice shook, not from fear but from fury. "You fucking used him."

"I didn't think he'd die, Vik! At worst, I thought he come back to the bar and say he felt something was watching him."

Vikram's hands balled into fists. "A *fucking* logging company packed up and ran. They surrounded this place with barbed wire and cameras, paid off employees to shut up, and you — *you* —decided to send my brother up here to confirm a hunch?"

Vikram's face darkened.

"You son of a bitch," Vikram said. "You used my brother.

Like bait. Chickenshit mother—"

Vikram launched himself at Mike, fists flying in wild haymakers. Mike didn't flinch. He sidestepped the blows with practiced ease, ducking one, pivoting around another. Vikram, driven by pure adrenaline and grief, kept swinging until his own exhaustion caught up to him. His breath hitched, his arms fell to his sides, and without warning, he collapsed against Mike, sobbing into his chest.

"You're lucky I don't know how to fight, dick face," Vikram mumbled through his tears. "Or you'd be down."

Mike wrapped an arm around Vikram's back, steadying him. "I know. I'm sorry, kid. I'm sorry. I didn't think he'd get hurt. I didn't think..." His voice trailed off.

Vikram pulled back, sniffling. "You can stuff your sorries in a sack, Mike. Your apologies won't bring Venu back."

Mike nodded solemnly. "I know. Nothing I do or say will make that better either."

Mike loosened his grip. Vikram took a shaky step back, his face unreadable. Then, without warning, he swung and sucker punched Mike square in the jaw.

"Ouch! Shit!" Vikram yelped, doubling over and cradling his hand. "I think I broke my hand. Damn it, that hurt!!!" Mike rubbed his jaw, eyes narrowing for a moment. He considered responding in kind, then exhaled and let it go.

"Did that make you feel better?"

"No! I think I feel worse! I *definitely* think my hand is broken." Vikram winced in pain as he flexed his fingers.

"Let me see," Mike said, stepping closer. He gently examined Vikram's right hand.

"It's not broken," he said after a moment. "But it's going to feel like crap for a while. We've got less than an hour of daylight. You ready to move on? We're getting close to the road."

Vikram nodded, wiping his eyes. "Yeah. Let's go."

CHAPTER 20: LEFTY RELIEF

They moved together in silence, trudging through the thick underbrush. The canopy above was growing darker, shadows stretching between the trees. They had gone no more than a hundred meters when Vikram suddenly slowed.

He sniffed the air. "Mike... I can smell it."

Mike came to an abrupt stop beside him. His posture shifted. "Me too..."

From somewhere behind them came the telltale rustle of branches signaling that something huge and heavy was forcing its way through the forest. Then… silence. A beat later, a rock thudded harmlessly into the dirt a few feet to their left.

Both men stopped in their tracks, heads whipping toward the sound. Their chests rose and fell with rapid, shallow breaths. After several moments of strained silence, Vikram whispered, “Did he just underhand that rock?”

Mike didn’t look back. “His right shoulder’s injured, remember?”

A pause.

"Oh my God," Vikram muttered, eyes wide with the absurdity of it, "Bigfoot can't throw left-handed."

"Maybe," Mike muttered, "but he can still tear us to pieces if he gets close enough."

He drew his revolver again, unholstering it with a calmness that belied the urgency simmering under his words. The steel caught a faint glint of the dying daylight.

"Stay behind me," he said, low and steady. "He's going to charge us. Just like he did at the clearing."

The woods fell into an unnatural hush. Even the insects seemed to sense the weight of what was coming. Vikram could hear his own heartbeat pounding in his ears, feel the heat of fear rising in his chest.

Then came the chuffing. Low, guttural, just off to their right. Close.

Mike's body tensed as he thumbed the hammer back on the revolver. The metallic *click* seemed to echo in the silence. Suddenly, the brush exploded with movement. Branches snapped like dry bones, twigs crushed beneath something massive as it barreled forward.

Mike spun toward the sound and fired three times in quick succession. The muzzle flashes lit the darkening trees like lightning through a storm. The forest screamed back.

A shriek tore through the air, wild and raw and filled with rage. A beat passed, then the sound receded. More branches broke, farther away now. The crashing and stomping faded into the woods.

Then, quiet again.

“I think you hit it,” Vikram breathed, voice trembling.

Mike exhaled slowly. “Maybe. If I did, it was the luckiest shot of my damn life. I never saw him, I just fired where the noise was coming from.” He glanced around warily. “This forest’s so thick, it’s a miracle a bullet made it past the trees at all.” He glanced into the darkness. “Still... scared him off. That’s something.”

CHAPTER 21: STICK TO IT

Vikram and Mike continued pushing through the dense forest. Their heads scanned from side to side, tracking every whisper of movement in the underbrush, every creak of a branch.

Occasionally, they stopped in their tracks when a rustle or crack echoed from deeper within the woods. Each time, their hearts pounded until the silence resumed. Mike's revolver remained fixed in his grip, his trigger finger just outside the guard, disciplined and ready. Vikram stayed close behind, his eyes flicking nervously over his shoulder every few steps. Suddenly, something moved through the trees off to their right. A deliberate rustling, too heavy to be a deer.

"Stop," Mike ordered.

Vikram froze mid-step. "Is he close?"

Mike studied the woods, squinting through the thick underbrush. "Hard to tell. But we need to head that way soon. That should be where we meet the road."

"You think?" Vikram asked, voice tight.

"Yeah, pretty sure. Not exactly where we entered, but close."

They started walking in the new direction. After a few yards, Vikram paused and picked up a thick, six-foot stick from the forest floor. He gave it a couple of test swings, then jabbed it into the air a few times. A flicker of inspiration crossed his face.

"Mike! Mike!"

Mike, several meters ahead, turned around with a scowl. “Try and keep it down, will ya? What is it?”

“Look, Bigfoot already knows we’re out here,” Vikram whispered loudly, “not sure why we have to be all I Spy sneaky. Anyway, I was thinking we should tie that knife I bought to the end of this stick, use it like a spear if he charges again. What do you think?”

He looked up at Mike, eyes wide, hopeful like a kid showing off a science project to a skeptical dad. Mike stepped forward, extended his hand. “Let me see that thing.”
Vikram handed him the stick. Mike gave it a few testing wobbles, inspecting the grain and heft.

“That’s not a bad idea,” Mike said. “If he charges us again, we’ll need something between us and him. Need to break about a foot off of this though, it's too long to pivot between all these trees."

He nodded to Vikram, "Let’s get that knife out, I’ve got some twine in my pack.”

They both dropped to their knees and began rummaging through their gear. Vikram pulled out the large survival knife, still sheathed. He passed it to Mike, who slid the blade out and examined it with an impressed grunt.

"This is actually a really good knife," Mike muttered, eyes narrowing as he inspected the finish. "Serrated and sharp. Nine-inch blade. Micarta handle... this isn't a prop replica."

He looked up. "How much did you pay for this?"

A sheepish look crossed Vikram's face. "Uh... they told me it was a Jimmy Lilly or something? I paid $1,500. Did I get ripped off?"

Mike froze mid-wrap of the twine, staring at him. "You paid fifteen hundred for this?"

Vikram cringed. "Yeah. I did. So...yeah?"

Mike blinked once, then gave a slow shake of his head.

"No," he said at last. "Not even close. And it's Jimmy *Lile*, not Lilly. He was the knifesmith who designed the original First Blood knife. These go for two grand, easy. This thing'll do some damage. Good purchase, kid."

Vikram let out a sigh of relief, hiding a grin. It wasn't much, but finally, he received a nod of approval from Mike.

Mike finished lashing the knife to the stick, tight and deliberate. When he was done, he gave the makeshift spear a once-over, nodded at the craftsmanship, and handed it back to Vikram.

Vikram held it like a warrior preparing for a charge, beaming. "Thanks, Mike. Really."

Mike just grunted. "Let's move."

They re-entered the forest, two men armed with grit, fear-fueled adrenaline, and a $1,500 handmade spear that might be the difference between life and death.

"This looks pretty badass," Vikram said, turning the spear in his hands with an impressed grin.

"It is badass," Mike replied, taking it gently from him. "But be careful. Hold it like this."

He stepped to Vikram's side and showed him how to cradle the shaft across his forearm, with the blade resting high against the right shoulder.

"You want it tight and steady like that," Mike said. "Fast to raise, easy to maneuver if it charges."

Vikram took it back, mimicking the hold with a nod. "Got it. Just hold it like a Spartan in *300*."

Mike frowned. "Is *300* a movie or something?"

"Yeah," Vikram laughed. "And it's awesome. It's about three hundred Spartans who held off thousands of Persians. Now we're the Spartans... and that thing is a giant, walking Persian rug."

Mike rolled his eyes, shaking his head. "Is everything a movie to you?"

"You gotta understand," Vikram said, walking alongside him now. "I loved American movies growing up. They were huge for me. Larger-than-life guys like Rambo. All the Arnold movies. They made an impression, especially for a young Indian kid who didn't always feel like he belonged. Those movies gave me and Venu something to aspire to." He hesitated. Voice softening. "Especially the *Rocky* movies. Man, those hit different. They gave us hope, you know? That if you work your ass off, you can go toe-to-toe with Apollo Creed, be the champ. That's what drove Venu to the outdoors, he was chasing a dream. He was putting in the work... and..." Vikram's voice cracked. His pace slowed. He turned away slightly, blinking hard to clear the tears.

"I know," Mike said quietly. "I'm sorry, Vik."

"Venu and I..." Vikram continued, his voice barely above a whisper. "Even when we weren't getting along, we always had *Rocky IV*."

Mike gave him a sympathetic look and nodded. "I used to watch all the *Tinkerbell* movies with my daughter. And the Disney Princess ones. We'd sit there and debate which fairy was stronger, or which princess had the best character arc. Snow White was her favorite... until Belle came along. I miss those times."

"At least you still have a chance to watch them with her again," Vikram said, wiping his eyes. "Venu and I don't. You know that."

They walked in silence for a while after that. The only sounds were the crunch of their boots against the forest floor and the soft breath of wind through the trees. Mike finally opened his mouth. "Vik, I—" Vikram stopped and held up a hand.

"Don't," he said firmly. "I'm stopping you right there. I know you're sorry, but I don't know if I'll ever forgive you for sending Venu up here knowing that thing might still be around."

He turned to face Mike fully. "I don't need another apology.

Not now. Just get me out of here. That's all I'm asking. Apology not accepted."

Mike nodded slowly; lips pressed tight. His hand drifted over his close-cropped head before resting at the back of his neck.

"Okay," he said. "Let's keep moving."

They resumed their hike, weaving through the underbrush in tense silence. A few minutes passed before Vikram broke it with a quieter, lighter tone.

"So..." he said, glancing up at Mike. "Which princess was your favorite?"

Mike snorted and gave him a sidelong look. "I always liked that Jasmine. *Aladdin* was solid start to finish. Funny genie. Good music. Jasmine had spirit."

"I can see that," Vikram grinned. "What about..."

The sounds came from everywhere, branches cracking, foliage shifting, something massive displacing the forest around it. Both men froze.

Mike's hand instinctively dropped back to his revolver, drawing it with practiced efficiency. Vikram, heart pounding, planted his feet wide and held the spear high like he was bracing for a medieval joust.

Mike glanced over. His eyes narrowed at Vikram's ridiculous, exaggerated stance.

"Vik," he hissed, "hold the spear with a split grip. You've got no leverage like that."

Vikram blinked, confused. “I don’t know what that means. Split grip?”

“Yeah. One hand lower than the other—slide them apart. You want control, not whatever it is you think you're doing.”

The snapping intensified ahead of them. Heavy, deliberate movements pressing through the underbrush. The creature wasn’t being subtle anymore.

Mike’s brow furrowed as he turned back toward the noise.

His voice dropped to a grim whisper. “He’s cutting us off. Herding us.”

Vikram’s stomach turned. “What do you mean?”

“Shhhhhh,” Mike snapped, raising a hand to silence him as the woods fell still again.

CHAPTER 22: TIP OF THE SPEAR

The sounds stopped.

The forest, moments ago alive with crackling movement, dropped into an unnatural silence.

Then came the scream.

It started high—a shriek that pierced the canopy like a siren and then plunged into a guttural, almost inhuman roar that seemed to shake the earth beneath their feet. It bounced off the trees in all directions, reverberated in their chests, disorienting, as if the very woods were howling at them.

Vikram jerked in place, eyes wide. "What the *fuck*, Mike?" Another howl tore through the woods. Vikram edged closer to Mike, spear clutched tightly, arms trembling. "Mike?" he whispered.

Mike was spinning slowly in place, eyes scanning the dense growth ahead. His revolver was already raised, cocked and steady.

"I can't see him," he muttered. "I can't see him."

"I can't smell him either..." Vikram said. "We usually smell him first."

Mike nodded slowly, then stiffened.

"Yeah... but I do now. Real strong. He's close."

A sharp *crack* came from the left, something heavy breaking a branch. Mike spun toward the sound, gun trained. A large rock hurtled through the brush and crashed into the earth just feet from Vikram. He stumbled back. Mike's jaw clenched. "He still can't throw as hard as before."

Another series of snaps rang out, this time behind them. Both men turned. Then more breaking branches from the front.

"He's messing with us," Mike said through gritted teeth. "Trying to confuse us."

Vikram's voice cracked. "Yeah, he's doing a good job of it. What do we do?"

Mike looked up. The sky had deepened into a bruised navy. Darkness was descending on them, fast. "I don't know."

More cracking from deeper in the forest. But this time, the sound drifted away. Fading.

Then the birds returned. The bugs. The low rustling of ordinary life.

"Is he gone?" Vikram asked.

"For now. Maybe." Mike didn't lower the revolver. "But he's cutting us off. The direction he just moved—he knows it's our way out. He wants us boxed in."

Mike finally exhaled. "We've got fifteen minutes of usable daylight left. After that, it's going to be pitch black. We need to find a place to build a fire and rest. Or at least *try* to rest. We can't let him push us too far off course."

Vikram looked toward the thick woods, then up at the sky again. His voice wavered. "How are we supposed to *rest* with that thing out there?"

Mike finally lowered his weapon and turned to him. "We find a small clearing, build a perimeter with dry twigs and branches. If he gets close, we'll hear it. He's too big to move through without making noise."

Vikram was shaking his head before Mike even finished. "I don't know, Mike..."
"That's all I've got, Vik," Mike snapped, frustration bubbling up. "We are *completely* fucked right now. That thing has every advantage. We've got three bullets left and your goddamn Rambo spear. That's it. Building a fire and trying to catch our breath is the best idea I've got."

Vikram stood in silence for a beat, then said, "Then maybe we stop reacting and start pushing back."

Mike blinked. "What?"

"If he's trying to cut us off—fine. Let's go *toward* him. Let's counter. Let's make him think *we're* hunting *him*."

Mike stared at Vikram for a long moment. His eyes narrowed at first, then softened. The corner of his mouth curled upward in a reluctant grin.

"Vik," he said slowly, "that's so dumb, it might just be brilliant." He nodded. "He's been king of the hill up here for years. Apex predator. No one's ever challenged him. If he thinks *we're* coming for *him*, he might back off. Or at least throw him off his game long enough to give us a shot at the access road."

Mike checked his smartwatch compass then shrugged off his pack and rummaged through the main compartment. He pulled out a headlamp and tested the battery. There was still some life. Mike placed the lamp on his head. "This will help, but there's no telling for how much longer...it's been stored away in here for over a year."
Vikram, buzzing with adrenaline, pulled out his iPhone. The screen lit up. No bars. Battery: five percent.

"Yeah," he muttered. "Didn't think so. Don't you people believe in cellphone service up here?" he muttered. "I haven't had service since I left town. Not a single bar. And now my battery's circling the drain."

Mike didn't look back as he shrugged his pack onto his shoulders. "Twenty years ago there was talk of putting up a cell tower near the camp. Management even floated the idea of making it a hub for the area. That didn't exactly work out."

"Sasquatch ruined that too," Vikram grumbled.

Gripping his makeshift spear, he struck an exaggerated battle stance and began marching off with exaggerated bravado. "It's time to show him who's boss of these woods."

Mike watched him disappear into the dark for a few paces, then called out, "Hey, boss of the woods... you're going the wrong way."

Vikram stopped in his tracks and turned back, sheepishly.

"Which way, then?"

Mike jerked his head to the right. “That way.”
The two men set off again, deeper into the darkening forest.

Vikram flicked on his phone flashlight every few seconds to scan the ground behind Mike. Up ahead, Mike’s headlamp cast a steady cone of light onto the trail.

“Good thing you brought that headlamp,” Vikram said. “My phone is gonna be D-U-N, ‘done’ any second now.”

Mike sighed. “Then shut it off. We might need that battery when we make it back to the vehicles. I don’t have a phone.”

Vikram scoffed. “Of course you don’t, Mike.”

He powered down the phone with an exaggerated sigh. They walked on in silence for a few moments.

A single, deep knock echoed through the trees, sharp and sudden, like a baseball bat slamming into a telephone pole. Both men froze.

“That sounded close,” Vikram said, instinctively raising his spear.

Mike’s eyes narrowed. “One knock. That makes it harder to tell where it came from.”

“It sounded like it came from *everywhere* ,” Vikram whispered. They waited, breathing shallow, listening. Nothing. The forest came back to life. Crickets resumed their chatter, branches rustled gently in the breeze. Mike relaxed slightly, and they resumed walking.

Another *crack* , louder this time.

Vikram flinched. Mike reached for his pistol.

“That was definitely closer,” Vikram said. “Mike... where is he?”

“Quiet,” Mike hissed. “He’s close.”

“I don’t hear anything.”

Mike held the revolver steady. “Get ready…”

“Get ready for *what* ?!” exclaimed Vikram.

A sudden explosion of sound behind them—branches snapping, twigs splintering. Vikram spun instinctively, raising his spear wildly.

The butt of the shaft slammed into Mike’s headlamp, knocking it clean off his forehead. The beam tumbled into the underbrush and landed facedown, plunging them into near-total darkness. “Shit!” Mike barked.

“Sorry! Sorry, Mike!”
Around them, the woods erupted again—snapping branches, shifting leaves, something huge moving fast and with purpose.

Vikram dropped to his knees, frantically feeling for the headlamp.

Mike crouched down and tucked the revolver in one of the front pockets of his jacket. With both hands free, he turned in a circle, frantically feeling for the headlamp. The creature was closing in.

"Got it—stop grabbing!" Mike snapped, wrestling the straps of the headlamp from Vikram's hands.

"Okay, okay..." Vikram gasped, still crouched low. "I can smell him, Mike!"

Mike fumbled with the straps, cursing under his breath as he finally secured the headlamp back onto his head. The light snapped on with a harsh beam, illuminating the surrounding woods in stark relief.

"Yeah," he said, voice low. "I smell him too..."

The forest had gone unnaturally still again. Mike turned, his eyes scanning the darkness, heart thudding against his ribs. He shifted the light slightly to his left—and froze. Just beyond a twisted cedar, a huge face appeared, watching, half-lit by the trembling beam. The headlamp beam caught its eyes burning red and locked directly onto his. A wall of matted fur and taut muscle stood nearly motionless, except for the steady rise and fall of its barrel chest.

Then, in a blink, it vanished back into the trees.

Mike let out a sound, guttural, involuntary, something between a gasp and a groan.

Vikram spun around, eyes wide. "What?! Mike, what?!"

"It was there," Mike said, stepping back, his voice tight. "By that tree. Looking right at me. And then it was gone. It's still close."

Vikram gripped his spear tighter, his voice trembling. "What do we do?"

"I don't know, kid," Mike said, his hand fishing for the revolver he had stuffed into his jacket pocket. He drew it slowly. "I think we keep moving. We're maybe a thousand meters from the road, give or take. We need him to back off. Keep pushing, like you said. Make him think we're not afraid."

Suddenly, two sharp tree knocks cracked through the woods like gunshots.

Both men pivoted toward the sound.

Then another knock. This one solitary. And from a different direction.
Vikram turned, nearly bumping into Mike. His voice was shaking now. "Where's he at? Mike, those knocks...they're coming from all around us!"

"I don't know," Mike muttered. "Just don't panic!"

"Don't panic?!" Vikram snapped, barely holding it together.

"Shut up, kid! Just listen!"

They stood shoulder to shoulder, eyes darting through the darkened forest, the headlamp casting frantic shadows across the undergrowth. The sound of snapping branches and rustling limbs began to echo all around them—left, right, behind, ahead. Everywhere.

Vikram spun to his right, spear up and trembling in his grip, pointing it into the trees.

"He's everywhere, Mike!" he shouted.

Mike's hand tightened on the revolver. The woods around them felt like they were closing in. Whatever was stalking them wasn't just hunting anymore.

It was playing.

CHAPTER 23: PHONEBOOTH

“Easy, Vik,” Mike said, trying to keep his voice steady. “Don’t panic. He’s trying to confuse..." He didn’t get to finish.

The woods erupted as the creature exploded from the undergrowth, a mountain of fur and fury barreling toward Vikram. The scream that tore from Vikram’s throat was primal. He raised the makeshift spear and lungedforward, but it was awkward, desperate. The beast swatted at the weapon with one massive hand, easily deflecting it to the side. The force of the blow wrenched Vikram off balance, but somehow, he held on, stumbling to his right as the creature swung again. Its thick, clawed arm just missed his head.

The dense trees hemmed the monster in, limiting the full range of its massive limbs, a narrow advantage that kept both men alive for the moment.

Mike raised the revolver, but before he could fire, the creature lashed out with its left arm, striking Mike’s hand and sending the gun spinning into the darkness.

The beam from Mike’s headlamp sliced through the dark in wild arcs—catching glimpses of fur, bark, mud—until it found the monster’s face again, just in time for both men to hear another shriek. Louder. Closer.

Furious.

Mike backed away quickly—but his foot twisted over a knotted root, and he went down hard, a jolt of pain flaring through his left ankle as he crashed into a tangle of gnarled wood.

The creature saw its chance.

It stepped toward him with a feral snarl, upper lip peeled back to reveal the long incisors. One arm raised high, its enormous fist was clenched like a sledgehammer.

And then it screamed.

The monster staggered, lurching to the side as Vikram plunged the knife-tipped spear into its back—just below the right shoulder blade. The blade tore through thick hide and sinew. Vikram yanked it back, the serrated edge raking across muscle, eliciting another bellow of pain. The creature turned on him, its red eyes blazing with rage. Vikram didn't hesitate. He dipped low, driving the spear forward again—this time catching it just above the hip. The knife punched through flesh, and when Vikram pulled it back, blood sprayed in a wide arc.

It howled.

Staggering, the creature took several retreating steps.

"Mike! Mike!" Vikram shouted, his voice cracking. "Shoot it! Shoot it!"

Mike was scrambling to stand, fighting through the sharp pain in his ankle. But the creature was fast, much faster than it had any right to be. It pivoted on a heel and lunged toward Vikram, who tried to reset his grip and bring the spear up. He was too slow.

The backhand came like a freight train. Vikram instinctively curled inward, arms across his chest, but it wasn't enough. The blow landed with sickening force and sent him flying, his body slamming into a tree with a dull, awful thud. The spear fell from his hands.

Mike was up now, breath ragged, eyes wide. The monster turned to Vikram, who was barely moving, slumped at the base of the tree, blood trickling from his temple.

"Hey!" Mike shouted. "Hey! Over here!"

He waved his arms, trying to draw its attention, adrenaline numbing the throb in his ankle. "HEY!"
The creature turned toward him slowly, eyes narrowing, nostrils flaring. It took a step forward.

Mike swallowed.

"Shit."

Mike's eyes darted from the snarling creature to the spear lying just two meters away—so close, yet guarded by the monster's enormous, leathery foot. The beast bared its teeth and unleashed an eardrum-shattering roar that sent a bolt of terror through Mike's chest and down his spine.

And then it lunged.

Bracing on his good ankle, Mike surged forward, ducked low, and rolled just beneath the creature's outstretched arm. The monster reached for him, but a sharp cry of pain stopped it short, the injury in its right shoulder flaring again. Mike scrambled on hands and knees, heart pounding thunderously, fingers clawing at roots and soil until he reached the spear. He grabbed it and used it as a crutch to hoist himself to his feet, planting it hard into the earth to stay upright.

"Back off, you son of a bitch!" Mike shouted, voice hoarse. "Back off!"

The creature paused, its heavy breath rising in misty clouds. The bloody patch on its shoulder glistened. Fresh blood oozed from the stab wound above its hip. The dried, crusted stain across its ribs still marked the second shot Mike had landed.

Mike looked up, panting, fear thick in his eyes, but something else too. "I don't want to do this," he said, softer now. "Okay? I just want to get my friend out of here. I don't want to hurt you. Let us go."

The creature locked eyes with him. Something passed between them in that moment — recognition, maybe. Weariness. The beast's head tilted slightly, its breathing slowing.

Then its expression hardened.
It charged.

Mike let out a sharp breath and stepped forward—not back — pivoting slightly to the right. He raised the spear and slashed downward as the creature reached for him. The blade ripped through the creature's left arm, opening a deep gash from elbow to wrist. The monster screamed in rage. Mike didn't hesitate. He slashed again, this time across the beast's left side, just under the ribs.
"Enough!" Mike shouted, chest heaving. "Back off! Enough!"

The creature faltered. Its eyes, glowing red in the flickering beam of the headlamp, moved to the wounds. Blood ran freely down its arm. It looked back at Mike. Only this time, it hesitated.

Mike raised the spear again and feinted forward.
The creature flinched.

Then, with a final snarl, it turned and bounded into the darkness, vanishing into the trees. The sounds of its passage, branches snapping, underbrush shredded, faded quickly.

Mike, spear in hand, rushed to Vikram's side.

"Hey... hey, kid," he said, urgently. "Wake up. C'mon."

Vikram stirred with a groan. His eyelids fluttered. "Am I dead?" he mumbled. "I think I'm dead again. Everything hurts."

Mike chuckled, relieved. "Can you stand? We've gotta move. We can't stay here."

Vikram tried, bracing one hand on the tree trunk, then hissed in pain. "I think some of my ribs are broken," he said. "Feels like they're scraping together when I move."

"Could be," Mike replied. "But we've got no choice. You need to be on your feet."

He crouched, slipped his arms under Vikram's, and heaved upward. Vikram screamed in pain as he was lifted.

"Ahhh! Let go! I'm standing, okay?!"

Mike eased off and gave him a nod. "Sorry, kid. But we gotta get out of here. This headlamp's almost dead. There's too much blood on the ground and it's going to bring in all kinds of scavengers. We need to move. Find a place to make camp until sunrise."

"Okay," Vikram said breathlessly. "Fire. Camp. Got it. Can we make s'mores?"

Mike shook his head, smiling in spite of the chaos. "Wish we could, Vik. Let's go."

"Why didn't you shoot it, Mike? It was right in front of you!" Vikram asked.

Mike sighed in frustration. "It knocked the gun out of my hand, sent it flying into the brush."

Vikram glanced around, "Shouldn't we try and find it?"

"Needle in a haystack," Mike said. "No idea which direction it went. I'd feel better if we had it too, but we don't have the time. We've got maybe a mile of trees to get through. Then it's a couple more back to camp."

Vikram nodded, wincing. "Alright. Let's get moving, I guess."

Mike glanced at his smartwatch, checked the compass, then turned slightly to his right. "This way."

Slowly, they set off, two battered shadows moving deeper into the dark, bloodstained woods.

CHAPTER 24: IN THE PAINT

The two men stood in what could be loosely described as a small clearing, less than 10 feet in diameter. Mike began to gather up small branches and twigs for a fire.

"How much further, Mike?" Vikram asked, voice strained with exhaustion.

"We've been at it forty-five minutes and barely covered half a mile," Mike replied. He crouched slowly, favoring his ankle as he picked through fallen limbs. "Between my ankle and all of your injuries, we just aren't moving very fast."

"I don't want to stop," Vikram muttered. "I just want out of these woods."

"Same, kid," Mike said. "But we're both busted up. You need to rest a bit, and I need to try and wrap this ankle. And it's getting cold."

Vikram tried to straighten his posture. "Didn't I rest enough when Squatch knocked me out?"

Mike turned and looked at him, the failing light of the headlamp illuminating his face. "What you did back there is why we're still alive, okay? Your knife is paying off. You stood your ground and fought. Now you're going to rest a couple of hours."

Mike helped Vikram shrug off his backpack. Before setting it down, he dug through the compartments and pulled out the ferrow rod. He then propped the pack against a tree trunk and eased Vikram into position so it could support him.

"This," Mike said, holding up the farrow rod, "is the second best thing you bought."

He crouched over the pile of dried leaves and brittle twigs he'd arranged, then struck the farrow rod. A shower of sparks leapt forward. On the third try, a wisp of smoke appeared. Another strike and a small ember glowed. Slowly, it grew into the beginnings of a fire.

Vikram looked toward the flame. "Next time we do this, you know what we'll need?"

"What's that, Vik?" Mike asked, feeding a few longer sticks into the growing flame.

"We'll need to remember not to do this again."
Mike let out a low laugh. Vikram joined him, but the moment the chuckle escaped his lips, he winced and clutched his ribs.

"Shit," Vikram groaned. "Laughing hurts."

The small fire flickered between them, casting long shadows that danced in the trees surrounding the clearing.

Mike stood and added a few thicker branches to the fire, coaxing it into a strong, steady burn. He set his pack down beside him and carefully pulled off his left boot and sock, grimacing as he turned his ankle toward the light. The headlamp was fading fast, casting weak light across the bruise already blooming across the bone. He rummaged through Vikram's pack, pulled out the first aid kit, and started wrapping the joint with an ace bandage.

Vikram stirred. He sat up suddenly, groaning and clutching his side.

Mike jumped, his eyes darting to the dark tree line. "What is it? Did you hear something?"

Vikram held up a finger. "Shhhhh..."

"I didn't hear anything..." Mike reached slowly for the spear.

Vikram twisted in place, winced again, and wrinkled his nose. "I can smell it, Mike."

Mike sniffed at the air, frowned, and stood to do a slow walk around the edge of their tiny clearing. "I don't smell anything."

Vikram inhaled deeply again, narrowed his eyes, then pointed to Mike's bare foot. "Nope. I definitely smell something."

Mike blinked. "Are you sure?"
Vikram let out a wheezy laugh that ended in a groan and pointed straight at Mike's foot. "It's your feet, Mike. Jesus. We've gotta get you some foot powder or something."

Mike stared at him, slack-jawed. "You serious? You had me thinking it was back."

"Nope," Vikram grinned. "I think your swampy-ass foot

scared it off."

Mike chuckled and sat back down, shaking his head. "I should kick your ass for that."

He finished wrapping his ankle while Vikram leaned against his pack, pretending to sleep. A few minutes passed in silence before Vikram spoke again, his voice low and mischievous. "Hey, Mike? Mike?"

"What?" Mike said with a sigh. "Why aren't you sleeping?"

"Just hear me out. What if we caught it, trained it, and turned it into a basketball player?"

Mike blinked at him. "What?"

"I'm serious," Vikram went on, animated now. "Did you see that first step? He's got serious lateral quickness! We trim him up, teach him a few post moves, get him in a jersey and he'd dominate the paint. No one's blocking his shot."

"You're an idiot," Mike said. "Go to sleep."

"I mean, Seattle's due for an expansion team, right? Bigfoot would sell out every home game. He'd rewrite the record books."

"Sure," Mike said dryly. "Game recap: 'Bigfoot scores 70 points on 35-of-38 shooting, pulls down 27 boards, blocks 19 shots, and kills three men in the fourth quarter. He really filled up the stat sheet tonight, especially in the murder column.'"

Vikram laughed, then hissed through his teeth and held his ribs. "Yeah, he'd have to work on the anger management."

"Hell," Mike said, leaning back against a tree trunk, "he'd make a better defensive end. You teach him snap counts, let him run wild...he'd obliterate quarterbacks."

Vikram shook his head. "Nah, the NBA's where the real money is. As his agent, I've gotta think long-term. Endorsements, shoe deals. I'd go after everyone using his image on mugs, shirts, bumper stickers. We're talking generational wealth, Mike. Bigfoot's gonna get *paid*."

Mike smirked. "Flat fee for me. Up front. You're gonna have a hell of a time insuring that contract."

"Just thinking big, man."

There was a pause. The fire crackled. Somewhere in the distance, an owl called out once, then fell silent again.

Mike finally grunted. "Why am I even entertaining this?"

Vikram leaned his head back. "Because you know it's a great idea."

"Go to sleep, kid."

"Nighty night, Mike."

The two men sat in the faint orange glow of the fire. Around them, the forest was thick and black and endless. Overhead, a faint sliver of moonlight cut through the trees, casting long shadows across the clearing. Two survivors wrapped in fatigue and firelight, fading laughter, and the raw edge of survival, tried to rest.

CHAPTER 25: REBOUND

The mist hung low over the forest floor, curling through the trees. Pale morning light filtered through the dense canopy in streaks, illuminating the clearing in a ghostly gray-blue haze. What remained of the campfire smoldered quietly, its last wisps of smoke rising to meet the mist above.

Vikram slept propped against his backpack, arms crossed tightly over his bruised ribs. His face twitched slightly in the cool air. A few feet away, Mike sat upright against the base of a tree, the spear cradled across his chest like a rifle. His boots were back on, the edge of the bandage wrapped around his ankle bulged above the cuff. His breathing was slow, heavy.

Then Mike's eyes snapped open.

He jolted upright and scanned the woods around them with a frantic look. He gripped the spear and struggled to his feet, bracing himself against it like a crutch. Each shift of weight onto his injured ankle sent a jolt of pain up his leg, drawing a hiss through his teeth.

"Not moving too fast, are ya?" Vikram's voice came dry and scratchy from the other side of the fire pit.

Mike turned, surprised. "Didn't know you were awake."

"Hard to sleep with all the groaning and moaning," Vikram said, wincing as he pushed himself upright.

"Yeah, sorry about that," Mike muttered, adjusting his grip on the spear. "This ankle's shot. How are you feeling?"

"Like a Bigfoot threw me into a tree," Vikram said. "Everything feels broken."

Mike offered a hand. "Let's get up and get outta here, okay?" Vikram hesitated, eyeing the hand like it might bite him.

Then he reached up and immediately yelped in pain.

Mike didn't flinch, just nodded at him to try again. "C'mon."

Vikram took a breath, clenched his jaw, and reached again. Mike leaned back and hauled him up in one motion. Vikram screamed as his ribs protested violently.

"You never realize how much you use your ribs," Vikram gasped, hunched over, "until a Bigfoot bashes them."

"Yeah," Mike said with a grim smirk, "and now everything within a mile knows how bad they hurt."

Still bent slightly, Vikram reached for his backpack, teeth gritted. He tried to lift it onto his shoulders but gave up halfway through. Mike stepped over, grabbed the pack, and helped slide one strap over Vikram's arm, then the other.

Vikram winced and hissed all the way through.

"This sucks," Vikram muttered. "It hurts to breathe."

“Yep,” Mike replied. “But we gotta move. At our speed, it’ll take the whole damn morning to reach the road.”

Vikram stood quietly for a moment, staring up into the mist-draped trees. “He’s still out there,” he said softly. “Do you think...?”

Mike adjusted the spear in his hands and followed Vikram’s gaze into the canopy. “I think he’s hurting, bad. We tore him up. He’s lost a lot of blood and burned a lot of energy. He’s tired. Beat to hell. Just like us.”

Vikram nodded. “I still wish we had the gun.”

Mike shrugged. “This spear’s done its job. It’ll do it again if it has to.”
For a moment, the forest felt unnaturally still. Then Mike motioned with his chin. “Let’s move.”

They began walking, slow and ragged, disappearing once more into the fog-choked woods—two battered men held together by adrenaline, fear, and a threadbare sense of hope.

Branches slapped against Mike’s forearms as he hacked his way through the thicket with the spear, using it like a machete. The forest grew denser here and the gnarled brush pulled at their legs, low limbs snagging on backpacks. Every few feet, Mike winced as his bad ankle bore weight it clearly didn’t want to. Vikram trailed close behind, hunched slightly, his breathing ragged. Pain rode his every step.

"Hey, Mike," Vikram said quietly. "What are we going to tell people about all this when we get back to town?"

Mike didn’t turn around. “We don’t.”

“What do you mean we don’t?”

"If anyone asks, we say we ran into a bear. Maybe crashed mountain bikes. We sure as hell aren't going to say we fought a Bigfoot," replied Mike.

Vikram stumbled over a root. "Why not?"

"Because I don't want those horseshit-peddlin' 'Bigfoot hunters' up here," Mike said, slicing through a tangle of ferns. "That's why."
Vikram shook his head in disagreement. "Why not tell the truth? Finally get the word out?"

Mike stopped and turned to face him, expression stern. "One, ninety percent of people won't believe us. The other ten percent? They'll turn this place into a circus. Drones. Infrared cameras. Thermal scopes. You think this thing is dangerous now? Wait until it's cornered. Wait until some brodozer-driving morons come stomping through these trees with high-powered rifles and Monster energy drinks. I'm not doing that. It deserves better."

Vikram bristled. "It deserves to die, I don't care what you say. If I get the chance, I'm killing this fucking thing. It killed my brother, Mike. It's killed other people too."

Mike's jaw tightened. "Yeah. When they encroach on its territory."

Vikram shook his head, eyes wild. "Where's all of this coming from? I'm killing it. End of discussion. And since you're suddenly all buddy-buddy with Bigfoot, maybe *you* shouldn't be the one carrying the spear."

He lunged for it, trying to wrench it free from Mike's grip. Mike easily yanked it back with one hand, a look of calm amusement on his face.

“Kid,” he said, “you can barely hold that backpack upright. Your ribs are wrecked. You’re not gonna do much with this thing except hurt yourself.”
Vikram stepped forward again, grabbing for the spear.

“Give it to me, Mike! You can’t be trusted to...” Something moved in the trees.

Both men stopped, their hands frozen on the spear between them. Mike’s eyes narrowed. He tilted his head, listening.

“That’s not him,” he whispered.

Vikram didn’t look convinced. “What makes you say that?”

Mike’s voice was low, cautious. “Too... I don’t know. It doesn’t feel menacing. It sounded casual.”

“Casual?” Vikram hissed. “Something is casually stomping through the woods? Just out on a morning stroll?”

Mike gave the spear a sharp tug, Vikram released his grip. His hands went to his damaged ribs. "Geez, Mike! That friggin' hurts!"

Mike turned away, spear in hand. "It was an elk, maybe a deer. It wasn't him." He began limping his way back through the forest. “We’re less than a half mile from the road. Let’s move.”

Vikram stood for a moment, brow furrowed as he took in the silence. No birds. No rustling. Not even wind. Just stillness. Suffocating, unnatural.

"It's too quiet," Vikram murmured.

Mike gave a short nod. "Yeah. Stay alert. Be intentional with your steps. Let it know we're not afraid." He looked back at Vikram. "Let's go."

Without another word, they pressed forward, threading through the trees, each step a prayer for daylight and distance from what stalked them.

The creature stood at the lake's edge, framed by mist and early light. It cradled its right arm across its torso, the limb limp and wounded, held as though in an invisible sling. Its matted fur was streaked with dried blood, crusted black against thick muscle, the aftermath of its first true battle in years.

With labored steps, it shuffled down to the water's edge, sinking into the soft shoreline mud. The creature crouched low, letting its weight settle slowly, and dipped its massive left hand into the cold water. It drank carefully, deliberately, scooping and slurping, the motions heavy with pain. Again and again, until its thirst was slaked.

Then, with effort, it reached its good hand into the muddy shoreline. Thick clay and earth squelched through its fingers. It brought the slurry to the wound in its side, just beneath the ribs. The bullet had traveled deep.

It pressed the mixture into the wound. A bellow erupted from its chest, furious and raw. Birds exploded from the canopy in a chaotic riot of wings. Then the forest, so recently alive with sound, fell silent in response.

The creature rose to its full height. Its breath came in deep, ragged pulls, chest heaving with effort. For a moment, it stood perfectly still, listening.

Somewhere in the distance, faint, but clear, the snapping of branches.

The two men were still alive. Still moving.

It breathed once more. Then, with astonishing speed for something its size, the creature vanished into the shadows of the forest.

CHAPTER 26: YELLOW RIBBONS

They moved slowly through the woods, each step an act of will. Pain clung to both men—Mike limping heavily, Vikram clutching his bruised ribs—but neither dared to complain aloud.

The creature's roar split the silence, reverberating through the trees like a thunderclap from hell.

Both men froze.

Mike turned his head toward the sound, eyes scanning the shadowy thicket ahead. "That didn't sound good."

Vikram's voice rose with a rare note of hope. "Hey! Mike, look!" He pointed to a tree just ahead. Wrapped around its trunk, fluttering faintly in the breeze, was a yellow logging ribbon.

"We're close, Mike!"
"Yeah... we are," Mike said, though his voice trailed off. His eyes were still scanning the trees beyond the ribbon.

Vikram picked up on the change in tone. "Do you see something?"

Mike shook his head. “No. Nothing. But we’re near its lair. Back in its territory.” He paused, lips tightening as he weighed the risk. “I’m tempted to have us doubleback. Cut through the old growth. Could hit the road from a safer angle.”

Vikram shook his head, eyes narrowing with resolve. “We’re too beat up. We’re out of water. We push through.”

Mike hesitated a beat longer, then nodded slowly. “Alright. We push through. But once we hit that road, we move fast. Pain be damned.”

Vikram gave a small, crooked smile. “*Pain be damned.* That’s going on the T-shirts I’m making to commemorate this whole nightmare.”

Mike exhaled a tired laugh. “Let’s move.”

“*Let’s move'* goes on the back,” Vikram muttered with a wince as he fell in behind.

They pushed through the bramble, chasing yellow ribbon after yellow ribbon. Heads down, mouths shut, every step driven by the same thought—get out alive.

Branches cracked beneath their weight as they stumbled on, every step heavier than the last. Then, between the trees, a sliver of gray cut through the green—fractured and uneven.

The road.

Mike froze for a moment, staring through the trees. His voice was low, tight with adrenaline. “There it is. Head on a swivel, got it? We move fast.”

Vikram grimaced, adjusting the weight of the backpack slung over his shoulders. “Move fast. Easier said than done.”

They didn't wait another second. Mike stepped forward, spear in hand, eyes scanning every shadow. Vikram followed close behind, ribs searing with every breath. The woods around them remained silent, but both men knew that silence meant nothing.

Not anymore.

They pushed forward, toward the road.

CHAPTER 27: FULL CIRCLE

Mike staggered down the slope, spear gripped tightly, his limp more pronounced with each jarring step. As he reached the edge of the roadside drainage ditch, his good foot landed awkwardly on a slick patch of gravel, nearly sending the blade of the spear into the side of his face.

“Shit,” he hissed, steadying himself.

Vikram was right behind him, stumbling across the ditch with a grunt of pain. Every breath was a battle against the sharp fire in his ribs.

“Look at that,” Vikram wheezed. “We made...”

A rock screamed through the air, slicing just inches past Mike’s head.

"He’s got his fastball back!” Mike shouted, already ducking low.

“Where is it?!?!” Vikram spun in a panicked circle, scanning the trees.

“I don’t know! I don’t...”

Another rock, bigger this time, nearly the size of a playground dodgeball, hurtled out of the tree line. It slammed into the road several feet away, the force of it scattering gravel like buckshot.

Mike instinctively stepped in front of Vikram, planting himself between his unlikely friend and the trees, the spear in his left hand, his right arm extended behind him to keep Vikram close. Their breaths came fast and loud, the only sound on the otherwise silent mountain road.

Then came the cacophony of limbs breaking, branches snapping, and trees shaking.

The creature emerged.

It stepped out from the shadows of the woods and onto the road less than twenty yards away. Towering, massive, its right arm dangling at its side like dead weight. Its left hand clutched a rock the size of a small watermelon. Blood had dried in thick, matted streaks across its fur, mixed with smears of mud. Its eyes were yellowish, rimmed with red, but sharp and alert. They burned with something deeper than rage.

The monster's gaze locked onto Mike.

And Mike... stared right back.

Something passed between them. Recognition.

Mike's breath caught. His fingers tightened around the spear. The pockmarked scars on the creature's face—around its eyes, the ridge of its brow, its cheeks. They weren't random.

They weren't from this fight. They were old.

The memory slammed into Mike like another rock, a memory from a lifetime ago, buried under denial and fear. The shrieking. The smell. The Caterpillar cab rocking like it was being picked up by a storm. The hands reaching for him through broken glass.

His voice was barely more than a whisper. "It's you..."

The creature took one step forward.

Mike shifted the spear, sliding his right hand around the front of his body, bracing the shaft with both hands. His knees bent slightly as he settled into a balanced stance, one learned by instinct, not formal training. Vikram moved out from behind him, sidestepping to Mike's left. The two now stood shoulder to shoulder in the middle of the road, facing down the creature.

The monster loomed, its massive chest heaving, one arm hanging limp, the other curled around a rock. Its head swiveled slowly, first to Mike, then to Vikram. And for a brief moment, Vikram's face softened. His own pain and fear, the terror of the hunt and the weight of his brother's death, all gave way to something startling...sympathy.

The creature's eyes locked on him, then they turned back to Mike.

With a sudden inhale, the beast curled its cracked lips over jagged yellow teeth and let out a roar that seemed to tear open the sky. A scream so primal, so furious, it rattled the breath from Vikram's lungs. He stumbled backward instinctively.

Mike didn't move.

"Easy, kid..." he said without looking. "Don't get jumpy."

Vikram said nothing. His eyes never left the beast. Mike stared right into the monster's eyes, trying to keep his posture calm, unthreatening.

"We don't have to do this," he said, voice low and even. "We just want to leave. That's all. We're going home, and you can go home too."

Mike took his left hand off the spear, just for a second, just long enough to give Vikram a near-invisible motion—*go.*

Vikram began stepping backward. One foot, then another. The creature's gaze followed the motion.

It growled. Deep and low.

Mike regripped the spear. "Easy, big guy. Just stay with me. We're leaving. We won't bother you again." The creature shifted its stance.

Its eyes narrowed.

And then it hurled the rock.

Mike barely had time to twist. The rock grazed him above his left hip, but carried enough force to knock him off balance. He stumbled hard, nearly falling. His right ankle gave out, and he dropped the butt of the spear like a walking stick, catching himself. Gritting his teeth, he straightened, wincing.

" *Run!!!* " he shouted.

Vikram hesitated, then turned. His legs pumped furiously as he sprinted down the road. Gravel slid and popped beneath his boots, breath ragged in his throat.

But something made him stop.

He turned.

And what he saw would haunt him forever.

There, in the road, stood Mike and the creature, locked in stillness like ancient rivals that had been summoned together by fate. One man, one beast, poised between worlds. From Vikram's vantage, the creature loomed impossibly tall, a living shadow carved from rage and the forest itself. Yet Mike did not yield any ground. He stood rooted, spear raised and resolute.

“Mike!!!” Vikram screamed.

Mike half-turned his head.

It was all the creature needed.

It lunged.

Massive strides closed the distance in less than a heartbeat.

Mike pivoted back, swinging the spear wide, jabbing hard. The monster roared - *he hit it* —but the beast pressed forward, knocking Mike down like a wrecking ball. The spear clattered across the road.

“M*ike!!*” Vikram screamed again, watching in horror as the creature loomed over him.

He saw the monster reach down. Saw it lift Mike off the ground like he weighed nothing. Vikram’s heart buckled. Mike locked eyes with him, blood at the corners of his mouth, pouring from his nose. He choked out a single word, "Run!"

Vikram turned and ran again, harder than before, the trees

spinning at the edges of his vision. Each stride sent a sharp, grinding pain through his ribs, and he instinctively cradled his side with one arm as the other pumped awkwardly. Tears streaked down his face, unbidden. He didn't know if he was crying from grief or pain or terror.
His lungs burned like fire had taken root in his chest. His thighs were seizing, every muscle straining past its limit.

But he couldn't stop.

At last, the battered yellow swing gate at the rear of the camp came into view. He made it to the barrier, then collapsed over it, bracing himself with trembling arms, gasping like a man drowning in air. He turned his head, eyes scanning the empty road behind him.

Nothing.

No crashing through the trees. No monstrous silhouette.

He whimpered, a soft, pitiful sound, and pushed himself off the gate, stumbling into a run through the camp. Everything was a blur. The ghost-town buildings. The abandoned equipment.

He skidded to the chain-link fence. No opening. No gap. Just more fence. Where had it been? Where was it? Where?

"Shit, where did we come in? Shit!" He grabbed fistfuls of his hair. "C'mon, Vik...figure it out. Get it together." He sucked in a deep breath and tried to orient himself. "Okay, okay...there's the main building. We came through the fence and the building was to the left...I gotta go up further then."

He ran along the fence line, scanning the metal links for the opening they'd used the day before. Then movement. Between the buildings. A flicker of shadow. Something was out there.

"C'mon, where is it?" he muttered. "Where is it?" He sprinted harder, legs screaming in protest, until finally— *there*! The sagging gap in the fence. He shoved at it with his good arm, widening it just enough to wedge his battered body through.

His backpack caught.

"Shit!"

He struggled, twisting his shoulders, wincing as metal bit into fabric and flesh. Finally, he slipped out of the pack's straps and fell forward, landing hard on his injured side.

His scream was equal parts pain and terror. But he didn't stay down.

He scrambled to his feet, took three desperate steps toward his car and then stopped. "The keys!"

He spun back to the fence. His backpack was still tangled in the chain-link. He forced himself into a clumsy half-run, half-limp. His eyes never left the camp, every breath tight with dread. He tore the backpack away from the fencing with a snarl, ripping the nylon. Then he was sprinting again, plowing through the brush and thick scotch broom, ignoring how it tore at his clothes and skin.

His car came into view.

He dropped the bag at the door and slapped the handle. Nothing.
The car door remained locked.

His heart sank. The key fob wasn't close enough to the door sensor. He grabbed the backpack, lifted it, shoved it closer to the handle:

Click

The door unlocked. The headlights flashed once. His eyes shot back towards the camp in the distance.

And somewhere in that instant he saw something move.

Vikram flung his backpack into the passenger seat, dove behind the wheel, and jabbed the ignition button. The engine came to life with a deep, confident growl—the reassuring voice of German engineering saying *you're not dead yet.*

He threw it into reverse.
Eyes flicked from the side mirrors to the backup camera, guiding himself past the concrete barriers that framed the narrow access road. The adrenaline had sharpened his vision, narrowed his focus to just the image of the road behind him. He brought his eyes forward again—and everything shattered.

A bowling ball sized rock smashed through the front windshield with a deafening *CRACK* , glass exploded inward in a shower of jagged shards. The rock slammed into the passenger seat and embedded itself deep in the upholstery, tearing through leather and foam.

Vikram screamed and instinctively stomped the brake. The car jerked to a stop.

Ahead, framed in the gaping, fractured hole of the windshield, the creature stood at the chained front gate—its hulking form a living mountain of rage. It was covered in blood. Not just dried remnants from their fight in the forest, but new wounds. Fresh crimson smeared its chest, face, and claws. It howled a bone-rattling roar of fury and pain as it repeatedly slammed its good arm against the gate. The chains held, but the steel posts trembled with each blow.

"Oh God—no no no no—"

Vikram threw the car into reverse again and floored the pedal. The tires spun, gravel and dirt erupting as the car swerved slightly, lurching backwards down the narrow road. The backup camera came alive with a
chorus of warning beeps—closer, closer, something behind him.

He glanced down just in time to see the concrete barrier flash across the camera screen.

WHAM.

The rear bumper slammed into the concrete, jarring the entire vehicle. Vikram's head snapped forward, nearly striking the steering wheel.

"Shit! C'mon, c'mon!"

He shifted into drive, pulled forward sharply, trying to straighten out, then back into reverse. The camera was useless now—either shattered or too obscured by debris from the impact. He checked the side mirrors, trying to guide himself into a clearer path.

BANG.

Another crash—he clipped another barrier. Panic flooded his chest like a second heartbeat. His hands trembled on the steering wheel. He threw it back into drive again, breathing hard.

Then he looked up.

The creature had *broken through* the gate. Steel screeched as it tore away from the post. The chain links held, but the frame itself buckled. Now the creature stood in the road, just five meters away. Its massive chest heaved, its breathing loud and ragged. One arm was curled around a rock the size of a basketball.

And it was looking directly at him.

Vikram stared through the fractured remains of his windshield, his own chest heaving, hands locked white-knuckled on the steering wheel. His eyes flicked to the massive rock cradled in the crook of the creature's left arm.

With deliberate, almost ritualistic care, the creature shifted the stone into its open palm. It was like watching a weightlifter position for the final lift—controlled, practiced, and purposeful. Then it brought its ruined right arm up to steady the rock.

A sharp grunt tore from the creature's throat as the movement reawakened its injuries. Its lips curled back in pain, baring teeth like aged broken ivory. The wounded arm trembled and dropped back to its side like a dead branch, useless and limp.

But the rock was still cradled in its left palm, and the look in its eyes hadn't changed.

It was going to throw.

Inside the car, Vikram's world compressed into a single

breath. Time stretched. His thoughts screamed louder than the warning beeps from the console.

If it throws that rock, I'm dead.

He couldn't outrun it. Not now. Not hurt. Not in this car. The engine idled beneath him, a caged beast waiting for a command, but even it might not be fast enough. Vikram's lips parted slightly, as if to speak. As if *pleading* might stop what was coming.

Outside, the creature's fingers curled tighter around the rock.

Its red-tinged yellow eyes locked on Vikram's, narrowing.

CHAPTER 28: GERMAN ENGINEERING

Vikram took a breath so deep it felt like it scraped the bottom of his soul.

He dropped the car into drive.

With his left foot, he jammed the brake pedal to the floor, steadying the growl of the engine with his right foot that hovered just above the accelerator. His right hand slid to two o'clock on the wheel, gripping tight. He adjusted the angle slightly, lining it up, just enough.

His breath hitched.

Then he released the brake and slammed down on the gas. The Audi exploded forward, tires spitting a cloud of gravel and dirt behind it. Vikram screamed—a sound born of terror and fury, fear and freedom. A final act.

The creature tried to sidestep, but it wasn't fast enough. The sedan clipped its left leg just below the knee. The impact lifted the beast off its feet and sent it crashing onto the hood. Glass shattered, the last fragments of the windshield caving under the crushing weight of the monster's body.

The airbags detonated in Vikram's face.

The world went white and muffled. Pain bloomed across his cheek, his nose, his forehead. Then came the second impact—hard, sudden—when the car slammed head-on into one of the concrete barriers. The Audi groaned to a halt, hissing like a dying animal.

Vikram was dazed, barely conscious, blood running from his nose, a hot line of it seeping down over his lip. He blinked and tried to orient himself, but all he could smell was the rank, rotting stench pressing into the cabin. It was suffocating.

It was the creature.

It was still there.

He moved instinctively, blindly, crawling under the deployed airbag, reaching with his good arm for the door handle. He slid out of the seat like a wounded animal and pushed himself away from the massive body draped across the hood. His shoulder screamed. His ribs burned. He hit the ground hard and lay on his back, gasping for air, blinking up at the gray morning sky.

Two breaths. Then three.

He rolled over and tried to stand.

Every part of him protested. Pain knifed through his ribs, his arm dangled uselessly at his side, and he could feel swelling in his face. But he got to his feet, staggering, stumbling like a boxer in the twelfth round.

He turned back toward the car.

The creature was rising.

Slowly, groggily, but rising.

It pushed up from the dented hood, its shoulders hunched and shaking. The car creaked beneath its weight as it stepped down onto the road. It was bleeding badly. The left leg was bent strangely, and its right arm still hung at its side.

The creature turned and looked at Vikram, the rage in its eyes unchanged.

Vikram took two steps back.

The creature growled. It bared its teeth again, saliva glistened along its lips. It limped forward, dragging its injured leg slightly.
Vikram managed a shaky smirk, even as his body begged him to fall over.

"I guess I hurt you a little bit after all," he said. The beast said nothing. It only reached down, scooping up the same rock it had wielded moments before.

"No," Vikram whispered.

He turned to run, but he was too slow. He managed three steps before the rock clipped his right shoulder with bone-shattering force. He collapsed, sprawling into the gravel.

He tried to push himself up, but his arm refused. He gagged and spat blood onto the road. His chest spasmed. He rolled onto his back and stared up at the sky.

Venu.

He thought of Venu.

Tears streamed down Vikram's face, but a smile bloomed through the blood.

"Looks like I'll be seeing you soon, big brother," he whispered.

The crunch of footsteps—massive, deliberate—echoed across the road.

Vikram didn't look. He didn't need to. He could smell the death and decay, the unrelenting malice.
It stood over him now.

He forced his eyes upward.

"Goddamn," he croaked, "you stink, Squatch... Christ..." The creature gazed down at him, its chest rising and falling in ragged cadence. The monster's lips parted into a grotesque smile.

And still, Vikram didn't flinch.

From the stillness came the thunder.

The roar of a diesel engine tore through the silence like a chainsaw. The creature's head snapped toward the main road, eyes wide with animal instinct. A moment later, tires slid across gravel, and vehicle doors flew open with shouts.

Then gunfire.

The first crack of a rifle echoed through the forest like a lightning strike. The creature reared up, snarled, and turned on its heel. It sprinted back toward the camp, just as more rounds split the air.

Another shot.

Then another.

A furious, guttural howl tore through the sky. The sound of something massive crashing into the camp gate sent a tremor through the ground.

Vikram, barely conscious, lifted his head. The world swam in front of him. The trees, sky, and smoke from the Audi's engine swirled together in a bleeding blur. Boots pounded the road. A shadow dropped beside him. "Hey, buddy, take it easy," a calm voice said. A hand pressed gently on Vikram's shoulder. "You're gonna be okay. You're gonna be okay..."

Vikram turned his head and blinked at the man beside him.

A uniform. A badge.

Deputy Grimes.

Vikram tried to speak. His mouth moved before sound came. "Mike...Mike is still out there...we can't...we can't leave Mike..."

"You let us worry about that," Grimes said, his voice low and reassuring. "We're going to get you outta here, okay?"

"Don't forget...about Mike..." Vikram whispered, the edges of the world going black again. "Don't forget..." His voice trailed into silence.

And then he was gone, slipping into unconsciousness as the sounds of shouted commands and ringing gunfire echoed around him.

CHAPTER 29: AFTER PARTY

Vikram stirred beneath a thin hospital blanket, his body broken and bandaged, the pain stitched into every breath. The soft beeping of monitors kept time with his pulse. An IV drip ticked steadily beside him. His right arm was immobilized in a sling; his ribs were bound tight in layers of tape. Scrapes and bruises covered his face, and a padded bandage wrapped his forehead like a crown of war. Footsteps echoed from the hallway. A shadow paused in the doorway, backlit by sterile light from the corridor. The figure stepped into the room.

Sheriff Baker.

He stood silently at Vikram's bedside, taking in the state of the young man. His eyes were heavy with something deeper than exhaustion. Guilt. Grief. Resignation.

"You're beyond lucky, kid," the sheriff said quietly. "Beyond lucky."

He lingered for a moment more, then turned to leave.

"Sh...Sheriff?"

The sheriff stopped. Turned. Walked back to the bed, his boots padding softly on the linoleum.

“Hey, kid,” he said gently. “You should be sleeping.”

Vikram’s voice was faint, raw. “Sheriff...what about Mike?”

The sheriff glanced away, “Don’t worry about that, okay? You need to rest and heal up.”

"Did you find him?” Vikram’s voice cracked.

Baker looked at him long and hard, then sighed. “Vik, we can talk about all that later. No need to worry about Mike anymore. Go back to sleep. Me and Grimes will come by tomorrow or the next day to sort this shitshow out.”

Vikram tried to sit up, his whole body igniting in pain. A sharp cry escaped him. Within seconds, a nurse rushed in. “Sheriff,” she snapped. “You need to leave. He needs rest.”

“I was just leaving, Carol.”

“Did Mike make it?” Vikram shouted, as loud as his battered body would let him.
The sheriff stopped in the doorway. He didn’t turn around. His gaze dropped to the floor. After a pause, he walked out, the sound of his boots fading into the distance.

Vikram stared up at the ceiling, his vision blurred by tears. A sob wracked his chest, and another followed. He didn’t care who heard him.

The nurse stepped to his side, placing a gentle hand on his shoulder. “Easy, kiddo,” she whispered. “Shhh... I’m going to have the doctor bring something to help you sleep.”

“I don’t want to sleep,” Vikram said, voice shaking. “I just want to know what happened to my friend."

"I know," she murmured. "I know. Just rest for now, okay? I'll be right back."

She slipped from the room. Vikram lay alone in the silence, sniffling, his head slowly shaking back and forth against the pillow. Outside, the wind rustled the trees beyond the window—soft, indifferent, and unconcerned with human sorrow.

"Someone just tell me what happened to Mike," Vikram muttered, voice barely above a breath. His eyes were glassy, red-rimmed with emotion and pain.

Nurse Carol returned, followed closely by a man who looked more like a time traveler than a physician. He was in his early sixties, white hair untamed and curling at the edges like smoke. A white Civil War-era-looking beard covered his chin, and if he'd been wearing a white suit and bolo tie, he'd have been the spitting image of Colonel Sanders.

"Doctor's going to take care of you now, okay?" Nurse Carol said gently, giving Vikram's shoulder a soft squeeze.

The doctor stepped forward with a warm, grandfatherly presence and a soft southern cadence that felt like it had been lifted from a frontier novel.

"Hello, son," he said, peering over half-moon glasses. "You've been through quite the ordeal. You're all busted up and rest is the only thing that's gonna fix that."

Vikram winced as he tried to shift, face scrunching in pain. "I just want to know what happened to my friend, doc," he said, fighting to keep his voice steady.

"All in good time, my boy. All in good time," the doctor said, his tone so calm it was infuriating.

He reached into his coat pocket and pulled out a syringe. With practiced ease, he found Vikram's IV line and injected the clear medication. Vikram inhaled sharply, then exhaled through his teeth as the familiar floaty warmth began to spread through his chest and limbs.

"Do all backwoods doctors have to talk like they're narrating *Little House on the Prairie*, doc?" Vikram mumbled, already slipping. "Callin' me 'my boy'... that's good stuff..." The doctor chuckled as he capped the syringe.

"You're a good kid," he said. "This'll put you out a spell. I'll check on you a bit later. For now, just rest."

"Put me out a spell..." Vikram muttered, his words slurring. "Maaaaaan, that's country talk... Doc, I just... Mike... did he..."

His voice drifted off into silence as his eyes fluttered shut, sleep pulling him down like a warm tide.

CHAPTER 30: JUST THE FACTS

The next day.

Vikram sat propped up in bed, looking less like someone who'd been tossed around by a myth and more like someone recovering from a bar fight with gravity. His slung arm rested on a pillow, his ribs were taped so tight he could barely breathe, and his face was a patchwork quilt of scabs and gauze. But his eyes? Sharp. Awake. Ready.

Sheriff Baker stood at the foot of the bed, arms crossed. Deputy Grimes leaned casually in the doorway.

"You're lookin' a little more lively there, Vik," Baker said. "How ya feelin'?"

Vikram grinned, wincing slightly. "I'd say, 'strong enough to pull the ears off a gundark,' but I don't think you'd get it, Sheriff."

Baker's eyebrow ticked up. "That's an *Empire Strikes Back* reference, Vik. Of course I get it. How old do you think I am?" He jerked a thumb at Grimes. "If anything, he's the one who won't know it."

Grimes straightened up. "Hey, I get it. OT's the only *Star*

Wars trilogy worth watching."

Vikram chuckled dryly. "I'd high five you both, but one arm doesn't work and if I raise the other, I might cough up a quarter cup of blood."

"Yeah," Grimes said with a small smile. "Let's not."

Vikram's smile faded. "No flowers, no card. I'm guessing this isn't a social call?"

Baker cleared his throat and stepped closer. "You're right. We're here to make sure we got your statement correct."

Vikram's brow furrowed. "Wait—*got* my statement? I haven't given you a statement."

The sheriff's voice stayed casual.

"Well, just to confirm," the sheriff looked down at his notebook, "we understand that you and Mike encountered a large, territorial grizzly bear out near the privately owned, securely gated logging camp. You both entered the area illegally, ventured off into the protected old growth forest, and were stalked and attacked by said bear." He closed the notebook and looked directly at Vikram. "That sound about right?"

Vikram blinked, stunned. His eyes bounced from Baker to Grimes. Grimes met his gaze and gave him the slightest nod—a slow up and down, paired with a raised eyebrow that said, *Just go with it.*

Vikram didn't.

"What is this bullshit?" he snapped. "You want me to sign something that says a grizzly bear did this? Are bears your go-

to scapegoat for everything around here?"
He laughed bitterly. "No fucking way."

"Grimes," the sheriff said calmly, "would you mind shutting the door?"

The deputy pressed his lips together but obeyed. The soft *click* of the door closing turned the hospital room into a confessional.

Vikram tensed. "What's happening? Are you two about to smother me with a pillow? You know forensics can prove that, right? You backwoods hobos might not be up to speed on modern science, but..."

"Will you shut up?" Baker cut in, his voice sharp but not angry. "We're not gonna hurt you. Promise."

Vikram looked to Grimes, who held up both hands. "No one's gonna hurt you, Vik."
Baker dragged a chair up beside the bed and sat down. His boots creaked as he settled in.

"Listen, kid," he said. "I know it wasn't a goddamn grizzly bear that attacked you. And I know it wasn't a bear that killed your brother. Okay?"

Vikram stared at him, silent. He nodded once. "I hear you," he said quietly.

Sheriff Baker leaned in closer, his expression stern but not unkind. "Good," he said. "Now, I know what attacked you and Mike. I know what killed your brother. Grimes knows now too. We've had ourselves a... problem in this area for over a hundred years."

Vikram stared back at the sheriff, trying to process what he was hearing.

“But here’s the thing,” Baker continued, his voice lowering. “You can’t tell anyone it was a Bigfoot that came after you. If word got out, this place would be crawling with hunters, wannabe cryptid experts, and YouTube assholes with night vision goggles and podcast microphones. They wouldn’t know what they were dealing with. Hell, we barely know what we’re dealing with. All we’ve ever done is try to give it space , respect its boundaries. That’s when everything’s fine. We only get trouble when someone crosses the line. Mike knew that, but he drew Venu a map anyway. Then you two ventured past the boundary. A price was paid.”
The weight of the sheriff’s words settled heavily in the air. “We can’t have this thing hunted,” Baker said. “I can’t have that. We’ve got to leave it alone. You understand?”

Vikram mulled over what the sheriff had just said. “It’s still out there, though,” he said softly. “It killed my brother. Probably killed Mike too.”

“Only because that line was crossed,” the sheriff replied.

Vikram clenched his jaw. “I’m having a hard time with this ‘live and let live’ bullshit, sheriff.” He turned to the other man in the room. “Grimes?”

The deputy gave a small, regretful shrug. “I’m with him on this one, Vik. You’ve got to keep this to yourself. If people start thinking there’s a Bigfoot up here, this place will turn into a circus. We’re a two-person department. We can’t handle that kind of attention.”

Sheriff Baker stepped forward again, his voice dropping even lower. “And just so you’re clear...if you go public with this, you'll get zero support from me, from Grimes, or from anyone else in this region. You'll just be another internet whack job giving interviews, talking about how you survived a Bigfoot encounter." He paused, letting that image settle in.

"And if you even think about bringing up the logging camp, understand this: that area is being secured again. Not by mall cops with pepper spray, but by ex-Blackwater types. Real mercs. The kind of men who shoot first and bury the body before anyone asks questions. You understand me?"

Vikram's face tightened. "Why are you guys being like this?"

"Because it's about respect," Baker said firmly. "Maybe in a few years, once things quiet down, you can tell your grandkids. But for now? You lock that truth up tight."

"I don't know if I can do that," Vikram said.

"Oh, I think you can," the sheriff replied. "You're a smart kid. You'll do what's right...even if it's not what you want to do."

He stood up and looked Vikram square in the eyes. "I like you, Vik. You're a good person. I hate what happened to your brother. I hate what happened to you and Mike. But boundaries were crossed. A price was paid. That's how it's always been out here—long before my little speed-trap town even existed."

He nodded at Grimes, who walked over to the door and opened it. Baker paused briefly, as if he wanted to say more, then turned and left the room.

Grimes lingered for a moment longer in the doorway. "There's a lot of stuff you don't know, Vik. I wish I could tell you all of it. But just know that you kicked the mother of all hornets nests out there. Sheriff and I'll be back tomorrow. Try to get

some rest."
Vikram gave him a half-hearted glare. "I don't think I want to play basketball with you anymore, Grimey."

"That's okay," Grimes said, smiling faintly. "You can barely walk right now. Wouldn't be a fair game anyway."

Despite himself, Vikram managed a small grin.

Grimes tapped the doorframe twice. "See you tomorrow, Vik."

He stepped into the hallway, closing the door gently behind him. In the waiting room, Sheriff Baker was already standing, arms crossed, looking out the window. "What do you think?" Baker asked as Grimes joined him. "Is
he going to cooperate?"

Grimes looked uncertain. "Hard to say, sir. He's seen a lot. Lived through even more. And I'm pretty sure he's got a lot he wants to say."

Baker narrowed his eyes. "Does he know?"

"Know what?"

The sheriff gave him a hard look, lifting both eyebrows.
"Does he *know*?"

Grimes hesitated. "I don't think so. He didn't ask."

Baker exhaled slowly. "Gotcha. Guess he'll find out either way."

"Yeah," Grimes said quietly. "I guess he will."

Together, they stepped out of the waiting room and walked into the parking lot, the automatic doors sliding shut behind them.

Morning sunlight filtered softly through the blinds, casting long slats of gold across Vikram's hospital bed. Nurse Carol bustled into the room with her usual efficient warmth, clipboard in hand and a patient smile on her face. "Let's see if we can get you to sit up a little more today," she said, walking over to the bed. "Maybe even get you standing for a bit."

Vikram nodded, his voice hoarse but eager. "That would be great. I really want to try to take a shower, ya know?" He sniffed the collar of his hospital gown and made a face. "I'm starting to smell like that Big...bear. Big, upright-walking bear." He tried to play it off with a weak chuckle.

Nurse Carol smiled politely, not fully catching the subtext, or perhaps simply choosing not to. "We can arrange for that," she said. "It'll be painful though. Not much we can do for broken ribs except let them heal, but a shower might lift your spirits." She made a few quick notes on his chart, checked the IV bag, and gave him a reassuring pat on the foot before heading out of the room.

As the door clicked shut behind her, Vikram shifted restlessly under the sheets. He winced at the sting that radiated from his ribs, then lifted his left hand and studied the IV catheter taped to his skin. It flexed slightly with the twitch of each finger, a quiet reminder of how broken his body still was.
A shadow suddenly darkened the doorway.

He turned his head slowly toward the entrance of the room,

brow furrowing.

Someone was standing there. Watching him.

CHAPTER 31: YOU GOTTA SEE THIS

"Oh, hey, Sheriff," Vikram said, turning his head slowly toward the door. His voice was dry, laced with sarcasm. "Here to try to coerce another statement out of me?"

Sheriff Baker didn't smile. He stepped into the room, letting the door close softly behind him. The look on his face was unreadable.

"Nope," he said flatly. "You and I are going to take a walk. Got something you need to see. Think you're up for it?"

Vikram raised an eyebrow. "Yeah, I think so. I was hoping to shower before I go out in public again."

"We aren't leaving the hospital," Baker replied.

Vikram eyed him warily. "Well, that sounds vaguely terrifying, Sheriff."

That earned a small chuckle. "Guess that came out more serious than I meant it to. If you're ready, I'll flag down the nurse and we'll take our little field trip. Sound less terrifying now?"

Vikram sighed and nodded. "Yeah, I guess. Let's do this."

The sheriff gave him one last look, then disappeared into the hallway. A few minutes later, he returned with Nurse Carol, who was pushing a wheelchair, accompanied by a young male orderly.

"Okay, let's see what you've got today, tough guy," Nurse Carol said, flashing Vikram a warm, encouraging smile.

With the help of the nurse and the orderly, Vikram eased himself out of bed. His face twisted in pain as his feet touched the cold floor, and sweat beaded on his forehead as he slowly pushed himself upright.

"That... really sucked," he muttered, gripping the side of the bed for balance. "I really need that shower now."

"When you and the sheriff are done, we'll talk about it," Nurse Carol said gently.

"Sounds good." Vikram looked over at the sheriff, who had stepped back into the corner of the room to give them space. "Sheriff?"

"You good to walk?" Baker asked, his voice quiet but firm.

"I can walk," Vikram said. "It only hurts when I breathe, talk, cough... you know. Walking can't be any worse."

"Let's try a couple steps here in the room first," Nurse Carol said, ever the voice of calm practicality.

Vikram took a cautious step forward. Then another. He nearly forgot the IV stand until it pulled at his arm. Muttering under his breath, he turned back, grabbed it with his good hand, and limped toward the sheriff.

"I'm good," he said through gritted teeth. "Let's go check out whatever it is you've got to show me."

The hallway looked like every hallway in every mid-sized hospital Vikram had ever seen—if not in person, then in movies. The chairs lining the walls were upholstered in that strange patchwork of browns and greens, a pattern seemingly designed to hide stains and suppress emotion. The color scheme extended to the walls and tile flooring—bland, institutional, unmemorable.

Posters lined the walls, touting flu vaccines, nutrition tips, and seasonal health awareness campaigns. Between them hung framed photos of the Pacific Northwest: evergreen forests in fog, placid lakes beneath snowcapped peaks, aerial views of familiar small towns. Vikram's eyes caught on one, an image of towering trees veiled in mist, the same sort of trees that had nearly swallowed him whole just days before.

They continued down the hall, Vikram shuffling slowly. "Hey, Sheriff Baker."

Baker turned to face Vikram, never breaking stride. Vikram continued, "Do you think it's weird that your last name is Baker and you work around Mt. Baker?"

"Never really thought about it," Baker said dryly.

They approached a pair of heavy doors at the end of the hall. Unlike the rest of the hospital's muted and passive aesthetic, these looked industrial. Ominous.

Vikram slowed and eyed the doors suspiciously. "What are we doing here, Sheriff?" he asked.

"You'll see," Sheriff Baker replied without looking back. He stepped ahead and opened one of the doors, disappearing inside and letting it shut quietly behind him.

Vikram was left standing awkwardly in the hallway, his loosely tied hospital gown fluttering slightly with the building's circulating air. He looked down at himself and let out a quiet, dry chuckle. "Jesus, this is a hell of a look," he muttered.

Feeling exposed and curious, he ambled toward one of the framed forest photos nearby—not because he wanted to admire the scenery, but because he was hoping to catch a glimpse of his reflection in the glass. His bruised face stared back at him: tired eyes, bandaged forehead, hair matted and unwashed. A survivor, barely.

The metal door creaked open behind him.

"Alright, c'mon, kid," said the sheriff's voice.

Vikram turned, took a steadying breath, and limped toward the threshold.

CHAPTER 32: STATUS REPORT

Vikram shuffled through the heavy ICU doors, the sterile air cool against his hospital gown. The main reception area was subdued and quieter than the rest of the hospital, with softer lighting and voices that never rose above a whisper. Nurses and doctors moved through the space in hushed, coordinated motion, like dancers performing a sacred routine. Three rooms branched off the main corridor, each one enclosed in glass walls that allowed for near-total visibility. One of the rooms stood empty. Another held an elderly woman fast asleep beneath pale hospital blankets. The third, closest to Vikram, had its curtain drawn halfway enough to hide its occupant from view.

Sheriff Baker motioned silently toward it. "This way," he said.

Vikram followed, walking slowly, his IV stand squeaking softly with each step. As they approached the room, the sheriff stepped aside and gestured for Vikram to go ahead. He hesitated for a moment, casting a curious glance at the sheriff before turning toward the door.

He didn't recognize the person lying in the hospital bed. Whoever it was had been savaged by something monstrous. Their head was swathed in thick layers of gauze and bandages. A ventilator tube ran from their mouth, and a leg—brutally broken in multiple places—was suspended in traction, held together by an array of rods and pins. The left arm was wrapped in heavy gauze and bandages, and the face, bloated and bruised, was nearly unrecognizable.

Vikram stared in disbelief, his voice uncertain. "I don't understand," he said softly. "Who is this?"

"Take a closer look," the sheriff replied.

Vikram stepped cautiously into the room and studied the swollen face again, squinting through the damage, the bruises, the grotesque swelling.

Then it hit him.

"...Mike?" Vikram whispered. "Is this Mike?"

The sheriff nodded. "Yes, son. That's him."

Vikram's mouth fell open slightly. His mind reeled, trying to stitch together the unthinkable shape in the bed with the gruff, grumbling man he knew.
"We chased that 'bear' off with our rifles—me and Wade Coombs," the sheriff said. "Grimes got you in the back of his cruiser and brought you here. Wade and I doubled back to look for Mike."

He paused for a moment, shaking his head.

"Hell, you boys did a number on that thing. I'll give you that. It ran off into the tree line behind the camp. I can't say for sure if we hit it. If we did, it wasn't anything serious. Those 'bears' are damn hard to hit. Nimble, too." Sheriff Baker took a step into the room, glancing once at the array of machines monitoring Mike's battered body. "It tore up the gate something fierce, which turned out to be lucky for us. Wade and I managed to wedge it open enough to get the ATVs inside. We hauled ass through the camp and found Mike near where we found your brother's pack." He paused again, quieter now.

"I didn't think he'd survive the ride back down the hill. Hell, I wasn't sure we would. That monster was screaming, banging trees... the kind of sound that makes your bones crumble. We loaded Mike into Wade's Trailmaster and got out of there fast. Figured maybe it'd had enough for one day and wouldn't give chase."

Vikram stood there, stunned. He looked from Mike to the sheriff and back again, his eyes wide with a new mix of horror and disbelief.

"Wait," he said slowly. "Not only is Mike still alive—but that monster is, too? You didn't kill it?"

"I think Wade might've winged it once, maybe twice," the sheriff said. "But you and Mike did the real damage. That thing was bleeding badly. It's flesh and blood, Vik. Not some mystical ghost or unkillable nightmare. It can die. I'd be shocked if it survived the week."

Vikram turned back to the bed, staring at Mike's shattered body. "Is he... is he going to make it?" His voice cracked. "Christ, he's..."

"I'm not a doctor," the sheriff said. "But Mike's tough as they come. The fact he's still breathing is a miracle. He's got a long road ahead of him, but if anyone can pull through this, it's him."

"I want to stay," Vikram said suddenly. "With him. Just for a while."

"You can't," Baker replied gently. "This is ICU. I had to call in a favor just to get you in here at all. You're not family." He shifted uncomfortably. "His daughter's flying in from Spokane. She'll be with him soon. And I made sure your parents were notified. They're flying in from California tonight."

Vikram nodded absently. "His daughter...good. That's good. My parents, though...that's gonna be rough. They've had a lot thrown at them lately."

He took one last long look at Mike before turning away from the glass. He didn't speak again as the sheriff guided him slowly back to his room. The only sound was the soft shuffle of their footsteps echoing in the sterile hallway.

CHAPTER 33: THE AGREEMENT

Vikram eased himself carefully onto the edge of the hospital bed, wincing as his ribs protested the movement. Sheriff Baker stepped forward cautiously, watching his movements.

"Need help lying back down?" the sheriff asked.

Vikram shook his head. "No. I'm sick of lying down. I really want a shower... and to go home."

Baker gave a slow nod. "Can't help you with either of those right now. But I'll go grab the nurse in a minute. Before I do, we need to settle up on what we talked about yesterday."

Vikram's shoulders tensed. "Yeah, I know. But I'm not a liar, Sheriff. If someone asks me to give a statement, I'm going to tell them the truth."

The sheriff sighed, his jaw tightening. "This isn't about truth, Vik. It's about protecting what matters to the people who've lived with this for a long time. People who understand the history around here." He took a step closer.

"And if that's not enough for you, think about this; if you go telling your story to the press, or what passes for the press these days, you'll hurt Mike more than he's already hurting."

Vikram's eyes snapped to him, blazing.

"Leave Mike out of this," he growled. "He's suffered enough. He's gotta live with getting my brother killed, almost getting me killed, and getting himself torn apart."

The sheriff nodded solemnly. "Yep. All of that's true."

"Then leave him out of it," snapped Vikram.

Baker rubbed his forehead and looked up at the ceiling, as though searching for the right words among the cracked white tiles. Then he leveled his gaze at Vikram again, more serious than before.

"When the timber company shut down, Mike and the others signed lifetime NDAs. Not just 'don't talk about it for a while'—I mean *lifetime,* airtight. They can never talk about what they saw up there. Not to the press. Not to their families. Not even to each other. You break that, and they claw back *everything.* All of it. His severance. His house. His savings. They'll come after him with lawyers, bury him in lawsuits, and they won't stop until he's got nothing left."

Vikram stared at the sheriff, hands trembling. "I don't want that. I don't want Mike to lose everything. But the truth's going to come out eventually. Somehow, some way."

"Maybe," the sheriff said, "but not from you. Not directly, not indirectly, not in a way that traces back to you in any way. That's the deal. The truth you'll tell is that you and Mike got jumped by a rogue grizzly. They've been talking about reintroducing grizzlies to the Cascades for years—maybe one was released early. Happens all the time in bureaucracies, right?" As he spoke, the sheriff pulled a folded map from his back pocket and smoothed it out on the tray table. He pointed to a remote area on the opposite side of the Mt. Baker–Snoqualmie National Forest from where Vikram and Mike had actually been.

“You weren’t at that logging camp. You were here,” the sheriff said, tapping the map.

“This is crazy,” Vikram muttered, staring at the paper.

“Crazy or not,” Baker said, folding the map again, “this is your truth now.”

Vikram didn’t answer at first. He stared hard at the point on the map. Then he slowly shook his head.
“I don’t like it. None of this feels right. But I’m not going to make things worse for Mike. That’s the only reason I'll agree to this bullshit.”

He looked the sheriff in the eye. “If he dies... all bets are off.”

Baker let out a long breath and smirked. “Yeah. That’ll be quite the story. A Bigfoot tale among a thousand others. No one’ll believe it. That's not true...other whackadoodles will have you on their podcasts to tell your story. And you'll have no evidence, not even a photo, to back it up."

Vikram narrowed his eyes. “I don’t know if I’m supposed to hate you or respect you, sheriff. You feel like a good guy doing bad things. It’s... confusing.”

Baker shrugged. “Welcome to adulthood, kid.”

He moved toward the door. “I’ll go grab the nurse. You want me to call anyone else while I’m out?”

Vikram shook his head. “No. Just really hungry... and that

shower's still high on my list."

"Roger that," Baker said, stepping into the hallway.

Left alone, Vikram stood slowly and walked toward the hospital window. He gazed down at the parking lot below, then glanced at the hallway beyond his door. Quiet. Empty. He returned to the window and watched as Sheriff Baker emerged outside, deep in conversation with two men—one dressed in casual golf attire, the other in tactical gear. They exchanged a few quiet words, shook hands, and then disappeared into separate vehicles. Each car drove off in opposite directions.

Vikram muttered under his breath, "What was *that* nonsense?"

A voice startled him.

"What was what nonsense, dear?"

Vikram turned quickly. Nurse Carol had entered the room carrying a stack of towels.

"Hey, I didn't hear you come in," he said, still unsettled.

"I'm here to help you with that shower," she said brightly. "Got some towels and what not. You sure you're up for it?"

"Everything hurts," Vikram said, offering a tired smile. "I can only use one arm... but yeah, I'm up for it." He walked back toward her, slow and stiff. She helped him get prepped, steadying him with calm and practiced hands. Despite everything, the warm thought of hot water and clean skin gave him something small—something human—to hold onto.

And far from the hospital, several miles deep in the forested valley, men with blueprints and rifles were making sure Mike and Vik's encounter stayed buried.

At the edge of the old logging camp, the sound of industry roared back to life.

Several heavy-duty work trucks rumbled over flattened brush and torn asphalt, kicking up dust clouds in their wake. The skeletal remains of the old chain-link fence were being ripped away by bulldozers and clawed up by earthmovers. New foundation posts were already going in—massive, steel-reinforced footings that would anchor fourteen-foot palisade fencing.

Welders sparked as crews fastened the metal walls into place. Every section was topped with two feet of coiled razor wire, transforming the perimeter into something that looked less like a dormant lumber operation and more like a high-security prison. The workers moved at a breakneck pace, their coordination suggesting more than just urgency—it suggested a practiced response plan, one they'd rehearsed before.

Armed guards in tactical gear flanked the worksite, watching from the tree line and along the dirt access roads. Some stood at static posts, rifles slung but ready. Others moved in constant patrols, scanning the forest, saying little. Their uniforms bore no insignias, and their vehicles—military grade pickups and matte-black SUVs—were just as unmarked.

Toward the back of the camp, a second team began trenching out a new fence line, this one running parallel to the access road. It would serve as a secondary barrier, an internal checkpoint to isolate the road even further from public approach. As the first layers of fencing went up, signs bearing stark red letters were hammered into place: **NO TRESPASSING – FEDERAL CONTRACTORS – DEADLY FORCE AUTHORIZED**.

The forest beyond loomed tall and dark, but the message was

clear: this was no longer just a defunct logging camp. It was a cordoned zone—erased from maps, protected by secrets, and bristling with firepower.

CHAPTER 34: BACK TO LIFE

In the dim hush of the ICU, a young woman stood in the doorway, motionless, her hands slowly rising to cover her mouth as her eyes filled with tears. Her gaze was fixed on the man in the bed—her father, the once indestructible figure of her childhood, now reduced to a fragile shell of bruises, broken bones, gauze, and tubes. His chest rose and fell in uneven rhythms, a ventilator hissing beside him.

She stepped forward, her legs trembling with every inch, and reached down to take his hand into hers. The skin was warm but slack, the fingers unresponsive—until, suddenly, one of them twitched. Her breath hitched. The fingers curled slightly, and she felt a small, faltering squeeze.

Mike's eyes blinked open, glassy but aware. "Dad..." she whispered, barely able to form the word. It came out cracked and soaked in disbelief.

In the quiet of a cramped county office, Sheriff Baker stood alone in front of a large wall map, its surface peppered with faded pushpins, each marking a call, a sighting, a report whispered but never confirmed.

One by one, he reached out and pulled them free. Blue, red, yellow. Each one plucked from the cork with finality. As the last one came loose, he let it fall into a shallow dish on the desk and stared at the now-blank forest expanse. He turned away.

Beth flipped the pull chain that illuminated the neon 'OPEN' sign in the bar's front window. The glass flickered to life in a pink and blue glow. She walked slowly toward the front door, pausing before it to take in the wall covered in fading, sun-bleached flyers.

MISSING — names, ages, dates. Some barely legible now, others newer. All unanswered. Her eyes lingered on one in the middle, a young man with dark hair and a wide smile. She reached out, touched the corner of the flyer, and let her hand fall away.

In a clean, bright hospital room, Vikram lay nestled beneath crisp white sheets. His mother sat beside him, gently stroking his hair with the kind of soft touch only a mother could give. His father stood at the foot of the bed, pulling cartons of takeout from a brown paper bag, trying to mask his own emotions with the simple act of unpacking food. Without warning, Vikram's mother leaned in and wrapped her arms around her son, burying her face into his shoulder. A sob broke free from her chest. Vikram, startled at first, soon joined her, tears streaking down his cheeks. His father moved to them both, resting a steady hand on his son's arm, the only strength he could offer.

Across town, on a sunlit softball field nestled at the edge of the Cascade foothills, an 18U team practiced under the watchful eye of their coach. The girls in the outfield laughed and bantered as they chased fly balls. A thick greenbelt framed the field's edge, trees casting long shadows over the grass.

At the crack of a bat, a ball soared over the centerfield fence, vanishing into the woods beyond.

"Alright, pick 'em up!" Coach Terry called out from near the third base dugout, clapping his hands.

Three girls jogged along the outfield fence, gathering stray balls. The centerfielder, Morgan, stopped near the fence line, scrunching her nose.

“Ewwww. I think someone dumped garbage back there,” she said, waving a hand in front of her face.

“Jump the fence and check it out!” the right fielder, Kaylie, teased.

“No way,” Morgan replied. “It smells *disgusting*.”

“What about the ball Katelyn hit?” asked Jossy, peering into the trees. "She might want to keep that one."

“That ball’s stayin’ in the woods,” Morgan said firmly.
“Let’s go, it’s gross.”

The three turned back toward the infield, beginning to jog—until a softball, worn and slightly scuffed, came sailing back over the fence and landed with a soft *thud* in the grass in front of them.

They froze.

Two deep tree knocks rang out from the greenbelt, heavy and purposeful.

CHAPTER 35: ORDER TAKERS

Mike woke to the sound of breathing that wasn't his own.

For a few seconds, he didn't know where he was. Everything hurt. Not sharply—just everywhere, all at once, like someone who didn't care if things lined up properly had pulled apart and then hastily reassembled his body.

Then the beeping resolved into a monitor. The smell of antiseptic cut through the fog. Hospital.

He tried to move his right hand. Nothing happened. Panic flared, brief and animal, before the pain arrived and crushed it back down.

"Easy," a voice said. Calm. Male. Not a nurse.

Mike opened his eyes.

A man and a woman stood at the foot of his bed.

The man was heavyset, dressed in dark slacks and a button-down shirt that strained against his considerable belly. His hair was thinning, his complexion pale from too many hours under fluorescent blue light. He could have been forty-five or fifty-five, it was difficult to tell from the sagging skin of his face. A visitor's badge hung from his shirt pocket. Mike squinted, trying to make out the corporate logo stitched above it.

The woman beside him was younger—early thirties. Light brown hair fell neatly to her shoulders, sunlight from the windows catching careful highlights. She wore a sharp charcoal suit over an aqua blouse, her makeup minimal, emphasizing high cheekbones and an effortless composure. A leather-bound folder rested under one arm.

The older man smiled.

"Good morning, Mike," he said. "You gave us a scare."

Mike swallowed. His throat felt like sandpaper.

"Who...?" he managed.

"Logging company," the man said easily, as if that explained everything. "Risk management. My name's Jeff Daniels. This is Erica McKenzie, legal counsel."

Erica nodded once. No smile.

Mike tried to sit up. Pain detonated along his ribs and spine. He hissed and fell back against the pillows.

Jeff raised a hand. "Please don't do that. You're in no condition to hurt yourself any more than you already have."

Mike stared at him. "You shouldn't be here."

Jeff's smile thinned, just slightly. "We disagree."

Erica stepped forward and placed the folder on the rolling tray beside the bed. She opened it, revealing a familiar stack of papers.

The NDA.

Mike's stomach sank.

Daniels glanced at the monitor, then back at Mike. "Let's not waste time. You violated the agreement you signed with us. Multiple times. You disclosed restricted information to a civilian. You entered a controlled area without authorization. And"—he paused and glanced down at a clipboard he was holding—"on a separate occasion, you stole several chainsaws, a stump grinder, and four Husqvarna 545RX brush cutters. That's over five-thousand dollars worth of logging equipment, a class B felony. You're looking at serious prison time and a hefty fine of what, Erica?"

"Twenty-thousand dollars, easily," she replied matter-of-factly.

Mike closed his eyes.

"So," he said. His voice was hoarse. "You knew about that."

Daniels nodded, as if Mike had just confirmed the weather. "Of course. But we don't really care about the equipment. Cost of doing business after such an abrupt closure." He paused, a humorless grin on his face. "We're here to discuss the NDA. Now, ordinarily, we'd already be in court. Civil penalties. Asset seizure. Garnishment. The works."

Erica slid a second document out of the folder and set it on top.

Mike recognized the header.

Property records.

Daniels continued. "You own your house outright. No mortgage. That's good. Makes things simpler."

Mike opened his eyes again. "You can take my house, I don't care."

"That's not true," Erica said gently. "You care very much. You just don't want us to know you do. Your ex-wife destroyed you in the divorce. That house is all you've got."

Silence filled the room, broken only by the steady beep of the monitor.

Daniels leaned forward slightly. "We could also pursue damages. Loss of operational secrecy. Environmental violations. Federal land-use complications. That number gets very big, very fast."

Erica spoke again. Her voice was calm, but flat. "You'd spend the rest of your life paying it off."

Mike laughed. It came out as a rough bark that sent fresh pain through his chest.

"So do it," he said. "What's stopping you?"

Daniels studied him for a long moment. Then he sighed, almost regretfully.

"You survived," he said. "That complicates things."

Mike frowned.

"If you'd died," Daniels continued, "your silence would've been permanent. Tragic, but efficient. Instead, you woke up. Which means now we have to negotiate."

Mike stared at him. "Negotiate what?"

Daniels straightened. "Your future."

Erica slid another sheet forward. One page. Typed. Clean.

"Here's how this goes," she said. "You say nothing. Ever. Not to the press. Not to law enforcement. Not to your family, and not to the family of the men you dragged into this." Daniels' voice hardened just a fraction. "Especially not to them."

Erica took over. "If you cooperate, we make this go away. No lawsuit. No seizure. No penalties. Your medical bills will be your own." She tapped her pen on the tray and smiled. "Price of doing business, Mike."

Mike's eyes flicked to Erica's. She smiled, and he could see in her eyes that this was a conversation she did not want to be having.

"Discretion," Erica said. "Is expensive."

"And if I don't?" Mike asked.

Daniels' spoke, a smile returned, thin and practiced. "Then you'll wake up one morning to find your accounts frozen. Your house tied up in litigation. Your name attached to things that will follow you forever."

He leaned in close enough that Mike could smell his cologne.

"And the kid?" Daniels said quietly. "He'll learn exactly how expensive your principles are."

That did it.

Mike's breathing changed. His eyes sharpened, the fog burning off.

"You leave him alone," Mike said.

Daniels straightened again, satisfied. "That's entirely up to you."

He tapped the single-page document.

"All we need is your signature."

Mike stared at the paper. His hand trembled as Erica placed a pen between his fingers.

After a long moment, Mike signed.

Daniels took the paper, glanced at it, then slid it back into the folder.

"Good choice," Erica said. "Get some rest."

Then the two of them turned and walked toward the door.

Just before exiting, Daniels stopped.

"One more thing," he said without turning around. "This isn't over. It's just contained."

The door closed softly behind them.

Mike lay back against the pillows, staring at the ceiling.

Outside the room, somewhere down the hall, a nurse laughed.

And Mike finally understood the true cost of surviving.

The apartment still smelled like him.

Not in any obvious way—no cologne, no lingering food—but in the faint, lived-in warmth of a place that hadn't yet accepted its owner was gone. Vikram felt it the moment he stepped inside. The air was too still.

His ribs protested as he bent to set a box down. A sharp reminder that his body hadn't caught up to what had happened. Breathing still came in careful increments. His head pulsed, dull and insistent, the afterimage of pain lingering behind his eyes like a bad echo.

His mother folded clothes at the dining table, stacking them with methodical precision. His father stood by the window, arms crossed, watching the city as if it might offer an explanation if he stared long enough.

They worked in silence.

Every few minutes Vikram had to stop—not because of the ribs, but because of the dizziness. The room would tilt, just slightly, as if reminding him he didn't fully belong upright yet. His mother noticed but said nothing. That, somehow, hurt more.

He picked up one of Venu's jackets. It was still dusted with pine needles, still faintly smelling of cold air, and folded it into the box.

“I’m going to take some time off,” Vikram said.

The words sounded louder than he expected as they broke the silence.

His mother froze, a shirt half-folded in her hands.

“Time off?” she said. “From work?”

“Yes.”

His father turned from the window.

“And then what?” he asked.

Vikram swallowed. His throat was dry.

“When Mike is released from the hospital, I’m going back to Glacier.”

Silence snapped tight.

“To do what?” his mother asked.

“Help him,” Vikram said. “He’s not… he’s not okay.”

His father’s voice sharpened. “You do not owe that man anything.”

“I know.”

“No, you don’t,” his mother said, her tone rising despite herself. “You nearly died. Your brother did die. And now you want to go back there?”

Her hands shook as she set the folded shirt down.

"What were you doing there in the first place?" she asked. "And why was Venu there?"

The question had been waiting. Vikram had felt it hovering since the moment they arrived.

He closed the box and leaned against the wall, careful with his ribs.

"You know Venu," he said quietly. "He was always outside. Always off chasing something. A trail, a view, a story."

His father shook his head slowly, the way he did when disappointment hardened into something colder.

"Life is not a national park," he said. "It is not a vacation where you wander off and expect the world to wait for you. You have obligations—to your work, to your family. Not honoring those obligations cost Venu his life. And now you want to do the same."

The words hit Vikram hard.

"That's not fair," Vikram said, heat creeping into his voice. "Venu didn't—"

His mother cut him off. "Then explain it," she said. "Explain why my son is dead!"

Vikram opened his mouth. Closed it.

The concussion fog pressed in, a dull pressure behind his eyes. He stared at the floor, at a small scratch in the hardwood that he'd never noticed before, and felt the weight of everything he couldn't say. Lying to his parents felt wrong, but he also couldn't tell them the truth.

His mother's eyes brimmed. "Why was Venu out there?"

Vikram didn't answer right away. Instead, he crossed the room and reached for the mantle.

The photo was exactly where he remembered it.

Venu stood in the foreground, red beanie pulled low, wind cutting across his smile. The Enchantments rose behind him —jagged, vast, indifferent. He looked impossibly alive in the frame, like someone who belonged out there.

Vikram held it out.

"This is why," he said.

His mother stared at the photo, her mouth tightening.

"He loved those places," Vikram continued. "You both know that. Being out there made him...whole."

His father looked away, refusing to look at the photo. When he finally spoke, his voice was low, almost calm — which made it worse.

"Whole," he repeated. "That is the word you choose."

He turned back now, eyes sharp, wounded.

"We did not cross an ocean so our sons could feel whole," he said. "We did it so you could be safe. So you could have stability. A future."

His hand rose, gesturing around the apartment — the clean

lines, the view, the quiet proof of success.

"This was the point," he said. "Not that."

Vikram felt his chest tighten. "Baba—"

"No," his father said, louder now. "I am not finished."

He stepped closer, the years of restraint finally burning off.

"I drove taxis at night," he said. "Buses before sunrise. I came home smelling like diesel and sweat. Your mother and I lived in apartments where the water ran cold half the time, where the heat barely worked. We counted every dollar so you and your brother would never have to."

His voice cracked, then hardened again.

"And for what?" he demanded. "So Venu could walk away from all of it? So he could chase mountains and forests like some kind of tourist in his own life?"

"That's not what he was doing," Vikram said. "You know he wasn't shallow. He wasn't—"

"He was selfish," his father snapped. "He chose himself. Every time."

His mother gasped softly, but said nothing.

"That photo," his father said, pointing at it now, unable to stop himself, "is not a symbol of freedom. It is a reminder. Of everything we gave up that he refused to carry."

Vikram's hands trembled around the frame.

"He didn't abandon you," he said quietly. "He was still your son. And he didn't deserve—"

"Do not tell me what my son deserved," his father said, voice rising. "He had obligations. He had responsibilities. And he treated them like optional things."

Silence filled the room, thick and suffocating.

Then his father's gaze locked onto Vikram.

"And now you stand here," he said, "talking about leaving your job. About going back to that place."

Vikram swallowed. "Mike saved my life," he said. "I owe him—"

"You owe him nothing," his father said flatly. "You owe us."

The words landed like a prison sentence.

"You will not take a leave of absence," his father continued. "You will not go back to Glacier. You will not throw away the life your brother already did."

His mother turned away, quietly crying now.

Vikram stood there, ribs aching, head pounding, the photo still in his hands — a dead brother between him and the people who raised him. He drew a slow breath, steadying himself. When he spoke again, his voice was quieter, stripped of heat.

"I do not wish to dishonor you," he said. "Or the sacrifices you and Amma made for Venu and me. I carry those with me. Every day."

His father didn't respond.

Vikram looked down at the photo in his hands, at his brother's smile, frozen in a place that had claimed him.

"But I am going back there," he said. "Mike is alone. He saved my life and needs help. That is the only way I'll find peace with any of this."

His father inhaled, slow and deep before speaking, then turned toward Vikram. "You will not find peace up there," he said.

"Maybe not," Vikram replied. "But I won't find it here either."

Sheriff Baker was sitting in his office when he heard the front door open, followed by the sound of his deputy's tactical boots thudding across the floor.

Deputy Grimes peeked into the sheriff's office and offered a subtle wave. "Mornin', Sheriff."

"Mornin'," he grunted back, then stood up from behind his desk and turned towards the area map on the wall to his left. He had pulled out the pushpins of where search and rescue had looked for Venu. As he moved toward the office door, he paused. His eyes caught the hole in the map where a red pushpin had been, the one marking the lumber camp. That area, including the road leading up to the gates, were now closed to the public. And him. He ran a hand through his reddish hair, blew out a breath of air, then stepped into the main office.

Grimes's head snapped up from behind his monitor. "What's the plan for today, Sheriff?"

Baker smiled wanly, "Plan? Wade will be here any minute.

We've gotta lot to talk about." He turned towards the coffee maker, hit the power button, then frowned when the "Add Water" indicator flashed in a shade of blue he found most annoying. "Goddamn it, Grimes. How many times have I told you to refill the water reservoir in this thing if you're the last one to use it?"

"Sorry, Sheriff," Grimes replied sheepishly. "It won't happen again."

A loud sigh escaped from Baker. "Yeah, it will."

The front door swung open and in stepped Wade Coombs, dressed in standard-issue search and rescue Carhartt gear. His face was pale and puffy, his eyes noticeably bloodshot. Baker sighed again. "Looks like you hit it hard last night, Wade."

Coombs laughed, then broke out in a deep, rattling cough that doubled him over. Grimes stood from his desk, Baker raised a hand and motioned for him to take a seat. The message was clear; Wade made this bed, let him drown in it.

Coughing fit over, Coombs staggered over to the empty seat in front of Deputy Grimes's desk. He wiped his mouth with the back of his sleeve. "What did you want to talk to me about, Baker?"

Sheriff Baker hit the "Brew" button on the Keurig out of habit, then turned to face Wade and Deputy Grimes. "It's what I wanted to talk to you and Deputy Grimes about, Coombs." He half-turned to reach for his coffee mug — a replica of Rust Cohle's "Big Hug Mug" — then stopped when he remembered.

"Still needs water," Grimes offered from behind his monitor. "Thing isn't going to refill itself."

Baker turned and fixed him with a flat stare. Grimes straightened. A beat passed before the corner of Baker's mouth pulled into something that wasn't quite a smile.

He set the empty mug back down.

"What do you two know about Haven Corporation?"

The room was too big for what they were doing in it.

Once, it had been the lumber camp's meeting hall—a high-ceilinged, open space meant for safety briefings and shift changes, maybe the occasional half-hearted pep talk before men went back into the trees. Haven had scrubbed it clean and dressed it up just enough to feel modern: whiteboards on rolling stands, a ceiling-mounted projector, long folding tables arranged classroom-style. Power cables snaked across the concrete floor, feeding laptops and radios.

It looked like a place where you'd learn new compliance procedures.

Now there were twelve armed operators sitting in it.

Rifles rested against chair legs. Plate carriers creaked when someone shifted. Helmets sat in a neat line along one wall, night-vision mounts catching the overhead light. The contrast was almost absurd—like a corporate training seminar that had wandered into the wrong genre.

Morton stood at the front, turning a dry-erase marker between his fingers. He didn't bother with the projector.

"You've all read the packet," he said. "That was the clean version."

He went to the board and wrote a single word, block letters, no flourish.

PREDATOR

"This isn't a bear," he said. "It's not a gorilla. It's not some freak throwback somebody forgot to tell biology about. Whatever it is, it sits at the top of the food chain out there. Nothing hunts it. Nothing pressures it. Except us."

He underlined the word once.

"And we're behind."

A chair creaked. Someone adjusted their vest.

"It moves intelligently. Not human, but not dumb either. It throws rocks—accurately. It makes noise where it wants you to look, then comes from somewhere else. A team up in Alaska ran thermals and night vision, thought they had it boxed in. Six hours later they were exhausted, disoriented, and staring at their own tracks."

He let that sit.

"It let them go."

He added another word beneath the first.

STRONG

"Seven to nine feet. Eight hundred pounds. Vertical leap over five feet from a dead stop. It runs uphill through timber faster than any of you can sprint on a road. We've recovered rounds from previous encounters—rounds that should have dropped an elk. They didn't slow it much."

No one smiled.

"It prefers darkness or weather bad enough you'd rather be anywhere else. It leaves tracks when it wants to. When it doesn't, it might as well not exist. If you think you're tracking it at night, understand this—it already knows where you are."

Morton paused, then added the part no one liked.

"This one's alone. Cast out. Why doesn't matter. Lone animals don't posture. They don't bluff. This thing has already killed a civilian and put two more in the hospital. When it commits, it finishes."

He capped the marker and set it down.

"Up close, you won't outrun it. You won't out-muscle it. Firearms are the only thing we know that work, and only if you're disciplined and fast. If it closes inside ten meters, your odds drop hard."

He finally met their eyes.

"This team is on standby," Morton said. "You are not here to hunt."

That got their attention.

"You'll establish a patrol corridor from the access road up to the trailhead leading to Hidden Lake. Two-man elements rotating through the timber, daylight and night cycles. You'll also secure the perimeter of the camp itself."

He tapped the board.

"Checkpoints go up on the main road immediately. No civilians past that point. Lost hikers, hunters, tourists—everyone gets turned around. No exceptions."

Morton let that settle, then continued.

"We'll also be placing listening posts near the popular trailheads. Passive only. Audio, motion, observation. Anything that suggests movement outside the known boundary line gets logged and reported up the chain."

A pause.

"You do not pursue."

Some operators exchanged brief looks.

"This creature stays within its territory most of the time," Morton said. "That's benefited us for years. As long as it does, we maintain distance and deny access. That is the mission."

A hand went up—Nicks, steady as ever.

"Rules of engagement?"

Morton nodded. "Observe and report only."

He scanned the room, catching the hesitation on Nicks's face.

"If it charges, if it attacks, if it breaches the perimeter and you're the last line—then you defend yourselves. Center mass. Controlled fire. Otherwise, you do not escalate."

Morton tossed the dry erase marker into the tray at the bottom of the whiteboard.

“We’re here to keep people away from something they don’t need to know exists. Nothing more.”

No one argued.

“Gear check in twenty,” he said. “We step off at dusk.”

No more questions.

Chairs scraped softly as the operators began to rise, reaching for helmets, checking straps, the room shifting from classroom learning and back to muscle memory.

“One last thing before you leave,” Morton said.

They stopped.

“Major Robinson will take tactical lead on this operation.”

A few heads turned. No one spoke.

Morton’s eyes swept the room again, slowly and deliberate.

“Act accordingly.”

That was all he said.

The projector hummed quietly overhead, still unused, as the team moved to gear up.

The room felt different without the team in it.

Empty chairs sat in neat rows, whiteboards wiped clean, the projector still warm from earlier. Sunlight filtered in through the high windows, catching dust in the air that had been ground into the concrete decades ago, back when the room smelled like sap and diesel instead of disinfectant.

Robinson stood near the windows, helmet tucked under one arm, watching the tree line beyond the clearing. Morton closed the door behind them, the latch clicking softly.

“For most of my career,” Robinson said, still facing the glass, “the monsters had names. Flags. Bank accounts.”

Morton didn’t reply. He waited.

“We hunted people,” Robinson continued. “Foreign cells, domestic extremists, traffickers, even the cartels moving product across both borders. You could map it. Follow the money. Take one piece out and the rest of it collapsed.”

He turned then, a faint, humorless smile crossing his face.

“Still doesn’t sit right that we’re standing guard over something we used to joke about around a campfire.”

Morton leaned against the table. “At least we’re not hunting it.”

“I know,” Robinson said. “Not yet.”

He took a breath.

“In the past, our job was to keep human problems away from them. Push smugglers out and shut down meth labs. Close off roads no one was supposed to be on. We weren’t the spear—we were the fence.”

He stepped closer, lowering his voice.

"So why are my people here now? The personnel that have been called up all have extensive combat experience, not containment."

Morton picked up the marker Robinson had left behind and rolled it between his fingers.

"Because the fence is getting crowded," he said. "We're seeing pressure near the boundary—nothing crazy, but enough to make certain paygrades nervous that there could be a loss of containment."

Robinson raised an eyebrow, skeptical.

"Pressure near the boundary?" he said. "From what I've been able to piece together, we had one over-motivated hiker find his way to Hidden Lake that wound up dead. Then that hiker's brother and a local survive an attack when they go looking for him. That's it. There haven't been any other confirmed encounters since the camp shut down—what, almost twenty years ago?"

Morton didn't answer right away.

Carlton shifted his weight, finally turning from the window.

"Something isn't adding up," he said. "Hidden Lake isn't marked. It's not on public maps. There's never been a maintained trail. It's only accessible from an access road that's inside the camp or through miles of dense uncharted old growth forest. So how did the first hiker know how to get there?"

"Exactly," Morton said. "And that's something we need to discuss."

Robinson's eyes narrowed slightly. "What's there to discuss?"

Morton met his gaze. "Sheriff Baker may have over-disclosed where the first hiker was found."

"That doesn't sound like Baker," Robinson said.

"No?" Morton argued. "Well, the good Sheriff had a map hanging in his office with a goddamn red pushpin marking where the camp is. He then questioned the brother about how the deceased knew about the camp and the lake. One thing led to another, next thing you know the brother is being given a guided tour of the camp and lake by a local he met in a bar."

Silence settled between them, heavy but controlled.

"It's a shit show, Major and it has the potential of growing exponentially shittier," Morton said at last.

Robinson adjusted his grip on the helmet, considering that.

"What do we know about this local?" Robinson asked.

"That is something I was hoping you could fill me in on." Morton took a seat and gestured to Robinson to do the same as he reached for a notebook on the table

CHAPTER 36: HOME AGAIN

Two weeks later, the room had started to feel less like a place to recover and more like confinement.

The machines were quieter now. Fewer alarms and fewer people rushing in with clipboards and urgency in their eyes. Even the smell had changed—less antiseptic, more stale coffee wafting in from the nurse's station and whatever industrial cleaner the night crew used to wipe down the linoleum.

Mike sat upright in the hospital bed, propped against angled pillows, the thin gown gaping at the collarbone. His hair—what was left of it—had grown back unevenly, exposing the male-pattern baldness he had begun to hide in his late twenties by shaving his head. Stubble shadowed his jaw, gray at the chin, aging him past his years. Mid-fifties on paper, but some days he wore it like seventy.

His injured leg lay elevated in a rigid brace, swelling still pronounced. The external pins were gone, but the damage hadn't vanished with them.

Vikram stood at the foot of the bed, arms folded to keep himself from fidgeting. His ribs still chirped when he breathed too deep, but the concussion haze had thinned enough for him to feel present again. Still, he was exhausted, like his body had finally caught up to what his mind had already lived through.

A doctor stepped in—early forties. He projected a calm, practiced neutrality that made even bad news sound manageable. A name badge hung from his coat. Vikram didn't catch the name. He barely cared.

"Morning," the doctor said, glancing between them. "How're we feeling today?"

Mike gave a one-shoulder shrug. "Restless, but still banged up."

The doctor nodded as if he'd heard worse. "That's fair."

He moved to the foot of the bed and flipped through the chart. "Okay. Your external fixation pins were removed three days ago. That's good progress. But it's important you understand—removal of the pins doesn't mean the fracture is healed."

Vikram leaned in slightly.

"The tibia and fibula were both fractured," the doctor continued. "Clean breaks in places, complicated in others. We stabilized them with a plate and screws. That hardware is doing the heavy lifting now."

Mike's eyes narrowed. "For how long?"

"Minimum six months," the doctor said. "But in your case..." He hesitated—not dramatic, just honest. "It's very possible the plate and screws remain permanently."

Mike stared at him. "For life."

"For life," the doctor confirmed. "Age plays a role. Bone healing isn't what it was in your twenties. But the bigger factor is compliance."

Mike made a sound that could've been a laugh, could've been a cough. "Compliance."

The doctor ignored the tone. "Non-weight-bearing means non-weight-bearing. No 'just a few steps.' No limping to the bathroom because you don't want help. The minute you put full weight on that leg too early, you risk shifting the fracture, and then you're back in surgery."

Vikram nodded, already cataloging the rules.

"Physical therapy starts in earnest once you're cleared," the doctor said, "but for now, we focus on range of motion where we can, swelling management, and preventing complications."

"Complications like what?" Vikram asked.

The doctor glanced up. "Blood clots. Infection. Loss of function if he doesn't keep up with therapy. The usual."

Mike stared at the ceiling, jaw working. He didn't look scared. He looked… trapped.

The doctor turned a page. "Now. Head injury."

Mike's eyes flicked down.

"You had a severe concussion," the doctor said. "And the symptoms you're reporting—dizziness, headaches, nausea, sensitivity to light—that's not unusual. It can last weeks. Sometimes months."

"Months," Mike repeated flatly.

"Sometimes," the doctor said again. "Rest helps. Hydration helps. No alcohol."

Mike's gaze sharpened at that. Like the doctor had just taken something from him.

Vikram seized on it. "Diet," he said. "What should he be eating? Protein? Calcium? Anything specific for bone healing?"

The doctor's expression softened slightly—he was used to family members trying to take control of the chaos with a checklist.

"A balanced diet," he said. "Adequate protein. Vitamin D. Calcium. But nothing replaces time and compliance."

Vikram nodded. "Okay. And pain management?"

The doctor glanced at Mike. "We've already been tapering the medication during your stay. You'll go home with enough to manage the pain for the next week, maybe ten days. After that, barring a setback, there won't be refills."

Mike nodded once.

"That's fine," he said. "I don't mind the pain."

The doctor studied him for a moment, then gave a small nod.

Vikram kept going. "Physical therapy schedule—how often? And home mobility—stairs, showering—"

"We'll coordinate that," the doctor said. "Home health will be involved at first. He'll need help."

Vikram glanced at Mike, as if to say: I can do that.

Mike didn't meet his eyes.

"And alcohol," Vikram said, returning to the word like it was a loose thread. "He can't drink at all?"

The doctor didn't flinch. "Not right now. It interferes with healing. It worsens concussion symptoms. It increases fall risk. It doesn't mix well with the medications he's on."

Vikram nodded again—practical, receptive, absorbing.

Mike's jaw tightened.

Vikram's mind kept sprinting ahead. "Driving. When can he drive? He has a truck—"

"Not until cleared," the doctor said. "And not with the dizziness. He needs to be stable before he's behind the wheel."

Vikram asked another question, then another. He didn't mean to. It was just… if he kept talking, if he kept gathering rules and guidelines and timelines, then maybe he could make this make sense.

The doctor answered patiently, ticking through checklists and cautions like a man describing the weather.

Mike listened the entire time without saying much. He sat there, hands on top of the blanket, looking outwardly calm, but Vikram could see it—the tension in his forearms, the controlled breathing. The way his eyes kept flicking toward the door like he expected someone else to walk in at any moment.

Finally, when Vikram asked about follow-up appointments,

Mike exhaled hard.

"Do I get a say in any of this?" he asked.

The room went still.

Maddy shoved the couch forward an inch, then another, the wooden legs scraping loudly across the hardwood.

"Seriously?" she muttered, bending to check the clearance again.

The hallway wasn't wide, but it wasn't narrow either. Still, she kept adjusting—angling the couch just so, nudging a side table closer to the wall, pulling a framed photo down and setting it carefully in the hallway closet so it wouldn't get knocked over when they brought Mike home.

She stood at the front door and looked down the path she'd made. Clear. Wide enough for a walker. Wide enough for a wheelchair if it came to that.

She exhaled and moved on.

The kitchen was next. She cleared the counter closest to the sink, shoved a stack of unopened mail into a drawer, and pushed the trash can back until it sat flush against the wall. She rearranged chairs around the table, then stepped back, assessing it like she was staging a house for sale.

She pulled clean sheets from the hall closet—flannel, not the cheap stuff—and folded them over her arm along with a blanket and two pillows. She paused by the couch, unfolded the hide-a-bed, and laid everything out with more care than she meant to.

"For Vikram," she said aloud, like the house needed an explanation.

The place felt too quiet without her dad in it. Too orderly. Mike had always been messy in a way that suggested motion—half-finished projects, stacks of papers that meant something only to him, a jacket tossed over the back of a chair because he might need it again soon.

Soon.

Maddy moved down the hall, stopping in front of the framed photos that lined it.

There were dozens.

Mike in a windbreaker, standing behind a dozen grinning girls in softball uniforms. Mike kneeling in the dirt, pointing something out to a cluster of players who hung on every word. Mike holding a trophy he didn't look like he cared about, surrounded by kids who clearly did.

She stared at them longer than she meant to.

"You always had time for them," she said quietly.

The words came out sharper than she intended—dismissive, almost. She crossed her arms, tilting her head as if daring the smiling version of her father in the photos to argue.

She moved on.

There were photos of her, too. Of course there were. Mike had never missed an opportunity to document her life.

Maddy in a leotard, hair slicked back, arms raised at the end of a routine. Maddy on a school stage in costumes, mid-song, mouth open wide in exaggerated expression. Maddy holding programs, certificates, diplomas—all proof she had existed, that she had done things worth framing.

She didn't stop at those.

Her eyes kept sliding past them, returning to the team photos. The group shots. The candid ones. The moments that screamed presence.

Practice after practice. Tournament weekends. Long afternoons under bleachers and sun.

She told herself she wasn't being fair.

She told herself he'd shown up for her plenty of times.

But fairness wasn't the point. The point was how it felt.

She thought about the night she told him she wanted to be a teacher.

Not a lawyer. Not an engineer. Not something that sounded impressive at dinner parties or justified the long hours and missed events.

A teacher.

She could still see his face—how he'd tried to hide the disappointment, how it had leaked out anyway as questions that sounded like concern but felt like doubt.

You sure?

You know how hard that is, right?
You ever think about doing something… more lucrative?

That had been the start of it. The first crack.

Maddy reached the end of the hall and turned into Mike's bedroom. She'd already moved the nightstand to give more clearance, already shifted the bed an inch toward the wall. She straightened the lamp, tugged the cord so it wouldn't be a tripping hazard.

She did everything that needed doing because someone had to.

Because he was coming home.

She sat on the edge of the bed for a moment, elbows on her knees, staring at the floor.

She wasn't sure how he was going to react when he found out about Kadee.

The thought sat heavy in her chest, unspoken, unformed—but there. Waiting.

She stood, smoothed the blanket, and left the room.

In the hallway, she paused one last time and glanced back at the photos.

Not the ones of her.

The others.

She didn't take any down. She didn't turn them around.

She just kept walking, the scrape of her footsteps echoing

softly through a house that was about to be full again—of crutches and walkers and truths she wasn't ready to unpack yet.

A car pulled into the driveway.

Maddy froze.

Not just a car—the car. A boxy rental SUV, beige and anonymous. She moved to the front window and watched from behind the curtain, heart ticking faster than she wanted it to.

Vikram climbed out first.

He circled the SUV quickly, like someone who'd rehearsed this part in his head the entire drive home. He opened the passenger door with exaggerated care, one hand braced on the frame, the other hovering like he expected Mike to shatter if handled incorrectly.

Mike did not look pleased.

Even from the window, she could see it—the tight mouth, the way his shoulders were taut in irritation. He sat there for a moment, unmoving, staring straight ahead like a man considering whether pride was worth the pain.

Vikram said something she couldn't hear. Whatever it was, it earned him a look.

Mike finally shifted, swinging his good leg out first, then carefully maneuvering the rest of himself forward. His movements were slow, deliberate, and clearly infuriating to him. Vikram hovered the entire time, hands out, ready to catch him, steady him, manage him.

"Easy," Vikram said—Maddy could read that one on his lips.

Mike shot him a glance that said don't start.

Maddy pressed her forehead lightly against the glass.

So this was it.

The man who once hauled coolers and gear bags without breaking stride now needed a valet. A spotter. A handler.

Mike straightened as much as he could once he was standing, chin lifting, posture asserting itself out of habit more than strength. Vikram immediately reached for the crutches in the back seat.

Mike waved him off.

"No," he said—loud enough that Maddy heard it through the glass.

Vikram froze. He knew that tone.

"You can't put weight on it," Vikram said, keeping his voice level. "The doctor was clear."

"I know what he said," Mike replied. He leaned against the SUV, buying himself a second. "I just need to get to the door."

Maddy watched as her father lingered there longer than he meant to, shoulder pressed to the vehicle like it was part of the plan. Then he took a careful step toward the house.

His jaw clenched. The muscles at his temples flared, sharp and unmistakable.

Vikram moved again, the crutches in his hands now. “Mike. No exceptions.”

Mike tried to wave them away, but the shift in weight made his face tighten. Still, he pushed forward, injured leg barely grazing the ground in a weak, awkward hop. Sweat beaded along his hairline.

“I can do this,” he said, breath clipped.

Vikram caught Maddy’s reflection in the window and lifted his hands in a helpless gesture. She nodded—once.

He stepped directly into Mike’s path.

“This isn’t about what you can do,” Vikram said. “I know you can walk to the door. Not until the bones set.”

“Move,” Mike said. “Or I’ll move you.”

Vikram gave a short, incredulous laugh. “With what? Just take the crutches so we can get you inside.”

“Inside for what?” Mike snapped. “To sit on my ass? Get out of the way.”

“No.” Vikram held the crutches out between them like a gate. “Not until you take these.”

Mike tried to straighten again. His balance wavered. Vikram reached to steady him—Mike swatted his hands away.

That was when Maddy bolted outside.

“Dad,” she shouted, “just take the damn crutches!”

Mike's face was flushed now—rage, pain, exertion all bleeding together. "I don't want them. It's just a few goddamn steps."

"You're going to hurt yourself," Maddy said. "Please."

"I don't need them," Mike shot back. "And you're not a doctor, so stay out of it."

Maddy stopped cold. "Wow. Really? Just use the crutches."

Vikram took a breath, forcing calm where there wasn't any left. "Mike, listen to her. You put weight on that leg and you risk shifting the plates and screws."

Mike turned on him. "I don't want to use the stupid crutches."

That did it.

"Well, you fucking have to, Mike!" Vikram snapped, shoving the crutches into his chest—hard enough that Mike stumbled, barely catching himself.

For a long moment, no one moved.

Mike stood there, breathing hard, the crutches pressed awkwardly against his chest. His hands hovered, uncertain.

Then he sighed.

Not in defeat, but in resigned acknowledgement.

"Fine," he said quietly.

Vikram didn't react right away. He waited, the way you do with someone you don't want to push into a corner again.

Mike took the crutches, adjusted his grip with deliberate care. Tested them once. Then again. The motion was clumsy, but controlled.

"There," he said. "Happy?"

Vikram nodded. "Relieved."

Maddy stayed where she was, watching closely. When Mike finally shifted his weight onto the crutches, really committed to them, she let out a breath she hadn't realized she was holding.

"Okay," Vikram said gently. "Door's right there."

"I know where the door is!" barked Mike. He then took a step. It wasn't graceful. It wasn't fast. But it worked.

He looked up at the house, then back at the crutches in his hands.

"Don't get used to this," he muttered.

Maddy didn't react. She stepped aside and held the door open wider.

"Path's clear," she said. "All the way to your room."

Mike glanced past her, down the hallway. Took it in.

"Of course it is," he muttered.

Vikram appeared behind him, grinning faintly, carrying a bag from the hospital with Mike's medication and personal items.

"You did a great job, Maddy," Vikram said. "Everything's out of the way."

Maddy shot him a look—half gratitude, half warning.

Mike stood in the entryway, taking in the house like it was both familiar and newly hostile terrain.

"Alright," he said, mostly to himself. "Let's get this over with."

Maddy watched him start down the hall—slow, stubborn, unsteady—and felt something shift in her chest.

It wasn't pity, it was responsibility. She realized in that moment just how isolated and lonely her father's life had become. Another deep breath, then she fell into step beside him, close enough to catch him if he stumbled, careful not to touch unless he asked.

Vikram followed a half-step behind.

The house closed in around them, the spaces between pride and necessity, of being carried and being helped, narrowing.

Vikram and Maddy occupied the kitchen carefully, circling one another like they were still negotiating where they fit. She sat at the table, thumb flicking through TikTok without really watching it, while Vikram opened cabinets and closed them again, one by one.

The silence stretched—thick, uncertain.

Finally, Vikram broke it. He stood staring into the last open cabinet, shaking his head.

"Does your dad eat anything that isn't seasoning or condiments?" he asked. "Because there's, like... no food in this house."

Maddy snorted despite herself.

"He used to stop at the store every day," she said. "Buy whatever he needed for dinner that night."

Vikram frowned. "Why not just buy groceries for the week?"

She laughed and pushed back from the table. "You're asking me to explain my dad. That's your first mistake."

He turned slightly, curious now.

"He said planning meals felt like giving up control," she went on. "Like if he planned ahead, he was locking himself into something he might not want later."

Vikram blinked. "Control over... dinner?"

"Everything," Maddy said. "Meal prep made him feel trapped. So he kept spices, sauces, random stuff—and figured the rest out on the fly."

She drifted toward the counter, her eyes catching on a stainless-steel utensil holder. She spun it absently, then reached in and pulled out a small, faded spatula—white once, now stained pink with old tomato sauce.

"This was mine," she said. Then, after a beat, "Is mine."

Vikram turned fully now. "Yeah?"

She nodded, turning it over in her hands. "I was his little chef.

Like in Ratatouille." A small smile tugged at her mouth. "I mostly just stirred pots of sauce, but we cooked together. That was our thing."

The smile faded.

She placed the spatula back in the container, more carefully than necessary.

"Then he left," she said. "And that was that."

Vikram shifted his weight, suddenly unsure where to put his hands. He thought about the long hike to Hidden Lake, how the subject of Maddy carried a visible weight, that seemed to press down on him the longer they walked.

"He misses you," Vikram said finally. "More than he knows how to say. And if there was something he could do to change the past—"

Maddy scoffed, cutting him off.

"Oh God, no," she said. "I don't need him and my mom back together. That would be so bad."

She crossed her arms, then uncrossed them, restless.

"What I need from him is acceptance," she said. "Of who I am. Of what I choose to do with my life. Not the version of me he planned out in his head."

Vikram nodded slowly. He understood that kind of disappointment more than he wanted to admit.

"He just wants the best for you," he said.

Maddy smiled at him—not unkindly, but knowingly.

"Yeah," she said. "Whose best?"

She tilted her head. "Mine—or his?"

Vikram didn't have an answer for that.

CHAPTER 37: THAT'LL DO

Coombs sat alone in a rear booth near the pool table at The Thirsty Badger, nursing his fifth beer of the afternoon. A handful of locals—mostly part-time county employees—were half-heartedly playing pool. From what Coombs could tell, their game of chasing the eight ball around the table was a pretty good metaphor for the dead-end futility of their lives.

He stared into his pint, watching carbonation bubbles rise and vanish into a thin foam.

Maybe that sums up the dead-end futility of my own life, he thought.

He snorted softly and drained the glass. As he slid out of the booth, he caught a snippet of conversation from the pool table.

"Those two dumbasses got what they deserved," said a wiry man in his early twenties. He wore the uniform of someone who thought he looked like an outdoorsman—Carhartt jacket, Red Wing boots, an unruly mullet shoved under a trucker hat. He lined up a shot and missed badly. "Especially Mike. Fuck that guy."

Coombs stopped.

Two others laughed.

"I saw that Indian guy in here with him," said a stocky man Coombs recognized—an aimless drifter who survived on odd jobs and government assistance. "Right before they got their asses handed to them. Guess he was the brother of that other dipshit that got himself killed."

He leaned over the table, squinting at a shot he was about to miss.

"Fuckin' turban-wearing assholes got more money than sense."

The third man was older—at least twenty years on the others. Coombs knew him too. A relic from the lumber camp days. Did a little time in county for pushing meth and weed up in Blaine. He spoke like a sentence was something he had to wrestle into submission.

"Mike's a fuckin' know-it-all sack of shit," the man said. "Should've died too." He grinned. "But I'll take that dead Indian as a consolation prize."

That did it.

Coombs stepped up to the table.

"You three idiots have a lot to say about things you don't understand," he said.

The older man laughed. "I understand there's one less job-stealing Indian in the world." He smirked. "I'm fine with that."

Coombs picked up the eight ball, rolling it once in his palm.

"Job-stealing Indian?" He looked at each of them in turn. "You're all too stupid to be threatened by anyone. Indian or otherwise."

"Fuck off, Wade," the older man said, stepping forward. "Mike thinks he's better than us. That bear should've killed him. Done everyone a favor."

Coombs didn't hesitate.

He hurled the eight ball.

It caught the older man square in the mouth. Teeth exploded. Blood sprayed. The man staggered back and crashed into the jukebox, sliding down it in a crumpled heap.

The stocky man tried to retreat.

Too slow.

Coombs grabbed him by the collar and drove two hard punches into his face. The nose went with a dull crunch. Coombs let him fall.

The third man froze—caught between fight and flight. One fist raised, the other hand out, useless.

"I'm sorry," he stammered. "I'm sorr—"

The apology ended with a short, clean right cross.

He dropped like a sack of flour.

Beth rushed out from behind the bar the moment she understood what had happened. Her eyes took in the scene—the three men on the floor, blood-smeared across the worn hardwood floor, the jukebox humming uselessly in the corner.

"What the hell, Wade?" she said.

The stocky man with the broken nose lay on his back, hands clutched to his face, wheezing through his fingers.

"Oh my God," Beth said. "I've gotta call an ambulance."

She turned on Coombs, voice urgent now. "Get out of here, Wade. Right now."

He didn't move.

Instead, he slid back into the booth, sat down heavily, and pulled out his phone.

"Sheriff," he said when the call connected. "It's Coombs. I just beat the shit out of three guys at The Badger."

A pause.

"Yeah."

Another pause.

"I'll be here."

He ended the call and set the phone on the table, hands flat. He looked at Beth and said, evenly, "Mind grabbing me another beer?"

Coombs sat slumped on the bench in the holding cell, forearms resting on his knees, hands dangling uselessly between them. The knuckles on his right hand were bruised and bleeding.

Baker stood outside the bars, hat in his hands.

"You can't just attack people, Wade," Baker snapped. "You don't get to decide who deserves what."

Coombs looked up slowly. His eyes were heavy, unfocused, the afternoon beers dragging his thoughts half a second behind his words.

"They were talking shit," he said. His voice was thick, but steady. "About Mike and the kid...and the kid's dead brother."

Baker exhaled through his nose. "Shutting them up is not your job, Wade."

Coombs shrugged, the movement sloppy. "Can't have it, Sheriff."

Baker studied him. This wasn't bar-fight Wade, the brawler who'd had one too many. This felt different. Protective. Purposeful. Like something had been waiting for an excuse to come out and start unloading on people.

Something Baker wasn't sure he wanted explained.

The front door opened behind him.

Deputy Grimes walked in, boots echoing across the floor. He crossed to his desk, set his hat on the chair, and pulled out his notebook.

"Well?" Baker asked.

Grimes flipped the notebook open. “Older guy—Jackson—had enough crystal on him to flirt with federal charges. That gave me probable cause to search the vehicle.”

Baker’s eyebrows lifted slightly.

“Car belonged to the one with the busted nose,” Grimes continued. “Found an unlicensed revolver in the glove box. No CCW.”

Coombs snorted softly from the cell.

Grimes glanced at him, then went on. “Those two aren’t pressing charges if we look the other way on the crank and the handgun.” He reached behind his back, drew a .38 from his waistband, and handed it to Baker. “Made that deal—but only after confiscating this.”

He looked back down at his notebook. “Third guy’s clean. He wants to press charges. Says Wade jumped him.”

Baker winced. “Any witnesses saying otherwise?”

“Bar back says Jackson stepped to Wade first,” Grimes said. “But that’s a tough sell to a jury when three guys have busted-up faces.”

Grimes closed the notebook.

“But,” he added, locking eyes with Coombs, “I convinced him to drop it.”

Baker turned. “How?”

Grimes’s mouth twitched. “Wade’s covering the dental work. All of it.”

Baker exhaled slowly. “How much?”

“A lot,” Grimes said. “But it keeps Mr. Coombs out of jail.”

Silence settled over the room.

Coombs leaned his head back against the cinderblock wall and closed his eyes.

Baker watched him for a long moment, then shook his head.

“Jesus Christ, Wade,” he muttered.

He turned to Grimes. “This office will pay for the dental work.”

Grimes frowned. “Sheriff—”

“The department has the money,” Baker snapped. “And I’m not letting this turn into something bigger than it already is.”

He slipped the revolver into his desk drawer and shut it.

“Paper it the way we discussed,” he said. “Then get him out of my holding cell.”

Later that evening, Sheriff Baker sat alone in the silence of his office. His eyes were fixed on the area map of Mount Baker hanging on the wall.

That’s when his phone rang.

“This is Baker.”

A familiar voice answered. “Sheriff. Commander Morton.”

Baker straightened slightly.

"Patrols and listening posts are in place," Morton said. "The camp perimeter has been secured." A brief pause followed. "You shouldn't have anything to worry about."

Baker's eyes never left the map. "And if I do?"

Another pause—longer this time.

"Then you call Major Robinson directly," Morton said. "Keep me out of it until you can't. Understood?"

A dozen questions surged through Baker's mind—about jurisdiction, about authority, about what exactly had been unleashed up there—but he swallowed them all.

"Understood," Baker said.

The line went dead.

Baker lowered the phone slowly, still staring at the map, and wondered when exactly not worrying had started to feel like the most dangerous option.

"Way to go, tough guy," Vikram said, watching as the medical technician wrapped the final layers of plaster around Mike's leg. "You just had to try walking from the bathroom to the kitchen without crutches. Now look at you."

Resignation—and regret—escaped Mike in a long sigh. "I don't want to hear it."

"You have to hear it, Dad," Maddy said, leaning in. "Just like you have to use the crutches."

The technician, a seasoned veteran of casts and family squabbles, smoothed the last edge and nodded. "All right. Let's give this about twenty minutes to set before you try standing. The doctor will be in shortly."

She slipped out, closing the door softly behind her.

The room settled into an awkward quiet. Vikram shifted his weight, about to say something, when a quick knock sounded and the door opened again.

"You got lucky, Mike," the doctor said. He couldn't have been much older than twenty-five. "The plate and screws held. But we're putting you in this cast for two weeks to limit movement." He glanced at the chart. "Any questions?"

Mike shook his head.

Vikram's hand shot up like an overeager second-grader. "Does he have to use the crutches, Doc?"

The doctor didn't hesitate. "Absolutely."

Vikram pointed at Mike. "You hear that? Absolutely. No exceptions. Not even from the bathroom to the kitchen."

"Not from the bathroom to anywhere," the doctor said, firm now. He tapped the cast lightly with his pen. "You put weight on this leg, you risk pulling the hardware out of place. That means spiral fractures in both bones."

Mike winced.

"Recovery from this break will take time," the doctor continued. “Spiral fractures take twice as long—if they heal properly at all. Understood?”

Mike nodded. “Understood.”

Maddy rested a hand on her father’s shoulder. He reached up and squeezed her fingers, a quiet acknowledgment of both the pain and the humiliation.

“I’ll have the tech bring in your discharge paperwork and home-care instructions,” the doctor said, already turning for the door.

The door closed, leaving the three of them alone again.

CHAPTER 38: BROKEN

The dark was thicker here.

The lair breathed with him, damp air rising and falling, carrying the sharp mineral scent of water and old earth. He lay on his side, pressed into the cold, muscles coiled tight despite the pain that burned through his shoulder and down his flank. The wounds throbbed with each breath. The tearing bite of metal still lived inside him.

He shifted carefully.

Pain flared, bright and immediate, but he did not cry out. Sound traveled too easily now.

He remembered when this place was quiet.

When the boundary was open.

Now the air carried something new.

Oil.
Metal.
The sharp crack from the sticks they carried.

They moved along the old paths again—slow, deliberate. Not lost. Not wandering. The ground remembered their boots. The trees did not want them.

He had watched from above as they came, spreading like ants along the hard road, setting up their lights and listening boxes. He had heard them speaking into the air, calling to one another without voices.

The boundary was closed.

Not by him.

By them.

He flexed his fingers, claws scraping faintly against stone. Blood had dried in the fur along his arm, stiff and dark. He would heal. He always did. But healing took time, and time was no longer his alone.

He turned his head.

The stump stood where it always had, pale against the dark.

The head rested there, just as he had placed it.

The smell was wrong now—old, fading—but still different from the others. No oil. No metal. No black powder. Only death.

This one had not been like the rest.

It had come alone.
It had looked instead of taken.
It had crossed without knowing.

He had watched it before the strike.

He had waited.

The boundary mattered. It always had. Crossing it was not allowed. Not by those who cut trees. Not by those who brought fire. Not by those who killed for sport and left rot behind.

But this one had not smelled like them.

Still, the line was crossed.

He had acted because that was what kept balance.

Or so it had always been.

Now, lying wounded in dirt and shadow, listening to the distant hum of human machines, he wondered—only briefly—if the balance had shifted before the strike.

The thought unsettled him.

He pushed it away.

Regret was a human thing.

Yet...

Beyond the far ridge, deep where the trees grew wrong and the ground dipped into places even he avoided, something moved. Not often. Not loudly. But it had been closer lately. Testing. Listening.

That thing did not respect boundaries.

It did not protect.

It took.

He inhaled slowly, tasting the air, and felt the old warning tighten in his chest. The humans were loud now, but predictable. Dangerous, but fragile.

The others in the deep woods were neither.

His territory was smaller now. His wounds slowed him. The balance he had kept alone for so long was no longer stable.

He lowered his gaze from the stump and closed his eyes.

When he rose again, it would be different.

It would have to be.

HE'S HERE

Book Two Of The Mount Baker Bigfoot Chronicles

CHAPTER 1: THE FARM HOUSE

The old farmhouse sat at the edge of dense, untamed forest, its wooden bones weathered by years of rain and wind. Around it stretched fallow fields and uneven pasture, hemmed in by towering pines and moss-dark fence posts. In daylight the place looked peaceful; in the predawn dark, it fell eerily silent.

A faint yellow glow seeped from a single kitchen window. Inside, James Reed stood at the sink, finishing the last of his lukewarm coffee. He held the mug in both hands, staring into nothing. By this point the coffee was ritual more than drink.

Reed was in his early sixties, though his posture suggested younger. Broad-shouldered, with hands built for work — leathery, stone-hard. The lines on his face came not from stress but from sun and wind. His gray hair was cropped close, sawdust and wisps of alfalfa clung to the cuffs of his flannel shirt.

James set the mug in the sink and reached for the Carhartt jacket draped over the chair. The sleeves were stiff from years of use. He shrugged it on and muttered, "Once more into the fray..." before stepping out into the cold.

The motion light above the back door flickered on with a soft *click*, casting a pale glow onto the stone path that cut across the backyard. Beyond the circle of light, the yard vanished into black. The forest loomed beyond the property line, silent and watching.

James didn't like how heavy the air felt this morning. Something was off. “Should’ve run more lights,” he grumbled. “Stupid not to.”

He flicked his phone flashlight app to 'On', a thin beam cut across the frost that crackled beneath his boots. Nearing the shed, he slipped the phone back into his pocket and rubbed his hands for warmth. The padlock was cold under his fingers. He spun the dial, missed, swore under his breath, stepped back, and tried again.

“Damn it all," he grumbled as he fumbled with the combination.

The lock popped. James pushed the shed door open and reached inside to flip on the interior light. Dust floated in the dim amber glow of the exposed bulb as he grabbed the cloth-lined basket from a hook.

“Alright,” he muttered. “Let’s see what you’ve got for us this morning.”

Basket in hand, he turned to leave, then hesitated.

The weak glow from his phone flashlight was not enough. Not out here. Not this morning. Frowning, he reached back inside and grabbed the larger flashlight that was purposely hung near the door for mornings like this one.

He stepped out and walked around the side of the shed toward the chicken coop.

He stopped. Too still. Too quiet. The usual cacophony of clucking hens that greeted him every morning was absent.

James squinted into the dark, but his flashlight beam told the story before his brain could catch up.

The chicken coop was destroyed.

Wire fencing had been shredded and torn apart like paper. The wooden frame was splintered. Feathers blanketed the ground in a thin layer of white, but it was the red that stood out. Bright, wet splashes of blood stained the snow-like fluff. Several hens lay twisted and broken in the dirt, their bodies torn in half or tossed aside like toys.

James stood frozen, his breath fogging in front of him. The basket slipped from his hand and hit the ground with a dull thud.

"Jesus..." he breathed, taking a cautious step closer. "Tore right through the wire...."

He trailed off. The flashlight beam trembled in his hand.

"...something had a great fucking time in there."

He didn't wait to investigate further. He turned and ran, boots pounding across the flagstones, the quiet forest behind him suddenly loud.

Mimi jumped at the sound of the back door slamming shut. She was in the kitchen, kettle tilted mid-pour, the scent of steeping Red Rose black tea just beginning to fill the air. Her robe was cinched neat, hair swept up in the kind of no-nonsense twist that declared war on chaos, especially in the morning.

James strode in, boots heavy, face drawn tight.

"What's the matter?" she asked, startled.

He peeled off his gloves and tossed them onto the counter. "Bear got into the coop," he said, already moving toward the hallway. "Killed most of the birds. Tore the whole damn thing apart."

Mimi blinked. "Are you sure it was a bear?"

"Pretty sure," he called over his shoulder, opening the hall closet with a grunt. "Wires ripped clean, nesting boxes crushed. Not the work of coyotes, not a cougar. Just a nuisance black bear getting bold."

She followed slowly; tea forgotten for the moment. "What are you looking for?"

"My shotgun," James said as he pushed through boxes and storage bins on the closet floor.

Mimi leaned against the wall of the hallway. "You moved it

under the bed after those home invasions in Snohomish, remember?"

The rummaging stopped. A pause.

"...Right."

James emerged from the closet with a sheepish shrug and disappeared upstairs. She stared up at the noise of footsteps and shifting furniture.

Mimi moved toward the banister. "Don't suppose you'll fold the laundry while you're up there?" she called.

A moment later, he thundered back down, Mossberg 500 under one arm, a box of shells in his hand.

"That bear's still nearby," he said calmly, almost to himself. "I could smell it out there."

Mimi moved to block his path, gently. "It's still dark, James. Maybe give it a few hours. This doesn't need to turn into a hunt."

He shook his head. "I've gotta take care of this now. If a bear thinks our coop is easy pickings, it'll keep coming back. Maybe next time it tries the garage, or the porch, or goes after the dogs."

She sighed, arms folded. "But you're not really a hunter."

That gave him pause. He tilted his head, thoughtful. "No. I'm not. But this isn't hunting — it's protecting what's ours. Bake a pie, eat a pie. See a bear, shoot a bear. Simple as that."

Mimi's eyes softened but worry clung to her like fog. "Shoot a pie...bake a bear, you aren't making any sense. And what if it's not a bear?"

He blinked, thrown off. "What else would it be?"

"I don't know," she said. "It just... feels wrong."

James watched her for a moment, taking her seriously now. He set the shotgun down beside the door.

"Alright," he said. "I'll stick to the perimeter. Just check the field, nothing more. If I see anything that isn't a bear, I'll call Sheriff Baker, let him know we've got a problem. Sound fair?"

Mimi nodded slowly. "Just... please be careful."

"I will," he said, pulling on his gloves again. "Love you."

He stepped out the back door, into the mist-choked field. The morning was still half-formed, a pale, uncertain light wrestling with fog that clung low to the ground like gauze. The field stretched wide behind the farmhouse, uneven rows of spent corn stalks jutting from the soil like brittle bones. Most were weathered to husks, the harvest long past, silent sentinels standing stiff in the mist left to guard nothing but air.

James stepped into the field with deliberate caution, the ground soft and squelching beneath his boots. A fine sheen of dew coated the grass. A tractor sat rusting along the fence line, its faded green body now more ornamental than functional. Weeds curled around the wheels like the fingers of time reclaiming what once mattered.

He moved past the chicken coop. In the misty light, the wrecked coop looked less like an attack on hens and more like an act of violence. Something had torn it apart for the sake of destruction itself.

Then he saw them.

Tracks.

Not paw prints. Not hooves.

Too big. Too upright.

He crouched beside them, squinting in the gray light. The impressions were deep, the heel marks clear. Wide forefoot, long toes. Human-like, but wrong. Distorted. Heavy.

A tightness coiled in his gut.

He pulled out his phone and snapped a photo. The shutter sound was absurdly loud in the quiet.

The tracks led away from the coop, straight toward the trees at the edge of the property. The mist was thicker there, like it was guarding a secret. The shapes of the trees were smudged and ghostly, no detail, no depth.

He hesitated. The weight of the shotgun shifted in his grip. It didn't feel reassuring anymore.

Still, he followed the trail, step by careful step. The sound of his boots were swallowed by the fog. The field funneled him toward the trees, corn rows on one side, sagging wire fence on the other. He stopped at the threshold.

That's when he smelled it.

A rank, oily stench flooded his nose. Skunk and rotted meat, burnt hair and mold. It hit like a wall, thick and wet and wrong. His eyes watered. His grip tightened.

Ahead, through the veil of fog, something hunched and massive loomed.

Not a mountain lion. Not a bear.

He raised the shotgun slowly, stock pressed to his shoulder, breath held. The thing didn't move. Its outline blurred at the edges, a shape made of smoke and shadow.

"Got ya," he muttered under his breath.

Then it vanished, slipping back into the mist like a whispered threat.

RINGTONE.

His phone shrieked in his pocket.

From the fog, it lunged. A wall of motion and mass. James backpedaled on instinct and fired.

BANG.

The roar that followed wasn't that of a bear. It was deeper, primal, and close.

James went down hard, the back of his head cracking against damp earth. The shotgun slid out of reach. His hands clawed through the mud and grass, found metal.

Just as his fingers touched the barrel, something massive, leathery, impossibly heavy, slammed down.

CRUNCH.

The shotgun was flattened into the mud beneath a massive foot.

James froze.

His eyes crawled upward.

It towered over him, a living mountain, its breath pumping in hot, steaming bursts. Each exhale rattled in his chest like distant thunder. Its eyes, just shapes in the fog, glowed with something too intelligent. Too old.

And then, like a nightmare that knows when to retreat, it turned and melted into the mist.

James lay in the mud, his chest heaving, ears ringing, eyes wide and unblinking.

CHAPTER 2: SMOOTH OPERATOR

The kitchen was small but lived-in, a space that bore the fingerprints of years gone by. Faded yellow linoleum patterned with faint geometric diamonds curled at the corners. It gave underfoot with a soft groan. Knotty pine cabinets, dulled with age, lined the walls, their brass handles smudged with use. At the center sat a vintage Formica table with chrome legs, half-buried beneath unopened mail, dog-eared magazines, and a chipped mug ringed with stubborn stains.

Beyond the narrow window over the sink, the backyard pressed in, a patch of overgrown grass, a leaning bird feeder, the first green hints of moss creeping up the fence posts.

Vikram moved in the space, barefoot in sweatpants and T-shirt, slicing fruit with practiced efficiency. On the counter, a boxy, outdated juicer rattled and whined like it had one more job in it before it gave up the ghost. He fed chunks of carrot, apple, and orange into the chute, pausing only to wipe his hands on a dish towel slung over his shoulder.

At the table, Mike sat with his left leg propped on a second chair, the bulky fiberglass cast extending from his ankle to just below the knee. The bruising on his face had faded, but shadows lingered under his eyes. He looked older than he had a month ago. Worn. Thoughtful. His fingers drummed a soft rhythm against the table's surface as he stared out the window into the trees.

"Here you go," Vikram said, sliding a tall glass in front of him with a grin. "Carrots, apples, oranges, ginger, turmeric, and just a dash of black pepper. Boosts absorption."

Mike glanced down at the orange liquid like it had personally offended him. "I wanted a Denver omelet."

"You'll get an egg white and spinach omelet," Vikram replied, turning back toward the stove. "After the juice. You need it, you're still dealing with inflammation and a battered immune system."

Mike muttered into his glass as he took a sip. "I've been out of the hospital two weeks and I kind of miss the food."

Vikram scoffed, "You were fed intravenously for ten days, then graduated to ice chips and some chalky protein slush. What exactly are you missing?"

"Cinnamon apple sauce," Mike said wistfully. "Banana pudding."

Vikram glanced over his shoulder. "Lucky for you, I have to go to the store today. I'll pick up some applesauce while I'm there. Might even leave an egg yolk in the omelet. It's your cheat day."

Mike took another drink. "Gotta admit... this juice ain't bad. Could use some rum, though."

Vikram chuckled. "When the cast comes off, we'll celebrate with a real drink. Promise."

Mike didn't answer right away. His gaze drifted back toward the tree line, the dense wall of green that framed the backyard and spilled down into the valley. He watched it in silence, eyes narrowing like he was searching for something...or maybe remembering something he'd rather forget.

"I can't stop thinking about it," he said finally. "What we saw. What we went through."

Vikram lowered the spatula and turned to face him, leaning back against the counter. "Same. Every time I shut my eyes, it's right there. But hey, we survived, right? So did he." A faint smile ghosted across his lips. "He's probably out there thinking, 'Man, those two guys kicked my ass. Better lay low before the other Bigfeet find out.'"

Mike's brow furrowed. "Other Bigfeet, I've been thinking about that too. What if there's more?"

Vikram joined him at the table, setting down a plate. Mike picked up his fork, chewing not just food, but thoughts.

"He's flesh and blood," said Vikram, "a biological being. Science says there must be more. Breeding, survival, evolution, all that."

"I always wondered," Mike said quietly, "if this one was some kind of outcast. Like maybe it got pushed out of a group. A rogue."

Vikram stood and carried their empty juice glasses to the sink. "I think we've got bigger stuff to worry about than Sasquatch family dynamics and societal constructs."

He glanced at the clock.

"The nurse will be here in an hour for your therapy. I'll run into town while you two work—get groceries for tonight. Salmon and spinach salad. Omega-3s. High protein. Good for healing busted bones. And the banana pudding you're just dying for."

Mike looked up from his plate. "Hey... I appreciate this. Really. With Maddy back at school, and you still recovering...you didn't have to stay and help out."

Vikram shrugged. "You're welcome. If that was a thank you."

Mike gave him a slow nod. He turned his eyes back to the trees, "I'm never gonna look at those woods the same again."

Vikram followed his gaze. "That makes two of us."

He walked back to the table and motioned towards Mike's empty plate, "Now hand that over, tough guy. I'll wash. You sit."

Mike smirked and slid the dish forward. "Don't forget applesauce."

Outside, the wind picked up slightly, rustling the edge of the forest. The trees swayed silently in the distance.

CHAPTER 3: GAME OF CHICKEN

Deputy Grimes scribbled furiously across a legal pad, the phone cradled awkwardly between his shoulder and ear. His pen scratched a steady rhythm as he tried to keep up with the voice on the other end.

"Uh huh... okay... dead chickens... James had his shotgun? Really? Okay. Yes, ma'am, as soon as the sheriff gets in, I'll pass that along. Thank you."

He clicked the receiver back onto its cradle and sighed, long and heavy. For a few seconds he just sat there, staring at the notes he'd made. Then the office door creaked open, and Sheriff Baker stepped inside, brushing mist from his jacket sleeves and unbuttoning his coat as he moved.

"Deputy," Baker greeted.

Grimes straightened slightly. "Morning, Sheriff. Just got off the phone with Mimi Reed. Something tore through their chicken coop. Pretty bad, from what she says."

Baker crossed the room to the coffee station, fishing through the collection of dusty K-pods. "Why didn't they call Fish & Wildlife?" he asked while reading the top of each pod. "And why do we have so much goddamn hazelnut flavored coffee?"

Grimes gave a small, uncertain shrug. "Well, funny story. Apparently, James went out with a shotgun to deal with what he thought was a bear...came back yelling about how it wasn't a bear."

The Keurig hissed to life. Baker didn't look up. "Mountain lion?"

"Nope. His exact words were 'skunk ape."

That got Baker's attention. He turned, one eyebrow arched. "Skunk ape?"

Grimes winced slightly, holding up his hands like a man too close to a lit firework. "I know what you're thinking. I don't know if he means what we think he means. But Mimi sounded shook up."

The machine gurgled, then fell silent. Baker added two creams to his coffee, stirred it slowly, eyes distant.

Grimes cleared his throat. "Sheriff?"

Baker took a sip, then finally met his deputy's eyes. "Guess we better go take a look."

The coop looked like a war zone. Feathers littered the ground like snowdrifts, the red blood drying to a deep maroon. The back wall of the structure had been peeled away as if by a wrecking ball. Nesting boxes lay smashed in the mud, and a few chicken carcasses were still half-buried beneath splintered boards.

Baker's eyes lingered on the damage a beat longer than he meant to. Grimes caught the look, but neither said anything. Not yet.

James stood nearby, gripping his ruined shotgun, the stock cracked through, like it might vanish if he let it go. Mimi hovered behind him, arms crossed tight, her expression straddling the line between worry and weary exasperation.

"This whole back section," James said, motioning toward the wreckage. "Ripped clean out. Look at the poles, they're pulled right outta the ground."

Baker crouched to inspect the frame, eyes narrowed. "Yeah, I see it."

James pressed in closer, the muzzle of his shotgun uncomfortably close to the sheriff's head. The sheriff took half a step back. "Mind setting that shotgun down while we're here?"

James shook his head. "Not after what I saw."

He walked a few steps and pointed at the mud near the coop, "Look at these tracks, Sheriff. These aren't bear tracks. I've hunted bear. These are different."

Baker followed the prints slowly. They trailed from the woods, circled the coop, then drifted toward the open field and then back towards the trees.

He knelt beside one. "It's been raining. Mud's soft. Look at how my boot print spreads out here, how the water fills it."

James stepped over, inspecting the fresh boot print with a skeptical frown.

"What are you saying?"

"I'm saying the conditions distort prints," Baker replied calmly. "A big bear, for sure. But still a bear."

"No damn way," James said sharply. "It walked upright. Stank like skunk and garbage. Like one of those damn skunk apes they talk about down in Florida."

Grimes and Baker exchanged a glance. Then Grimes stepped forward, his tone even. "James, it was foggy. Early morning. You were rattled. Could've been your mind playing tricks."

James turned, quick and sharp, and closed the distance with the deputy. He jabbed a finger toward the field, shotgun still clutched tight.

"Boy, don't tell me what I did or didn't see. I know what I saw, and it wasn't no goddamn bear! It was huge. Two-legged. Stunk to high heaven."

Mimi took a cautious step forward, her voice soft. "James..."

Before she could say more, Baker stepped between the two men, his tone firm but not aggressive. "Easy. Back off. Both of you, simmer down."

James's face was red, his eyes wide and wild. "He's trying to tell me I'm crazy!"

Baker took a half step closer. "And what exactly did you see, James? Be honest. Heavy mist. Barely any light. A dark shape in the field. It stood up. You panicked, fell backward, fired your shotgun. Sound about right?"

James's mouth opened, then closed. "Yeah, but... it wasn't a bear."

"Maybe not," Baker said, his voice cooler now. "But that's not what you're going to say. Fish & Wildlife will be here by tomorrow. Let them handle it."

James looked stricken. "And what about my chickens?"

"What about 'em?" Baker said, shrugging. "Price of doing business out here. I'm surprised you haven't had cougars poking around. Chickens are an open invitation for predators, especially this close to the foothills."

That landed like a slap. James's face darkened, teeth clenched tight. Mimi exhaled sharply and looked away.

After a long pause, Baker sighed.

"Tell you what. Feed & Seed's got a fresh shipment of chicks. Go pick up a few. Rebuild the coop. Send the bill to my office, keep it within reason. No backhoes or fancy gadgets. My generosity has limits."

That softened James, just a little. "Thanks, Sheriff. I appreciate it. But I'm telling you...it wasn't a bear. I know it wasn't a bear."

Baker's voice dropped. "No, James. You don't know. You think you saw something, but the mist... fear...adrenaline... it plays tricks. So don't go around town running your mouth. I don't need this town in an uproar. And you don't need folks whispering that James Reed's losing it."

James didn't answer at first. His shoulders slumped, whatever fight he had in him drained. "Yeah... got it."

"And if it was a bear, and it's as big as you say?" Baker said, gesturing toward the shotgun. "Might be time to load up on slugs."

He gave Grimes a slight nod, and the two lawmen began walking toward the car. They were nearly to the driveway when Baker slowed.

His eyes wandered up the hillside. Mist clung to the trees, hanging low and still. The sheriff stood beside the SUV, one hand on the driver's side door latch, and watched the edge of the woods for a long beat.

Then, without a word, he climbed into the driver's seat and started the engine of the Ford Explorer. He sat still for a long moment, hands resting on the wheel, then let out a tired sigh and rubbed a hand across his face.

"What a friggin' mess," he muttered.

Grimes settled into the passenger seat, closing the door with a soft thud. His gaze was fixed on the windshield, unfocused, distant.

"You think it was here?" he asked quietly.

Baker's expression didn't change. He stared out the windshield, then gave a slow shake of his head.

"Nah. James saw a bear. Got himself spooked. Filled in the blanks with shadows and adrenaline fueled imagination."

Grimes didn't respond right away. He just kept staring, his thoughts churning behind his tired eyes.

"Yeah, but..." he said finally. "What if it was here?"

The sheriff turned his head slowly, looking at his deputy - not angry, not dismissive, but with the wary patience of a man who'd considered that same question more than once.

"That's a 'what if' we're not equipped to deal with," he said.

With a low groan of gravel under the tires, Baker threw the

SUV into reverse and backed out of the Reed driveway. The mist closed in behind them.

CHAPTER 4: TEMU TENT

They were already arguing before the tent was half up. Travis yanked at the poles, his face drawn tight with effort. Erin stood nearby with the instruction manual flapping in her hand like a paper flag of defeat. The clearing around them was soft with moss and grass, the dirt beneath still damp from the day's shade. Evening light stretched long through the trees, warm and golden, but the tension between them had saturated the air like humidity before a thunder storm.

"These aren't labeled," Travis said, frowning at the heap of identical tent rods. "They all look the same."

"They're supposed to be," Erin said, turning the instructions upside down. "'Insert Pole A into Segment A2 to bond the primary structure for support.' What the hell does that even mean?"

"You bought this thing off TEMU for nineteen bucks. It probably translates to "Good luck, dumbass."

Erin dropped the instructions. "It had good reviews."

Travis didn't look up. "It's not the reviews I'm doubting. It's the lead based paint and asbestos the Chinese manufacturer used to make it."

Erin's glare could've peeled bark. "Don't be racist."

He froze, mid-assembly. The sleeves of his brand-new Arc'teryx jacket bunched at his elbows as he gripped the pole. "How is that racist?"

"It just is. Saying stuff like that."

Travis spun one of the rods slowly in his hand, then pointed it at her. "It's not racist to say this tent sucks and that it was made in China. Facts don't care about feelings."

"Even facts can be racist," Erin snapped, her Patagonia fleece zipped all the way up despite the mild air. The neon laces on her spotless trail runners glowed against the mossy ground.

He stared at her for a beat, the last of the light slipping through the trees behind her. Then, slowly: "You're overcomplicating this. Let's just pick two poles that look kind of the same and jam 'em together. It's going to be dark soon and I don't want to sleep on a pile of aluminum tent poles and nylon."

Erin, after a long, eye-roll-worthy pause, handed him a pole. "You're a dick."

Travis accepted it. "Love you too."

They got it standing. Barely.

The tent sagged at the center, one side slumped in like a melting cake. It looked like it might collapse with the faintest breeze.

"Best nineteen bucks I ever spent," Erin said flatly.

"Yup," Travis agreed, hands on the hips of his hiking pants. "Five-star value."

They didn't say much more as they gathered kindling and cut small branches. A faint pink hue rimmed the treetops as twilight settled, painting the edges of their campsite in quiet, fading gold.

Then came the sound.

A deep, hollow knock, far off but deliberate. Like wood striking wood, too forceful to be natural.

Erin straightened. "What was that?"

Travis paused mid-swing, hatchet dangling at his side. He listened as the sound echoed once through the trees, then died. "Probably just some other campers. You know how people get out here."
She didn't reply. She glanced toward the tree line, then returned to arranging the wood.

The fire came to life quickly, a teepee of dry twigs and branches licked to orange by the ferrow rod's sparks. Warmth filled the clearing, wrapping them in comfort. Erin added a skillet over the pit and tossed in a couple foil-wrapped meals. They sizzled loudly, drawing smiles from both of them.

"Chicken fajitas," she said. "It's nothing but Mountain House dehydrated meals starting tomorrow."

Travis groaned dramatically, Erin laughed, stirring the skillet.

After dinner, Travis stacked the dirty dishes and filled a collapsible wash basin with water warmed over the fire in a large pot.

"I'll wash up away from camp," he said. "Be back in a sec."

"Don't dawdle," Erin replied, tossing him a dishrag.

He gave her a mock salute and disappeared into the woods.

Erin leaned back in her camp chair, eyes skyward. The fire cracked and hissed, its embers rising in bursts of orange, dancing against the dark. She smiled and poked the flames, coaxing the heat higher.

Minutes passed. A breeze stirred. Cold. She pulled the collar on her jacket up and snuggled down into the chair.

From deep in the woods, farther than Travis should've gone, came a loud SNAP.

She sat up straight. "Travis?"

Silence. Then movement, slow and deliberate. Something

heavy crept through the brush, just beyond the firelight.

"Stop messing around, Travis. You're not funny."

A plastic plate sailed out of the dark, landing at her feet with a clatter.

Her heart jumped.

"Are you fucking kidding me?" she snapped. "You almost hit me!"

Another plate flew past her head.

Erin shot to her feet, scanning the dark. The fire popped behind her, throwing wild shadows. She saw something, a shape, shift at the edge of the trees.

Then came the smell. Rancid. The stench penetrated the smoke from the fire.

"Travis?" she whispered.

Silence. Then something was tossed, almost casually, from the trees, and landed with a dull, wet, sickening thud in front of her.

She looked down.

It was Travis.

His head had been crudely severed, flesh and splintered bone jutting jagged from the neck. Blood sprayed across her boots in heavy, dark splatters. For a heartbeat she couldn't process it—her mind rejected what she saw. Then the scream tore free, raw and piercing, shattering the stillness of the woods.

She spun to run.

Something smashed into the back of her skull. A rock. Pain flared white-hot, the world tilting, vision blurring as she crashed to the ground.

Her hands scrabbled weakly at the earth. She tried to crawl.

A shadow fell over her. Towering. Massive. Its breath thundered above her, hot and ragged.

She lifted her head just enough to glimpse the bulk of it, just as a thick, gnarled branch swung down in a brutal arc.

Blackness swallowed everything.

CHAPTER 5: HYDRATE!

Mike braced himself against the cluttered bathroom counter, trying not to topple forward as he fumbled through an unruly sea of bottles, tubs, tubes, and foil packets. His crutches wobbled beneath him, and one of the plastic caps on the bottom squealed in protest against the tile.

"Jesus," he muttered, squinting at a small container with letters too tiny to read without a microscope, or at least a pair of reading glasses he refused to admit he needed.

He sighed in defeat and hobbled out of the bathroom like a disgruntled giraffe on stilts.

"Vik!" he shouted down the hallway. "Vik!"

Footsteps pattered from the kitchen, quick and light. Vikram appeared around the corner, spatula still in one hand, apron slightly stained with whatever he'd been sautéing.

"What's up?" he asked, brow furrowed. "Everything okay?"

"No, everything is not okay," Mike snapped, waving him forward like a man flagging down a rescue helicopter. "Get over here."

Vikram stepped into the bathroom doorway, eyes falling on the counter.

"What the hell is all this?" Mike asked, gesturing wildly at the mess of products. "The nurse had everything organized. Now it looks like a Sephora blew up in here!"

Vikram didn't flinch. He folded his arms, tilted his head, and raised an eyebrow with the confidence of someone who had absolutely no regrets.

"That," he said calmly, "is my skincare routine."

Mike blinked at him. "Your what?"

"Skincare routine. I use all of it." Vikram shrugged his shoulders, clearly flummoxed that Mike didn't get it.

Mike gestured at a sleek green bottle with a name that sounded like a concoction developed by a startup.

"What the hell is 'Orveda Bio-tech Sheer Brew Gel'?"

Vikram scoffed, grabbing the bottle like a teacher retrieving a textbook. "Seriously? This firms fine lines. Obviously."

He plucked another container from the counter. "This one's Eye Unveiler. Reduces puffiness."

Another. "And this…this is Age Reducing Serum. Eight straight hours of hydration, you unlearned savage."

Mike groaned and leaned his forehead against the mirror. "Age reducing serum? You're twenty-five."

"Twenty-seven," Vikram corrected, straightening his posture. "See? The stuff works."

Mike made a noise halfway between a growl and a sigh, rubbed his temple like he was warding off an aneurysm.

"I don't care if it works or doesn't work. I just want to find my meds without accidentally OD'ing on your grapeseed extract. Do you have a bag or something you can throw this all into?"

Vikram shrugged. "I guess."

"I'm glad you're here, kid," Mike said, voice softening. "Really. It's been a huge help. But with Maddy back at school, maybe move your skincare lab into her bathroom. No need to colonize mine. That bathroom is closer to your room anyway. Everybody wins."

"Okay," Vikram said, already half-turned toward the hallway.

"Dinner's ready, by the way."

He disappeared back toward the kitchen, trailing the faint scent of turmeric and whatever else was simmering on the stove.

Mike let out a slow breath, stared once more at the glossy countertop battlefield, then turned and made his way down the hall one cautious step at a time, navigating crutches and chaos with the weary dignity of a man who just wanted his antibiotics and a little peace.

CHAPTER 6: TRASH PANDA

Grace sat in her dimly lit living room, wrapped in a crocheted blanket that bore the faded pastel hues of an earlier decade. A lamp with a tasseled shade cast a warm pool of light beside her, illuminating the pages of a well-loved paperback. The rest of the house was cloaked in quiet shadows, the only sound the steady tick of the mantel clock.

At her feet, Colt, her aging chocolate Lab, lay snoring softly, his paws twitching with some dream of chases and uncatchable rabbits.

Grace turned the final page of her chapter, sighed with satisfaction, and slipped a handmade bookmark between the pages.

"Time for bed, Colt," she said, her voice low and gentle. "Let's go out one last time."

Colt stirred but didn't rise. Instead, his head lifted sharply. His ears pinned flat, tail vanishing between his legs.

"C'mon, don't be dramatic," Grace coaxed, rising from her chair. "Let's go potty."

Colt whimpered.

She reached for his collar with one hand, tugging gently. He flattened himself to the floor like he was trying to disappear into it.

Grace's brows furrowed. "What is it, boy? Nothing out there but bunnies that don't let you catch them."

She glanced toward the back door, then back at her dog, more curious now than concerned. "I'll go out with you, okay?"

Colt's eyes were wide and glassy. He didn't move.

Grace grunted as she bent over, easing him up in her arms—heavier than she remembered, but she managed. "You're going on a diet," she muttered, hobbling toward the door.

Her fingers closed around the doorknob.

It turned easily.

Too easily.

The door creaked open an inch.

It was already opened.

She froze.

In her arms, Colt squirmed violently, kicked free, and bolted up the stairs in a blur of fur and claws, barking frantically all the way.

Grace stood in the kitchen doorway, staring at the gap between her and the night.

"What the hell?" She wondered if she had forgotten to close the door behind her when she let Colt out earlier in the evening.

She reached out, flicked on the porch light.

The yellow glow blinked to life. Just enough light to reveal the chaos.

Her garbage and recycling bins lay overturned, their contents spewed across the yard like entrails. Soggy paper, plastic bottles, and food scraps glinted under the porch light.

"Goddamn raccoons!" she barked, reaching for the snow shovel propped by the door.

She marched onto the porch, the cold biting at her ankles beneath the robe.

"What did you little bastards get into now?"

The smell hit her before she made it halfway to the bins.

Rank. Oily. Heavy with rot. She gagged, pressing a hand to her face.

She banged the shovel against the bin lid. The clang echoed through the yard like a warning shot.

"Get outta here! Get!"

Silence.

Then from the darkness near the front of the house came a low growl. Deep. Resonant. Not canine. Not anything she'd ever heard before.

Her breath caught. Her eyes locked onto the source of the sound...

Movement.

A towering shape burst from the shadows. Massive legs. A powerful torso. It swept past her in a blur of impossible speed, clearing her backyard fence in a single, inhuman leap.

Grace dropped the shovel.

Her scream cut through the night.

She spun on her heels, nearly tripping over her robe, and bolted inside.

SLAM.

The deadbolt clicked home.

Deputy Grimes knocked firmly, the polished toes of his boots glinting in the porch light. From within, Colt barked, high-pitched and frantic.

"Grace?" Grimes called. "It's Deputy Grimes. Can you open the door, please?"

He stepped back, unhooked his Maglite, and swept it across the yard. Shadows leaned long from the trees at the edge of the property. Wind rustled the hedges.

KNOCK. KNOCK.

"Grace, I got a call there was a disturbance. You okay in there?"

Click. The deadbolt shifted. The door opened just an inch, chain lock taut.

Grace peered out, her expression wary.

"I asked for Sheriff Baker," she said flatly.

"Sheriff sent me," Grimes replied. "I'm Deputy Grimes. Just here to check on you."

She squinted at him.

"How old are you?"

"Twenty-four, ma'am."

"How long you been a deputy?"

Grimes exhaled slowly. "Long enough. Can you tell me what happened?"

There was a pause. Then she closed the door, unlatched the chain, and pulled it open.

"Come in."

Grimes stepped into the living room, removing his hat. Colt rushed to greet him, tail wagging like mad, eyes still wide with residual panic.

The house smelled faintly of tea and wood polish. The furniture was plush and old. A push-button phone sat on an end table beside a library of VHS tapes and a CRT television. The past lingered here in analog silence.

From the kitchen came the clinking of a spoon against porcelain.

"One second, dear," Grace called. "Finishing my tea. Take a seat."

Grimes sat on the edge of the couch, notebook open, pen poised.

Grace shuffled in a moment later, Colt on her heels. She settled into a recliner, blanket back across her lap like a shield.

"So," Grimes asked. "What happened tonight?"

Grace recounted it all - Colt's panic, the open door, the trash, the smell, the size of the thing, the way it moved.

"There you have it," she said at last, lips pursed. "A Bigfoot. In my yard."

Grimes paused, tapping the notebook with his pen.

"A Bigfoot. I see. Mind showing me where it all happened?"

Grace stood, folding the blanket and returning it to the wicker basket next to the recliner, "Of course."

Grace led him out back. Colt whined but didn't follow. Grimes swept the yard with his flashlight. The beam caught large, wide tracks in the dirt.

He followed them to the fence line, knelt down, shone the light into the woods beyond. Something about the depth, the stride, was wrong. Too long. Too deliberate.

His gut twisted.

He walked back slowly.

"The sheriff and I dealt with a similar situation earlier today," he said. "Big bear, real aggressive. Comfortable in people's yards. These prints? Same as the ones it left behind."

Grace stared at him. "A bear? Bullshit! That weren't no damn bear."

"Bears walk on their hind legs all the time, Grace. It's easy to misinterpret it in the dark, especially when you're startled," Grimes replied.

"I know what I saw. The sheriff would believe me." Grace folded her arms across her chest defiantly, dismissing the deputy's assessment of the situation.

Grimes kept his face calm. "I'll take photos of the tracks. I'll review everything with the sheriff tomorrow. I promise."

"I don't see you writing that in your notebook," said Grace, subtly nodding her head towards Deputy Grimes.

He held the notebook just out of her view, then scribbled

hastily. "There. 'Grace states what she encountered was not a bear.'"

"Not good enough," she snapped. "It was a Bigfoot. Write that down."

Grimes sighed. "Yes, ma'am."

He wrote it verbatim.

Satisfied, Grace nodded and turned toward the house.

In the dim glow of the patrol car's dashboard, Grimes flipped back through his notes. His eyes lingered on the words he'd written. He didn't realize he was grinding his teeth.

"Sheriff, you there?"

Static. Then: "Whatcha got, Deputy?"

Grimes stared out at the woods beyond the driveway. Cold sweat crawled down the back of his neck.

"We've got a problem, sir."

A pause.

"How big of a problem?"

Grimes's voice was quiet. Tight.

"About seven and a half feet tall."

CHAPTER 7: HOUSE CALL

The next morning. Sheriff Baker rapped his nightstick against the front door of Mike's house—two quick, heavy knocks, louder than necessary.

He exhaled through his nose, jaw tight. Beside him, Deputy Grimes stood with his hands in his jacket pockets, silent.

The door swung open.

Vikram leaned in the frame, arms crossed, his smile all teeth and challenge. “Well, well, well. Top of the morning, fellas. Here to coerce me into signing more paperwork or are you here to tie up loose ends by un-aliving me and Mike?”

Baker’s face was granite. “Neither. But we need to talk.”

“We already did,” Vikram said, eyes narrowed. “It was a bear. Remember?”

Baker sighed. Grimes stepped forward with a lighter tone.

“Hey, Vik. I know our last conversation wasn’t great. But we need to ask a few more questions about your...encounter.”

“Questions?” Vikram raised an eyebrow. “We’ve answered plenty. Or rather, you answered for us.”

Behind him, Mike appeared in the hallway, leaning on his crutches.

“Let ’em in, Vik.”

Vikram turned, stunned. “What? Why?”

"To see what these questions are all about."

After a beat, Vikram stepped back and opened the door wider. "I should charge you a king-sized chocolate Payday as a toll."

The foursome made their way into the small, cramped kitchen. Mike eased into his seat at the table, his crutches propped within reach. Vikram stood by the sink, arms folded. Baker hovered awkwardly before pulling out a chair. Grimes remained standing, his notebook ready.

Mike said, motioning towards the garage door. "Grimey, I can get you a folding chair from the garage if you like."

"I'm good, Mike. Thanks."

Mike looked between them. "So... what's this about?"

Baker sat forward, resting his elbows on the table. "Not gonna beat around the shrubbery. There've been a few...bear encounters in town. James Reed's coop got wrecked. Grace had her garbage bins upended last night."

Mike and Vikram exchanged looks.

The sheriff continued, "James, and now Grace, described a large, bipedal creature. Smelled like skunk." He let it hang. "Sound familiar?"

Vikram's brow tightened. He looked at the floor, then up again. "Sure. But what's that got to do with us?"

"You boys fought him on his turf," Baker said. "Now he's here. And that's not normal. Not by a long shot. This situation is beyond my job description."

Vikram scoffed. "That's rich, Sheriff. You're the authority around here until the shit gets weird. Don't you and the other local yokels have a secret pact to deal with Bigfoot if he comes knocking? Or are you all talk and a badge?"

Sheriff Baker glared at Vikram, visibly struggling to maintain his composure. He inhaled deeply, his patience rapidly deteriorating. "We've got protocols for *out there*. We don't have a damn playbook for this happening *in town*. It showing up on the edge of town is out of scope of our current protocols."

Vikram laughed sarcastically. "What, you're a program manager now, Sheriff? This situation falls out of scope of your protocols? Where's the tough guy that showed up in my hospital room? Just admit you don't know what you're doing and leave me and Mike out of this!"

Baker shot to his feet, boots scraping tile. His fingers hovered near his belt—not on his gun, but close enough to send a message.

Vikram didn't flinch. "You want to fight me now?" he said, smirking.

Grimes moved fast, stepping between them. "Sheriff..."

Baker didn't respond. He stared Vikram down for a long second, then stepped back.

"Watch your goddamn mouth," Baker muttered.

Vikram didn't move. Just folded his arms and smiled like someone who'd already won.

Grimes stayed planted between them. "Are you two about done fucking around?"

Silence. Even Baker blinked.

Grimes let it settle before turning to Mike. "What can you tell us? Anything useful to help stop this from getting worse?"

Mike nodded. "I'll answer your questions." He looked at Vikram. "You done?"

Vikram exhaled. "Yeah. I'll cooperate. Sorry, Sheriff. Couldn't resist."

Baker rubbed a hand over his face. "Any information you can provide would be appreciated."

"It can be hurt," Vikram said. "Fast as hell. Strong. Super accurate when flinging rocks. He's basically a big, hairy Josh Allen."

Mike leaned forward. "We were lucky, Sheriff."

"Lucky how?" Baker asked.

"I got a few shots in. It slowed him. Tight quarters levelled the playing field. Couldn't use its size in the old growth. Vik's spear helped. Made it a fight. If it had caught us in open space, we wouldn't be here today. Full stop."

"We also went on offense," Vikram added. "Not sure that worked, though. It still beat our asses."

Grimes scribbled in his notebook. "Any weaknesses?"

"It didn't like bullets. Or spears. Or cars," Vikram offered.

Mike nodded. "It's flesh and blood. Not invincible. But smart. It was herding us, cutting off escape routes, driving us where it wanted. Vikram's idea to go after it flipped the script. It's an ambush predator, as much as something that big can be. Going after it gave us the opportunity to get back to the road. But that was open space, and you can see how that worked out for me."

A heavy silence hung in the room for several beats.

"Where were these new sightings?" Mike asked, breaking the quiet.

"Cook Road," Baker replied. "No more than half a mile apart."

"Close to the foothills," Mike muttered.

"Appears that way...for now," Baker agreed.

Vikram tilted his head. "Why leave a safe zone just to raid garbage? There's plenty of food for it out there in the woods."

"That's what's bothering me too," Mike said.

"We've got a busted coop and a few trash cans," Baker said, guarded. "This could still be an actual bear. Both witnesses were under heavy duress. Their stories have to be taken with a huge grain of salt."

"I'm leaning towards bear too," Grimes said, but it sounded more like hope than belief.

Vikram and Mike exchanged a glance, not doubt, just quiet agreement that something wasn't adding up.

Then Vikram spoke, "Guys...I know I'm on thin ice with both of you, but come on, it's not a bear."

Sheriff Baker shifted on his feet, visibly uncomfortable. "You're probably right, Vik. But until it's confirmed to not be a bear, that's what I'm going with."

Baker's radio chirped to life, breaking the silence.

"This is Baker."

DISPATCH:

"911 call. Two missing campers near Pine Lake. Car found at dispersed campsite car lot. SAR en route. They're asking for you."

Baker stood. "Roger that. On my way."

He clipped the radio back to his shoulder, turned to Mike and Vikram.

"Missing campers. Thanks for your time. We'll be in touch."

Vikram walked them to the door. He watched the SUV back out, taillights glowing red before vanishing down the road.

He returned to the kitchen.

Mike looked up at him. "What do you think, kid?"

Vikram walked to the sink, leaned forward, stared out the window. The Cascade foothills stood silhouetted in the distance, dark and patient.

"I don't know," he said. "I just hope this is a real bear situation... and not a 'bear' situation."

Mike nodded slowly. "I'm gonna lie down for a bit. Head's killing me."

"Dizzy? Lightheaded? Should I call the nurse?"

"Nah. Just a headache."

Vikram gave a small nod. "Alright. Let me know if it gets worse."

"You bet." Mike crutched his way toward the hallway.

Vikram called after him.

"Mike?"

Mike stopped.

"What if it's here looking for us?"

Mike smirked over his shoulder. "It doesn't have my address, Vik."

The door to his room shut behind him.

Vikram stood alone at the kitchen window.

The morning light had begun to break, soft and gray, filtering through the trees.

But the foothills in the distance still loomed quiet, unmoving, and full of secrets.

CHAPTER 8: STAND DOWN

The gravel popped beneath the Ford Explorer's tires as Sheriff Baker pulled into the overflow parking lot, a weathered wooden sign creaking slightly in the breeze:

OVERFLOW PARKING / DISPERSED CAMPING AHEAD.

Parked nearby was a dusty Search and Rescue truck, its side panel emblazoned with the SAR logo. Wade Coombs, broad-shouldered and sunburned, leaned against its hood, flanked by Deanna Moore, lithe, sharp-eyed, and visibly impatient.

"We've gotta stop meeting like this, fellas," Wade said, offering a hand as Baker stepped out of the Explorer.

Deputy Grimes climbed out behind him and immediately found his attention snared by Deanna. Their handshake lingered just a second too long.

"You gonna give me my hand back, Deputy?" she teased.

Grimes cleared his throat, flushing. "Yes, sorry. Of course."

Sheriff Baker shook his head, suppressing a smirk. "No dogs today?"

"They're over at Icicle Creek Canyon tracking some lost climbers," Deanna said.

The sheriff frowned. "Got it. What do we know here?"

Wade led them over to the trail map mounted on a faded kiosk. "Couple named Travis and Erin. Checked in three nights ago. Erin's mom reported them missing when they didn't come back this morning. Had a set return time to make an appointment."

Grimes folded his arms. "Sure they didn't just extend the trip? Weather's been decent minus the rain two nights ago."

Wade shook his head no, "Mother was adamant. Said her daughter doesn't miss appointments."

Sheriff Baker squinted at the map. "They say where they were headed?"

"Sort of," Deanna said. "Their car's parked a couple miles up, near the dispersed camping trailhead. Likely went in from there."

"So why'd you two wait for us down here?" Baker asked.

"Given the recent 'bear' activity," Wade said, choosing his words carefully, "figured you'd want in on the ground floor."

Grimes drifted toward the road, staring into the tree-lined slope that crept into the misty foothills.

"You good, Deputy?" Deanna called, arching an eyebrow.

Grimes nudged a sprout of fireweed with his boot. "Yeah. Let's go find them."

At the remote parking area, a faded silver Saab sat locked and undisturbed. Rain-splattered dust clung to its windshield. Baker tugged at the handle. Locked. He circled to the rear hatch. Also locked.

Grimes peered inside through the passenger window. "No forced entry. Nothing broken. Guess they took off on foot up into the foothills"

"Downhill trail follows a creek," Baker noted. "Why not camp near the water?"

"Against the rules," Deanna replied. "No dispersed camping within a quarter mile of water."

She tapped the back window, covered in eco-conscious bumper

stickers. “They’re rule followers.”

Wade tossed Deanna a backpack and strapped another over his shoulders. “Bear sprays in both. Sheriff, need any? Grimes?”

Sheriff Baker patted his holstered sidearm. “Brought my own.”

The deputy glanced down at his own sidearm, "Same."

“Alright then,” Wade said. "Let's get going."

They hit the trail that led them up into the hills.

The campground clearing was eerily still. A cheap tent slumped awkwardly to one side. Camp chairs sat undisturbed beside a cold firepit. A few plastic plates were scattered around the perimeter, their placement odd. Flung, not dropped.

Deanna poked the firepit with a long stick. “Haven’t had a fire in at least a day. Cold ash.”

Grimes approached the tent, pausing just outside the entrance. He gave the nylon fabric a light tap with his nightstick.

“Sheriff’s Department,” he called out. “If you’re in there, I’m unzipping the tent.”

No response. No movement.

He waited a beat, then rapped again—firmer this time.

“Sheriff’s Department. Coming in.”

Still nothing.

Grimes crouched and slowly unzipped the flap. “Sleeping bags are still rolled,” he said, scanning the interior. “Backpacks haven’t been touched. They never stayed here. Or they are out on a hike and left their tent seriously squared away.”

Baker spotted the tent’s instruction manual crumpled in the dirt and picked it up, flipping through the pages with a scowl. “Jesus,” he muttered, squinting at the diagrams. “It’s a miracle they got this thing standing. These instructions are garbage.”

A few feet away, Wade crouched near the fire ring, holding a red plastic plate up to the light. A dried smear of mud stretched across the surface, vaguely palm-shaped, but off. Too broad.

"You're gonna want to see this," he called.

Baker stepped over and examined the plate. His eyes narrowed. "Could be the guy's. Big hands."

"Too big," Wade muttered.

Baker didn't bite, "Still to be determined."

"Guys?" Deanna's voice drew them back to the firepit. She pointed with the toe of her boot to a scatter of dark, tacky droplets smeared across a flat rock. "Is that...blood?"

Sheriff Baker squatted down to get a closer look and removed a pair of latex gloves from his pockets, wriggled them onto his hands, and then gently touched one of the smaller stains. Still tacky. He lifted his gloved finger, examined it. His face tightened as he lowered his head. "Yeah. More in the grass. Hit this place with UV and it'll glow"

Grimes stepped back, unsettled. "What's our next move here, Sheriff?"

Baker stood, face unreadable. "Tape off the area. 100-foot perimeter. Tag the car, too. Bag the plates, utensils, everything in the tent. Grimes, block off the fire pit, mark anything else that seems out of place. Wade, anything jump out at you about this campsite?"

Wade squinted his eyes towards an area of tall grass. He moved closer, examining the ground as he walks. He stopped and took a knee and places his hand next to a large impression in the soft ground. Stalks of tall grass have been compressed deeply into the mud. He stands, carefully steps around the impression and finds another matching print a few yards ahead. He straightens, stares into the dense woods. Wade then turns towards the Sheriff, "Yeah Sheriff, we seem to have ourselves a bear problem."

The team finished their grim work at the campsite and regrouped near the trailhead, where Travis and Erin's Saab sat quietly beneath the trees. Deputy Grimes moved with mechanical focus, stringing yellow crime scene tape around the vehicle. Orange cones marked out a rough perimeter, bright against the dirt and pine needles.

Deanna sat sideways in the open passenger door of the SAR truck, legs swinging gently above the ground. Her gaze was distant, fixed somewhere beyond the tree line.

Sheriff Baker stood near the edge of the trail, arms crossed, eyes on the forest. Wade Coombs stood beside him, their voices low, nearly swallowed by the hush of the woods.

"What does she know?" Baker asked quietly.

Wade shook his head. "Nothing that should worry you. She's still talking about that bear we ran into near the lake a few weeks back, the one that nearly tore the rookie's arm off."

Baker's gaze drifted upward, scanning the trees like he expected something to be watching. "Let's keep it that way, then. I don't want her involved in this." He squinted into the dense canopy, then added, more firmly, "In fact, we're not bringing SAR into this at all."

Wade turned, blinking. "Wait, what? You're saying we're handling this—just you, me, and Grimes?" He let out a short, nervous laugh. "We got lucky last time. I'm not going after this thing on its turf. It knows the terrain. It's stronger. It's faster..."

Baker smirked, a low chuckle slipping out. "*Its* turf? No, Wade. It's in *ours.* And it's the one dictating the rules right now. Mike and Vikram turned the tide when they went after it. Maybe it's time we do the same."

Wade took a step back, hands raised. "Whoa, whoa—no. I'm out. I don't want any part of this."

But Baker closed the distance, resting a firm hand on Wade's shoulder. Gave it a squeeze. "I didn't say we're going after it. I'm calling up to the camp. They'll clean this up."

Wade's expression twisted. "You can't be serious. You're bringing in those wannabe SEAL Team Six clowns? With their M4s and laser sights? They'll tear up the forest...and they won't be quiet about it."

"It's them or us," Baker said simply. "I'm not sending a SAR team out to get shredded. And I sure as hell don't need them coming back to town with stories, especially if they find our missing campers in pieces. If they find them at all. Christ, Wade, half the SAR team can't even legally order a drink."

Wade let out a long breath. "I hear you. I'll back you. But if this goes sideways, you better have a damn good Plan B."

Baker turned, started back toward Grimes, then paused, glancing over his shoulder. "We'll see how it plays out. If it goes to hell, we deal with it then. But I'm not bringing in outsiders."

Wade stood frozen a moment longer, then gave a slow, incredulous shake of his head. "You can't protect this secret forever," he said quietly. "Someone's gonna survive. And they're gonna talk."

Baker sighed. "Pics or it didn't happen, right? Isn't that what the kids say?" He looked back at Wade. "The internet's full of Bigfoot stories. Not a single one with a clear photo. No credible video. Until that changes, I protect the forest, the town, and the secret. You with me?"

Wade didn't answer. He turned and walked toward the SAR truck, frustration bleeding through his every movement. Deanna glanced up from the open passenger door as he approached. "What was that all about?"

Wade exhaled slowly. "Just a disagreement on how to handle the bear situation."

"You two looked fired up," she said. "Don't we have standard protocols for this? Wildlife Services? Fish and Game?"

"Normally, yeah," Wade said. "But this is... different."

She narrowed her eyes. "Different how?"

Wade hesitated, then offered a clipped response. "We're standing down. Sheriff's calling in another team."

Deanna jolted upright. She stepped directly in front of him, eyes blazing.

"Stand down? Why the hell would we do that? That makes no sense! Those two missing campers could be out there right now, hurt and waiting for us to find them!"

"I get it," Wade said, keeping his voice even. "But the Sheriff wants SAR away from this one. After what happened last time, he's trying to limit exposure."

"Limit exposure, that doesn't make any sense!" she snapped. "Does he think we can't handle it?"

"It's not about us or you," Wade said, raising both hands. "You're damn good at what you do. This isn't personal."

A beat passed. Then—quietly—Wade added, "I'm driving the Sheriff back to his rig. No radio or phone reception here. He's gonna make the call."

Deanna didn't reply. She just paced alongside the truck, arms crossed, tension radiating off her in waves.

Across the clearing, Grimes finished taping off the Saab. He gave the perimeter a once-over, satisfied, and headed toward them.

Sheriff Baker approached from the trail. Deanna stepped into his path, planting herself by the passenger door, her expression sharp, unyielding. "You're pulling us from the search?" she demanded.

Baker stood firm. "I'm calling in a specialist team, predator control. I think we're dealing with a rogue grizzly or brown bear."

Deanna scoffed, "What are you talking about? This isn't grizzly territory, Sheriff. That doesn't track. Those missing campers could be out there."

The Sheriff looked directly at Deanna, firm, "There's been talk about reintroducing them to the area. Or one migrated here following an elk herd. Either way, I'm not risking someone from our team getting mauled again."

Deanna's face softens as she recalls the bear attack on her teammate on the last operation. "I don't like it. If something's out here, we should be involved. This is our backyard, it's where I trained!"

"Duly noted," the Sheriff sighed.

Deputy Grimes strolled up to the SAR truck and came to a stop beside Deanna, his hands resting on his duty belt. "What's going on?" he asked, glancing between her and the Sheriff.

Sheriff Baker pinched the bridge of his nose in frustration. "Nothing's going on. Radio's useless out here, hills are blocking the signal. I need to call in a wrecker for the Saab."

Deanna set her hands on her hips, cheeks flushed with anger. "You're leaving something out, Sheriff."

Without a word, Baker brushed past her and climbed into the truck. Grimes looked like he was about to speak, but the Sheriff cut him off with a cold, warning glare. "I'm calling in a specialty team to conduct the search," Baker said flatly. "You and Deanna tape off the trailhead. Wade and I will be back shortly." He paused, eyes narrowing. "Don't do anything stupid."

The word *stupid* landed like a slap. He looked directly at Deanna as he said it, then slammed the door hard enough to rattle the frame. The truck pulled away in a spray of gravel.

Deanna stared after it, seething. "What an ASS!"

Grimes raised his hands in a calming gesture. "Take it easy, Deanna. He's a good guy...he's just trying to do what's right."

She recoiled. "*Take it easy?* You take it easy, Grimes. He looked right at me when he said 'stupid.' *Fuck that guy.*"

Grimes looked down, then over at the taped-off Saab, then the trailhead. A muscle in his jaw twitched. He didn't say anything, just nodded toward the trees and started walking. After a beat, he motioned with his head for Deanna to follow.

She hesitated, then fell in step beside him, still fuming, but not done. Not by a long shot.

Grimes dutifully retrieved the crime scene tape from the hood of the Saab. “We still need to tape off the trailhead.”

“I’m going back to the site. Wade saw tracks, we missed something.”

Grimes moved to stop her. “Deanna, the area is sealed off. We can't go...”

“Oh no, it’s sealed off! What will we *do*?” She shoved past him without breaking stride, marching up the trail.

Grimes stood there for a moment, conflicted, weighing something unspoken. Then he sighed, muttered a curse under his breath, and followed her in.

CHAPTER 9: THE CLEARING

The interior of the Ford Explorer was quiet, save for the soft crackle of the two-way radio. Sheriff Baker leaned back in the driver's seat, eyes fixed through the windshield at Wade. He stood beside the SAR truck, one boot crossed over the other, nursing a cigarette like it might be his last. The air outside was still, the afternoon light beginning its slow descent into amber.

Sheriff Baker pressed the radio's transmit button. His voice was low, measured, but tense. "Yeah, you heard me correctly. We've got an active situation here. I need your best team to come neutralize this threat. Quietly."

The radio hissed before a clipped, confident voice replied.

"How soon?" It was Carlton Robinson, commander of the lumber camp's private security force.

Baker's gaze dropped to the floorboards of the SUV, a flicker of doubt he quickly buried. "ASAP. Like I said, active threat."

There was a pause on the other end, filled only by static. "Roger that. I'll have a three-man team up there, and I'm coming with them. Always wanted to see a 'bear' up close."

Baker didn't smile. "When can I expect you?"

"Ninety minutes. We'll need to gear up for a long night," Carlton replied, tactical and efficient.

"Roger that," Baker said, ending the transmission. He returned the receiver to its mount with a soft click, then opened the door and stepped into the gravel lot.

Wade flicked the cigarette butt into the dirt, grinding it under his heel as the sheriff approached.

“All good?” Wade asked.

“Ninety minutes,” Baker said. “They’re on their way.”

Wade smirked, rubbing the back of his neck. “It's official then, you called them in off their little compound.”

Baker didn't respond. Wade let the silence sit for a beat. Then, "Just funny, is all. You’ve spent your years as Sheriff saying you didn’t want those guys anywhere near town business. Called them a liability. Said they’d bring heat we couldn’t control."

Baker’s eyes narrowed. “We don’t have a choice this time. This thing’s not staying in its corner.”

Wade’s voice dropped, lower now. More serious. “Alright. So, what happens when this goes sideways? When they don’t come back? When they leave a bigger mess than we already got?”

Baker didn’t answer immediately. Wade continued, "I’m serious, Sheriff. You bring them in, you own what comes with it. Carlton’s not subtle. His people aren’t trained for quiet. You think this town won’t start asking questions when blacked-out SUVs roll through town with that thing mounted to the hood? What if ten more people go missing?"

Baker turned to him then, calm but firm.

“You’ve got it wrong. Carlton’s not some loose cannon, Wade. He’s former Recon. We served together. Twice. I trust him with my life.”

Wade’s expression didn’t soften.

“His team isn’t just muscle." Baker continued, "They’ve been training for this *exact threat.* Quiet approach, coordinated tracking, non-lethal options if they can manage it. They don’t go loud unless it’s the only option.”

He took a step closer, voice low. "They're not here to light up the forest. They're here to make sure no one else disappears. Trust me, they've got secrets to protect too."

Wade looked at him for a long moment, weighing the words, the risk, the history behind them. Then he exhaled and looked away, muttering, "Better hope they're as good as you say."

Baker didn't answer. His gaze drifted to the half-crushed pack of cigarettes in Wade's shirt pocket. "Thought you quit."

"I did," Wade replied. "But this bear situation got me started again."

Baker gave him a look. Not judgment, just a weary kind of understanding.

"You heading back up?" he asked.

"Yeah. I'll grab Grimes and Deanna, get 'em down before your reinforcements roll in. Hopefully she's cooled off."

Baker gave a slow nod. "I'll stay here, wait on the wrecker for the Saab."

Wade climbed into his truck and cranked the engine. As he rolled forward, he leaned out the window, flashing a tired grin. "Watch out for bears now."

The truck pulled away, kicking up a light spray of dust as it disappeared up the winding road. Sheriff Baker stood there for a long moment, alone again with the quiet rustle of trees and the weight of too many secrets pressing against the dusk.

Deanna and Grimes stepped back into the campground clearing, the woods pressing in around them. The light had shifted, it was lower now, colder. Deputy Grimes scanned the tree line with wary eyes, the unease etched plainly on his face.

Deanna moved ahead, toward the spot where Wade had stopped earlier. She crouched low, hand hovering over a wide, deep impression in the mud.

"Grimey, come check this out," she said. "I don't think these are bear tracks. They're huge."

Grimes approached slowly, eyes fixed on the ground. His apprehension deepened into visible concern. "We should go back," he muttered. "I've got a bad feeling about this." A beat passed. "And... can you not call me 'Grimey'?"

Deanna straightened, caught off guard. "Wait... I thought you liked being called 'Grimey'?"

Grimes winced. "Yeah. When I was nine."

He shifted awkwardly, trying to soften the sting in his voice. "I mean... I'm not nine anymore. I'm in law enforcement. I'm gonna be Sheriff someday. I can't have people calling me 'Grimey.'"

Deanna reached out and gently placed a hand on his arm.

"I'm sorry, Deputy Grimes," she said, the name deliberately formal. "I guess I just thought it was kind of... cute. I used to hear my brothers yelling it during your games, "Grimey, I'm open!' 'Grimey, take the shot!' It stuck."

She studied his face for a moment. Her smile softened, touching the laugh lines at the corners of her eyes. "You're not a high school kid anymore."

Grimes flushed, cleared his throat, and looked away. She pulled her hand back, the moment settling between them like dust.

"We should head back," he said, voice quieter now. "Sheriff's gonna be pissed we're up here."

Her expression shifted, still playful, but edged with determination.

"I want to follow these tracks a bit," she said. "Then we'll go."

"Why?", asked Grimes, "I don't think that's a great idea."

"C'mon," she coaxed. "Let's just see how far they lead into the trees. Then we turn around. Promise."

Without waiting, Deanna moved forward, tracing the faint path into the underbrush. Grimes hesitated, then sighed and followed reluctantly, but unwilling to let her go alone.

Deanna and Deputy Grimes moved cautiously through the forest, the hush of the trees wrapping around them like a veil. Deanna kept her eyes on the ground, tracking. Grimes followed close behind, his right hand resting on the grip of his holstered Sig Sauer, eyes sweeping the tree line with quiet tension.

She halted suddenly, crouching low. "There," she said, pointing.

Partially hidden in the underbrush was a collapsible wash basin, dirt-smudged and out of place. Deanna knelt to reach for it.

"Hey," Grimes said sharply. "Don't touch that. It's evidence. This whole area's part of the crime scene now."

She pulled her hand back and stood, brushing her fingers against her pants. Her eyes scanned the forest floor again, thoughtful. "I don't see any more plates..." she murmured, her voice trailing off. Then,"...utensils. Over there."

Scattered among the pine needles and fallen leaves were plastic forks and knives, some snapped, others buried halfway in the soil.

A beat passed.

"And can I just call you by your first name?" she asked, glancing back. "Saying 'Grimes' makes me want to add the *ey*."

Grimes exhaled a quiet laugh. "First name's fine. Just don't touch anything we find out here."

"Got it, *Patrick*," she said with a grin.

He tried not to smile, but failed. The sound of his own name from her mouth hit different, more intimate somehow.

He stepped carefully around the basin and the utensils, scanning the area again. Ahead, Deanna had already started moving farther up the trail.

"Now where are you going?" he called.

"Just a little further," she replied over her shoulder. "Looking for anything that might tell us what happened or where they are."

Grimes glanced back toward the main trail and then followed her, deeper into the woods.

The trees grew thicker as they pressed deeper into the forest, branches knitting overhead and casting long, skeletal shadows across the mossy ground. The late light barely filtered through now, just a dusky glow trapped in the canopy.

"Nothing else out here," Deputy Grimes said, voice tight. "Let's head back."

Deanna didn't stop. She gestured ahead, eyes locked on the thinning tree line in the distance.

"Just a little further. Looks like there's a clearing up ahead."

Grimes sighed and followed.

They walked another ten meters in silence.

Then Grimes slowed, nostrils flaring. "Do you smell that?"

Deanna sniffed the air, nose wrinkling. "Sulfur...and..." she hesitated, "...rancid deli meat."

"That can't be good," Grimes muttered.

He grabbed his radio, brought it to his mouth. Static. He adjusted the dial, tried again. Nothing. Just a dry, broken hiss.

Somewhere to the right, something moved, low to the ground, heavy. Deanna stopped cold.

"What was that?" she whispered.

SNAP.

Branches cracked. Grimes moved instinctively, stepping in front of her, hand on his holstered pistol.

"Stay behind me," he said, voice low, steady.

CRACK.

Another snap. This time behind them.

Then left.

Then right.

The forest closed in. Every sound echoed louder, sharper. They were surrounded.

Grimes drew his weapon, sweat forming on his brow. His eyes swept the dense brush, but he saw only flickers of shadow.

Deanna stayed close, one hand gripping the back of his jacket.

A low growl rumbled through the trees, deep, guttural, wrong. It didn't sound like a bear. It didn't sound like anything that belonged in these woods.

Then chaos.

The forest exploded in motion. Branches whipped and bent, something massive circling them at speed, too fast to track. Leaves churned. Bark shredded off trees.

Panic overtook Deanna. She bolted.

"Deanna!" Grimes shouted, spinning after her.

She screamed - piercing, terrified, lost in the trees.

"Deanna!" he yelled again, voice cracking. "*Deanna, where are you?!*"

Another scream.

"*Patrick!!*" Her voice rang out desperately, fading. "*Patrick!!!*"

Grimes tore through the underbrush, chasing her voice, crashing toward the clearing. Heart pounding. Pulse roaring.

And from all around him, the forest roared back.

Grimes found her at the edge of the clearing, frozen mid-scream.

Deanna stood motionless, eyes wide, arms limp at her sides. In front of her, Travis and Erin's corpses lay grotesquely staged, ritualistic and obscene. Their heads had been placed in a cradle of alder branches, twisted together like a crude crown. Blood streaked the bark. Shredded clothing hung like flags, soaked in rot and gore.

Travis's ribcage was crushed inward, ribs snapped and bent like broken fence posts. Both bodies were half-eaten, bloated, decomposing in the humid, stagnant air.

Grimes froze, the sight knocking the breath from his lungs.

Deanna trembled, her skin ghostly pale, pupils blown wide. She was locked in place, paralyzed by whatever her brain could no longer process.

"Deanna!" Grimes shouted. "We have to go!"

SNAP. A branch broke nearby.

The air turned. Thick. Rancid.

Grimes recoiled at the stench. He stepped to Deanna, grabbed her by the shoulders. She was ice-cold, unblinking.

"Deanna!" he barked. "Snap out of it!"

But she didn't move. Didn't blink. Just stood there moaning, a hollow sound caught in the back of her throat. Her eyes were glassy now, staring through the scene in front of her as if reality had come undone.

The creature emerged.

From the shadows beyond the bodies, it stepped forward.

It was massive. Over seven feet tall, shoulders hunched and bulging beneath matted black fur. Its head was conical, eyes burning orange like coals in a fire. A mouth split open in a grin—wide, unnatural, lined with jagged yellow teeth.

The smell hit like a punch: wet earth, blood, rotting meat, and something...primal, ancient.

The thing growled low and slow, almost mockingly. A sound full of menace and intelligence.

Grimes stepped between it and Deanna, raising his sidearm.

The creature stopped, eyes locking onto the weapon. Something flickered in that gaze. Recognition. Or curiosity.

Grimes fired.

Three quick shots. The report of the pistol shattered the stillness.

The bullets hit, one in the forearm, another in the shoulder, a third square in the torso.

The beast staggered, howling a choking, nightmarish scream that echoed across the trees, it crashed backward into the forest; branches snapping under its retreat.

Silence. Smoke curled from the muzzle of Grimes's pistol.

Deanna didn't move.

He rushed to her, dropping to one knee. "Deanna," he whispered, gently shaking her shoulder. Nothing.

No time.

He hoisted her over his back in a fireman's carry and rose with effort, staggering at first, then finding his footing. He didn't look back. He couldn't.

He carried her into the trees, away from the clearing, away from the crown of branches and the carnage beneath it.

Into the shadows. Into the silence.

CHAPTER 10: AFTERMATH

Wade's truck rumbled to a stop beside the abandoned Saab. The tires crunched over loose gravel as he threw it into park, eyes scanning the immediate area.

No sign of Deanna. No sign of Grimes.

The place was still, unnervingly so.

He killed the engine. Silence swallowed the cab, broken only by the ticking of the cooling motor. Wade grabbed the radio off the dash and brought it to his mouth.

"Grimes? Deanna? You copy?"

He released the button. Nothing. Just dead air and the faint hiss of static. He adjusted the frequency and tried again, louder this time.

"Grimes, Moore…this is Wade. Respond."

Still nothing.

Wade lowered the radio and stared at the trailhead. The crime scene tape fluttered in the breeze, but the trail itself was undisturbed. No movement. No voices. No footprints visible from here, but he knew.

They'd gone up.

He cursed under his breath, dropped the radio on the passenger seat, and climbed out of the truck. He took a few steps toward the trees, then stopped, heart beginning to hammer in his chest. The light was falling fast. Shadows lengthened across the forest floor like reaching fingers.

This wasn't just a protocol breach, this was a risk.

He spun back to the truck, slammed the door shut behind him, and fired the engine. The tires kicked up dust as he reversed, he then gunned it down the road the way he came, back toward the Sheriff.

He needed backup. And fast.

Sheriff Baker stood near his Explorer at the edge of the gravel lot, arms crossed, eyes fixed on the tree line as the late-day sun filtered through the pines.

Wade's truck tore into the parking area, tires spitting up dust and stone as it skidded to a stop just feet away.

Baker turned, already sensing something was wrong.

Wade threw open the driver's side window, his face flushed and tight.

"Sheriff! We gotta move! Grimes and Deanna weren't at the trailhead. I think they went up to the campsite."

Baker didn't hesitate. He yanked open the passenger door and climbed in.

"Sweet Jesus."

The moment the door slammed shut, Wade shifted into drive. The truck shot forward, back wheels kicking out as they tore onto the winding gravel road.

"You don't think that bear got 'em, do you?" Wade asked, gripping the wheel hard enough to whiten his knuckles.

Baker stared straight ahead, "Not if they stayed put. But if they went poking around that site..." He slammed his palm against the dashboard in frustration.

They hit a bend too fast; the rear tires slid dangerously close to the ditch before Wade corrected.

"Damn it," Baker muttered. "I shouldn't have left them. Grimes is sweet on Deanna, he'd follow her straight into hell if it meant looking brave."

"He's a good kid," Wade said. "He can handle himself."

Baker shot him a look. "Wade, the kid's never fired his weapon outside the range. Never even written a damn speeding ticket. You think he's ready for what's out there?"

The truck skidded to a stop beside the empty Saab, gravel spraying from beneath the tires. Baker and Wade jumped out, eyes scanning the clearing.

"They're not here," Wade said, grim. "They must've gone up."

Baker's gaze swept the trailhead, a muscle twitched in his cheek. "You bring a gun?"

Wade hesitated. "I've got a not-quite-legal sawed-off in the toolbox."

"Perfect," Baker muttered. "Grab it. We'll talk legality later."

Wade popped the latch and yanked open the truck bed. In seconds, he was armed. Without another word, they broke into a run, boots pounding against packed dirt as they disappeared up the trail.

They stumbled into the clearing, bent over, gasping. Wade was drenched in sweat, one hand on his knee.

"Jesus Christ," he gasped. "I really gotta quit smoking."

Baker straightened, both hands on his hips. "I gotta quit aging."

Gunshots. Distant. Three sharp cracks.

They froze.

Baker's revolver was in his hand in an instant. Wade racked a round into the sawed-off, the metallic *click-clack* loud in the quiet clearing. They exchanged a glance. And then they moved.

They sprinted through the trees, brush scraping at their legs, low branches whipping past. The Sheriff ran like a man half his age, adrenaline burning through the stiffness in his joints. Wade trailed behind, breath ragged.

"Sheriff! Wait up!" he called out, wheezing.

Baker stopped, spun around. "Suck it up, Wade! Jesus!"

Wade doubled over, hands on his thighs. "I don't jog for fun, alright? I drink! I smoke! I hang out at the *fucking bar!*"

Baker looked like he was about to curse again but froze.

Rustling. From the trees.

Both men raised their weapons in unison, feet planted, eyes locked on the shadows.

A shape staggered toward them.

Deputy Grimes burst through the underbrush, Deanna slung across his shoulders, blood streaked down his cheek, his eyes wild but clear.

Baker rushed forward. "Is she hurt? Are *you* hurt? We heard shots..."

Grimes didn't stop moving.

"She's in shock. I'm fine. We found the campers." He met Baker's eyes. "What's left of them. And the bear. That's what you heard."

Wade reached out. "Here kid, let me take her."

Grimes shifted Deanna's weight higher on his shoulder. "No. I got her into this. I'll get her out."

And without waiting for a response, he pushed past them - bloodied, battered, but resolute -disappearing into the trees as Baker and Wade fell in behind him.

The Ford Explorer sat idle beneath the shadowed trees. Outside, Wade's truck rumbled away in a spray of diesel, dust and gravel, Deanna unconscious in the back seat.

Sheriff Baker sat behind the wheel, his hands clenched into

fists atop his knees. His jaw twitched, teeth grinding.

He turned toward Grimes.

"What the fuck were you thinking going up there?" His voice was low, deadly. "I told you two not to do something stupid and that's exactly what you did."

Grimes sat in the passenger seat, hunched forward, eyes fixed on his lap. His cheeks were streaked with silent tears.

"Crying's not gonna fix it," Baker snapped. "You could've gotten yourself hurt. Got Deanna killed."

Grimes rubbed his thumbs together, knuckles white.

"She thought you were hiding something," he said quietly. "She just wanted to make sure we didn't miss anything."

Baker's face twisted with rage. He slammed the heel of his hand against the steering wheel with a sharp *thud.*

"You're goddamn right I was hiding something!" he shouted. "She didn't know what was out there. You did. That was your chance to lead, Deputy and you followed her like a puppy."

Grimes sat up straighter, voice trembling but earnest. "Is she going to be okay?"

Baker stared at him, the anger draining slowly from his eyes. He let out a long breath and rubbed the back of his neck.

"I don't know," he said. "She was damn near catatonic. Wade's taking her to the same hospital we took Mike and Vik to. We'll see."

Grimes swallowed hard. "Can we go see her?"

Baker blinked, stunned. "Now? Are you fucking kidding me?"

He reached for his revolver, checked the cylinder, snapped it shut with a flick of his wrist. "I've got Carlton and his team showing up any minute. That and the goddamn wrecker for the Saab. This is now a body extraction and bear eradication job. *You're* gonna brief them. Fully."

Through the windshield, a blacked-out GMC SUV rolled into

view, tires crunching on loose gravel.

"Did you hit it?" Baker asked.

Grimes wiped his eyes with the back of his hand, gaze distant. "Yeah. But this nine mil might as well have been a BB gun. I don't think I hurt it. Just pissed it off."

Baker nodded grimly. "This crew will have heavier gear. They know what 'bear' means. You give them everything...description, location, behavior. All of it."

Grimes reached for the door handle. Baker stopped him with one last look.

"What you did was incredibly reckless," the sheriff said, voice low. "And now she knows what we mean when we say 'bear.' That's on you. We'll deal with that when she recovers."

Grimes hesitated. "She was gonna go up there no matter what I said, Sheriff. I couldn't stop her."

Baker shook his head slowly, the fury replaced by something heavier — disappointment, patience worn thin. "Couldn't stop her?" he echoed. "Let me tell you something, Deputy. If you're ever gonna make it in this job, you've gotta understand one thing and that's *you* are the law. That badge means something. You wear it, you back it up. Even if you've got a fucking crush. Am I clear?"

Grimes nodded. "Crystal, sir."

"Good. Now get the hell out of my car and go brief Carlton and his team."

Grimes stepped out, shutting the door behind him with a quiet *click*.

Baker watched his deputy walk toward the approaching SUV - slightly hunched, shoulders tight - and exhaled a long, bitter breath.

"What a friggin' mess."

He pulled his hat off the dashboard, placed it on his head, and stepped out of the vehicle to meet the team.

CHAPTER 11: THE C-TEAM

The blacked-out GMC Yukon came to a stop with practiced ease. Doors opened in sync, and four figures emerged in matching olive-drab tactical gear. Their boots were spotless. Rifles slung tight. Movements crisp.

Carlton Robinson stepped out first.

A Black man in his mid-fifties, he carried himself with the quiet authority of someone who had spent decades in command. Fit and broad-shouldered, he looked like he'd been lifted straight from a recruiting poster. His posture was ramrod straight, his close-cropped salt-and-pepper hair framing a strong face carved in resolute lines. Hawkish eyes scanned the treeline. Even his GoRuck boots seemed to land without a sound. Military bearing at its finest.

Behind him, his team filed out with silent discipline and precision.

Sergio Lara, wiry and sharp-eyed, barely older than a recruit but moving like he'd done this a hundred times.

Nicks, early thirties, short black pixie cut peeking out from under her helmet. Calm, no-nonsense, second-in-command stamped on her presence.

Madden, a slab of tactical meat and muscle, buzzcut flat-top, the kind of guy who looked like he bench-pressed two of his teammates for warm-up.

Deputy Grimes stood waiting by the trailhead. He swallowed hard, adjusted his stance, and stepped forward with forced confidence.

"You Carlton?" he asked.

Carlton gave him a quick once-over, not unkind, just efficient. He extended his hand.

"Yep. Carlton. This is Lara, Madden, and Nicks."

Grimes nodded at each as they shook hands. "Deputy Grimes. I had the, uh... recent Bigfoot encounter."

Carlton raised his brows with a theatrical gasp, hands flying to his chest.

"A Bigfoot encounter? What the?!? I thought we were here to track down a rogue bear!" he said, voice dripping with exaggerated surprise.

The team chuckled. Grimes flushed.

A beat of silence stretched awkwardly.

From behind him, Sheriff Baker's footsteps approached.

"He's just messing with you, Deputy," the Sheriff said, voice dry. "Carlton, good seeing you."

The men shook hands. Grimes exhaled silently, grateful for the save.

"Sheriff," Carlton said, then turned back to Grimes. "Alright, Deputy. Give me the what, where, and when."

Grimes squared his shoulders. "We tracked it to a clearing about 800 meters northeast of the campsite. Found the campers. What's left of them."

Carlton's smile faded. "Go on."

"There were signs it might be a den. Heads were...displayed. Like a warning. The area was tight. Maybe twelve to fifteen feet across. Thick cover. Bones everywhere."

Carlton gave a nod, impressed. "Lara, you getting this? This is how you brief. Succinct. Detailed."

Lara nodded. "Roger that, sir."

"Anything else, Deputy?" Carlton asked.

"I hit it. More than once. Nine mil. Didn't do much."

"We brought appropriate gear," Carlton said, patting the side of his vest. "Thanks."

A diesel engine rumbled up the road—the tow truck. Sheriff Baker stepped away to intercept it.

Carlton turned to Grimes again. "You said 'we' during the debrief. Sheriff with you?"

Grimes shook his head. "No. The other person's getting medical treatment."

"Seriously injured?" Carlton asked.

The deputy shook his head, "Shock. No physical wounds."

"Understood." Carlton nodded and turned to his team.

Grimes took that as his cue to step away. He jogged down toward the Sheriff and the arriving tow truck, grateful to be dismissed.

Nicks adjusted the sling on her rifle. "What's the play, sir?"

"Line formation," Carlton said. "Nicks, take point. Madden, rear security. We maintain sound discipline. Listen for tree knocks, heavy steps, anything unusual."

Madden cracked his knuckles, casually. "We bringing the deputy?"

Carlton glanced after Grimes. "Negative. He's seen enough for the day."

"So..." Lara hesitated. "Ambush this thing?"

Carlton locked and loaded his weapon, the *clack* of the bolt echoing sharp and final.

"Nope," he said. "It's already gonna know we're coming. Be ready to fight."

The team checked gear, toggled safeties, and fell into silent readiness. The air had changed, it felt thicker now. Charged. They moved forward as one.

The campsite was quiet. Still.

Carlton ducked beneath the yellow crime scene tape, his boots moving softly on the damp pine needles. He swept his eyes across the ragged campsite, taking in the sagging tent, the disturbed fire pit, and the pile of evidence bags like a man sizing up a chessboard mid-match.

The air was tinged with the faint odor of burnt wood and something more primal, blood and rot clinging stubbornly to the underbrush.

Behind him, his team fanned out with tactical precision.

Lara, light on his feet and alert, veered into a patch of tall grass near the rear of the campsite. He crouched low, studying the flattened blades with a finger extended.

Carlton turned his head slightly. “Whatcha got there, Lara?”

“Prints, sir,” Lara replied. “Deep. Wide set. Entry point’s here.”

Carlton gave a single nod. “You heard the man. Line formation. This campsite is fallback. Maintain your discipline," he emphasized. "No talking unless necessary.”

All three team members echoed the response.

“Clear.”

Carlton pivoted to face them fully, his silhouette tall against the misty edge of the woods. His voice lowered, direct and unwavering.

“None of you have engaged with the target before. It's big. It's fast. It’s strong. It *will* defend its territory. It throws rocks, sometimes the size of your head. Uses them to stun, maim, and kill. You’ll smell it before you see it.”

He let the weight of those words hang in the air. The forest swallowed the silence, like it agreed.

Nicks, already adjusting the scope on her weapon, added: "Shadows will mess with your head. Stay sharp."

Carlton pointed to her with the edge of his rifle. "Nicks, you've got point. Run thermal from here on. If you catch a large heat signature, call it. Don't hesitate."

"Copy," she said.

"Lara. Madden. You're hybrid, visual and thermal. Foliage is dense, so don't count on clean shots. If we confirm contact, it's weapons free. This is a kill mission. Understood?"

Three heads nodded.

"Understood, sir."

Carlton slung his rifle back into a ready position and took one last look at the dimming tree line.

"Lock and load. This thing's smart. Crafty. It *knows* it's being hunted. Don't underestimate it. Move out!"

The chorus of clacking bolts and softly whispered affirmatives followed. They moved, each step deliberate, each breath measured.

The team dissolved into the trees, swallowed by the thick ferns and low-hanging cedar limbs, boots barely whispering on the ground. The sound of the forest returned in strange, scattered bursts — wind through leaves, a raven calling once in the distance.

Somewhere ahead, something waited.

And it already knew they were coming.

CHAPTER 12: HAPPY HOUR

The kitchen was quiet, bathed in the warm amber light of early evening. The scent of turmeric and ginger still lingered faintly in the air. Mike sat hunched at the table, poking halfheartedly at a smoothie with his straw, the thick, nutrient-packed blend slowly separating into layers of orange and green.

Across the room, Vikram loaded the last of the dishes into the washer and shut the door with a satisfying *clunk*. He hit the start button, and the machine whirred to life.

Mike glanced down at the glass in front of him, then back up. “Kid, I’ve about had it with smoothies.”

Vikram turned, one brow raised. “What’s wrong with it?”

“It’s not bad,” Mike admitted, “I’m just not feelin’ it. Too much liquid, not enough food.”

Vikram leaned back against the counter, arms folded. “I can make that salmon you like. The one with the Asian Zing sauce from B-Dubs.”

Mike let out a groan, leaning his head back. “I’ve had nothin’ but salmon and smoothies for two weeks. I want a bacon double cheeseburger. From the bar.”

That got Vikram’s attention.

His face lit up like someone flipped a switch. “The bar? For real? You up for that?”

Mike didn’t answer. He just reached for his crutches, pulled himself upright, and gave Vik a look that said *let's go before I change my mind.*

Vikram clapped once, pivoted, and bolted out of the kitchen.

Mike blinked. "Where the hell you goin'?"

From somewhere down the hallway came Vikram's voice, muffled by distance. "Washing my face and changing shirts! Give me five minutes!"

Mike checked the clock. "You've got *three* minutes, kid. I want to make it for happy hour."

There was a pause.

"Five minutes for the moisturizing mask to take," Vik called from the bathroom, "then eye cream. Then I gotta iron. I need thirty!"

Mike groaned and started hobbling after him, half-laughing, half-exasperated. "*Thirty?!* That's horse shit, Vik! I'm not paying full pri—"

Before he could finish the sentence, Vikram reappeared in the hallway, his face fresh, hair perfectly tousled, shirt crisp, confidence dialed to eleven.

"Take it easy, you frugal bastard," he said with a grin. "I'm ready."

Mike just shook his head.

"I'll get the truck started," Vik added, already moving toward the door.

Mike stood there for a beat, the weight of cabin fever melting off his shoulders.

"Hell yes," he muttered to himself. "Let's get a damn burger."

And with that, he walked out into the cool evening, the sound of crutches tapping against the porch followed by the rumble of a pickup engine coming to life.

Mike and Vikram stepped into the bar, and for a moment, the

din paused—just a beat—as a few heads turned their way. Familiar faces, most of them, and all clearly surprised to see Mike out and about.

They made their way to a corner booth near the jukebox. Mike settled in with a sigh of relief, his crutches resting against the bench. Vikram slid in across from him, eyes scanning the room.

From behind the bar, Beth looked up, did a double take, then broke into a smile.

“Well, well, well,” she said, making her way over, “what have we got here?”

“Hey there, Beth,” Mike said, his voice warm.

Beth leaned into the booth, giving him an awkward but heartfelt hug. Across the table, Vikram pulled a face, his wide eyes with mock surprise, like a middle schooler watching his friend flirt for the first time.

Mike shot him a glare. Beth grinned and turned her attention to him.

“And how are you, turkey club?”

“I’m good, Beth,” Vikram said brightly. “Had to get ol’ Mike outta the house before he killed me. Speaking of turkey clubs, can I get one?"

"Of course," she said, "Crisps on the side?”

“You remembered!” Vikram beamed, throwing her a goofy grin.

Beth winked. “Naturally. Anything for you, Mike?”

“Double bacon cheeseburger, double order of fries, and a Diet Coke,” he said. “Tartar sauce for the fries.”

Vikram blinked. “Diet Coke?”

Then he turned to Beth. “I guess Mike is watching his weight and doesn’t believe in drinking empty calories. In fact, he’s so calorie aware he’ll only have *one* order of fries. He doesn’t need all that starch and inflammation-inducing seed oil in his diet right now." He turned to Mike. "Double fries? Really?"

Mike threw up his hands. "You've had me eating nothing but salmon, salad, and smoothies for *three weeks*!"

"Yeah," Vikram shot back, "and you look great! Beth, tell him. He's glowing from the Omega-3s and collagen peptides. His clothes fit better. His scowl lines are fading."

Mike leaned in hard against the table, "I just want some *real* food." He turned to Beth, almost pleading. "Double order of fries."

Vikram sat back and tossed the menu on the table in frustration. "I've had you on a *real whole food* diet. Fries aren't real food! Christ, you're so ungrateful!"

Mike glared. "One order of double fries isn't going to kill me. I'm having the fries, Beth. And a cup of chowder, too."

Vikram reached over and snatched the menu from his hands. "Get the fuck out of here with that chowder!"

Beth stood frozen, pen hovering over her notepad, an expression of stunned amusement on her face. Then she burst out laughing.

"I'm gonna give you two a few more minutes," she said, shaking her head as she walked away. "I'll be right back."

"Scratch the chowder," Mike called after her, "but not the fries."

Vikram tossed the menu back on the table and leaned back in his seat with an exaggerated sigh. "Fine. Whatever. Have your fries."

Beth scribbled something into her notepad and disappeared into the kitchen.

A silence settled between them. Mike stared down at the condensation sliding down his glass. Then he chuckled.

Vikram looked up, apologetic. "Sorry, man. I've just been so locked in on helping you get better, I guess I got carried away."

"You're good, Vik. I appreciate it." Mike paused, then added with a sigh. "I really wanted that chowder though."

Vikram slid out of the booth. "I'll go tell Beth to add it."

Mike waved him off. "Nah, it's okay. You're right. I don't need it."

Vikram hesitated, then nodded.

They both leaned back in their seats, finally relaxed. The bar noise returned around them—easy, familiar, safe. For a moment, it felt like they had outrun the shadows in the woods.

Vikram's brow furrowed. He turned back toward Mike.

"Everything okay?" Mike asked.

"Yeah, I think. I'm probably being paranoid, but... I think Beth and that nurse were talking about us."

Mike twisted around just in time to catch the nurse glance toward them, then quickly look away.

"Yeah," Mike said. "They're definitely talking about us. She probably recognizes the strong, distinguished gentleman who fought off a bear while his younger, unprepared friend ran for his life."

Vikram chuckled. "More like she recognizes the older gentleman who got horrifically mauled by said bear and the handsome young Indian buck who saved him."

"Both versions can be true," Mike said with a wink.

Beth returned with their food: a towering turkey club, a heaping basket of fries, and a cheeseburger that seemed to defy structural logic.

"Turkey club with chips," she said. "Double bacon cheeseburger, double fries, a gallon of tartar sauce... and a diet Coke for our calorie-conscious patron. Anything else?"

Mike tilted his head toward Vikram. "Yeah, Beth. My paranoid friend thinks you were talking about us."

Beth hesitated, then smiled crookedly. "Mind if I sit?"

Vikram scooted over. Beth slid into the booth beside him and leaned in.

"There was some kind of bear incident up near Pine Lake this morning," she said, voice low. "Wade Coombs brought in that dog handler from SAR... Deanna or Diana or something. She was in full shock. Wouldn't speak. Just... vacant."

"Was she hurt?" Vikram asked, instantly serious.

Beth tilted her head slightly. "No. No wounds. Just... whatever she saw, it broke her."

"She was with Grimes, right? They both okay?" Vikram asked, voice heavy with concern.

Beth nodded. "Physically, yeah, she's fine. No word on the deputy. But people are talking. You two showing up here with Mike still looking like hell…"

"Thanks, Beth," Mike deadpanned. "Really appreciate that."

"Sorry. Just saying what people are saying. And with James and Mimi's chicken coop getting wrecked a couple nights back... it's like everyone's got their hackles up. And this? This is making it worse."

Mike removed the straw from his drink and set it aside. "Why'd you bring me a straw? You know I hate straws."

Beth blinked. "Did you hear anything I just said?"

"I heard you," Mike said quietly. "And it's not helping that you're sitting with us right now. People are watching."

Beth exhaled, hurt flickering across her face. "Right. Okay."

"If you hear anything else," Mike said, softening, "let us know. For now, I just wanna eat and not think about bears. Sound fair?"

Beth nodded slowly. "I close tonight, like always, but if I hear anything, I'll swing by tomorrow morning. That okay?"

Mike hesitated. "Uh, I guess. I mean, my place is kinda—"

"That works!" Vikram interrupted loudly, slapping the table. "Tomorrow morning. Ten o'clock. Perfect."

Beth blinked. "Okaaay...see you then, I guess?"

"Yep, see you tomorrow morning!" Vikram said before Mike could speak.

Mike nodded in agreement.

Beth walked away. Mike watched her go.

"She's totally into you, idiot," Vikram said.

Mike snorted. "I don't know about that."

"Oh my God! She invited herself over to *see you.* That's an unmistakable sign. You two are practically married now. She'll be pregnant by next month. Then—"

Mike threw his straw at Vikram, pegging him right between the eyes.

"Shut up! I just want to eat my stupid double cheeseburger and mountain of fries and go home."

Vikram grinned. "Yeah, we gotta clean up before Beth moves in. Maybe I'll..."

Mike slammed the table, rattling the silverware. "*Enough!*"

Other patrons turned to look. Mike stared straight ahead, pretending he didn't notice. Vikram was still smirking.

"Hey, Mike?"

Mike ignored him.

"Mike?"

A sigh. "What?"

"You think it's our... bear? Missing campers, traumatized dog handler, Grimey involved... feels like it's back."

Mike dipped a long fry in tartar sauce and took a slow bite.

"If it is, kid," he said, chewing, "I'm in no shape to do much about it."

Vikram stared down at his turkey club, then began slowly peeling the sandwich apart, one slice at a time.

CHAPTER 13: THE HEAT IS ON

The forest pressed in around them like a living, breathing thing. The squad moved in tight file formation through the dense, darkening woods, every step deliberate. Twilight filtered through the canopy in thin, fading streaks just enough to distort depth, just enough to play tricks on the eyes.

At point, Nicks moved like a ghost, rifle raised, her sharp eyes scanning ahead through the glow of her thermal sight. Carlton followed, tall and composed, his face a hardened mask of focus.

Lara flanked left, rifle swinging with practiced fluidity, his hybrid optics overlaying green-tinged night vision with bursts of infrared whenever he toggled the scope. Madden brought up the rear, his own hybrid rig humming faintly, switching between night-enhancement and heat when he swept the trees. A wall of muscle and vigilance, he kept flicking his scope skyward, scanning the canopy as though expecting something to drop from above.

Their boots whispered over pine needles and dead leaves. Then the woods opened up.

The clearing was exactly where Grimes said it would be.

They fanned out, rifles up. One by one, optics flipped up and of the way — Nicks pulling her thermal aside, Lara and Madden flipping their hybrids to standby.

For a heartbeat, the world was muted — all pale ghosts, grainy silhouettes, and warping heat blooms. Then beams of white light snapped on, cutting into the clearing. The harsh glow stripped away the mystery, revealing everything in brutal detail: wet blood black against moss, bones gleaming slick and pale, and the terrible clarity of what the dark had been hiding.

"Jesus," Lara muttered. "This is brutal."

Nicks's beam landed on the crumpled form of Erin. Her headless body lay draped in moss and blood-matted leaves.

"My God," she breathed. "It tore her head off."

Madden's flashlight swept the clearing. His breath caught.

"Heads," he said grimly. "They're on the ground...arranged in some kind of messed up nest."

Carlton took it all in, the bodies, blood, ritualized staging. His temples flared, his jaw was set tight.

He'd seen things like this before in war zones where men turned savage, where tribal vengeance played out in symbols and mutilation. Heads arranged like trophies. Limbs twisted for display. Cruel messages carved into human remains.

But never animals. Never like this.

This wasn't instinct. It was intention. And that made it worse.

"We'll bag and extract once the threat's neutralized," he said, voice flat.

A crack cut through the woods. Then another.

They froze.

Then came the knock, one loud, deliberate knock, heavy wood on wood.

Carlton's voice dropped low. "Back to work."

The team powered down their lights. Night vision goggles slid into place. The forest became a world of green grain and heat blooms. They moved like shadows, silent and low.

The team had gone less than twenty meters before Nicks raised a fist. Halt.

Through her thermal lens, a distorted patch of heat bled through the trees. For a moment, Nicks thought it could have been a misread of the scope, a signature anomaly. Then the shape shifted, massive, hunched, and impossible to mistake.

"Tango," she whispered. "One hundred yards out."

"Do you have a shot?" Carlton asked.

"Negative. Not clean. Too many trees." Nicks replied.

Carlton's mind worked fast. "Delayed split flank. Nicks right. Lara left. No more than fifty yards. If you've got the shot, take it. Shoot to kill."

"If it charges?" Lara asked.

"We retrograde back to this clearing. Concussion grenades if needed. Madden and I will suppress. Defensive line here. If it runs, pincer and pursue."

Madden nodded. "Got it, sir."

Carlton scanned his team, then gave the nod. "Lock and load. Stay sharp. This thing's smart. Crafty. Don't underestimate it."

Nicks and Lara peeled off, fading into the trees.

And just like that, the woods swallowed them.

CHAPTER 14: TAKE ME OUT

The bar had quieted some, the low hum of conversation blending with the soft clink of glasses and the distant rhythm of classic rock from the jukebox. Mike sat alone in the booth now, the remains of his double bacon cheeseburger and fries pushed aside. His crutches leaned against the edge of the table as he tapped away at his phone.

The screen lit up with a new message.

MADDY: *How are you doing, Dad?*

Mike smiled faintly, thumbs hovering over the screen of his phone. He typed, backspaced, retyped. Finally:

MIKE: *I'm good, kiddo. Vik got me out of the house. At the bar.*

(SEND)

A few seconds passed.

MADDY: *The bar? You can't drink with the meds you're on, Dad!*

Mike chuckled under his breath.

MIKE: *No drinks, just food. Tired of smoothies and fish.*

(SEND)

He shifted, the cast on his leg heavy, a dull ache reminding him how not good he really was. Still, the faint smile stayed on his face as he watched the typing bubble appear on the screen.

Her response was almost instant, rows of laughing emojis.

Mike's fingers paused, then typed again.

MIKE: *When are you coming home?*

(SEND)

The delay in her response felt longer this time. His expression darkened just slightly as he stared at the screen.

MADDY: *Maybe next weekend.*

Mike pursed his lips. He typed back quickly.

MIKE: *Okay. Miss you.*

(SEND)

MADDY: *Miss u too. Hey, there's a game tonight. Maybe you and Vik can check it out. I know the girls would love it if you stopped by.*

Mike read that twice, his heart tugging just a bit.

MIKE: *Might do that. Goodnight. Love you.*

(SEND)

Her reply came with a row of heart emojis.

MADDY: *Love u 2! Say hi to Vik for me!*

Mike slipped the phone face-down on the table, exhaling slowly.

Just then, Vikram returned from the bar, slipping the receipt into his wallet with a satisfied grin.

"Ready to roll, tough guy?" he asked.

Mike reached for his crutches, using the edge of the table for balance as he rose slowly.

"Yep," he said. "Mind stopping by the fields? I want to watch Maddy's old softball team play."

Vikram raised an eyebrow, skeptical. "Are you up for that? I mean, you're just barely cleared to put weight on that leg. No hero stuff."

Mike was already moving toward the door, one crutch at a time. "Yeah. I'm up for it."

Vikram slung their jackets over his shoulder and followed. "Okay then," he said, holding the door open as they stepped into the evening air. “Let’s go.”

CHAPTER 15: FIRST CONTACT

Through the green-tinted lens of her thermal monocular, Nicks tracked a massive, motionless heat signature just beyond the tree line. Her breathing was steady, finger moving to the trigger of her AA-12 automatic shotgun, the drum magazine loaded with FRAG-12 explosive rounds.

She whispered into her radio.

"On my shot."

She squeezed the trigger.

BOOM!

The first round exploded, shredding a sapling into a confetti of bark and splinters.

BOOM!

The second flared white-hot in her scope as it hit the target's right shoulder.

BOOM!

The third detonated against the dirt, kicking up a wall of soil and debris.

The AA-12 hammered into her shoulder, the stock jolting with every shot. Nicks adjusted her stance, keeping the massive weapon steady.

For a heartbeat, nothing. Smoke and debris clouded her vision.

Then, in the haze, the heat signature shifted. It dropped low, the bulk of it flattening against the earth and moved too fast for something that size.

"No effect! No effect! It's moving on you, Lara!" she barked.

Lara flipped down his thermal scope, sweeping the trees. The lens swam with static heat noise from the muzzle flashes, splintered trunks bleeding warmth, ghost signatures dancing through the distortion. "I've got nothing on thermal! No visual!"

Carlton's voice came cool and commanding over the radio. "Weapons tight."

The crashing came fast, barreling through the brush. Lara swept his rifle in a tight arc, adrenaline humming through his fingertips. The sound was closing in. Fast.

Snap. Crack.

A flicker of movement in thermal. Low and spider-fast.

He opened fire.

The SCAR barked in controlled bursts. Something howled in an inhuman shriek that made the air itself shudder.

Silence.

Lara dropped to a knee, swapped mags, breath catching in his throat.

"No movement," he called. "Repeat, no movement. Can't confirm neutralization. Target dropped about twenty meters out."

Carlton's response came swift over comms. "Base team advancing. Switch to precision fire. Nicks, hold and engage if it heads your way."

"Roger that." Lara steadied his rifle.

Carlton and Madden moved through the underbrush, rifles raised, scanning through scopes. They stepped lightly, boots muffled by layers of pine needles and moss. The air was thick with tension.

Lara caught a whiff of something acrid and foul.

"You weren't lying about the smell, sir," he muttered.

"Stay alert," Carlton said. "We're close."

He broke formation slightly, forming a loose triangle with Madden and Lara.

"Lara, fire three rounds at anything you think looks suspicious."

Lara visually swept the area directly in front of him. "Everything looks suspicious, sir."

"Then fire at what feels extra suspicious." Carlton ordered.

"Roger that."

Lara fired a three-round burst into the brush. Debris flew, but nothing emerged.

"Noth..."

His words choked off.

Through thermal, the forest flared. A massive shape rose where before there had been only heat noise. It had been crouched low in the brush, utterly still... waiting.

Now it moved.

It unfolded in a blur of molten heat, bursting upright. Branches snapped, earth shook.

It charged.

"Contact!" Lara screamed, stumbling backward, tangled in roots. He landed hard, scrambling, his rifle firing wild bursts. The creature lunged with terrifying speed.

A massive foot slammed into Lara's chest.

CRACK.

Bone gave way beneath a crushing weight. Lara's scream turned into a ragged, gurgling breath. The creature lifted its foot, ready to crush again.

Gunfire ripped through the forest.

RATATATAT

Carlton charged forward, emptying his magazine into the creature's flank. Blood sprayed. The beast recoiled, staggering back from Lara's broken form.

Carlton's mag dropped, a fresh one slapping home with practiced speed. He racked the bolt and flipped on his tactical light, the beam cutting across the clearing.

The light swept past tree trunks, undergrowth, shattered saplings—then caught on movement.

The creature froze.

It was a monstrous nightmare: fur matted and blackened, its shoulder shredded from the previous explosive hit. Blood poured from its chest, legs, torso. It should have been down, finished, yet it stood there, trembling with life, wild-eyed and unbroken.

Then it turned and bolted.

Carlton raised his rifle again.

Gunfire ripped through the forest.

"Madden! Nicks! Target moving to your positions!"

Madden sprinted to intercept. Fired and missed, trees exploded, bark torn apart by rifle rounds.

The creature swerved toward Nicks.

She was ready.

Thermal showed the beast glowing white-hot.

Twenty meters.

She steadied her stance, breath slowing.

Ten.

It burst through the trees, an avalanche of fur, blood, and rage. Their eyes locked through the scope.

She fired.

BOOM. BOOM. BOOM.

Three explosive rounds slammed into the creature's chest. Each burst lit the woods in flashes of fire and smoke, the concussions rattling the air.

The creature screamed one final, rage-choked shriek.

Then it collapsed, silent.

For a moment, the only sound was Nicks' own breathing in her headset.

She edged forward, boots silent over the pine-strewn forest floor. Her voice crackled low over comms.

"Tango down. Approaching."

Carlton's voice came through, cool and clipped.

"Careful, Nicks."

She flicked on her tactical light. The harsh beam sliced through the lingering smoke and floating debris, illuminating the wreckage of the forest—and what lay at the center of it.

A low, rasping breath crawled through the dark.

Her light found the creature slumped, matted fur hanging in blood-slick ropes, patches of flesh torn away by the explosive rounds. It lay in a twisted coil of limbs and gore, but its chest still moved. Shallow. Wet. Struggling.

Nicks tightened her grip on the AA-12. Her finger hovered over the trigger. For a moment, she froze. Its eyes found hers, and something flickered there. Something almost human.

She took in a deep breath, then exhaled hard, training reasserting itself.

With a flick of her wrist, she ejected the FRAG-12 magazine and slapped in a fresh drum loaded with slugs. She racked the action—clack-chunk—and took aim.

BOOM.

BOOM.

Double tap to the chest.

The body jerked, then went still. The breathing stopped.

Nicks lowered the shotgun. Smoke curled through her light beam, her breath fogged in the cold night air.

"Target neutralized," she said quietly, her voice steady over the radio.

Silence answered.

And then came Carlton's voice, calm and final.

"Roger that."

CHAPTER 16: BALLGAME

Bright field lights cast a crisp glow over the infield as a sharp grounder screamed toward short. The shortstop fielded it clean, flipped to second, and the second baseman pivoted, firing to first.

Bang-bang. Double play.

The crowd erupted in a burst of cheers and clapping. On the third row of the bleachers, Mike clapped louder than anyone, his crutches leaning beside him, his injured leg carefully propped on the seat in front. Beside him, Vikram watched the game with the curious concentration of a man trying to learn a new language.

"So same rules as baseball," Vikram said, squinting at the diamond, "but different pitching motion?"

"Mostly," Mike replied, still clapping. "Field is smaller. The ball bigger. Base paths, pitching distance is shorter."

Vikram nodded thoughtfully. "Gotcha. And you used to coach this team?"

"Helped out when Maddy played," Mike said. His eyes lingered a moment on the shortstop's jersey number before he continued. "Strength stuff. Mental prep. Most of these girls are crazy talented, they just don't always believe it."

Vikram turned to him, a slight smirk pulling at the corners of his mouth. "Wow. Big Mike the motivational speaker and girls softball coach. Would not have guessed."

Before Mike could reply, a couple of local spectators spotted him. They made their way over, clapping him on the shoulder, asking about his recovery. Mike grinned, joking that the bear didn't like how he tasted. Laughter followed, and they moved along.

Moments later, a small group of players in dusty uniforms jogged toward the bleachers. One of them, Katelyn, leaned over the rail and gave Mike an awkward, heartfelt hug.

"Thanks for coming to see us," she said, pulling back. "When are you coming back to coach again?"

Mike nodded toward his leg. "Soon as I can stand without these damn crutches."

"Good! We need you back before spring season. We're getting weak!" Katelyn grinned.

"Then hit the gym, kid. You know what to do."

"Yeah, yeah, I know," she said with a smile.

Another girl, more reserved, stepped forward. Jossy. "Hey, Coach. You doing okay?"

"I've been better," Mike admitted. "But I'm coming around. Decent night at the plate for you."

Jossy shrugged, shyly, but confident. "Three for four. A couple doubles in the center-left gap."

"Should've been four for four," Mike said. "You beat that throw to first."

She grinned. "Yeah, but this ump low-key hates me."

More girls joined, Kaylie and Morgan. Mike greeted them like a proud uncle.

"How are *you*, Coach?" Kaylie asked. "You look really beat up."

"Thanks for noticing, Kaylie. I *am* really beat up." He turned to Morgan. "And those were some serious swings you were taking tonight."

Morgan flashed a grin. "Thanks, Coach. I chose violence at the plate, just like you taught us."

"Always." Mike beamed.

Vikram sat quietly, watching the girls circle Mike. He seemed to be seeing Mike for the first time. This wasn't just a grumpy, lonely, old guy with a leg injury. This was someone these girls admired. Trusted.

Then Morgan wrinkled her nose.

"Something *really* stinks out by centerfield."

Vikram's head swiveled, alert.

"It's like garbage or something," Morgan added, fanning her hand in front of her face. "Kind of like it smelled at the other fields last week."

"Wasn't that just a hobo camp?" Katelyn asked. "Maybe they moved to these woods."

Vikram leaned in. "Hey there, I'm Vik...Mike's Indian friend. You said something stinks out there? And not just the arm on the other team's centerfielder?"

The girls giggled, but Morgan nodded. "No, for real. It's *nasty.* Like something's dead. It smells like garbage and skunk. Really gross."

Vikram subtly elbowed Mike.

"You hear that?" he murmured. "Garbage and skunk."

"You hear any strange sounds out there?" Vikram asked aloud.

Katelyn rolled her eyes. "Don't freak Mo-Mo out. Now she's going to be listening for weird sounds instead of paying attention to the game."

"No weird sounds," Morgan said. "Just the smell."

Mike glanced at Vikram, the concern already creeping in. Together, their eyes drifted toward the dense line of trees beyond the outfield. The woods looked darker than usual, more foreboding. Only a flimsy four-foot mesh fence separated the players from that wall of blackness.

The scoreboard lights buzzed faintly as the sun dipped lower, leaving only the artificial glow over the well-kept field. Jossy lingered near the bleachers, ball in one hand, glove on the other. She shifted her weight, rolling the ball across her palm.

"I gotta go warm up," she said. "I'm pitching this game. Are you staying?"

Mike didn't answer.

"Mike?"

His eyes were locked on the dark wall of trees beyond the outfield, his expression unreadable.

Jossy tilted her head. "Are you staying for the next game?"

Mike blinked, snapped his head toward her like he'd just returned from somewhere else.

"Yeah," he said. "Yeah... I'm staying. Get that shoulder loose."

Katelyn and Morgan had already started walking off. "We've gotta warm up too," Katelyn called. "See ya, Coach."

"Bye, Mike!" Morgan added.

The girls jogged toward the dugout, laughing and chirping like teenage girls do, the easy rhythm of their pregame rituals settling back in. Vikram slid a little closer to Mike, glancing casually over his shoulder to make sure no one was listening.

"What the hell, Mike?" he asked under his breath. "Do you think... you know... is he here?"

Mike clenched his jaw. A small vein on his temple throbbed beneath the skin.

"I don't know," he said, voice low. "I think we need to call Sher —"

The scream cut through everything.

Shrill. Raw. Terrified.

It came from deep in right field where the opposing team had been warming up. A moment later, the whole outfield exploded into chaos as girls scattered, sprinting toward the dugouts in a panic. Coaches shouted. Parents stood up in alarm. The players' faces were pale with fear.

Someone in the crowd shouted, "Did they see a mountain lion?"

"Is it a bear?"

Then silence, for just a heartbeat, enough to feel the wrongness in the air.

A figure stood near the left-centerfield fence.

Massive. Shoulders rising above the flimsy mesh. Arms too long, hanging below the knees. The field lights caught just enough to make it clear this was no man.

Something small — a calf, or maybe a goat — was slung over one shoulder, limp. The thing paused there, half-lit in the glow of the lights. Then with two enormous strides, it vanished into the tree line.

The silence shattered.

Screams. Yells. Chaos.

Parents yelled for their kids. Coaches tried to herd players toward the parking lot. Umpires barked orders no one followed. The bleachers rattled as people scrambled down, the air alive with the sharp slam of car doors and headlights flicking on in the parking lot.

"Was it a bear?"

"Call 911!"

"Did anyone get video?"

"That wasn't a bear..."

Mike was already rising, steadying himself on his crutches. Vikram stood, positioning himself protectively between Mike and the surging wave of people.

"We gotta get out of here," Vikram said, eyes scanning. "Ready?"

Mike didn't answer right away. "Are the girls okay?"

Vikram looked toward both dugouts. The benches were empty.

"I think so," he said. "Everyone bolted when the first girl saw our friend."

A new commotion caught their attention. Two men in their forties shoved through the crowd, rifles slung across their backs. Not hunters but dads, still in ball caps and jeans, who'd sprinted to their trucks the moment things went south. One had a scoped .308. The other cradled a shotgun, hands shaking but determined.

They stormed onto the field.

"Hey!" an umpire shouted, stepping in front of them.

They didn't stop. One shoved the ump aside, sending him sprawling to the dirt. Then the men vaulted the mesh outfield fence and charged into the woods.

Mike winced.

"That's not going to end well."

A few moments later—gunfire.

Sharp. Aggressive. Controlled.

Then a scream.

Not like before.

This was worse. Higher. Desperate. Something was happening in those trees. Something wrong.

The crowd froze.

From the woods, one of the dads burst back into view, bloodied and wild-eyed. His shirt was torn, his cheek split open, one arm hanging limp. He hit the mesh fence at full speed, flipping over it and crumpling into the dirt. He staggered onto hands and knees, wobbling, trying and failing twice before he forced himself upright.

A rock the size of a cantaloupe screamed out of the treeline, whistling through the night.

It hit him in the back of the head with a sickening crack.

He dropped instantly, boneless, to the turf. Blood pooled beneath him, dark and immediate.

Screams broke loose again. Panic exploded. The crowd surged for the parking lot in a frenzy of shouts and pounding feet.

Mike and Vikram stayed still.

Frozen.

Staring.

A roar tore from the woods, deep and guttural, like the earth itself had opened up. It rolled across the field in a low, vibrating wave, shaking ribs and rattling the air.

Then it changed.

It climbed in pitch…warped, twisting into something shrill and broken. It wasn't just a roar anymore. It was layered. Something wounded. Something enraged. Something that knew *exactly* what it was doing.

And at the edge of it all…something *human.*

Almost.

Then came the *knock.*

Just one.

Loud. Final. Like a warning shot.

"He's here," Vikram whispered. "Let's go."

Mike nodded, still pale. They moved fast, Vikram clearing a path through the rush of bodies, Mike hobbling behind on his crutches.

Behind them, the lights on the field kept shining.

The game was over. The nightmare had just begun.

CHAPTER 17: EXTRACTION

Carlton knelt beside Lara, his hand firm on the young man's trembling shoulder. Lara's breaths came in ragged pulls, each one a wet gasp echoing against the quiet trees. His eyes, once sharp and alert, were glassy now, unfocused.

"You did good, son," Carlton said quietly. "Real good. Just breathe. You're going to be okay."

Lara tried to speak, but only a gurgle escaped his lips.

"Shhh." Carlton's hand moved to Lara's cheek. "Don't talk. I'm with you. You don't have to fight anymore. Let it slide over you. You're okay."

Lara's chest hitched one last time, then went still. Carlton held his breath, watching for movement. None came. He leaned in, pressed his hand gently over Lara's eyes, closing them. Then he bowed his head.

"Lara's gone," he said into his comm.

Nicks stood over the creature's corpse, its grotesque bulk sprawled out beneath the beam of her flashlight. The fur was soaked with blood, its torso cratered from her final shots.

"He stood his ground," she murmured. "Did some damage to this thing."

"Yep," Carlton replied over comms. "He did good. Madden is en route to your position. He'll assist in securing the body."

Nicks raised an eyebrow. "Sir?"

“You heard me. Guard the body. I’ll bag Lara and carry him to the fallback point. I've already put in a sat-phone call into command. A second team is inbound and will take over the recovery operation.”

“I really don’t want to be out here longer than I have to be,” Nicks muttered. “This thing stinks. And something doesn’t feel right.”

“You’re my second, Nicks,” Carlton said. “Act like it. Hold your position. Relief’s coming.”

She sighed. “Understood.”

"Good. I'll see you back at camp." With that, Carlton ended the communication.

A moment later, Madden arrived, his rifle slung, expression grim as he looked down at the corpse.

“Christ,” he said. “This thing’s huge. What do you think…eight hundred pounds? Half a ton?”

“No idea. Don’t care,” Nicks replied. “You got any gum?”

“Nope." Madden sucked his teeth, then looked down at his boots. "Sucks about Lara. He was a good teammate.”

Nicks removed her helmet. “I don’t get it,” she said. “Why the hell are we guarding it? It’s dead. Lara's dead. He deserved better than this bullshit assignment.” She hurled her helmet at the creature's corpse, it bounced off the ribcage and into the brush.

“When I signed up, dead Bigfoot corpse sitting wasn’t on the checklist,” Madden said, half-joking.

Nicks whirled on Madden, but before she could respond, a single, loud *knock* echoed from deep within the trees.

They both froze.

Carlton emerged from the trees and into the campground, breath labored, Lara’s lifeless body slung over his shoulders.

He lowered the young man gently to the ground just as two camouflaged ATVs rolled into the clearing, headlights off. The contractors moved quietly, focused. From the second vehicle, Jacob Morton, lean and stone-eyed, stepped out like he was arriving at a boardroom. Morton approached Carlton. “I understand there was a bit of a situation,” he said.

Carlton nodded. “Yes, sir. Target neutralized. The body’s about a click east. Two of mine are holding position.”

Morton’s gaze shifted to the black body bag behind Carlton.

“That one?”

“Casualty. The target killed Specialist Lara.” Carlton's voice was low, measured.

Morton gave a tight nod, his expression unreadable. “Unfortunate. Can you brief the team on what to expect?”

“Of course. Mind if I call the local sheriff first? Let him know it’s over?”

Morton nodded. “Go ahead. I’ll go shoot the shit with the team until you’re ready.”

Carlton stepped away and pulled out a sat phone.

“Sheriff, it’s C,” he said. “Target’s down. We got it.”

There was a pause on the other end. "Sheriff?"

“What are you talking about?” Sheriff Baker’s voice crackled. “We had an incident in town less than an hour ago. At the ball fields. A hundred people saw it.”

Carlton froze. “You sure?”

“Absolutely. Walked off with a goddamn calf. Two locals followed. One of them is dead.”

Carlton’s voice dropped, low and guttural. “What the shit? Sheriff, I lost one of my men tonight to this thing." He takes a deep breath, "I’ve got two more guarding the body of the target a thousand meters from me. We took it down.”

“And I’m standing over a dead body with a caved in head in the middle of a ballfield. Witnesses are posting shaky video of the whole thing online." Baker said flatly.

A long silence passed between them.

"There's two of them," Baker said.

"I gotta go," Carlton muttered. "I'll be in touch."

"Commander Morton," Carlton called. "A moment."

"What's up?" Morton asked with a hint of impatience.

Carlton pulled him aside. "Secondary contact. In town. At least one fatality."

Morton blinked. "Confirmed?"

"Direct from Baker. He's on scene."

Morton took a calculated breath. "Don't tell the team. Not yet. Let's secure the ghost first."

"Roger that."

Morton turned and raised his voice.

"Extraction team! Robinson's going to brief you on the operation."

Carlton stepped forward, command in his posture.

"We've got three bodies: two civilian, one ghost. No road access, manual carry only. Use the SKED stretcher. Rotate every fifty to seventy-five meters. Campers get packed out on litters. Questions?"

One team member raised a hand. "No airlift?"

"Canopy's too thick," Carlton said. "Drag is our only option."

As the team broke to gather gear, Morton pulled Carlton aside again.

"You heading to the secondary site?"

Carlton nodded, "I want to confirm what folks think they saw."

"I'll walk with you," Morton said. "Need to brief leadership anyway."

They started down the trail.

"Why aren't we taking an ATV?" Carlton asked.

"Left them for the team," Morton replied. "They'll need them to drag that monster down the trail. We've got a truck with a forklift waiting on the main road."

Carlton shook his head.

"What a mess."

Morton didn't disagree.

"Yep. What a mess."

They slipped down the trail, the darkness folded in around them.

CHAPTER 18: MEANING OF IT ALL

Vikram paced the kitchen floor like a caged animal, his socked feet sliding slightly on the worn hardwood. Mike stood near the hallway entrance, arms folded, his weight shifted awkwardly to one side to favor his injured leg. He watched Vikram silently, brow furrowed with the kind of patience earned only through pain and time.

"You're gonna wear a groove in the floor if you keep this up," Mike muttered.

Vikram stopped abruptly, exhaling hard. He leaned against the kitchen counter, fingers tapping nervously against its edge. His whole body seemed to hum with barely restrained energy.

"That was crazy, Mike," he said. "He's here. In town. Out in the open."

He reached into his pocket, pulled out his phone, and started thumbing through apps with frantic precision.

"Check this out," he said, stepping over to Mike. "Already on YouTube. The quality's garbage, because of course it is... every Bigfoot video ever looks like it was shot with a camera wrapped in gauze, but look at the crowd reaction. The panic's real."

Mike took the phone, squinting at the screen. The video was grainy, shot from a low angle by someone screaming mid-recording. The shot jittered wildly, but the silhouette was there, tall, broad-shouldered, unmistakably upright. Something hairy.

He handed the phone back.

"Could be anything," he said. "Looks upright and furry, sure. Could be a bear. What are people saying?"

Vikram swiped through the comments, reading aloud as he went.

"'Looks hella fake.' 'No way this is real.' 'I was there and it's totally for real.' 'Heard it killed someone.' 'Staged video, not real.'" He sighed. "Opinions are all over the place."

He switched to TikTok. His eyes widened.

"Shit," he said. "It's blowing up. Half a million views already. Probably hit two million by morning."

Mike shrugged and leaned on the wall behind him for support.

"What does that actually mean for us?"

Vikram set the phone down on the counter and straightened up, his voice steady now, colder and more serious. "It means the sheriff and Grimes are about to have a huge problem on their hands. Every Bigfoot hunter with a GoPro and a gun is gonna be here by tomorrow afternoon."

Mike didn't respond right away. He looked past Vikram, toward the kitchen window and the black silhouettes of trees lining the edge of town. The night seemed heavier than usual.

"Yeah," he finally said. "That's what I'm worried about."

CHAPTER 19: RELIEF

Nicks and Madden stood over the creature's corpse, beams of their tactical flashlights slicing through the dense forest gloom. The light bounced off twisted branches and moss-draped undergrowth, throwing long, shifting shadows that made the trees seem to twitch. The forest had fallen into an eerie silence.

Madden scanned the tree line, jaw tight.

"What do you think that was?" he asked, voice low.

Nicks didn't look at him. Her eyes were locked on the darkness beyond their perimeter, sweeping her light back and forth like a metronome.

"Not sure," she said. "But tree knocks, if you believe the folklore, are how these things communicate. So stay alert."

Madden turned toward her, his mouth parted in disbelief.

"Are you kidding me?" he said. "That would mean there's two of these things running around!"

Nicks chuckled, the sound dry and edged with nerves. Her light didn't stop moving.

"Look at it, Madden," she said, nodding toward the hulking body sprawled between them. "It's flesh and blood. Biological. Of course there's more than one."

Madden glanced down at the massive corpse, its fur matted with blood and dirt, its chest pockmarked with bullet wounds and burns. A shiver passed through him.

"I guess so..." he muttered. "Just never really thought of it that way."

Nicks turned to him, amusement flickering in her expression. "Do we need to have a little chat about the birds and the bees, Madden?"

He flushed instantly, a deep, visible red rising up his neck and into his cheeks.

"No, no, no—I get it," he said quickly, holding up his hands in surrender. "I get it."

A crack rang out behind them, branches snapping underfoot. They both spun around, rifles raised, lights cutting through the dark.

A few tense heartbeats later, beams of light pierced the trees ahead. Multiple flashlights. Figures moved closer, silhouetted shapes with gear slung across their shoulders.

Nicks relaxed, just slightly.

"Must be our relief," she muttered, lowering her weapon.

Nicks shrugged off her backpack and set it down, unzipping the main compartment. She pulled out a pair of high-powered LED lanterns and flicked them on one by one. Brilliant white light flooded the clearing, revealing the full, grotesque scale of what lay in front of them. Then she shouldered the pack again, eyes never leaving the body.

"Fire up your lanterns," she said to Madden, her voice carrying a tired edge. "Let 'em get a good look at what they're dragging out of here."

The lights illuminated the creature's body in stark detail, limbs twisted, ripped flesh, a face locked in a final, terrifying expression. The new team would arrive any moment. And when they arrived, they'd see with their own eyes what had taken Lara's life.

Nicks exhaled slowly and reset her grip on her weapon, eyes still sweeping the tree line.

CHAPTER 20: EXTRA INNINGS

The field was quiet now. The earlier chaos had thinned into a tense stillness broken only by the low hum of an ambulance idling near the first base line. Its back doors hung open as two EMTs worked wordlessly, lowering a gurney onto the grass. Stadium lights cast a cold glow across the bloodied dirt near home plate, illuminating the dark red pool that hadn't yet begun to dry.

Sheriff Baker stood nearby, his eyes trained on the body. Deputy Grimes lingered beside him, silent and still. A few feet away, the county medical examiner arrived on the scene.

Shelly Moretti was hard to miss. She was stocky and sharp-eyed, dressed in rumpled corduroys, an oversized denim shirt, and a well-worn fleece vest with the county seal embroidered on the chest. Her short boots made soft scuffs on the turf as she circled the body, squinting down at the mess of crushed bone and blood.

"You're telling me," she said flatly, "that someone threw that rock from the edge of the woods with enough velocity to crack open this poor bastard's skull?"

Sheriff Baker barely glanced her way. "Shelly, I don't have time to explain. Just need him off the field."

Shelly moved around the body, eyeing the blood-soaked rock with the detachment of a seasoned examiner. She gave it a gentle nudge with her boot.

“And stop putzin’ around with the evidence,” Baker snapped. “This is still an active crime scene.”

She shot him a look. “I’ve just got one question.”

He raised an eyebrow, exasperated. “What’s that?”

“Was the assailant a lefty?” she asked. “The Mariners could use a left-handed arm in their rotation.”

Baker’s face darkened. Grimes let out a breath that might have been a laugh if he weren’t trying so hard not to piss anyone off.

“Not funny,” Baker muttered. “Can you sign off so we can move him?”

He shoved a clipboard toward her. Shelly took it without comment, motioning to the EMTs.

“Take him to the morgue,” she said. “I’ll meet you there soon.”

They lifted the body carefully, slipping it onto the gurney. The wheels clicked into place, and the ambulance pulled away with a low, mournful whine. As the taillights disappeared around the far lot, the Sheriff thumbed through the paperwork.

“You put ‘undetermined’ as cause of death?”

Shelly smoothed her fleece vest, her tone matter-of-fact. “Actual cause of death is craniocerebral trauma with associated skull fractures. But I figured ‘undetermined’ would play better. For now.”

Baker exhaled sharply. “Yeah. That’s probably smart.”

He looked out toward the field. The blood remained.

“This is a mess,” he said quietly.

Shelly nodded toward the stain. “This? This can be hosed off, Sheriff. The emotional and psychic damage? That's what lingers.”

“I wasn’t talking about the field, Shelly,” he snapped.

She lifted her hands in mock surrender. “Okay. No more jokes.”

Her tone shifted, turned serious. “You know and I know what threw that rock. Half the internet knows. You’re going to have a circus on your hands. And when the family starts asking questions..."

Baker said nothing. His jaw was locked, his hand resting unconsciously on the grip of his sidearm. He stared at the tree line. Grimes did too.

"He's going to come back," the deputy said softly. "This feels... personal."

Baker gave a grim smile. "Personal, huh? I can make this personal too."

Shelly's voice softened with concern. "Hey now. You need to keep a level head through all this."

Grimes stepped forward, awkward but earnest. "Yeah, Sheriff. I'm not gonna be able to manage a bunch of gun-toting Bigfoot hunters on my own while you're off on a vendetta."

Baker wheeled on them, voice rising.

"Will you two shut the fuck up? Christ, Grimey, you couldn't even keep eyes on a car this morning. That's half the damn problem. And you, Shelly, cook your damn books and spare me the lectures."

Grimes turned away, swallowing hard. Shelly crossed her arms, staring into the woods.

"You knew this might happen when you put that badge on," she said calmly. "We've dodged bullets before. But this time... this time the lid's coming off. You either contain it, or someone else will. And then we really lose control."

Baker's eyes flared. "Of course I know that. But I thought the fight would stay out there. People can live with legends so long as they stay in the woods. But this thing stepped into our world. It didn't just kill. It sent a message. That's not folklore. That's calculated violence from an intelligent apex predator."

Headlights swept over the grass. Carlton's SUV rolled to a stop behind the mound. He stepped out, steel-jawed and alert. His eyes landed on Baker and Shelly.

"Tough day, Sheriff."

"Tougher night," Baker replied.

"This is Shelly," he added. "Medical examiner."

Carlton extended a hand. Shelly gave it one brisk shake.

"Nice to meet you," she said. "And I saw the look on your face, don't worry, I know exactly what's up. But I've got a dead body to attend to and no time for small talk or to swap recipes for apple brown Betty. You gentlemen enjoy your evening."

She turned and walked off without waiting for a reply.

Baker gave a slow nod. "Appreciate your help."

As she moved toward her vehicle, Carlton turned toward centerfield.

"There's a second body out there," Baker said. "I need to find it."

Carlton's expression turned flinty. "I lost a man to one of these things tonight. I'm coming with you."

Footsteps approached from the edge of the field. Grimes emerged from the darkness, carrying two shotguns.

"Sheriff," he said, offering one of them. "Figured you'd want this."

He turned to Carlton. "Didn't know you'd be joining us. Only brought two."

Carlton flashed a grim smile and drew the massive handgun from his thigh holster.

"Desert Eagle five-point-oh," he said. "If it comes near us, I'll break this off in its ass."

Grimes gave a nod of approval. The three men entered the outfield. Beyond the grass, the woods loomed thick and quiet. Baker stepped forward and pulled a section of mesh fencing aside.

"Sun won't be up for a few hours," Baker said. "How do we want to do this?"

"Arrowhead formation," Carlton replied. "I'm on point. Sheriff takes right flank. Deputy take left. Mount your lights."

The men nodded. Clicks and snaps filled the air as tactical lights were affixed to weapons. Carlton raised his hand in a silent signal. Without a word, they stepped into the forest.

Behind them, a lone custodian began hosing blood off the field.

CHAPTER 21: STICK TO THE PLAN

The lanterns cast shifting halos of light over the clearing as the secondary extraction team arrived. Four figures, clad in matching tactical gear, moved with quiet efficiency. At the front was Flores, their team lead, early thirties, focused, his eyes already scanning the tree line. He approached Nicks and Madden, who had been standing over the fallen creature's grotesque corpse, rifles at the ready.

"You two can stand down," Flores said briskly. "Head back to the campsite and wait for further instructions."

Nicks scoffed, exchanging a glance with Madden. "Good to see you too, Flores. We do all the dirty work, you fellas show up for the heavy lifting."

One of the new arrivals, a woman with dark hair tucked under her helmet, stepped forward. "Watch who you're calling 'fella' there, Nicks," she said coolly.

"Benes," Nicks said with a faint smirk. "Didn't see you there."

Madden stepped around from the opposite side of the body, slinging his rifle over his shoulder. "If you've got this, Flores, we're out. No active threats detected."

Flores bumped fists with him. "Roger, that. We'll bag the campers too. XO wants control of their processing."

Madden gave Benes a quick shoulder pat as he passed. "You have fun with that."

Nicks started to follow, then paused and looked back. “Be careful out here,” she said. “Stay alert.”

Flores racked his shotgun with a sharp click. “You’re not the only badass out here, Nicks. If something shows up, we’ll light its ass up.”

That earned a half-smile from her before she and Madden disappeared into the woods.

Flores turned to the rest of his team. “Alright, listen up! Bag the civilians, then prep the SKED. We’ll strap them to the ghost and haul everything out in one go.”

He nodded to Benes and Mendiola, a stocky male specialist in his twenties. “Benes, Mendiola, clear a path through the underbrush with your machetes." He glanced at King, an intense and brooding Black male in his early thirties. "King, you’re with me on bag duty. Stay sharp. Call out anything unusual.”

“Understood,” the group echoed.

Benes and Mendiola began hacking through the undergrowth while Flores and King circled the corpse. The body was a mountain, limp, grotesque, and reeking. They got to work, attempting to find angles that would move the monstrous form on the ground.

They struggled in silence for several minutes, grunts being their only means of communication. Sweat began to form on their foreheads.

“This isn’t working,” King muttered, wiping a hand across his jaw as he stepped back. Lifting straps lay tangled and useless on the ground.

They had looped the rigging beneath the arms and around the torso, anchoring the harness to the SKED. But the creature’s sheer mass and the awkward sprawl of its limbs made it nearly impossible to get proper tension.

“Straps won’t catch,” Flores said, frustration creeping into his voice. “They’re just sliding under the weight.”

They'd tried threading the webbing beneath its back, cinching it under the torso, even looping the legs, but nothing gave them purchase. The creature's body was too wide, too low, and too damn heavy. The dead weight had settled into the forest floor, unmoveable.

King scanned the tree line, then exhaled sharply. "We need leverage. Branches. Like crowbars."

He broke away, grabbed a thick limb from the edge of the clearing, and brought it back. Jamming the branch under the creature's shoulder, he leaned in, using his full body weight.

The branch flexed. The corpse shifted with a wet, sucking sound — not much, but enough.

"There," he said, gritting his teeth. "See that? Get a branch. We pry it up, wedge the SKED underneath, then strap and drag."

Flores stepped back from the creature's body, hands on his hips, studying the dead weight slumped across the forest floor. He toggled his comms.

"Mendiola, status?"

Mendiola and Benes were working over a hundred yards beyond the outer perimeter. Flores was growing impatient, then a crackle. Mendiola's voice came through, winded. "Still clearing with Benes. Got about three-hundred more meters to cut before vegetation clears out on its own."

"Negative," Flores said. "Abandon the machete. We've got a new plan. I need a big-ass branch, solid, at least five feet. Like a pry bar. Find one and head back to the clearing. We'll use it for leverage to slide the ghost on to the SKED."

"Copy that," Mendiola replied.

Mendiola turned away from Benes, flashlight flicking toward a deadfall. He began picking through the small mountain of limbs. Most of the branches snapped or crumbled in his hands. He grunted in frustration and moved deeper. He swept his flashlight, it flickered briefly over something dark, covered in fur, and shaped like a massive foot near the base of a tree. He snapped the beam back, but there was only moss and shadow.

Branches snapped. He spun around. Nothing. Another crack. Closer. And then, the smell.

"Fuck this," he muttered and broke into a run, crashing through the brush toward Benes.

She turned just in time to see him collapse at her feet. "What the fuck, Mendy?"

He lay on his back, gasping, face streaked with scratches. "I think... something's out there...I heard it."

She furrowed her brow, swept her flashlight through the trees. "All I heard was you running like a little bitch."

"I'm telling you, I smelled it. Heard it."

Benes helped him up. "That dead thing stinks up the whole forest. You're just catching whiffs of it."

"Yeah, maybe," Mendiola said, though doubt lingered in his voice.

Benes pointed to a nearby tree. "I heard Flores on comms. Lucky for you, I found a branch. Big enough to lift a Buick."

"Thanks," Mendiola said with relief, grabbing the limb and jogging it back towards the glow of light where Flores and King were waiting.

Back at the clearing, King and Flores were kneeling by the corpse, adjusting the SKED straps when Mendiola arrived, breathless, dragging the limb behind him.

"Hey," he called out, slowing. "I swear I saw something. Big. And the smell was awful."

Flores barely looked up. "Probably just your nerves playing tricks on you."

King grunted, adjusting the rigging. "This whole forest smells like a slaughterhouse."

"I'm serious," Mendiola said. "You should warn Benes. I tried, but she blew me off."

Flores rolled his eyes, toggled comms. "Benes, this is Flores. Heads up, Mendiola thinks he saw something out there. Probably nothing but keep your eyes open."

A pause.

"Copy," came Benes's voice. Dry. Unconvinced.

Flores clicked off and went back to the SKED. "Alright," he said, clapping his hands. "Let's get this bastard lifted onto this thing. Mendy, haul the SKED over here," Flores ordered.

He tried. It snagged on undergrowth. He hacked at the brush, cursed, finally yanked it free and stumbled backward.

"Get it together, Mendiola!" Flores barked.

As King stepped over the body to help, Mendiola paused, wiping sweat from his brow.

"I was thinking..."

"Oh shit," Flores muttered.

Mendiola took a beat, then ignored the insult. "I can use the straps to pull while you two use the branches to lift. Then we roll this thing onto the SKED instead of trying to wedge the SKED under it. It'll be face down, but who cares?"

Flores blinked. "That... might actually work."

"Hell yeah," King said, impressed. "It's not SOP, but it's better than trying to manhandle this greasy filth."

"Nice, Mendy," Flores added. "We might actually get out of here before sunrise."

They got to work. As Mendiola crouched to tie the straps around the creature's neck and legs, King and Flores braced the branches under its massive chest. On Flores's count, they lifted. Mendiola yanked on the straps.

The body shifted, just inches from fully flipping, when a sharp crack rang out behind them. Branches. Heavy. Breaking.

Mendiola's eyes widened. He let go of the straps and backed

away.

The body flopped back. Flores snapped his head toward Mendiola, furious. King began to speak, but froze.

Mendiola wasn't looking at them. He was looking past them.

King started to turn to look behind him, to see whatever it was that had Mendiola spooked.

Then he vanished. A massive clawed hand yanked him into the air, hurling him like a ragdoll against a tree. His body crumpled with a sickening crack.

Flores scrambled for his sidearm, but he barely got his hand on the grip before a second arm slammed down on his head. His helmet went flying. A gush of blood splattered across the grass as the creature descended, fists pounding.

Mendiola turned to run, but the creature sprang towards him, covering the ground between them in a heartbeat.

One clawed hand slammed onto his shoulder. The other gripped his helmet. A twist. A snap.

Mendiola dropped like a stone.

Silence.

The second creature stepped fully into the clearing. Leaner than the first. Smaller. Wiry, its fur a patchwork of shadowy browns. It sniffed the air, short, sharp bursts, its eyes scanning.

It knelt beside the fallen one and gave it three hard shoves.

Nothing.

A pause.

A deeper breath.

Then it screamed.

A sound torn from the gut, furious, raw, and mournful all at once. It echoed off the trees, high and piercing, full of pain no human would ever mistake for anything else.

The creature bent low, curled its fingers around the corpse's ankles.

One last glance toward the wreckage—the blood, the gear, the broken men.

Then it turned and dragged the body into the darkness of the woods.

CHAPTER 22: BACK AGAIN

The ATV sat quiet near the edge of the camp, its engine long cooled. Nicks and Madden sat shoulder to shoulder inside the roll cage, weapons laid across their laps. The predawn sky stretched above them, a shifting canvas of purples and smoky blues. Around them, the world was still.

"Why do you think they brought these things all the way up here and just left them?" Nicks asked, her voice a low murmur against the hush.

Madden adjusted his grip on his rifle, the stock resting against his thigh. "Woods are too thick to drive through. My guess? They'll use 'em to haul the body down the trail. Probably have a flatbed waiting in the parking area."

Nicks considered this, clicking her tongue softly. "Yeah... guess I buy that. Hauling that thing into a chopper would've been a massive pain in the ass."

Madden huffed a quiet laugh and nudged her shoulder with his own. "Yeah. Talk about dead weight."

Nicks smirked, about to respond, but the sound cut her off.

An inhuman howl filled the air.

Nicks was already moving before her brain caught up, leaping from the ATV and racking her shotgun in one fluid motion. "Let's move!" she barked.

Madden climbed out behind her, his six-foot-four frame

knocking against the roll cage as he ducked too late. He winced, cursed, and followed Nicks into the trees.

They tore through the woods, flashlights jerking wildly through trunks and shadows. A second scream pierced the darkness,high-pitched, soaked in terror. Nicks and Madden moved faster.

The camp clearing opened suddenly before them in a harsh pool of tactical light cast by the LED lanterns.

Benes stood at the edge of the carnage. Her machete trembled in her grip, her expression frozen somewhere between shock and disbelief.

The creature's body was gone.

Madden's beam followed the drag marks - long, messy scars in the dirt leading into the forest. His light landed on something else, something twisted near the base of a tree.

King.

Madden bolted forward, nearly slipping in the trampled grass. He caught himself, reached the body, and dropped to one knee. King's limbs were contorted, broken in too many places to count. Blood slicked his armor and pooled beneath his neck.

"Jesus..." Madden whispered, lifting him gently. King flopped like a doll, heavy and lifeless.

He scanned the trees with his light. Nothing. Only blackness.

Back in the clearing, Nicks kneeled beside Flores. What remained of his face was unrecognizable, a pulpy ruin of blood and bone. Mendiola wasn't far, his neck twisted grotesquely, eyes wide open in death. Nicks leaned in and closed them.

"What the fuck happened here, Benes?" Madden demanded as he returned, laying King beside Mendiola.

Benes didn't answer at first. Her eyes were locked on the spot where the creature had been, like she was still trying to process its absence. She clutched her machete to her chest.

"I... I don't know," she said finally. "I was clearing trail. About two hundred meters out. Mendiola left to help with the body. I didn't hear anything until that howl."

She looked at the empty space again. "Was it not dead?"

Madden stepped forward, scanning the area. "It was dead. There's two of them."

He pointed with his boot. "Look here...grass bent this way. Then here. Something dragged it off."

Nicks straightened. "We need to move. Now."

"Benes!" she called. The woman snapped to attention.

"Carry Mendiola. I'll take Flores. Madden, you've got King."

Benes hesitated, motioning toward the campers' remains. "What about those two?"

Nicks' expression faltered for the first time, her voice lower now. "We'll come back for them in the daylight. Just worry about Mendy for now."

Benes hoisted Mendiola's body into a fireman's carry without protest. Nicks and Madden did the same, lifting their fallen teammates with grim determination.

Together, they disappeared into the trees.

Behind them, the lantern light flickered harshly over the clearing. Over the blood. Over the place where the dead thing no longer lay.

The silence was back.

CHAPTER 23: BAG & TAG

The woods behind the ballfield were still now. Quiet in a way that made skin crawl. Sheriff Baker and Carlton Robinson moved in near lockstep, silent and deliberate, eyes forward and flashlights slicing through the dark. Behind them, Deputy Grimes scanned the underbrush, shotgun tight in his grip.

Broken branches, crushed leaves, deep and uneven impressions in the dirt, all clear signs something massive had moved through here. And fast.

Up ahead, Robinson raised a closed fist.

They froze.

With slow precision,Robinson shifted his flashlight into his left hand, unholstered the Desert Eagle with his right, and dropped into a low-ready stance. No words. He stepped forward alone, melting into a thicket of alder and vine maple.

Baker and Grimes waited in tense silence, hearts pounding, watching Carlton disappear into the undergrowth. The Sheriff glanced at Grimes, who gave him a look that said: *Should we go after him?*

Before either moved, a low whistle cut through the quiet.

They pushed through the brush and froze when they saw it.

A body, or what was left of it, slumped against a half-rotted stump. The arms were gone, torn clean at the shoulder. Legs twisted, crushed. The face contorted, mouth agape in a final, silent scream.

Carlton's eyes were flint. "It made sure he suffered."

Baker didn't respond. He stared, lips pressed in a hard, cold line. A storm churned in his eyes.

Grimes turned slowly, sweeping his light over the surrounding trees. His voice was low but steady. "It's long gone, Sheriff. I don't smell it. Don't feel it watching us."

Carlton kept scanning. "This was a warning. It's claiming this area. It'll be back."

Grimes nodded. "Then we need to deal with it before it does."

Baker exhaled through his nose. "We should've ended it a long time ago."

He took a step back, rubbed both hands over his face, then pulled out his phone. "Let's bag him. I'll call Shelly. Have her boys pick him up."

Carlton turned, studying the Sheriff. "You doing alright?"

A bitter laugh escaped Baker's throat. "No, Carlton, I'm not doing alright. There's a goddamn Bigfoot killing people in my town. Tomorrow, this place will be crawling with hunters and reporters, and I have to lie. Tell them it was a bear."

Grimes tried to offer something, anything. "Most of the old heads in town know what to say. If a reporter or some YouTuber asks, they'll say 'bear.' They always do."

The Sheriff shook his head. "That's no comfort to this poor bastard." He paused. "Or the one already in the morgue."

Carlton stepped past the stump, flashlight arcing out ahead. A smear of blood led deeper into the woods, wide droplets soaked into the moss and dirt.

"It carried the calf off this way," he muttered. "Back toward the old camp. Hidden Lake's not far. Either they shared a den, or this one's got its own."

The Sheriff turned without a word and started back toward the clearing. Carlton watched him go, concern etched across his face.

"Sheriff?"

Baker's voice came back through the dark, hoarse and tired. "I'm going to call Shelly. Then I'm getting a couple hours of sleep. You two carry our friend back to the field."

Grimes stepped beside Carlton as he pulled a body bag from his pack. They crouched wordlessly over the remains, flashlights steady, and began their grim work.

CHAPTER 24: BREAKFAST BUNCH

The town was different than the day before, buzzing and unsettled. Beth could feel it as she rolled past the coffee shop, the bakery, the small grocery store. Normally sleepy sidewalks had become rivers of flannel, fleece vests, and oversized backpacks. A woman posed on the corner with a selfie stick, lips pursed, voice raised in mock surprise: *"So this is the town where the Bigfoot attack happened—can you believe it?!"*

Beth exhaled hard through her nose and gripped the wheel tighter. A horn blared behind her. She startled, looked up. The light was green.

"Shit, sorry!" she called out her window, then drove on.

At Mike's place, she paused on the porch before knocking. Her eyes landed on a chainsaw-carved bear wearing a faded American flag bandana, hunched protectively over a pot of honey with *WELCOME* etched in pine. She snorted a laugh. For someone like Mike, it was oddly cute.

The door swung open before she could knock again.

"Beth! Good morning," Vikram grinned. "Come in. Hope you're hungry, we're just sitting down."

Inside, Beth took in Mike's living room. National Park mugs lined one shelf. A framed portrait of Mike in his ranger uniform rested beside a smiling picture of his daughter. A second-edition *Lord of the Rings* box set was prominently featured in the IKEA bookcase against the wall.

"Wow," she said, running a finger along the spines. "You know these would go for a good price online, right?"

Mike's voice called out from the hallway, accompanied by the familiar *thud-thud* of crutches.

"They're not for sale. My boss gave them to me when I left the ranger service."

Beth turned. Mike stood in a green-and-black flannel, matching dark joggers—clean, pressed, and maybe a little dressed up.

"I didn't know you were such a reader," she said, amused. "Never seen you with a book at the bar."

Mike moved toward the kitchen, carefully testing a bit of weight on his bad leg. "Being the 'book-in-a-bar' guy isn't a good look."

Vikram waved her in. "Let's move the book club to the kitchen."

Beth stopped short when she saw the spread. Fresh fruit, pastries, coffee, and something bright green was whirring inside the Vitamix. On the stove: an omelet station worthy of a bed and breakfast.

"Help yourself," Vikram said, placing a gentle hand at her back. "I'd start with the smoothie. Apple, kale, ginger, pineapple. It's dope."

Mike had already taken a seat at the kitchen table, crutches leaned neatly against the wall.

"The kid makes a mean smoothie," he offered. "He's not lying."

Beth poured half a glass and took a cautious sip. Tartness puckered her cheeks, but it finished sweet and sharp. She smacked her lips. "This is actually really good."

Vikram grinned and turned toward the stove. "What's it gonna be? I've got mushrooms, sharp cheddar, diced ham, bacon bits…"

"Mushroom, cheese, and peppers, please," Beth said, eying the counter.

"Got it," Vikram said with a salute.

As the spatula clinked against the skillet, Beth sat across from Mike.

"I drove through town," she said quietly. "It's a circus. Sprinter vans, satellite trucks, hiking gear is everywhere. And that's just local Sasquatch hunters from Oregon, Washington, and Vancouver. Someone is even selling cast molds of Bigfoot feet near the old gas station."

Mike stared out the window. His fingers curled around a coffee mug like it was the only thing keeping him grounded.

"Beth," he asked. "How much do you know about it?"

She turned in her seat to face him directly. "Enough. I was in high school when they shut down the camp. People talked. I always thought that Bigfoot junk in the shops was the town letting outsiders in on our open secret."

Mike nodded. "Yeah. But the secret was always *out there.* Never *here.*"

She frowned. "Why do you think it came into town? Why now?"

Mike looked up at Vikram. A knowing smirk tugged at the corner of his mouth. "Ask him. Vik thinks it's after us."

"I was half-joking," Vikram said, plating her omelet. "But yeah...part of me thinks it's out for revenge."

Beth raised an eyebrow. "Seriously?"

"Seriously," Vikram said. "We encroached on its turf. Now it's encroaching on ours."

She studied him for a moment, then glanced down at the steaming plate in front of her. The scent hit her, rich and savory. She picked up her fork and took a bite, chewing thoughtfully as her eyes drifted toward the window. Outside, the woods pressed close, their dark outlines barely softened by the morning light.

Mike shook his head. "I'm not buying revenge. It's an animal, not a movie villain."

"Animals grieve," Beth said quietly, between bites. "Some even hold funerals."

That made both men pause.

Vikram nodded slowly, "Exactly."

Mike scoffed, "That's sweet, but this doesn't feel like grieving." He turned his head towards the kitchen window and watched a robin flitter around his small side yard. After a moment, he looked back at Beth then let out a long, tired sigh. "I don't know what the hell this is."

For a few moments, no one spoke. Beth ate with slow, deliberate motions, her gaze lingering now and then on the tree line outside.

She set her fork down, surprised to find her plate empty. "That was amazing, Vik. Thank you."

"No problem," Vikram said, as he placed Mike's plate on the table in front of him. "Oh...your precious Tapatío. One sec." Vikram grabbed a small bottle off the counter and walked it over to the table.

Mike picked the bottle up, dumped hot sauce over his eggs, poked at them. "I don't think it's the same one. I think there's two of them. The one in town...it was younger. Smaller. Different coloring. Lighter fur, brown instead of grey-black."

"Mike here is a Bigfoot behavior theorist now," Vikram teased. "Societal structure, biology... he's got a whole lecture."

Mike rolled his eyes. "We know they're territorial. We know there must be a breeding population. With all the clearcutting and replanting going on around here, it makes sense one got pushed down. Carving out new turf. And it's aggressive about it."

Beth nodded, then glanced at her watch. "Makes sense. But what if you're both right? What if it's revenge...and territory?"

Vikram shrugged. "Then we're in for a hell of a week."

Beth stood, brushing off her jeans. "I've got to open the bar. It's gonna be a zoo. If you feel up to it, Mike, swing by later."

Mike nodded, smiling faintly. "I might."

"Thanks again for breakfast, Vik," she said, walking to the door. "When this all blows over, maybe you and I can start a breakfast-and-smoothie joint."

Vikram threw up his arms like he'd just won the lottery. "Yes! I'm *so* in."

He walked her out.

Mike sat quietly, watching the woods outside.

The door opened and closed again. Vikram returned, grinning.

"She invited you over to the bar. That's basically a proposal in small-town language."

Mike grunted. "Is it?"

Vikram started cleaning up the kitchen. "Totally. But if we *do* go to the bar later, no double fries. Got it?"

Mike groaned and stood. He leaned on his crutches, misjudged his balance, and winced.

"You okay?" Vikram asked, spinning around.

"Yeah," Mike said. He limped to the sliding glass door, staring at the tree covered foothills in the distance.

"I can't shake the feeling this is my fault," he muttered. "The wheels started turning the day I gave your brother that map."

Vikram turned, leaned against the sink. He dried his hands with a towel.

"You're not wrong," he said. "But this was coming one way or another."

Mike moved toward the hallway. "Still. I'll carry that for a long time."

Vikram tossed the towel on the counter. "Then carry it. But don't let it stop you from living. Beth likes you. Let yourself be liked. Don't let guilt keep you from whatever's next."

He checked his watch.

“You’ve got PT in thirty. Nurse is coming after. I gotta finish up in here.”

Mike turned to go.

“Hey!” Vikram called.

Mike stopped.

“Some days I forgive you. Some days I don’t. But I believe all this is happening for a reason. I just don’t know what it is yet.”

Mike nodded, silent.

“Good,” Vikram said. “Now go get ready for PT.”

CHAPTER 25: FILE IT AWAY

Deputy Grimes pushed through the crowd gathered outside the Sheriff's Department - journalists, YouTubers, bloggers, and fringe cryptid enthusiasts wielding selfie sticks and DSLRs like weapons. Their voices layered in a cacophony of half-questions and shouted accusations.

"Deputy! What can you tell us about the sightings?"

"Is something hiding in the woods?"

"How many has it killed?"

"Is this a cover-up?"

"Bigfoot or Dogman?!"

Grimes froze at that last one, casting a brief, confused glance toward the speaker before shaking it off and pushing through.

"Excuse me, please," he said, his tone strained but controlled. "I have to get inside. Please, step aside."

He reached the front door. Locked.

The questions didn't stop.

"Can you confirm multiple sightings?"

"What's your official statement?"

He fumbled with his keys, hands shaking slightly, finally slipping one into the lock and twisting hard. The door clicked open. Grimes darted inside and slammed it shut behind him, twisting the deadbolt with finality. He exhaled, letting the noise dull behind the thick glass.

The office was quiet, almost eerily so. He crossed the lobby, boots echoing softly, and paused in front of the Sheriff's door. It was closed. Odd. Sheriff Baker never closed his door unless...

Grimes knocked.

No answer.

He reached for the handle.

It swung open before he could grasp it.

Sheriff Baker stood there, hollow-eyed and disheveled. His uniform was wrinkled, his hair unkempt, the stubble on his face bordering on a beard. Not the sharp figure Grimes was used to seeing.

"Sheriff! What's going on? We've got a real problem outside... press, hunters, YouTubers...it's chaos."

Baker didn't respond immediately. He turned toward the small Keurig in the corner and began sorting through coffee pods with robotic precision.

"I came straight here," he muttered. "After we found the second body. You and Carlton get that handled?"

Grimes nodded slowly.

"Good. Good." Baker opened a packet of powdered creamer and stirred it in, his back still turned.

"Sheriff..." Grimes hesitated. "What's going on with you?"

Baker chuckled, a tired, joyless sound. His eyes drifted upward to the mounted deer antlers above a dusty sign nailed into the wall.

THE BUCK STOPS HERE.

He stared at it a moment, the old wood grain catching the morning light, then turned around with his coffee in hand.

"I've been here all morning," he said. "Reading old files. Some of them go back to the sixties. Missing hikers. Deceased hikers.

Thought maybe I'd find a thread. A clue. Some hint for how to handle this."

He walked back into his office. Grimes followed, standing awkwardly in the doorway.

"And… did you find anything?"

Baker slumped into his chair. The leather creaked under his weight. He stared blankly at the wall of paper and pin-maps behind his desk.

"Nope," he said finally. "Nothing. We're flying blind, Grimes."

Grimes stepped halfway out of the office and glanced toward the front door. The silhouettes of reporters shifted and rippled against the frosted glass like restless shadows.

"What's the plan, Sheriff?"

Baker didn't answer at first. His eyes tracked the topographical lines on a large wall map. Then, with a heavy breath, he stood.

"The plan?" He straightened slightly. "I'm going to take a few minutes to get my ass in gear, iron this uniform, shave, maybe comb my damn hair. Then I'm going to walk outside and give those people a statement."

Grimes nodded, lips pressed tight. "How long?"

Baker moved toward the credenza beneath the map. He opened a drawer and pulled out a standard military-sized toiletry bag. He didn't say a word as he passed Grimes, heading toward the rear bathroom.

Just before disappearing down the hall, he called over his shoulder.

"Tell 'em twenty minutes."

Grimes watched him go, then turned toward the waiting crowd.

"Roger that, Sheriff."

CHAPTER 26: BAR RUSH

Beth pushed open the back door of the bar, the hinges creaking with their usual resistance. Paul, the scruffy day-shift cook, trudged in behind her carrying a case of vodka. Dave, the wiry barback with too much energy and not enough filter, followed close behind, earbuds dangling and hoodie sleeves pushed to his elbows.

Beth flipped on the lights. The familiar hum and flicker of fluorescent tubes washed over the empty bar. Dust particles spun lazily in the sunbeams cutting through the front windows.

"Want these under the bar?" Dave called, hoisting a second case with surprising ease.

"Yeah, if there's room. Otherwise, stuff 'em in the back office," Beth replied, already halfway across the floor, checking booths and wiping off smudged tabletops with a rag from her back pocket. She tugged the chains on the neon signs one by one - Rainier Beer, Blue Moon, Bud Light - each flickering to life like old ghosts.

From the kitchen came Dave's voice again. "We need to order more 80/20 burger patties! And eggs! We're out of eggs!"

Beth shouted back without missing a step, "Then get on the app and order them!"

"And bacon! And chicken strips!" Dave's voice rang again, even louder.

Beth spun on her heel, exasperated. "Dave, just order. Don't announce it!"

He emerged from the kitchen grinning, iPad in hand, knife still tucked into his apron loop.

"I *was* ordering while calling it out. It's called managing up," he said, proud. "We're talking about it in my online business class. You are now officially informed!"

Beth blew out a sharp breath through her nose, fighting a smile. "That's great. Thanks. In the future just order. I trust you."

"Got it, boss. Thanks!"

She unlocked the front door and was instantly met with a surge of bodies, a group of forty or more pressed in before the door even finished opening. Regulars she recognized nodded or waved as they pushed past, but the majority were strangers. Out-of-towners. Stocking caps, tactical vests, flannel, and the unmistakable gleam of GoPro mounts. Bigfoot hunters. Some with printed maps. Others already filming themselves in selfie-mode.

The place filled in minutes. Booths, tables, barstools were claimed and crowded. Locals grumbled as they were elbowed aside by excited tourists shouting about trails and "the footage."

Beth weaved behind the bar, tying her apron as she moved, already taking mental inventory of who was waiting longest. She grabbed a notepad from beneath the register and turned toward the kitchen.

"Hey, Dave?"

He looked up from his prep station, halfway through chopping an onion.

"What's up?"

"You'd better double up on the burgers, eggs, and pretty much everything else. It's gonna be a long week."

Dave walked toward the kitchen door and peered out into the crowd. His eyes widened. “Holy shit! I might need Paul to help out back here.”

“No problem. I’ve got the bar,” Beth called over her shoulder. “I’ll let him know. If things get too crazy, I’ll call second shift in early.”

She slid back behind the bar just in time to greet three tourists waving laminated trail maps and shouting for Bloody Marys.

Beth plastered on her service smile, grabbed her pen, and started writing. Her hands moved on autopilot, but her mind was already racing ahead. This was just the beginning.

The town was full. The woods were going to be full.

And she had a feeling it was only going to get crazier.

CHAPTER 27: BRING OUT YOUR DEAD

Deep in the old-growth forest, where the trees were so ancient and thick they seemed to hold time itself captive, a massive creature clawed at the earth.

Its gnarled hands, powerful things the size of dinner plates, ripped into the forest floor with terrifying speed. Fistfuls of dark soil, rocks, and twisted roots flew through the air, scattering across mossy ground. The canopy above filtered the sunlight into mottled beams, barely reaching the floor where the creature labored in the shadows of towering trunks draped in lichen and age.

The grave it dug was crude but deliberate, wide and deep, over seven feet long. The creature worked without hesitation, but there was no rage in its motions. Only purpose.

When the pit was finally ready, it turned to the lifeless form beside it.

Another of its kind.

The body was heavy, slack, limbs contorted in unnatural ways. One shoulder was shattered, the chest caved in, fur matted with dried blood and scorched patches from man-made weapons. The creature lifted it with surprising gentleness and lowered it into the grave. It paused, repositioning a leg, shifting an arm across the chest as if laying the body to rest mattered. As if respect could be shown through placement.

Then it knelt at the edge, head bowed low, eyes locked on the still face. It remained there for a long moment, utterly still.

A low, guttural rumble rose in its throat, deep and vibrating, like a tremor from beneath the earth. The sound built, swelling into a chorus of sharp, pained shrieks that rang out through the trees. The forest, ever quiet, held the sound in its ancient boughs and then swallowed it whole.

When silence returned, the creature rose.

It began to bury its fallen kin.

Clumps of earth covered the body. Layer after layer. No markers. No stones. Just the rhythm of grief in motion.

When it was done, the creature stood tall above the grave, chest heaving. It let out one final, low grunt, something between a farewell and a promise.

Then it turned and disappeared into the trees.

The grave remained behind. Unmarked, unseen, but never unguarded.

CHAPTER 28: MORNING

The clearing had been stripped of its horror.

Only the dull thrum of diesel engines and the low murmur of voices remained as the fresh squad moved with purpose, boots moved over broken branches and disturbed soil. Ten operators, all in matte black tactical gear, fanned out into the forest with precise, almost clinical efficiency, on their way to retrieve the bodies of the two missing campers.

Off to one side, Nicks, Madden, and Benes sat slouched on a fallen log, eyes hollow, faces smeared with dirt and the shadows of exhaustion. None of them spoke.

Across from them, Jacob Morton stood tall in the soft morning light, clipboard in hand, his expression unreadable. Beside him, a wiry older man in khakis and a black fleece vest tapped quietly at an iPad, his face lit by the bluish glow of the screen, his demeanor more academic than empathetic.

Near the tree line, another scene played out. Riley, lean and wiry beneath her tactical vest, oversaw the last of the gear being photographed and tagged. She couldn't have been more than twenty-eight, her face angular and sharp with youthful intensity. A streak of hair had slipped loose from her helmet, brushing against her cheek as she barked instructions to her crew. Her team worked quickly, snapping photos of backpacks, boots, torn bits of fabric — all that remained of Travis and Erin's final moments. One of the operators carefully loaded the items into the back of a camouflaged ATV.

Riley stepped away from her crew and made her way toward Morton.

"Commander Morton?" she called, voice clear and firm.

He turned, squinting slightly against the morning light. "Riley."

"We're done here. I'm taking my team back to the camp," she said, gesturing toward the vehicle, now loaded and rumbling with anticipation.

Morton's eyes swept over the campground, no trace of blood, no broken branches, no sign that anything monstrous had ever happened here. It looked, somehow, exactly as it had the day the campers arrived.

"Make sure we extract what we need from their gear before the families get eyes on any of it," he said, his voice flat.

Riley gave a curt nod. "Understood."

She swung into the passenger seat of the waiting ATV, tapped the dash twice, and the driver rolled them forward, bouncing along the dirt path as the vehicle disappeared into the trees.

Morton turned back to the trio still seated on the log. Nicks looked up wearily, her eyes sharp despite the dark smudges beneath them. Madden and Benes sat silently, heads bowed, trying to catch their breath...or maybe just trying to forget what they had seen.

The older man beside Morton kept typing, never looking up.

The wind shifted slightly, bringing the scent of moss and pine.

And beneath it all... something else. Faint. Rotten. Lingering.

CHAPTER 29: UFOS & PORTALS

The bar was absolute chaos.

The booths were jammed, the pool table a no-man's-land now blocked by tripods and hard cases. Every surface, once home to pints of beer and baskets of fries, was now buried under field gear, open laptops, and maps of the surrounding forest scrawled with red circles and cryptic notations. The town's regulars lingered awkwardly in corners, shoulders hunched, glaring as their watering hole was overrun by Bigfoot chasers in camo jackets and trail runners.

Beth moved like a machine behind the bar, pouring beers, snatching tabs, answering questions with clipped half-smiles and eye-rolls she didn't bother to hide. Paul, the scruffy day cook, had been drafted into service as a temporary bartender. He lined up bottles on a tray, his lip curling at the unfamiliar labels.

"Why do they all want these shitty IPAs?" he muttered. "We're down to three cans of that one with the jackalope on the label."

"Maybe they'll leave when we run out," Beth said, wiping her hands on a bar towel. She eyed the crowd, her expression calm but calculating. "I'm gonna try to get second shift in early. This is nuts."

She scooped up a stack of receipts and weaved through the tables. At one corner booth, two men in cargo vests and knit caps leaned across the table, gesturing wildly over a printed map of local trailheads.

“I'm telling you,” one of them hissed, “they're interdimensional beings. Forest portals. Ancient energy grids. Look at the ley lines.”

“No, no,” said the other, slapping the table. “It's cloaking tech. Military-grade. Possibly even alien.”

Beth approached, gave them both a tight smile, and dropped their check without a word. She didn't wait to hear their theories.

The front door opened. A gust of air rushed in and with it, Mike and Vikram.

Beth spotted them immediately. Relief flashed across her face. “Back here,” she called, motioning them behind the bar.

Mike leaned on his crutches, carefully navigating the crowd. Vikram trailed behind, ducking past a guy adjusting a GoPro strapped to his chest.

As Paul whisked a tray of drinks to a booth, he shouted, “It's a madhouse in here, boys!”

Beth lifted the partition to let them through. “Come on,” she said. “I need a breather.”

She led them down a short hallway and into her cramped back office. The space was no bigger than a walk-in closet. Liquor cases were stacked against one wall, a weathered desk crammed against the other. A bulletin board overflowed with receipts and staff schedules. Beth collapsed into her rolling chair with a groan.

“This is the busiest this place has ever been,” she said, eyes wide.

Mike leaned on the doorway. “Are those all Bigfoot hunters out there?”

Beth nodded. “Yep. Every last one of 'em.”

“Where are they staying?” Vikram asked. “They can't all be van lifers.”

Beth shrugged and started scrolling through her phone. “Doesn’t matter. They’re gonna get themselves killed out there. They think it’s a game.”

She held up a hand and pressed a contact on her screen.

“Javier? Hey, it’s Beth. Can you come in early? Yeah, like... now? We’re getting crushed.”

A pause. Then she exhaled with relief. “Okay. Great. See you in twenty.”

She ended the call and slumped deeper into the chair, eyes fluttering shut for just a moment.

“Sorry, guys,” she said. “I gotta get back out there. But maybe I’ll swing by later? Heard some crazy stuff this morning... wanted to talk to you about it, Mike.”

Mike shifted, clearly flustered. “Uh... yeah... yeah, for sure. Come by. I’ll be... we’ll be home, right, Vik?”

Vikram gave him a look. “You can’t drive. And I’m not taking you anywhere.”

He turned to Beth, deadpan.

“He’ll be home.”

Beth grinned and stood, tightening the strings of her apron. “Good. I’ll see you later, Mike.”

She caught his eye one last time, then walked out the door and back into the noise.

Mike and Vikram followed, stepping into the bar’s main room just as the next wave of orders hit the counter. The din swelled — shouts, laughter, the clink of glass. Beth was already moving again, weaving between tables, balancing three pint glasses in one hand.

Mike and Vikram slipped through the front and out into the sunlight.

Inside, the hunt was on.

CHAPTER 30: Q&A

Sheriff Eric James Baker stood before a wall of cameras and pointed microphones, the early afternoon sun glinting off press badges and smartphone lenses. He kept his stance square, shoulders broad, uniform pressed and crisp, at least from the waist up. He'd spent the better part of the morning preparing for this.

A reporter thrust forward, voice loud and eager.

"Sheriff! What can you tell us about the Bigfoot sighting at the baseball fields?"

His jaw tightened.

"Softball fields," he corrected, without smiling. "And there's been no confirmed Bigfoot sighting. After reviewing all submitted footage, it's my belief the video captured a large grizzly bear, one that's responsible for several recent disturbances."

Another reporter elbowed in.

"Grizzly bear, Sheriff? Aren't grizzlies extinct in this region?"

Baker narrowed his eyes.

"Two were reintroduced to the northern wilderness," he said. "One appears to have migrated south. Grizzlies are scavengers if opportunity presents itself. They've been known to wander into foothill neighborhoods. They can walk upright and easily reach eight feet tall. In a moment of panic, it's easy to misidentify what you're seeing."

From the back, a skeptical voice rang out.

"What about the man killed by a thrown rock? Are these grizzlies trained to throw fastballs?"

A flicker of annoyance crossed Baker's face.

"The Medical Examiner ruled his death the result of a fall suffered while engaging with the animal," he said coolly. "There's no conclusive evidence that an object was thrown."

Another reporter, younger, wearing a lanyard from a cryptid YouTube channel, piped up.

"Sheriff, any advice for the Bigfoot hunters flooding into town?"

Baker rubbed the side of his jaw, scanning the crowd.

"The forest is dense. Unforgiving. If you're out there chasing shadows unprepared, it won't end well. Wear high-visibility vests. We have master hunters tracking the bear. Don't get mistaken for something you're not."

A hush settled for a beat. Then.

"What should they do if they do encounter the bear?"

Baker fixed the reporter with a steely look.

"Let's hope they don't."

He turned without another word, stepping back inside the precinct and locking the door behind him.

Main Street buzzed with last-minute urgency.

Gear was double-checked. Camera batteries were swapped. CamelBaks were filled and re-filled. GoPros blinked red as cryptid chasers narrated into lenses about what they *might* find out there. Theories flowed faster than orders at the local coffee shop — forest portals, government clones, cloaking tech. Every passing conversation was a crescendo of delusion and bravado.

The camera of the world, if there had been one, would have panned past the swirling madness and settled at the edge of the frenzy.

An old RV sat parked at the curb, rust-colored, moss-lined at the seams, and dead quiet. On its bumper sat Brenda.

She was in her early sixties, all sinew and shadow. A half-smoked Camel unfiltered hung from her lips. Her cargo pants were baggy, her flannel faded, her boots scuffed. The HOKA trail cap perched backward on her head made her look like a seasoned hiker who'd seen too much and talked too little.

Her eyes weren't on the crowd.

They were on the caravan.

New vans, shiny, covered in decals of national parks rumbled down the road one after the other, disappearing toward the trailheads. She didn't move. Didn't flinch. Just watched.

The last van's taillights vanished into the tree line.

Brenda dropped her cigarette butt onto the street, grinding it beneath the toe of her boot.

Still no words.

No expression.

She climbed into the RV. The driver's seat sagged, foam poking through worn upholstery. The engine coughed, shuddered, threatened to die, then reluctantly caught and growled to life.

She didn't follow the others.

She turned in the opposite direction.

CHAPTER 31: CLOSING TIME

The sky had begun to dim, tinged with gold as evening crept over the foothills. A breeze teased the treetops. On the front porch of Mike's house, Beth knocked twice, her knuckles light against the wood.

A moment passed.

The door swung open. Vikram stood on the threshold, casual, warm.

"Hey," he said, smiling. "Come on in."

Beth stepped over the threshold and into the living room.

Sheriff Eric Baker stood alone, staring at the large area map pinned to his office wall. Red pushpins pierced the landscape, each one marking something unspeakable. Each one a memory he didn't want to carry but couldn't set down.

He held the phone to his ear, his voice clipped, his stance rigid.

"I've marked those hot spots, Jacob," he said. "What are you doing to keep people out of the area around the camp?"

Jacob Morton's voice came through the receiver, worn thin by the recent events.

"We've got teams posted at the main road. But I'm worried about the more motivated types. The ones who might bushwhack through the old growth. I can't allocate resources to listening posts out there, not after the casualties we've taken in the last forty-eight hours."

Baker let out a low sigh, rough as gravel.

"Guess we better hope they're not that motivated," he muttered. "I'll check in with you in the morning."

He hung up, shoulders sagging beneath the weight of what was still to come.

The silence in the room was thick. He turned back to the map, eyes scanning the crimson constellation he'd built. A slow-moving war. One he never wanted. One he now knew he might not win.

The overhead lights buzzed faintly, casting a sterile wash across the pale hospital walls. Deputy Grimes stepped inside, careful, almost tentative.

He wasn't in uniform, just jeans, a maroon hoodie, and a worn pair of black-and-red Air Jordans. In one hand, a small bouquet of slightly wilted flowers. In the other, a tiny stuffed Labrador Retriever.

Deanna Moore looked up from her bed.

Her hair was tied back loosely. Dark circles shadowed her eyes. But when she saw him, something lit behind them. Warmth and recognition, a tired kind of relief.

A smile bloomed across her face, quiet but real.

Grimes smiled back, sheepish, as if unsure if he was welcome but deeply grateful that he was.

The only light in the farmhouse kitchen came from the pale glow of the laptop screen.

James sat hunched forward, elbows on the table, breath shallow as he fast-forwarded through hours of grainy trail-cam footage. The wind outside whistled faintly through old windows. A chicken clucked once, then fell silent.

He clicked to the next clip.

Nothing.

The next.

And then.

Movement.

A massive, upright shape moved from the edge of the trees. Shoulders broad, steps silent. The creature moved with eerie, unnatural precision around the chicken coop, past the shed. James leaned in, transfixed.

The creature stopped.

Slowly and *deliberately*, it turned its head.

Its eyes glinted in the infrared light. Pinpoints of reflected fire.

James went still. His pulse slammed against his ribs.

The creature stared.

It blinked once, slowly.

A deep exhale, guttural, low, *intentional*.

Then it turned and vanished, melting back into the dark as if it had never been there.

The chair creaked beneath James as he fell back, breath ragged, one hand pressed to his chest.

On the screen, the woods stood empty again.

But something had seen him.

And it knew exactly where to look.

CHAPTER 32: FIRE WOOD

The forest stood tall and wild, vibrant with life even as dusk settled in. Old-growth trees arched high overhead, their moss-draped limbs swaying gently in the breeze. Ferns rustled underfoot, and distant frogs chorused from a hidden creek. Firelight from the nearby campground flickered between trunks, casting dappled gold across the underbrush. But deeper in, past the last echoes of laughter, something moved, massive, silent, deliberate.

The creature crept from trunk to trunk, impossibly quiet for its size. A ripple in the dark. It paused, crouched low. Watching.

Up ahead, van headlights bled into the clearing, cutting through the trees in thick beams. A group of campers —five, maybe six — sat in camp chairs around a fire pit, laughing and drinking. Someone passed a bottle. A bag of chips crinkled. From a speaker, faint country music played under the crackle of fire.

"I'm gonna grab more wood for the fire."

One of them stood, flashlight in hand, and disappeared into the trees.

The creature remained still.

The camper's light cut a thin path through the black. He moved lazily, crouching to scoop fallen branches, stacking them against his hip. A rhythm formed - step, stoop, snap.

Then he paused.

Nostrils flared.

A smell.

Thick and cloying. Skunk musk, wet fur, the copper tang of blood. It hit all at once, a sick punch to the senses. The kind of scent that made your throat close and your instincts flare. It didn't belong. Not here, not in this forest alive with pine, fern, and damp moss. The stench was an open wound in the otherwise clean woodland air.

He stood slowly. Sniffed again. Wrinkled his nose.

"What the hell..."

The flashlight beam wavered. He turned in a slow arc, scanning the undergrowth.

Something shifted behind a log.

SNAP.

A branch cracked under weight.

The flashlight jerked toward the sound and then froze.

Two glowing orange eyes blinked from the dark.

The camper took one staggering step back. The smell hit harder now, fermented meat and rot baked into fur. It clung to the back of his throat. His stomach flipped, the flashlight trembled in his grip.

The eyes didn't move. Just watched.

His breath hitched. The flashlight slipped from his hand, landing hard against a root.

Darkness swallowed everything.

He ran.

ABOUT THE AUTHOR

Jesse L Taylor

Jesse L. Taylor has been afraid of Bigfoot since age ten, thanks to the Leonard Nimoy's In Search Of...episode that discussed the cryptid.

In 1980, his family moved to Bremerton, Washington, near a vast greenbelt bordering a dense state park. That show—and those woods—sparked an overactive imagination and a deep belief that something was watching him every time he stepped outside.

Now 55, Jesse lives in a new home backed by yet another thick greenbelt. The fear never fully left. It simply evolved—and became the seed for this, his debut novel.

When not writing, Jesse is a slow trail runner, even slower ultramarathoner, and proudly mediocre CrossFitter. He's also a dad to three amazing daughters and husband to the most supportive and amazing wife on the planet.

www.ingramcontent.com/pod-product-compliance
Lightning Source LLC
LaVergne TN
LVHW010628110826
845149LV00014B/2807